DREAMTIME DRAGONS

BY DREAMTIME TALE FANTASY AUTHORS

GUY DONOVAN
ASSAPH MEHR
JAQ D HAWKINS
NILS NISSE VISSER
NAV LOGAN
BENJAMIN TOWE
MARC VUN KANNON
A J NOON
RICK HAYNES
LESLIE CONZATTI
JONATHAN ROYAN
MARY R WOLDERING

WITH SPECIAL THANKS TO THE COVER TEAM:
LIA REES
CORIN SPINKS
MICHAEL CRITTENDEN

DREAMTIME DRAGONS

By Dreamtime Tale Fantasy authors
2017

ISBN Paperback: 9789082323887
Netherlands NUR CODE: 334 (Fantasy Fiction)

A CBS Green Man Publication
Cider Brandy Scribblers
Brighton, Sussex
England

Text copyright@
'Biters' & 'Shandikhaar' @Guy Donovan
'Modern Dragon' & 'The View from the Other Side' @Assaph Mehr
'Cloud Dragons' & 'Fear & Heat' @Jaq D Hawkins
'The Wyrm in the Tarn' & 'Freósan Draka Treów' @Nils Nisse Visser
'101 Uses for a Dragon', 'The Dragon Raid', 'Free Will' @Nav Logan
'Red Fire Dragon' @Benjamin Towe
'A Soft Spot for Dragons' @Marc Vun Kannon
'Hauling Fire' @A.J. Noon
'At the Red Boar' & 'Gold is Everything' @Rick Haynes
'Arthur and the Egg' @Leslie Conzatti
'Cold and with Dragons' & 'The Offering' @Jonathan Royan
'Ana's Dream of Flying' @Mary Woldering

All rights reserved. No part of this publication may be reproduced, stored in a retrieval system, or transmitted in any form or by any means, electronic, mechanical, photocopying, recording, or otherwise, without the prior permission of both the copyright owners and the above publisher of this book.

All the characters in this book are fictitious; any resemblance to actual persons living or dead is purely coincidental.

Cover design by Corin Spinks (paperback), and Michael Crittenden (e-book versions), typography by Lia Rees.

THIS ANTHOLOGY IS DEDICATED TO
THE MEMORY OF LINDSAY EDMUNDS
WHO STOPPED TELLING STORIES FAR TOO SOON.

Let me tell you a story...

Marc Vun Kannon

CONTENTS

Foreword	1
101 Uses for a Dragon	2
A work in progress by Nav Logan	
Shandikaar	36
From *Of Dragons and Men* by Guy Donovan	
Hauling Fire	43
By A.J. Noon	
Cloud Dragons	58
By Jaq D. Hawkins	
Modern Dragon	66
By Assaph Mehr	
The Wyrm in the Tarn	68
From *Escape from Neverland* by Nils (Nisse) Visser	
A Soft Spot for Dragons	86
By Marc Vun Kannon	
Cold and with Dragons	119
A Drabble by Jonathan Royan	
At the Red Boar	120
From *Heroes Never Fade* by Rick Haynes	
Red Fire Dragon	124
From *Death of Magick* by Benjamin Towe	
Arthur and The Egg	136
By Leslie Conzatti	
The View from the Other Side	164
By Assaph Mehr	
Ana's Dream of Flying	167
By Mary R. Woldering	
The Offering	183
By Jonathan Royan	
Gold is Everything	192
By Rick Haynes	
Free Will	197
From *The Black Knights of Crom Cruach* by Nav Logan	

Fear and Heat 207
From *Demoniac Dance* by Jaq D. Hawkins
Biters 212
From *Songs of Autumn* by Guy Donovan
The Dragon Raid 217
A Drabble by Nav Logan
Freósan Draka Treów 218
A Wyrde Woods Tale written for Gerrit, Anna & Rozemarijn by Nils Nisse Visser
About Us 281
Brief Bios & Links

DREAMTIME DRAGONS

AUTHORS OF
DREAMTIME TALE FANTASY

FOREWORD

The Dreamtime Tale Fantasy facebook group was set up a couple of years ago by a handful of Indie authors who despaired of the big book promotion pages where 'Buy My Book!' posts passed by in endless succession, as well as more enjoyable author groups where promotion was strictly forbidden. The idea was to interact with other authors and readers, with some limited promotion, but mostly fun and interesting discussions and meaningful exchanges on reading and writing.

The group grew into a flourishing little online community. On a few occasions we talked about the possibility of publishing an anthology, to showcase our collective work and lend that the strength of our combined social-media platforms. In the spring of 2017 we decided to stop talking about it and actually do it. We are immensely proud of the end-result, a varied collection of stories bound together by the theme of literal or figurative dragons, like a multi-hued coat of dragon scales.

There is bound to be something to your liking in this anthology which features extracts from existing books, but also a great many new stories, written specifically for this anthology. What better way to sample new authors than tasting a sample here, trying on a cloak there, or running – terrified – from a flame-spewing dragon intent on a barbeque?

Many thanks are due to Lia Rees, Corin Spinks, and Michael Crittenden who designed the cover, and the many Dreamtime Tale Fantasy authors who contributed stories or valuable time to help content and copy-edit each other's stories. Authors from the USA, UK, Australia, Ireland and the Netherlands. This truly has been a collective international effort and we all sincerely hope that you will enjoy the fruits of our labours.

101 USES FOR A DRAGON

A WORK IN PROGRESS BY NAV LOGAN

Chapter One: Burning Desire

"How do you like your steak, sir?" the waitress asked politely. In that moment, the realisation dawned on me. I needed a pet dragon.

"I'll take it crispy on the outside, and still pumping in the middle please," I responded with a cheeky grin.

"Sorry!?"

Clearly my linguistic skills were too much for her limited English, despite her thick Dublin accent. "Rare," I explained with a sigh. "I want it rare."

This is just one reason why I need a dragon.

I could order a slab of meat and have it incinerated to perfection within seconds. Nothing too big, mind, a big dragon wouldn't fit into my bedsit.

My steak arrived; looking like it had a false tan and barely bleeding. Infuriated, I took the bull by the horns and began a quest that would change my life.

I searched E-bay and Amazon, but I couldn't find any dragons for sale; large or small. I couldn't even find dragon eggs. There were some ornamental ones, and imitation Game of Thrones ones, but I needed the real deal.

I knew what I needed to do. I needed to find an old Chinese junk shop. That would be the sort of place you could find dragon eggs, if ever there was one.

Sadly, rural Ireland didn't really do Chinatown. The best I could come up with was my local Chinese takeaway.

The thought made my stomach rumble. I was starving anyway and fancied a change from my usual diet of Pot Noodles and slices of Batch loaf. There's a lot that could be said about a Pot Noodle butty, but a chicken chow mein with egg fried rice and prawn crackers ... I could almost feel those monosodium glutamates swirling around in my bloodstream. Once the craving had taken hold, there was no going back. I simply must have.

It was Friday night, and the drunken hen nights and stag parties were in full flow, filling the streets of the town with inebriated revellers.

Why they would want to travel to a shithole like this was anyone's guess.

They came from the big cities, and even from overseas, to spend their hard-earned cash on watered-down lager and shots of vodka. It was ironic that they should travel to rural Ireland to get pissed on Dutch beer and Russian spirits. Still, it takes all sorts.

Me, if I had my choice, I'd be out of this poxy orifice in a heartbeat and I'd never look back. Why was I still here, you might ask? That's a million-dollar question, and one that I've yet to find an answer for.

I walked into the mayhem of the chipper, jostling my way through a crowd of giggling middle-aged women in pink rabbit ears and wearing clothing more suited for a strip club waitress. A drunken Corkonian was shouting abuse at the short Chinaman behind the counter.

"Sal'n'vingah?" asked the owner, ignoring the drunken rant.

"Ya what, Boy?! I can't understand a feckin' word of ya prattlin'. Why don't ya speak da Queen's English!?" - The ironies of modern day Ireland.

A Corkman, barely able to articulate the English language himself and ignoring his own God-given native tongue, hurling abuse at a Chinese. At least, I presume he was Chinese. He could have been born in Belfast for all I know.

"Sal'n'vingah?" persisted the owner, before giving up. "I pour it on myself!"

I smiled at the image in my brain of the owner pouring salt and vinegar over his head. Sadly, the condiments were liberally sprinkled into whatever the stupid Corkonian had ordered instead.

"That'll be Fah fifty-two…pease."

The drunk stared at his blankly.

"Fah fifty-two! Fah fifty-two!"

"What da feck ya talkin' about, Boy?"

The owner took an audible sigh and then repeated the sentence slowly. "Fawh Euro… and fifty…two cent, pease!"

Comprehension slowly dawned on the Corkonian, and he fumbled in his pockets for money. Swaying like a sailor in a storm, he steadied himself and dumped a pile of coins, pocket fluff, and a five euro note on the counter. He peered long and hard at the money, his brain ticking loudly as he tried to figure out if there was enough money there.

The owner eventually interceded and slid the fiver to one side, and then slid some coins over to join it. Leaving the pocket fluff and remainder on the counter. He then slid this pile of money into his till.

"Next!" he said in dismissal.

The drunken Corkman didn't moved.

His muscular bulk blocked up the counter. Finally, he asked, "Have ya got any ketchup?"

"No ketchup! You go now!"

"I want some feckin' ketchup!"

"No ketchup! Sal'n'vingah! I pour it on myself! You go now, yes!"

"I want some feckin' ketchup, ya stupid bastard. Why can't ya understand plain English?"

An explosion of loud Mandarin flowed from the owner's mouth. He was clearly getting angry. I didn't understand what he was saying, but I was fairly confident that if Mandarin (or whatever it was) contained swear words, then a choice few of them had been liberally sprinkled into whatever the Chinaman's shouts.

The doors into the kitchen swung open and a sumo wrestler walked in carrying a wicked looking cleaver.

He wasn't really a sumo wrestler. He was dressed in white overalls, rather than a greased-up loincloth, but he was certainly big enough and beefy enough to consider the sport.

A brief and heated conversation was held in Mandarin, while the owner presumably explained the problem.

Grunting, the sumo wrestler stooped and disappeared from view. When he popped back up, he slapped a sachet of ketchup on the counter beside the change.

"Ketchup, twenty cent."

There was no trace of a Chinese accent in the sumo wrestler's speech. His accent was pure Cultchie. The man was born and bred in rural Ireland. For all I knew, he could have been weaned on Guinness and strong sweet tea, spent his summers on the bogs footing turf, and he could be a fee-paying member of the local G.A.A. club. He was a few years older than me, but I seem to remember him vaguely that he had gone to our local Vocational school. Even back then, people had given him a wide berth

The drunken Corkonian was considering further argument. You could see it in the gleam of his contrary eyes. Corkonians were known to be tight-fisted bastards, or so it was rumoured within the town. His eyes met the sumo wrestler's and they locked there.

Silence descended. Even the giggly hen party had stopped snickering, waiting to see what would happen next.

The sumo wrestler might as well have been a statue of Buddha. His eyes never flickered in the slightest. He lifted his cleaver and half whispered, "You want ketchup or not?"

"Feck ya ketchup. Stick it up ya hole!" grumbled the Corkman.

Swiping up his change, along with his bag of steaming food, he turned and shouldered past me. Soon he was lost in the crowd of other drunken bastards; another face in the busy street.

The cold eyes of the sumo wrestler turned towards me. "Are you next, McCann?"

I blinked in surprise. The sumo wrestler knew my name. Of course he knew my name. This was rural Ireland, after all. I probably knew his name too, if I thought about it hard enough.

"McCann? Have you gone to sleep?"

"Sorry," I said, flushing like a beetroot.

"What're you having?"

"A number seven, egg fried rice and chips, please Can I have half and half?"

He nodded.

"Oh, and some prawn crackers too."

He turned to relay the order in mandarin to his father.

"You want salt and vinegar on that?" he asked, without even turning around.

"Aye, grand," I replied. It was then that I remembered the real reason for my excursion into the town centre on a Friday night. "…Oh, and I need a dragon too!"

He spun around and glared at me. "Are you taking the feckin' mickey, McCann?"

"No, I'm serious! I need a dragon. I thought ya old man might know where I can lay my hands on one."

"Get out of here, ya wee shite! I've had enough guff for one night. You're barred!"

"What!"

He lifted the cleaver threateningly. "I'll not be taking guff from the likes of you, McCann. Get the feck out of here before I split ya!"

"But what about my dinner?"

"Feck ya dinner. Out. Now!"

My pleading puppy eyes were ignored, and dejectedly, I slunk outside.

I started to take my frustrations out on a nearby wall.

This proved to be a bad idea. My old Converse runners were ill-suited for a serious wall-kicking. They lacked the steel toe-caps required for that kind of thing.

In the end, after hopping around for a while on one foot, I recovered from the pain of the foot bruising, I slid down the wall to mope sullenly. I sat there, ignoring the soft summer rain that was gradually soaking through my hoodie.

My reverie was broken by the sound of footsteps approaching. "You want dragon?"

I looked up to see a wrinkled old Chinaman. He could have been taken straight out of a movie. All he needed was the foot-long nails and the long-stemmed pipe. He was dressed all in black, traditional clothing, and sported a long beard and plait.

I looked up at him blankly.

"You want dragon?" he repeated.

I nodded, expecting him to respond with ridicule. It was a stupid idea, after all. For my troubled I'd now been banned from the only decent chipper in town.

"Dragons are dangerous creatures, ...and rare."

I looked at him with surprise. "You mean they really exist?"

"Of course. But dragons are expensive. Dragons vely lucky, ...cost a fortune. Are you rich?"

I shook my head. Rich! He must be joking. I was a student, for crying out loud. I'd barely enough to cover the chicken chow mein.

"You not want buy dragon then. You want find dragon egg!"

"What?"

"Dragon egg! Hard to find, ... but not impossible!"

"In Ireland?"

The old man considered the question, screwing his wrinkled face up and shaking his head from side to side. Finally, he answered. "Perhaps ... if you vely lucky!"

"How do I find a dragon egg?" I asked.

"That is special secret. Not to be given to just anyone!"

"But I have to know!" I pleaded.

The old man chewed his bottom lip and looked at me for some time.

I waited, silently hoping.

"People drink too much! Make big mess in street!"

I looked around at the street. The night was still young and it was already littered with chip wrappers, empty beer bottles, vomit, you name it. By the time the nightclub closed, you could be wading knee deep in the stuff.

"Council always complaining! We provide bins, but fools no use them!"

"Mmm," I grunted, noncommittally.

"I get up early every morning and clean off street. Then council can't complain. It clean before they finish sleeping, yes! That way, they can't take away licence."

"That's a tough job."

"Someone has to do it! My son and grandson, they work all hours! Need sleep sometime."

I grunted again, wondering whether the old man had gone senile. "What has this to do with dragon eggs?"

He smiled knowingly. "I getting too old for this. My knees not what they used be. You help me. I help you. Yes?"

"You want me to help you clean up the mess?"

"You clean up mess. I have lie in for change."

"And you'll tell me the secret of how to find dragon eggs?"

"You do this for one month. I think you may be friend. A man can tell a secret to friend. Maybe I tell you. Maybe not. We see…"

"But…!" I protested.

Sensing my reluctance, he shrugged his shoulders. "Forget. Stupid idea. Me going daft." He waved his hand in dismissal and turned to leave.

His slippered feet were already shuffling away.

"No wait! I'll do it."

What did I have to lose?

If nothing else, I might get back into his grandson's good books and get my ban lifted. It was a long way to the nearest decent chipper. A thirty-minute bus ride to be exact, and buses were hard to come by in rural Ireland.

He smiled and nodded his head enthusiastically. "You start at dawn. Don't be late. I leave brush and mop in shed around back."

Every weekend for the next few weeks, I woke to the annoying bleeping sound of my alarm clock and fumbled around in the dark, getting dressed. By five a.m. I was on the street, sweeping and moping outside the chip shop.

Weeks went by and I never saw the old man, but I sensed that he would be watching me work, hidden somewhere.

I felt that the old man was testing me.

This had more to do with my worthiness to own a dragon, than it had to do with street cleaning. At least, that's what I kept telling myself as I dragged my sorry ass out of bed in the pre-dawn hours and shuffled, zombie-like, into the town centre.

I'd just finished cleaning, one miserable morning when the rain was more horizontal than vertical, when I heard a voice calling me, "Hey, McCann!"

Standing in the doorway of the Chinese takeaway was the sumo wrestler. By now, I'd remembered his name. It was Sue. I'm not sure about the spelling of it, but it sounded like Sue to me anyway.

Sue motioned me over and let me in out of the rain.

"Dirty morning," he said by way of greeting.

I was soaked through, and could only drip on the floor and nod in agreement.

"Here," he said, handing me a small brown envelope, no bigger than my hand. "A little something for your trouble. Don't spend it all at once."

Realising that I was getting paid for my work, I considered protesting, but he cut me off. "Shut up and take it. It's not much, but you've earned it."

I looked down at the envelope in my hand and wondered what was inside. It seemed rude to look inside while he was still standing there. Instead, I asked, "Does this mean I'm not banned anymore?"

He grinned at me. "Sorry about that. Yes, McCann, you're welcome back anytime."

"Thanks, Sue."

"It's Lao-Tzu, McCann, not Sue!" he said, shaking his head in exasperation.

I nodded and left, putting the mop in the shed around the back.

As I was locking the shed door, Lao-Tzu appeared again. "I nearly forgot," he said. "Grandfather had a message for you."

"Yes?" I asked. The old man had not forgotten then. Was he going to tell me the secret of how to find dragon eggs? I could hardly believe it.

"Don't get excited, McCann. My Grandfather is very old, very wise, but sometimes his wisdom is beyond this world."

"What did he say?" I pressed.

Lao-Tzu shrugged. "He said that you should search where the lightning falls. Does that mean anything to you?"

I shrugged. "Is that it?"

Lao-Tzu grinned. "I did warn you, McCann. That's all he said."

… And that was why I started chasing after thunderstorms.

* * * * *

I spent the next few weeks chasing thunderstorms. There was no shortage of rain, but storms were few and far between. I got drenched quite a lot, but had still to get near enough to a lightning strike to know where to dig.

Standing on Strandhill, soaked to the skin, I was getting frustrated. I cursed the gods vehemently. Waving my spade wildly about, I berated every god I could think of: Buddha, Jesus, Mohammed, and Vishnu. You name it, they all got a sound slagging.

In a spark of pure genius, I remembered Thor, and he got a mouthful too.

Bang! I was struck by lightning.

* * * * *

Some days later, I woke up in hospital, heavily bandaged. They told me that I was lucky to be alive after a billion volts had blasted through my body. My right-hand side was a mess of burn tissue and I was forced to endure days in therapy before I was finally given the all clear.

Each minute of recovery gnawed at my impatient spirit. I needed to get back to Strandhill and collect my dragon egg. If I didn't, then all I had been through would have been for nothing.

It was almost a week later when I finally climbed the sandy dune to retrace my steps. The glassy sand and melted spade showed me where Thor had smote me for my temerity.

Thankfully, the beach was deserted.

I started to dig.

* * * * *

I have to admit that the dragon egg didn't look like much on first viewing. The crazy sand sculpture caused by the lightning strike was far more impressive. The egg itself looked like an oversized pebble, shiny and a drab brown in colour. It resembled an old-style rugby ball, without the stitching lines, and weighed about as much as a bag of sugar. Had I not been told to dig beneath the lightning strike, I would have easily overlooked it.

Leaving a large hole in the sand dunes behind me, I tucked the egg inside my overcoat and shuffled home like a dirty old man on his way to the local school. My eyes roamed nervously, watching out for anyone who could have guessed my hidden treasure.

I tried my best to ignore the strange looks I received on the bus ride home. One little boy kept peeking over the top of the seat at me. His attention made me nervous. He knew! He must know. For an irrational moment I even contemplated murder, but thankfully an angry scowl finally scared the young scallywag off.

Still, as I watched the bus pull away, my eyes watched the little lad. I made sure that the bus was well out of sight before slipping down the back alley and taking the stairs up to my bedsit.

*****

Sitting on my bed I considered what to do next. I had my dragon's egg. At least, I hoped that it was a dragon's egg and not just a stupid lump of rock, but what was I supposed to do now? I spent hours trawling the Internet, looking up incubation techniques and incubators.

I tried looking at the egg with a bright light behind it, hoping to reveal the dragon inside, but to no avail. It looked just the same as any other shiny brown rock.

Heat seemed to be a common denominator when it came to incubation, but how hot did it need to be for a dragon to hatch? Did the egg need turning? If so, how many times per day? The more I read, the less I knew.

I decided to invest in an incubator.

It arrived in the post three days later.

My landlady, Mrs O., signed for the package and has been giving me strange looks ever since. She went as far as reminding me of her 'Strictly No Pets' clause in my tenancy agreement. I smiled and explained that it was for college. I assured her that there would be no baby chicks within the bedsit.

She didn't seem convinced, but eventually dropped the matter.

*****

After reading the incubator manual carefully, I opted for the settings for a goose egg. *Why a goose egg?* I hear you ask. Have you any better ideas? They didn't have ostrich eggs in the manual for some reason.

For the next four weeks, the incubator sat and hummed quietly in the corner of the bedsit, but no dragon appeared. I tried turning the settings up to maximum and waited another two weeks. Still there wasn't even a wobble from my lump of rock.

In desperation, I turned to extreme measures.

Clearing out all the clutter that I had previously stored in my Baby Belling, I turned the oven up to its hottest.

I needed heat, I decided, lots of it.

If there had been a volcano in the vicinity, I would have chucked the egg into that, but there wasn't, so my tiny cooker would have to do.

I shudder to think about my next electricity bill.

For days I lived in my underwear as the temperature in my little bedsit soared like a midsummer heat wave.

Idly, I watched the meter spin around like an overexcited hamster on amphetamines. I dared not switch on my laptop or the TV, in case the fuses had a meltdown. I had enough problems with the landlady as it was, without her asking why my oven was on full 24-7.

I spent a lot of my time sleeping. The deadening heat brought on a stupor that was hard to resist. Lying there, sweating in my boxers, I dozed on and off for the next week.

Something woke me in the middle of the night.

Looking around at the darkened bedsit, I wondered what had startled me out of my slumber. There was a soft glow coming from around the door of the oven. Apart from that there was no light in my tiny flat.

Thump!

I blinked with surprise as the tiny oven door rattled and went still.

Thump!

Getting nervously to my feet, I crept closer. I was not imagining it. There was certainly movement.

Thump!

The oven door rattled firmly, just as my hand reached out toward the handle.

In my haste I grabbed the handle.

Too late, I remembered about the heat. My palm screamed in protest at me as it started to blister.

"Feck!" I cried, clasping my wrist in the hope of easing the pain. "Fecketty-Fecketty-Feck-Feck!" I cursed as I ran the tap into my sink and plunged my hand into the water.

Thump!

Thump! Thump-a-thump!

For a few moments I ignored the urgent noises coming from the Baby Belling. I had a badly burned hand to deal with first.

My eyes had finally stopped watering and I'd run out of curses to mutter when I looked around for an oven glove to use. I had never used the oven since I had moved in, but still, I rummaged around in the desperate hope of finding a mislaid mitt amongst the clutter.

No such luck.

Eventually, I wrapped a couple of towels around my throbbing hands and hoped for the best.

Gingerly, I opened the oven door.

Heat blasted out like a furnace and momentarily blinded me as my glasses became acclimatized. Smoke and steam were billowing out of the tiny oven. Using one of the towels, I wafted the air around to clear it.

I had just noticed a large crack in the dragon egg's shell when a loud klaxon erupted in the hallway outside of my door.

"Gad Zeus!!" I cried.

The smoke alarm must have gone off.

I heard the sound of other tenants stomping around in a panic. It wouldn't be long until they were heading for the fire escapes. With visions of firemen breaking down my door with an axe, I hurriedly opened the tiny windows as wide as I could.

Next, I reached in and grabbed the egg, wrapping it up in the towels as I juggled it like a hot potato. Stuffing it under my bed, I grabbed my dressing gown and stumbled out into the hallway.

By now, a crowd was gathering, barging down the stairs in their slippers and heading to the safety of the open air.

Sirens were already wailing in the distance. I followed the herd, pretending to be as dumbfounded as the rest.

Chapter Two: Home is Where the Heart is

The firemen arrived and anyone not yet awake within a three-mile vicinity was rudely awakened by the sirens and flashing blue lights. The street became like an ad-hoc festival. Tea and scones appeared as if by magic, as the firemen went about their business.

I did my best to stay unobtrusive, though the temptation of freshly buttered scones was too much for my empty stomach. I'd been living on Tayto crisps and coke for the last few days, too nervous to switch on the kettle for a pot noodle in case the Electricity Supply Board should go into crisis mode due to the power drain.

I was just stuffing a second scone into my mouth, tongue wiping away any stray jam, when the firemen returned. Between them they carried a small cooker, which they set down on the pavement.

It was my Baby Belling.

The white enamel looking a bit charred around the edges. It was then I realised the grave error I had made. I'd forgotten to switch off the damned cooker!

The Fire Chief, (or whatever they are called when you didn't live in Boston,) motioned over the landlady. He stood beside her and they spoke in hushed tones. His expression was stern and occasionally he would point with indignation at the cooker on the kerbside. She listened patiently to his tirade. It probably had something to do with health and safety and the fire hazards of old cookers.

All the time, she glared silently at me.

You could almost see the smoke coming off her fluffy slippers, such was the heat in that stare.

The scone suddenly felt like old boots in my mouth, and I was having trouble swallowing.

Finally, the Head Honcho of the local fire brigade had vented his anger. He would head back to the station and his cup of tea and dominos game, safe in the knowledge of a job well done.

Turning crisply away, he signalled for his crew to pack up their gear.

As quickly as they had come, the fire engines retreated, though with less noise and less flashing lights. Not that it mattered. Half of the town was awake by now.

"Mr McCann, a word if you will."

I nearly jumped out of my skin.

While I was watching the firemen disappear around the corner, Mrs O'Reilly, the landlady, had teleported to my side. How could an old lady move so fast, especially in those slippers?

Crouching Tiger: Hidden Landlady!

She must have learned some serious kung-fu tricks in her younger days. Did landladies even have younger days?

I shuddered at the thought.

"Mr McCann? Are you with us?"

I shook myself out of the daydream and looked at the hideous face of Mrs O'Reilly. Smoke partially clouded the rougher crevices of her mouth, but did little to lessen the overall effect.

"Sorry, Mrs O., I'm still in shock."

Her eyes flickered as if she wanted to roll them but had managed to control the urge. "Mr McCann, we need to talk. Perhaps you'd prefer to do this away from the public eye?"

I sensed the angry glares around me like the heat of an iron, inches from your neck. Small town Ireland, everyone knew everyone else.

There were no secrets to be kept. Your mother probably knew which colour underwear you'd chosen this morning, even before you had. In fact, me old dear had probably already been made aware of my public humiliation.

I was dragged back to the present by a phlegmy clearing of the landlady's throat.

"Oh, right," I said. "Lead the way."

We left the festivities behind and entered the haloed shrine of Mrs O's living room. Her flat was much larger than my own humble abode, taking up most of the ground floor of the Edwardian house. The room was littered with religious effigies, all glaring benevolently down at me.

Above the fireplace, hanging slightly off centre, was the Holy Trinity: Jesus, Pope John Paul, and J.F.K. The sacred heart had its own mini altar, with an electric candle ever burning. No fear of stepping on Lego in the dark in Mrs O's sitting room, not that any child in their right mind would ever set foot in here. They would need years of expensive therapy to recover from the ordeal.

The heady reek of cat piss dominated the room.

Boxes of cat litter lay in each corner, but apparently, the smelly moggies had never been potty-trained. The culprits looked up at me from the settee. They seemed unperturbed by their guilt as they mocked me with feline eyes. They huddled together like a Cat-hydra, a big pile of multi-coloured fur with many heads.

There was potential for a horror movie here, I thought.

Looking around, I wondered whether I was going to be offered a seat, a cup of tea maybe, but neither was forthcoming.

Mrs O settled herself in a battered armchair and looked up at me with an expression that would curdle milk. Taking some initiative, I started to sit on the edge of the settee, only to be hissed away by the Cat-hydra.

I paused, half-sitting, like a man taking a dump in the woods, looking around and hoping no one would spot him doing the dirty deed.

I was caught between committing to the settee and possibly being mauled to death by feral beasties, and standing. Finally, with as much grace as I could muster, I opted to stand.

Visions of the Headmaster's Office at school came flooding into my head, waiting to be berated and possibly worse from the old tyrant. Guilt washed off me in waves and I did my best to hide it, but Mrs O's scrutiny would make the Gestapo envious.

"Mr McCann," she began.

"Please, call me Gerry."

Her lips pursed like a Venus Fly-catcher chomping on a fat bluebottle, "Mr McCann, about the fire…"

"Fire, what fire?"

The Fly-catcher seemed to have found a broken bottle in its fly. "Mr McCann. This is no time to be funny. The Fire Brigade will be sending me a bill in the morning. This is not a time for joviality."

"Oh, the fire alarm … sorry about that."

"Mr McCann. The Chief Fire Officer: Mr Bardon assures me that the cause of this evening's disturbance started in your quarters. He informs me that they found your oven turned on to maximum and smoking in an alarming manner. What exactly were you cooking at four o'clock in the morning? Was this another one of your whacky science experiments?"

"Erm ... well..."

Mrs O raised a hand to stop me. The Garda College in Templemore could learn a lot from this woman.

"I really don't want to know, Mr McCann. As you know I don't normally allow students into my residence..." The way she said the word 'students' made it sound like the worst swear word ever uttered. It was almost like she was performing a black mass.

"In your case I made an exception, due to your dear mother, but I'm afraid this is not working out."

"Mrs O, I can explain..."

"My mind is already made up, Mr McCann. I'm sure with a creative mind like your own, you'll be able to find a wonderful explanation, but it is beside the point. I will expect you gone by tomorrow evening. Give my regards to your dear mother when you see here next, won't you?"

"But...!"

"That will be all, Mr McCann. I don't know about you, but I have a bed to go to. You can see yourself out."

Rising, the landlady, or ex-landlady as I would now have to refer to her, shuffled off towards the other door in the room. Did this lead to the kitchen, or a bedroom?

I would never know. Perhaps it led to a dark cellar where she buried any tenant whose rent was overdue.

The Cat-hydra watched me leave.

Haunting memories of leaving the Headmaster's office flickering through my mind. I considered going back outside and seeking another scone for comfort food, but figured my chances were slim. The whole street had seen me being summoned into the landlady's rooms. I wouldn't find a friendly welcome out there.

I slunk back upstairs.

Only then did I remember the dragon egg, and the crack I had seen in the shell.

With a renewed pep in my step, I opened the door to my bedsit, ignoring the fresh axe marks in the woodwork.

Rummaging under the pillow, I pulled out the towels and un-wrapped the bundle.

The egg jumped in my hands. It was coming to life. My experiment had finally paid off. As I sat watching, the crack widened and a tiny head appeared.

A warm feeling of paternity washed over me, helping me to forget my homelessness.

I was like a father beaming down at his son's face for the first time!

* * * * *

The dragon was in truth a bit of a disappointment. I'd been expecting sleek elegant grace and shimmering scales that dazzled in the sunlight. At the very least, I was hoping for a twinkling intelligent eye and fabulous wings.

What I got was a serious understatement.

It looked more like an amphibian than any dragon I'd ever imagined. The movies and artwork had obviously been all overkill on artistic licence. My pet dragon was dull by comparison.

It was about the size of a decent rat, and of a similar dreary colour. To be fair, it had scales, but they were more of the type you would find on snakeskin, and they did not sparkle or shimmer.

Neither was it sleek. In fact, the word that came to mind was portly. It did have a set of wings, but they seemed out of proportion with the overweight body. Basically, it looked more like a winged frog than a dragon. If I'd have bought it in a shop,

I'd be rushing back right now to demand a refund, before the shop went bankrupt, or the owners did a runner.

The Office of Fair Trade would certainly be looking carefully at the small print of the Trade Description Act to check whether it fairly represented the adverts.

Was it worth getting evicted for? Probably not, but that had been on the cards anyway. Mrs O had never been fond of me. She liked her tenants to leave early each morning, work all day on some building site and then spend all evening down the pub. She also liked to be paid promptly each Friday evening, in advance.

I was a college student studying Sociology. Sociology is a course for people who want to be a student but don't really know what they want to do. It's one of those safe courses that attract the lost and desperate within the student population. The lecturers were indifferent to attendance or grades, and are pleasantly surprised when more than half of their class turn up on a Monday morning.

In terms of Mrs O, this meant that I slept in much later than she considered healthy, my rent came whenever my grant came through, so was invariably late, and I spent most evenings sitting in my digs. Add to this the quantity, quality, and volume of loud music that seeped through the floorboards from my bedsit down to her living room.

This could be having a serious long-term impact on her Cat-hydra.

There would also have been the students, male and female, who visited me.

Mrs O's demeanour had scared most of my friends away, including my girlfriend or recently ex-girlfriend to be accurate.

All told, my eviction was as inevitable as the spring tide.

*****

My bedsit could be easily described in one word: dingy.

If someone had bought a wild array of items as a job lot going cheap at an auction and then crammed them into a tiny closet-like room, they couldn't have done any worse.

That's to say nothing of the woodchip wallpaper, or the off-pink magnolia emulsion which covered both the walls and the ceiling. The colour had probably been designed to give a cheerful air, but the designer had clearly never visited bedsit-land when he was working on this particular shade.

Added to this was the weather-beaten effect. The wallpaper was torn in places, there was a large splash of tomato puree above my bed, (God only knew how it got there or why), and the tiny sash window, half of which had been covered with a piece of cardboard where the glass had been broken and never replaced.

In conversation with friends, I jokingly referred to the scratch marks on the walls as a place where someone had tried to swing a hamster around and failed.

One of the highlights of my guided tours was the visit to the communal bathroom. The toilet seat was split, and wobbled whenever anyone sat on it, having only one bracket holding it in place. That was of course, if you were foolish enough to actually make contact with its grimy surface. I preferred the hover method. Take deep breath before entering, hold and squat, and hope you can finish your business before passing out.

The inside of the toilet reminded me of an H-block protesters cell, or an abstract painting in various tones of brown. I am sure that a Victorian sewage pipe would have been cleaner.

The bath was just as bad. I doubted that it even knew what cleaning fluid looked like. It was blacker than a coal-miner's ass-crack and just as crusty. It would probably need battery acid to clean it at this stage. Eons of use by a variety of road-workers had left if looking like the lungs of a chain-smoker.

Needless to say, I took showers at the college and never ventured near the bath. I can't even recall the bathroom sink, so quickly did I dismiss it upon first perusal.

You would think that with such a limited space to work with, that packing up to move would be a simple task. Somehow, I had managed to collect a whole array of useless items. With only one rucksack at my disposal I began to gather together essential items: college books, a handful of clothes, my laptop, some toiletries, a sleeping bag, and a tent. These became my priorities. Everything else had to go, apart from the dragon, of course.

Stabbing holes into a plastic container, I lined it with a couple of old t-shirts and placed the newly-hatched dragon inside.

I then began to haul the detritus I'd gathered over the last six months down to the bins. This proved to be harder than first anticipated.

Let me explain.

All the doors in the building closed automatically.

Each staircase had a fire door which also closed automatically.

Each landing had an automated light switch, which inevitably timed out while you were still halfway down the narrow staircase, leaving you in total darkness and fumbling for the next fire door or light switch.

The bins were stored at the rear of the building.

This meant that in order to take out any rubbish I had to navigate four doors, including the front door which had a Yale lock and needed a key, two timer-light switches, before walking around the building and unlatching the gate to access the back yard. All this while juggling whatever rubbish I was carrying and hoping not to bump into anyone coming the other way.

Firstly, the staircase was a tight enough squeeze for two people passing as it was, let alone carrying baggage, and secondly, I was trying to avoid my neighbours after waking them up in the wee small hours.

As Murphy's Law would have it, I met more of my neighbours on the first two rubbish excursions than I had in the last six months.

It was while I was trying to cram the second batch of rubbish into the already overflowing bins that I had a revelation.

I had just been trying to stuff the stolen traffic cone into the bin, which was already full of the usual garbage, along with two blinking orange road lights, a "Men At Work" sign (don't you just love rag week?), and the my recently-acquired incubator when I happened to look heavenward.

Twenty feet above my head I saw the colourful logo for a well-known breakfast cereal. It was blocking up a hole where a plate of glass should normally be.

How odd, I thought. I have one just like that covering my own window. Surely it wasn't the same window.

With all the twists and turns in the varied corridors, I'd completely lost my sense of direction. I had never once bothered to actually look out of my window, not even when I was taping the cornflakes packet over the hole to cut out the breeze. The windows were so full of grime that they hardly allowed daylight to enter my cupboard of a room anyway, so what was the point? Stepping over the varied litter that covered the back yard, I checked the other windows I could see. There was only one window with a grinning, brightly-coloured cockerel smiling down at me.

Heading back upstairs, my clearing out became a whole lot quicker. A swift kick cleared the cardboard away from the hole and soon it was raining assorted detritus into the back yard.

I hoped that no one would decide to venture back into the yard at that point, or I might soon face murder charges. The room was soon cleared of unwanted clutter, with pots and pans, clothes, posters, and everything else that wasn't nailed firmly in place, flying out of the window as quickly as I could grab them. I didn't even bother checking if the coast was clear below, or aiming for the overflowing bins. Why bother? There was so much other rubbish down there, no one was going to notice a little more. There were scrap yards with less junk in them than the back yard. The only thing it was missing was an ugly looking half-starved mongrel frothing at the mouth and yanking on the end of its chain.

By mid-morning I'd reduced the clutter by half and the only things remaining were the ancient wardrobe, bed, chest of drawers, fridge, Belfast sink, table, chair, and the two-bar heater (which didn't work but wouldn't fit through the window).

My Baby Belling cooker was still standing out on the kerb, having been wrenched out of the wall by the firemen. All of the hard graft had left me feeling famished, so I tucked into the last of the batch loaf, covered in peanut butter. The unused pot noodles were hurled out of the window. They were about as much use as a tin of peaches to a starving man without a can opener.

With a bellyful of sandwiches in me, I hauled the rucksack onto my shoulders and grabbed the plastic utility box. I could hear the baby dragon hissing in protest as I manhandled the box through the many fire doors and made my way to freedom.

I stood on the front step for a moment and considered my options. Where should I go now? The first image that came to mind was my girlfriend, Fiona.

No, I corrected myself. She was now my ex-girlfriend, and I'd certainly burned my bridges there.

Hindsight was a wonderful thing.

Had I known I was about to be evicted, I might have handled our break-up with a little more tact, and a little less bad language.

No, there was definitely no rebuilding that particular bridge.

In fact, it might be a good idea to avoid the parts of town where her older brothers hung out. I didn't have the dental plan to deal with that sort of confrontation.

Next, my mind wandered to the tried and trusted: My Mammy.

I shuddered at the thought of it.

I'd prefer a large dose of humble pie and a good battering by Fiona's brothers before I'd face the wrath of my mother. I'm pretty sure that her and Mrs O were from the same breeding stock. They were the same strong-willed Irish women that would put the fear of god into a demented pit-bull terrier.

With a sigh of resignation, I headed towards the town centre, and the bus stop.

I had a plan in my head. I would head back to Strandhill.

I had a tent and sleeping bag with me, and the rain was still of the softer variety. It was quiet down on the dunes, far enough away from any tourist traps to keep the vultures at bay. The occasional local might walk his dog down along the strand, but few ventured into the dunes themselves, as I had found out to my pleasure on the few occasions I'd managed to persuade Fiona to take a stroll down there. That was, of course, before we had a falling out over her stubborn refusal to relinquish her virginity.

Chapter Three: Freedom of the Open Dunes

The plastic box in which I was carrying the baby dragon thumped occasionally during my bus ride. He/she/it was getting restless. By the time the bus had reached its destination, the thumping was getting louder and was attracting unwanted attention. Quickly, I hurried away. My neck craning this way and that in case I was being followed.

The rain was getting heavier. I could feel it soaking through my hoodie and leaking down my neck by the time I'd managed to erect the tent. Crawling into the tiny shelter, I zipped down the doors. Only then did I risk opening the box and peeking within.

The dragon started up at me, hissing loudly at his confinement. It hadn't changed much. It was still a sorry excuse for a dragon, but nevertheless, it was my dragon.

I removed the lip and extended a finger to touch the dragon. It snapped petulantly at me, hissing again. I barely got my finger out of the way in time.

"Hey, that's not nice!" I protested. I smiled. "You're probably hungry, aren't you? Let's see what I can rummage up."

I dug through my rucksack, looking for possible dragon food. I should have thought of this sooner. I started to stack my food in front of me:

A bag of Tayto salt and vinegar crisps. No, that wouldn't work.

One can of Red Bull. I shook my head. Definitely not. He was hyped up enough after his confinement.

The more I thought about the dragon, the more I sensed that it was a male. I'd have to start thinking of a name for him soon.

I dug further into the rucksack and found a half-full jar of crunchy peanut butter. That had possibilities. Peanuts were, after all, rich in protein and oil and all that other good shit.

Next, I found a tin of tuna in brine.

Finally, I found a rather squashed Mars bar. Remembering that I hadn't eaten much either, I unwrapped the chocolate bar and dunked it into the peanut butter. Mmmm, delish!

Sorry, Mr. Dragon, but this is mine.

Reaching for the tin of tuna, I peeled open the tin. Taking a fork, I scooped up a small portion and offered it to the dragon. He sniffed at it, unconvinced before nibbling cautiously at the fish. He chewed for a moment before screwing up his tiny face.

"Not impressed, eh?" I grinned. "Can't blame ya. Here, try this." I dipped the fork into the peanut butter and offered him that instead.

The dragon flickered his tiny tongue out, sampling the peanut butter, before snapping hungrily at the spoon. I had obviously found the perfect food for dragons.

Looking down at the jar in my lap, I hesitated. There wasn't a lot of it left, and it was a long walk to the nearest shop to get more. An idea flashed in my head.

I dunked the last of my Mars bar into the jar and stuffed it into my mouth, before tipping the contents of the tin of tuna into the jar and mixing it together. I hoped that it was going to work as I could hear the rain coming down with gusto outside now. It would be a long and miserable walk to the shops, if the dragon turned its nose up at the meal.

"There we go, Gerry McCann's own secret recipe: Tuna in peanut butter sauce. Enjoy," I announced as I placed the jar into the plastic box with the dragon.

The dragon took one tentative bite, licked his lips in relish and then attacked the jar like a starving crocodile. It soon had peanut butter and tuna all over its head as it tried to crawl into the jar to get every last morsel of the savoury meal.

I sat watching with a big grin on my face.

In the end I had to remove the jar, fearful that he would eat too much and get sick. As it was, his stomach was distended like a tennis ball.

"You'll have to save some for later," I reproached.

He gave me a baleful glare and burped noisily in response.

A short while later, he was sleeping peacefully, emitting the occasional purring snore.

It had been a long and eventful day, so I decided to follow his example. Peeling off my wet hoodie and hanging it from the tent poles to dry, I curled up in my sleeping bag and slipped into sleep.

*****

I woke up to find the tent engulfed in a rank sulphurous stench. Gasping against the reek, I fumbled for the zipper and managed to open it far enough to poke my head out, before I suffocated.

"Jayzus wept!" I exclaimed, as the odour slowly escaped from confinement and wafted passed me head. Desperate to clear the air, I opened the tent flaps fully and wafted the air to create a breeze.

I heard the distinctive sound of farting, and knew it hadn't come from my own bowels. As the stench again rose up to pollute the air, I looked down at the plastic container. The dragon was nowhere to be seen. Panic gripped me, and doing my best to ignore the putrid smell, I searched the tent frantically. It didn't take long to find the farting culprit. He'd crawled into my rucksack and had been busy chewing my clothing. Had it been my socks he was chewing, I wouldn't have minded so much. They were already threadbare and more holy than Mother Theresa.

Sadly, it wasn't my socks he had found so delectable. It was my favourite t-shirt: U2- Go Home, live concert at Slane Castle.

It had been my first ever venture out into the world beyond my small town, into a magical world of rock'n'roll and mud. It was almost like going to a foreign country. To Hell or to Connaught they had said. Meath was a long way away from the rushy fields and stony walls of the west of Ireland, and that t-shirt was filled with happy memories.

The dragon had shredded it with claws and teeth. Before I could control my emotions, I gasped, "Ya little bollix!"

The dragon looked up guiltily, shreds of cotton still hanging from the corner of his fangs as he gave me his best shot at puppy dog eyes.

"Don't give me that!" I protested.

It flinched and backed away from my wrath, cowering under my baleful gaze. Finally getting my anger in check, I relented.

It was too late now. My shirt was already ruined anyway. My dreams of making a fortune in later years from this collector's piece were shredded, just like the cotton in my rucksack.

"Shit happens!" I surmised. "Come on, the rain is stopping. I think we better take you for a walk before you take a dump on my hoodie."

With a lot of encouragement and some baby noises, the baby dragon eventually braved the outside world and began following me around like an overenthusiastic puppy dog. It even flapped its tiny wings but stayed firmly on terra firma. From the look of its fat little toad body and the pathetic wingspan, I doubted it was ever going to fly.

A name came to me then.

I was thinking about flightless birds and the puffin sprang to mind. Puffin… Puff the Magic Dragon. It wasn't the most butch of names, and he was far from heroic or awe-inspiring, but it suited the little critter. "What do you think, Puffin?"

The little dragon squawked, and a tiny cloud of smoke billowed out of its nose.

"I'll take that for a yes, shall I?"

Happily, we spent an hour walking along the deserted dunes. It proved to be a good idea, as the tuna/peanut butter dinner had given Puffin a bad case of the scours. I was going to have to rethink his dietary requirements. Clearly, much though he had enjoyed his meal, it hadn't gone down well.

* * * * *

Money was getting tight, tighter than usual. When we got back to the tent, I counted it and decided I would need a degree in trigonometry to make the figures add up. I had to survive until Monday morning when Lao-Tzu paid me my unofficial wages for my unofficial job. Despite my recent storm chaser antics, I'd managed to keep up my early morning excursions to the town centre to do the street cleaning. That is, apart from during my stay in intensive care for lightning burns. Thankfully, Lao-Tzu had heard about my accident before the weekend madness had hit, and had made other arrangements. He'd even sent me some grapes in the hospital with a note saying, 'Get well soon, ya gobshite!'

As soon as I had been released from hospital, I'd popped down there to see if everything was still cool with us.

Lao-Tzu had fed me my usual chicken chow mein meal and greeted me like one of the family. I'd even been invited into the back of the chipper, where the Ming's extended family lived.

It had been a good afternoon, all told. I'd even met Lao-Tzu's sister who kept giving me the eye. I hoped that it wasn't just a dodgy tick, or that she wasn't right in the head. I had to admit, she was pretty hot-looking. I was caught between the temptation to encourage her, or to ignore her and not rock the boat.

At one point, she had even sat next to me at the kitchen table and surreptitiously brushed her hand along the inside of my thigh. I nearly leaped out of my skin, and completely forgot what I had been saying. I still wasn't sure whether it was in innocent gesture, an accident in passing, or whether she was coming on to me. My mind might still have doubts about it, but my libido had been panting like a dog in heat.

I hadn't seen her since, but tomorrow was Friday. I would have to find somewhere nearer to town to sleep before tomorrow night. I could hardly walk all the way to the shop at 3 in the morning, and there certainly wouldn't be any buses running. Not that I could afford one right now.

It was time to face facts and bite the bullet, or to be more accurate, face the firing squad and swallow the bullet.

It was time to go back to the Mammy's.

She would welcome me with open arms, of course. That's what mothers did.

I would be fed until it was coming out of my ears, and mollycoddled like a long-lost grandchild, but there would also be 'the looks'.

There'd be a certain amount of sighing.

There may even be tears and recrimination.

If I was lucky, I might get away with a scolding, or a week of nagging, but that was a slim hope. By now, I was pretty sure that Mrs O would have gone out of her way to accidentally bump into my mother. They would have had a long heart to heart, shared commiserations and my mother would have the full, over-embellished facts of her son's life as a student.

On the bright side, I would not go hungry, and neither would my dragon. There was also a good hiding place for Puffin.

At the bottom of my Mammy's garden was a shed. It contained my father's tools and empty plant pots. No one ever went down there anymore. Not since his death.

Puffin hadn't been happy to be going back into the plastic box, and in the end, I had been forced to bribe the dragon with the last of the tuna and peanut butter.

I knew that I would regret it later, but the dragon had gorged himself out and fallen asleep, letting me place him in the box and leave. With a heavy heart, I packed up my few possessions and headed for the bus stop.

* * * * *

Mammy lived only a short walk from the town centre. The day was just starting to darken as I walked up the street to the front door. The house was a semi-d, with an attached garage and a tiny front garden. The back garden was larger and surrounded by a high wooden-slat fence. It backed onto the river, which meandered through the town on its way to the sea nearby. Our back garden had become a bit of a jungle since my old man had passed away, but my mother had maintained the front garden. Whatever would the neighbours say if she ever let it go to wreck and ruin? She'd never be able to show her face again in the supermarket or the hair salon. Such would be the shame.

She started to pay a neighbour's son, (a snotty-faced geek of thirteen), to mow the short front lawn, but the back lawn had been my responsibility. I'm sure the lad would have mowed the back too, if he'd been given a chance, but that would have meant releasing me from the burden.

She kept the back garden in a dishevelled state as a mute reminder to me of her expectations. I couldn't walk past the bay windows in our kitchen without feeling the heavy weight of shame crash down on my shoulders as the weeds glared at me for my neglect. My mother never said anything. She didn't have to. Before my teenage years, I had become well and truly institutionalised. A simple frown, sigh, or eye roll, said more than mere words ever could.

That was before I got sick…

That's how my mother referred to it.

It was before that heady cocktail of adolescent hormones took control of me. It was before I became possessed by the devil. That was when I was a nice lovable lad, who knew his place, before I became … a student.

My mother still blames Bono, and my trip to Slane Castle for the change. She can't even watch him on telly any more. She'd turn off The Late Late Show whenever he was on it. That's how much she hated Bono. If he started coming to our church, I'm sure she'd convert to Protestantism, rather than look at his smug supercilious face, standing up on the altar. If she had her way, he would have been thrown into prison for the crime of me sneaking off for a mad weekend at a festival at the age of fourteen. In her mind, I've suffered irreparable damage caused by loud rock music.

SHANDIKHAAR

FROM OF DRAGONS AND MEN BY GUY DONOVAN

Author's note

Of Dragons and Men is a prequel novella to The Dragon's Treasure Series. It takes place almost exactly one year prior to the beginning of *"The Forgotten Princess of Môna."*

Spring, 442 A.D. Somewhere in the Rocky Mountains of North America.

Run, Hugrekkur told Shandikhaar, his hide rippling with iridescent blues and greens. *Go to the other opening and fly. I will join you soon.*

They will kill you, Shandikhaar objected, her own body still a muted grey. *There are too many.*

And we are already too few. You carry the future of our kind. You, more than I, must survive. Hugrekkur punctuated his statement with a roar and a blast of white-hot flame as more spears flew through the cave's narrow opening.

Shandikhaar obeyed. She wound her way through the twisting maze of tunnels under the mountain while the vermin's mixed cries of attack and death faded behind her. The shame that burned in her was due more to Hugrekkur being her mate than that she had left him behind.

Dragons were solitary, proud creatures and had been throughout their entire history. They mated only out of biological necessity to further the race, and did not remain with those mates. That she had left Hugrekkur behind, almost certainly to die, was of little issue to Shandikhaar. That she had done so reluctantly was a different matter. It was just not their way.

The two-legged vermin however, like those attacking them, took mates for life. They did not live their lives proudly apart, existing by their own strength or failing through a lack thereof. Instead, they banded together and multiplied like no other creature in the world. Alone, they were weak, having neither claws nor fangs, but together they found strength. It was the antithesis of dragonkind, but Shandikhaar could not deny that they had proven more powerful than dragons in the end. That there were so few of her kind left was proof enough of that.

She also knew that there would be fewer still if she did not get to the tunnel's far opening before the vermin found it.

Shandikhaar was young, as dragons reckoned age. Like all of her kind, she bore the shared memories of her proud race back to when the world itself was young and lit red by the bloated orb that had swung so swiftly through the steaming air of the sky. Those memories, even if not her own, included other creatures that had once walked, crawled, slithered, or swum over the face of the world but did so no longer. At least one other kind of creature besides dragons and the vermin had survived the falling of the bright light though. Even in her own memory, she knew of some enigmatic creatures that had once lived on land, but had long since returned to the sea.

The world has changed many times, she told herself. *It changes still. Now even dragons live and breed in shameful groups like the vermin that have driven us to the edge of oblivion.*

The unaccustomed weight of the eggs within her brought on renewed feelings of shame to know that the one who had quickened them remained yet with her, even as she raced toward another exit that promised her and her offspring a chance at life. Compounding that shame was a part of her that hoped Hugrekkur would not fall to the vermin that had surprised them so early that morning.

This land is plentiful with game, she thought. *Even if we gorged ourselves to fat stupidity, the vermin could live all their short, vicious lives on what we left behind! They continue to kill us not for their own survival, but for the joy of causing death.*

Far ahead, her keen vision detected the first hint of daylight. Her equally keen hearing told her it might already be too late to escape. Focusing on her mind's shared vision of what Hugrekkur saw and heard far behind her, she knew that the vermin had begun prying at the rocks above that cave mouth with their long, stone-toothed sticks.

Leave there, she thought to Hugrekkur no matter the shame it caused her to think it. *They are already here at this end, but are few enough.*

I am coming, he answered.

In the long tradition of creatures who shared thoughts openly between them, she knew that he was neither coming, nor truly intended to.

Then Shandikhaar heard the distant rumble of falling stone. It echoed loudly through the tunnel, but was even louder in her head. The last thing she saw through Hugrekkur's eyes was the cave mouth's top collapsing. Then she felt a brief spike of pain before all went dark. Were he only unconscious, she would have known. Where his mind had once been though, was nothing.

Hugrekkur was dead.

Shandikhaar shot from the cave's other entrance, her body now engulfed in waves of scarlet and gold. With a roar of unbridled fury, she shredded the first of the vermin there with her open, many-fanged mouth. Then, that victim's blood still hot and dripping from her jaws, she turned upon another just as it thrust a spear into her right shoulder. She did not even register its high-pitched cry as she disemboweled it too, the spear's shaft snapping beneath her as the force of her advance drove the stone point deep into her muscle. Turning back the other way, she saw three more vermin facing her, frozen in their shock and fear. Shandikhaar incinerated them with a blast of searing, white flame before leaping over their burning, shrieking bodies to climb higher up the mountainside.

She nearly reached the mountain's jagged peak before pausing to look down upon the scene. Their enemies already occupied the place that she and Hugrekkur had presumed to be safe for laying and brooding over her eggs.

My enemies, she corrected herself.

They advanced toward her, spreading out to either side. Clearly, the death of one dragon was not enough to appease them that day. Spreading her wings, she bellowed her prideful outrage upon them all.

Though she knew the savages heard only her roar, she shouted in her mind, *I am your death if you continue!*

Grappling onto a rocky promontory with one wing claw, she leaned out toward the nearest knot of the hated beasts and vomited forth a long blast of flame. They were too far away though, rendering her most potent of weapons merely a show. Worse, she knew by the feeling within her that she had little flame left. While there was an ample supply of the foul-smelling rock there to chew and make more of the fire-producing gas, she knew the vermin would overwhelm her long before she could summon enough flame to kill them all. If she stayed there, she would die…along with the dragonets she carried within her.

The long ago memories of her race still came to her, but they now seemed much more distant and brief. That she could summon them at all proved that she was not yet the last of her kind, but the survival of her eggs had become even more vital in the wake of Hugrekkur's death. She decided then that she must surrender herself to seeking out whatever remained of her kind in the service of her young.

It is shameful to depend on others, she thought, *but I will not submit to a fate that seems inevitable when any possibility remains for my kind to continue.*

With another bellow of rage, Shandikhaar leaped into the cool air and gave a mighty flap of her wings. The downdraft flattened the nearest of the savages, and she reveled in the sight as she rose into the sky. In a final show of her hate and disgust, she released her bowels upon them and then swung about to wing eastward as the flashing colors of her anger faded back to grey.

Ice built up on and then flaked away from Shandikhaar's body as she climbed through high clouds crystalline with the stuff. The cold soothed her injury, but stung her sensitive wing membranes. Ignoring the pain, she focused again on her shame. For the entire history of dragonkind's long, collective memory, no mating of male and female had ever lasted beyond the single act of quickening the female's eggs. She and Hugrekkur had broken that time-honored tradition and adopted a trait of the small-but-vicious vermin. It was an arrangement borne of circumstance and necessity, but that did little to ease her mind.

Was our shame for nothing though? she asked herself. *Are there enough left of our kind to continue at all, or will the world that once belonged to us belong only to the vermin?*

A part of her wondered if the world really was so different from before. Many races of creatures had died off throughout the memories of dragonkind. Perhaps now it was merely their time to follow those others into oblivion. Such thoughts did her little good, so she concentrated on what lay ahead. The ground below steadily dropped away, flattening until it rolled in grassy waves as far as she could see. Lakes and streams dotted the lower areas of that loamy, fertile land, and the scent of plentiful game filled Shandikhaar's nostrils. What bothered her was what she did *not* smell—báldrangur.

Báldrangur was what dragons called the rocks that, when chewed and swallowed, provided the gas for their flame breath. Though that flame had made them the mightiest creatures the world had ever seen, it was merely a waste product of the rock's primary purpose. For as long as their common memories accounted for, the draconic race as a whole suffered from pain that only báldrangur could relieve. Without it, the pain would increase until it incapacitated them, leading to death. Shandikhaar had recently chewed a great deal of the pungent-smelling rocks, but she knew that without a new source of it, she and her dragonets were doomed.

The only pain she felt then was her wounded right shoulder. She had been lucky that the vermin's aim had not been true, but the pain was growing worse with each beat of her wings. Seeing no signs of any vermin below, Shandikhaar looked about for a good place to rest. Ordinarily, she would hunt as well, but her appetite had gone away as she had grown increasingly gravid with her eggs.

Spotting an outcropping of rock at the top of a tall hill, she spiraled cautiously downward. When she was satisfied no danger awaited her there, she set down at the rocky crest's edge. Her leathery, grey hide took on the brownish green of the grass and the moss-and-lichen-spotted appearance of the rocks as she lay down. Secure for the moment, she licked away the blood crusted over her wound.

Deep inside, between her heavily muscled legs, she felt one of her five eggs shift about minutely. She knew it was early yet, but they would soon be ready for laying. For that, she would need something better for her brood than the meager shelter of rocks crowning a windswept hilltop. It was, however, the best she could do then.

As evening fell, Shandikhaar curled herself around one of the larger boulders and laid her wedge-shaped head atop it. The night's first stars made their appearance, and she turned her bright yellow eyes up to them. As a much younger dragon, barely out of her own egg, the twinkling lights had always entranced her. Now that she was much older, and there were so very few dragons left in the world, she liked to think that they were in fact the blazing eyes of untold generations of dragons looking down upon those that had yet to make the journey to whatever lay beyond life.

HAULING FIRE
BY A.J. NOON

Bert took a step back to survey the crate in front of him. All he could see was the back of his nephew pushing hard against the cargo to try and get it in. He resisted the urge to sigh and instead tried to make his point. Again.

"I'm telling ya Luth' it won't fit, you're forgetting about the nodules. The blasted thing just won't fit."

Luther, who was currently making up for his lack of experience by grunting strenuously and using his inconsiderable weight, making sure he put his shoulder into it as Bert had shown him, "An' I'm telling ya it will go! Those nodule thingys are only for decoration, she won't notice if we knock a couple off."

Bert let out the sigh he had been holding onto, "Well I for one don't want to be around if you do knock some off and she notices. Why don't you wait here while I go and get a bigger crate?"

Though his cheek was pressed firmly into the leather hide of the cargo, Luther managed to shake his head, "Take too long… this will go." The lad let out a roar of determination, which to Bert sounded more like someone blowing out a candle, and used every ounce of his scrawny nine stones to no effect.

Despite his growing impatience Bert chuckled at the sight of Luther's feet scrabbling for grip on the wooden platform. He had twice the years, and twice the weight, of his nephew and had been moving things for his whole life. When he had first started out with his brother he had been as keen as Luther but had soon learnt that haulage was not only about muscle. There was a knack to moving things, and the lad was yet to find it. It was that knack that had made Rubbler Brothers Transportation, in Berts' mind at least, very successful, having moved people's belongings across the kingdom. Whilst he and Luther did the hard work, though currently he was acting in his favoured supervisory role, his wife Mabel did the accounts and they made a great team.

Luther leant on the side of the wagon to catch his breath. The paintwork had once been a brilliant cream colour which Bert and his brother Syd had acquired from the local tavern. It had cost several beers and, of course, they had asked no questions, and they had sourced enough to re-paint the whole wagon. No-one had passed comment on the fact it was the same shade as the newly refurbished Merchants' Guild.

"Make people notice us it will," Bert had said at the time. The exertions of washing off the dust and mud that accumulated had soon taken its toll and on short attention span and the once gleaming wagon was now different shades, and textures, of brown.

That had been three weeks ago and hours later Syd was dead. They had loaded a piano for delivery and shortly after setting off the thing had slipped. Syd had gone to the back of the wagon to secure it whilst Bert had hitched the horses. There had been a thump and a groan and Bert had found Syd's shoes sticking out from underneath the piano, unfortunately still attached to his feet. There was an incriminating piano sized skid mark in the paint on the floor of the wagon that was still wet and still very, very slippery.

Once Bert had moved the wagon to a less inclined part of the road, and let the paint dry, he had manhandled the piano back onto the wagon, cleaned Syd's shoes, and then delivered the musical malady to the customer, 'A timely service' was the company motto after all. Then he had taken Syds' body back to Lucille, Syd's wife. Naturally she was distraught as Bert recounted his carefully rehearsed version of events, involving spooked horses and an unfortunate fall onto a rock, and she had accepted Syd's death as an accident.

To help assuage his guilt, it had been his idea to paint the wagon and he was not totally heartless, he had given Lucille two gold pieces and taken on his nephew Luther as an apprentice. Lucille had three other sons, each better built, but she had said Luther's likeness to Syd only reminded her of her loss. Faced with her grief, and the image of Syd's paint covered shoes flashing through his mind, he had taken Luther on.

Now Luther's usually pale face was bright red with beads of sweat rolling down it onto his leather jerkin. The lad had restarted his pushing, "She'll go in and we'll get our bonus or my name's not Lu…"

There was a deep grating sound as the cargo finally squeezed into the crate, with a gentle undertone of popping as nodules flew off in every direction.

Bert cussed, closely followed by the strongest cuss he knew when he realised how many nodules had come free. They lay in the dust around the crate, dark and leathery, and they seemed to be watching him incriminatingly, "Get them picked up and into the crate and let's get it locked down. They came off natural like if anyone asks." He shook his head and pulled a hammer from his tool belt with one hand, taking a handful of nails from a pouch with the other, "She'd better not notice!"

It took half an hour and three horses to pull the crate onto the wagon, and a further hour before Bert was satisfied everything was secure. He prided himself on the savings he made by using the least amount of packing materials but for this he had used all the nails he kept in his pouch and every rope he could lay his hands on. Unable to lash anything else down, and suppressing the voice within that was crying out for a jug of wine and an excuse to quit this job, he called Luther up to the pillion seat. They set off slowly, heading out of the Eastern gate of the town.

For the first mile Bert only looked back at the crate every ten steps, after which he reduced it to twenty steps. At the second mile he had to alternate shoulders as his neck was complaining about the abuse it was receiving. Meanwhile Luther was happily leaning out over the side of the wagon, one hand clutching a rope for support and the other grabbing any piece of foliage that was over four foot high and within reach.

By midday Bert was up to his knees in a pile of what he could only describe as weeds. He knew he would regret it but he asked despite himself, "Go on then, what's it for?" He nodded to the grass, flowers, and occasional branch that were currently tickling his ankles and calves.

Luther shrugged, desperate to make his great idea seem unimportant and yet desperate to receive praise for it, "Well if she wakes and is hungry then we're sorted. We can just throw this lot to her."

As serious goes Luther was up there with a broken axle, maybe even death, and Bert was unable to tell if the lad was joking. He took another glance at the crate behind him and then at the pile around him. After a long inhalation to suppress his misgivings he forced himself to ask, "So, she wakes up and we feed her... grass?"

Luther smiled, reminding Bert of a puppy getting his first bone, "We have to please all our customers, regardless of which side of the box they are."

Bert ploughed on, "And, just for arguments sake like, what if she doesn't want to eat grass. Maybe doesn't like grass?"

The frown that appeared in Luther's forehead was deep enough to be called a rut, something Bert always tried to avoid, but it was too late. The lad surveyed the wagon and spotted Bert's travel bag, "Cheese! We've got cheese. I don't know no-one who don't like cheese?" He paused for a second, thinking hard, "Shame we haven't any ham to go with it."

Bert looked at Luther, trying to fathom out what, if anything, was behind the bright shining eyes. Despite Luthers' lack of muscle and flesh an image came to Bert's mind, "Oh, I think she probably could find some ham to go with it, if she really wanted."

Luther nodded enthusiastically (his mother had raised him not to believe in *Sarcasm*), "Oh yes, very resourceful I reckon she is." Luther chuckled to himself as another thought slotted into his head, "Ham and cheese toasties, reckon she'll like them."

Bert took a long look at the crate before deciding a little more speed would do no harm and he flicked the reins. It was several miles before he dared look behind him again.

# # # # #

That first night they camped out under a grey sky with the stars hiding behind a blanket of cloud. The wizard, whose cargo they were transporting and the first Bert had ever dealt with, had been clear: stay away from inns and public places. Before loading up Bert had managed to get in a quick drink at the tavern and when he told his drinking pals who had employed him they had pulled their tankards up protectively to their chests: "You wanna watch him."

"Heard about that one, who hasn't!"

"Never trust a man in a pointy hat, 'specially one with a 'W' on it."

Bert had nervously laughed them off, a job is a job, yet now he was sat in front of a pathetic campfire longing after the comforts of blood red wine and a dripping side of roast boar. He was also trying to avoid thinking about the contents of the crate. He turned the skinny rabbit he was roasting and risked looking at the wagon, checking the wind was blowing the smoke away from it. The ropes that lashed the wagon and the crate to a withered tree, the only solid object to be found on the barren plains, were obvious from his vantage point, appearing very solid and almost re-assuring.

It would be a further two nights of camping before they reached the city where the wizard resided and if they got there within four days a bonus might be paid, though Bert doubted the wizards' reasoning. The cargo was needed by the full moon but how long would it actually remain asleep? Out here, on a quiet road and with a rapidly growing sense of unease; four days might be an overly generous estimate.

The logs on the fire settled and Bert watched as the rabbit he had so carefully balanced over it slipped. Bright blue flames flashed as the fat caught alight and the tender meat began to burn. He was not a man who believed in signs or omens but in his mind's eye he was the rabbit, his skin blackening against bright blue flames.

That night he slept a long way from the fire and the wagon, finding an old rabbit warren he half excavated so he could sleep as low and as hidden as possible. He managed to ignore the rumblings from his belly, the cheese he carried had lost its appeal, reminding him of ham and cheese toasties. Luther had cheerfully made his bed on top of the crate, finding the warmth emanating from it comforting.

# # # # #

Bert was relieved to wake the following morning and find himself still in one piece. It was with some trepidation that he peered over the edge of the sandy burrow. He was surprised to see that Luther had the horses harnessed to the wagon and was waiting for him. The crate was still intact on the back and, from this distance, appeared as a normal, though large, packing crate.

He stood, shaking out the sand that had managed to find a way into his unmentionables, and made his way back to the wagon. Pressing his ear to the crate, quite softly, he heard nothing and climbed aboard, taking the brew Luther offered him and setting the mug into the hole the lad had cut into the woodwork. It was a simple thing that allowed Bert to keep his drink upright and not have to juggle the reins at the same time, yet it was something Luther had invented.

It took another several minutes to move the somewhat wilted foliage so his feet were comfortable before Bert guided the wagon back to the road. How accurate were wizards? He was a quarter way into the journey and if the wizard was a bit out with his magics then maybe she would wake sooner than four days? How long had she been asleep for when they picked her up? He fixed his eyes on the road ahead, anxious to reduce the miles and most definitely avoid any potholes. A broken axle, out here and with no help… he shuddered at the thought.

# # # # #

Judging from the pale orange sun that was high overhead Bert reckoned it was close to midday and the heat of the barren plains had a ferocity matched only by Luther packing a crate. Bert was intently watching the road when his nephew broke his concentration, "What?" the youth asked.

Bert realised he was being spoken to, "What?"

"What? What did you say?"

Bert's mind was a blank since the coffee this morning, he had been that focussed, though he was sure Luther had been chattering along beside him. "I didn't say anything."

"Yeah you did, sounded like you were singing, like them monks do down on Chanty Street."

Bert shook his head, "Not me. Don't go in for that sort of thing. If I can't touch it it 'aint real."

He resisted the urge to check the crate behind him. He was not going to touch that!

Luther persisted, "Chanting. That's what you were doing, it was like, 'Two nights hmmm two nights ahhh, two nights hmmm, two nights ahhh.'"

Luther paused then nudged Bert with his skinny elbow, "Thinking of Aunty Mabel were you?" He chuckled to himself and then leant out of the wagon to reach for a particularly tall purple flower. He plucked it with some aplomb then laid it across the crate. "That'll be a treat for her. I'll leave 'em with the wizard once we get there so he can give 'em to her. Won't even charge 'im for it."

Bert stayed silent. Somewhere deep inside Luther's head was a set of instructions oblivious to the rest of the world. Most people had instructions that helped them walk and talk and had little routines to help them run away when required, or at least know when to shut up. Somehow Luther had made it to the age of nineteen not only alive but with all his limbs intact. Whatever it was that made the lad function was either so simple that it scared anything dangerous away, or so complex that Luther was always three moves ahead. Bert was pretty sure which it was as he watched Luther talk lovingly to the flower he had picked.

The afternoon progressed slowly, with Bert's stomach growing increasingly vocal at having missed rabbit the night before, charcoaled or otherwise, and as the sun set and the air cooled Bert saw smoke drifting into the sky ahead. His mouth watered as he recognised the inn it was coming from. They did a particularly fine side of beef and the landlady there was also particularly fine.

Bert watched the crate for several moments. There were still no sounds coming from within, no signs of anything waking, and his eyes dragged his focus back towards the smoke.

Surely the wizard knew what he was doing? He must have drugged her for longer than four days, must have put some safeguards in place? As the wagon drew up alongside the inn, Bert, with the help of his stomach, had made up his mind. The crate was silent, he was hungry, and wizards didn't get things wrong. The people round here would pay no attention to the crate, so there was no chance of it being robbed, and there was sure to be a steak for his supper and a proper bed for the night, one with no sand in it.

As he stopped the wagon Luther questioned him. "Uncle?" He asked tentatively.

"Told you not to call me that outside the house," he grunted, "It's Bert or boss when we're working."

Bert had one final listen for any untoward sounds from the crate. There was nothing. "We're stopping here for the night and that's that. Wizard or not!"

Luther shrugged, "Okay boss" he intoned, and then jumped off the wagon to unhitch the horses. Luther led them to the stables and Bert climbed down. Though there was no-one in sight he took a few minutes to double check, ostensibly stretching the miles of road out of his back, before tying the wagon to one of the hitching posts.

He patted the side of the wagon, 'You're going nowhere' he muttered, then entered the inn for the steak and wine he deserved for having taken on such a dangerous cargo. Inside he was greeted with such friendship and warmth that by his fourth tankard he had forgotten about the crate. Luther sat by one of the windows, watching the crate and sipping on his own tankard, full of refreshing, wholesome milk.

# # # # #

The following morning Bert woke to find the world had grown considerably smaller. His eyes were stinging, his tongue swollen, and whatever lived at the back of his skull was pounding on it trying to find the exit. He rolled onto his side and lay there, staring at the floor and wondering why his stomach was doing a re-enactment of a particularly strong high tide. Ebbing and flowing, ebbing and flowing. The movement finally tipped Bert over the edge and watched as his steak re-appeared in soggy chunks that floated across the wooden floor in a sea of red wine, now somewhat paler and with a greenish tinge.

When he finally managed to raise his head he saw Luther standing by the window.

"Uncle…"

A groan was all Bert managed.

"The wagon…"

The groan from Bert this time was one of disinterest. Couldn't the lad tell he was ill?

"It's gone."

Bert tried to get up but had to stop half way with one foot resting in the remains of his steak, the other trembling violently.

Finally he managed to stand and propped himself up on the window ledge. He squinted out of the window. The sun was already high in the sky and made his eyes sting. He shaded his brow with one hand and rested his head against the cool glass. Down in the road was the wagon still tied to the wooden post.

He tried to shake his head, which was not the right move for the illness that currently assaulted him. "Daft boy, it's still there."

"Yes Uncle, the wagon is still there." Luther's forehead was wrinkled, "But it has gone."

Bert checked again. The wagon was there, with some effort to focus he could make out the greenery still piled up in the foot well. Surrounding it were snapped ropes and pieces of splintered crate. He stared for a while. Where had his crate gone? Had some joker from the inn decided to swap it for a broken one? He examined the wooden shards more closely and realised it formed a pattern. The crate was definitely his crate, something had broken out of the top.

Realisation made his head throb. She was awake. And she was free.

# # # # #

It took a few minutes for Bert to brush the worst of the previous nights' meal from his clothes and gingerly get dressed. He found himself standing outside with a piece of rope in one hand and a piece of crate in the other. How he got downstairs was hazy, and he was pretty sure if he could remember it would account for his newly grazed shins and bloody nose. There was no mistaking from the remains that she had indeed broken free. Luther was standing a few paces away, looking up and down the road.

"Which way do you think she went Uncle? Sorry… which way do you think she went boss?"

Bert looked at the barren lands surrounding the inn. A bead of sweat ran down his neck, managing to miss his collar completely and run down his spine. Luther did not notice the dread filling Bert.

"Well boss? Which way?"

Now Bert was sweating profusely. Behind and above him he heard a tile dislodge from the inn roof and there was a long slow grating sound as gravity pulled on it. There was a second of silence before it hit the ground, shattering as it struck. The sound made Bert jump.

Luther heard nothing. "I reckon she's heading back westwards. That's where she came from. She'll be hungry I reckon. I'm always hungry after a decent sleep."

"Luther!" Bert managed to whisper and took a step backwards towards the safety of the inn.

"She wouldn't have gone North, or South. Nothin' there worth looking at."

"Luther!"

"Hmm, might have gone East. That's where we're going anyway. That'd make life a bit easier for us. Self-delivery."

He turned to face Bert, smiling as if he had solved a mystery. "Wouldn't that be great, her going straight to the wizard for us!"

"Luther will you shut up." Bert tried to whisper. His ears told him that despite his efforts to stay quiet he was shouting.

Another tile slid from the roof and Bert slowly turned.

Perched on the tiles, and most definitely watching them, was the cargo. He had to admit, as dragons go, beauty was not a word to use, even with his current predicament of a heavy hangover and a real possibility of being eaten colouring his judgement.

She was a little over eight foot tall with hips almost as wide. Her skin was green, but not a sparkling emerald green or a fresh lime green. If Bert had had the presence of mind to categorise the colour then dirty swamp green, with rotting logs floating on top, might have been on the tip of his tongue. She had two tiny arms sticking out at the front, below her long snout and her particularly sharp teeth that glinted in the sunlight. Her bottom legs were long and muscle bound, giving her the ability to jump great distances. Bert knew that dragons jumped places, they only flew if it was absolutely necessary as their wings were tiny and took a huge amount of effort to give any sort of lift. He had heard they only breathed fire when they were stationary, as she was now. Behind her a short stubby tail, tipped by a sharp spike of hardened skin, flicked back and forth.

Rivulets of drool ran off her front teeth and took several seconds to drip onto the ground in front of him.

Luther finally noticed. 'Oh well done boss! But how are we going to get her down?'

"Keepin' quiet and keepin' still would be a good startin' point I reckon," Bert whispered over his shoulder.

Luther scratched his head, then smiled. "Go on Unc… I mean Bert. Riddle it!"

If Bert had not been so scared he would have looked at Luther with incredulity, "Riddle it? A riddle 'aint going to fill its belly. A riddle 'aint going to feed its fire. You can try riddlin' it if you want. As soon as it looks away I'll be runnin' not riddlin'!"

"Go on! They say you can riddle a dragon. You can talk it down and we can then tie it to the wagon and be on our way. It'll only take a day or so to get to the wizard from here if we really hurry."

"I think we're past that. I reckon we need to get into the inn and wait 'till she gets bored and jumps off. We'll just have to tell the wizard we got set on by bandits and they loosed her."

"Think of the gold Unc… boss." The lad scratched his head, "And I don't think I want to upset a wizard."

"It's a hard choice lad. Wizard a hundred miles away or dragon here?" Bert stopped talking and watched the dragon carefully. Every few seconds she lifted her head, sweeping it from side to side, testing the air with her nostrils. Bert waited and as she lifted her head then he took one step towards the inn, reckoning he had another ten steps to go.

Before he took a second step the dragon leapt from the roof and landed right in front of him. She leaned over and sniffed him, she licked the side of his face, her rough tongue scraping his skin, but something upset her and she pulled back. Bert could still feel the remains of vomit and wine on his skin.

It was then that Luther walked over with a handful of the grass and flowers he had collected. He stopped when he was beside Bert and offered them up to her.

The dragon leant forward and sniffed the bouquet then, very gently, exhaled a small flame onto the offering. Though it was a small and gentle flame for a dragon it took off most of Luther's hair and his leather jerkin was most definitely alight.

Luther yelped, dropped the ashes he was now holding and rushed over to the water trough, which he threw himself into. The dragon tensed her giant leg muscles and jumped to the side of the trough, where it proceeded to sniff the singed, and slightly steaming, Luther.

Bert foresaw the events about to unfold and he ran into the inn. As a stifled scream, accompanied by sounds that he usually associated with an abattoir, rang out Bert kept going forward. He made it through the door and slammed it shut, cutting off the noise. The two patrons who were there looked curiously at him.

The landlady called over. "Did you want a late breakfast luv? I can rustle something up at a push?"

Bert shook his head, locked the door, and then sidled up to the window where he peeked out. There was no sign of the dragon and, apart from some smouldering grass and flowers, there was no sign of Luther.

Bert checked the eaves, making sure there were no sounds coming from the roof. When he was satisfied nothing was trying to get in, at least for now, he walked over to the bar and pointed to the wine jug. The landlady went to fill a tankard for him but he grabbed the jug from her and drunk deeply. Then he ordered a side of the rabbit that was roasting on the fire and sat at the table that was furthest from the door.

The scrawny roast rabbit she served him he thought briefly reminded him of Luther, not an ounce of real meat on it.

Instead of pushing his plate away he picked up the rabbit and ripped off some of the meat with his teeth, washing it down with long gulps of wine.

The landlady came over, "Can I run you a nice hot bath? Clean you up for the road? You're a bit fresh there my love."

Bert looked down at his clothes and sniffed. The scent of stale wine and the beef from last night greeted his nostrils. He dipped his fingers into the wine and dabbed them onto one of the few clean spots on his jerkin, "No thanks, this will do nicely."

Mabel was always on at him to sober up and eat less but, by his reckoning, it had kept him alive. The dragon had rejected his wine soaked flabby meat, it had been quite happy to go for milk fed Luther. More wine and meat it was for him from now on, maybe even with a bit of cheese if he could ever get over the image of a Luther toastie.

He counted out the coin remaining in his purse. There was enough for a couple of nights in the inn, giving the dragon time to vacate the area, then he might head back. Lucille would demand some more gold after the loss of one of her sons, but understanding came quickly to her, especially once she had the solid weight of coins in her hand. Maybe another of her lads might become his new helper, though this time the strongest one who did not think too much.

As for the wizard, he would stay away from him for a very long time. Bert had been paid up front with no questions asked. If anyone came for him then it must have been someone else, there were plenty of other hauliers around. Bert shuddered as the thought of the scaly tongue licking his face flashed through his mind. He put one hand up in the air and gestured for the landlady to bring him some more wine and started checking his jerkin for other clean spots, just to be on the safe side.

CLOUD DRAGONS
BY JAQ D HAWKINS

"Mister Bale!"

Through the fug of an opium haze, Jeremiah Bale recognised the timbre of the Captain's voice calling for his First Mate. With a few extra breaths, Mister Bale pushed his portly frame from the deck, grasping his rum flask in one hand while perching the opium pipe in his mouth to free the other hand for grabbing supports. On a dirigible originally constructed for racing, tethers and hand-holds were plentiful for airship pirates to keep themselves on deck during sudden turns and sharp manoeuvres.

Bale approached Captain Bonny, making no effort to conceal his intoxicants. What might have been a disciplinary offence on one of Her Majesty's airships was easy for Captain Bonny to overlook, considering Bale's piloting skills in a crisis, no matter his level of inebriation.

Bonny, the picture of air corps propriety in his starched uniform jacket and shining brass goggles perched neatly on his flight cap, stood in contrast to his dishevelled First Mate, but made no reference to either the tunic hem hanging partly out of Bale's rumpled trousers or evidence of his compromised state. The sweet aroma of opium emanating from the pipe Bale held in his mouth and the ever-present rum flask left no doubt as to Bale's condition. Had it been another man or anything but Bale's usual habit, Bonny might have hesitated to put him at the wheel.

"We're being pursued by a Company ship, Bale. Are you capable to pilot?"

"As I'll ever be, Cap'n. Best grab onto something."

With that assurance, Bale turned his steps down the stairs towards the pilot booth without waiting to be dismissed.

Captain Bonny, a veteran of Bale's uncanny ability to steer the airship even between buildings on a London street to pick up stragglers and vagabonds, shouted orders for all crew not required on deck to get below and for deck crew to secure themselves for turbulent manoeuvres. If anyone could shake off pursuit by one of the skilled pilots of the East India Company frigate airships, it was Mister Bale.

Bonny had only just got himself secured with one of the tethers when the ship plunged downward in a spiral that would have made many air corps men heave their most recent meal. Chances were, some of those below deck probably did, but the open deck crew were seasoned air men who had been with Bonny's crew long enough to expect the sudden drop, as well as the defiance of international air traffic laws that were sure to follow. If it weren't for the need to watch for the Company ship's movements with an open view, Bonny would have scarpered below decks himself to the comforts of the illusion of safety from within enclosed walls.

Before he had quite recovered from the weightless feeling of a sudden descent, Bonny felt the pressure of the deck beneath his feet pushing him upward at what should have been an impossible speed for this class of craft. How Bale always managed to get such a performance out of the unmodified dirigible was one of the mysteries of life that Captain Bonny left in the hands of the gods.

"*Aide*," Bonny prayed softly to his patron air goddess. "*Guide Bale's hand, and don't let us lose any men this time. He flies in the wake of the dragon...*"

It was a Chinese phrase meaning the smoke that follows the opium pipe or the state of being high that accompanies the use of opium. Bonny shuddered to think what would happen when they accomplished the raid on a London warehouse where crates full of the exotic drug had been stored. Having possession of effectively unlimited supplies of opium might challenge even Mister Bale's ability to function despite his continual inebriated state.

Information had come to Captain Bonny of a shipment to the East India Company that had been diverted by a private businessman and naturally he and the crew had made plans to commandeer the ill-gotten merchandise for quick sale across the channel. It was pure irony that a Company ship had spotted the airship pirates and engaged in pursuit before they had even accomplished the raid.

Presumably the Company didn't have as good an information network as could be found in the underworld and the captain of the pursuing ship might well be hoping that he had found the culprits. Had the opium crates been on board, the airship's manoeuvrability would have been greatly hampered. Bonny shook his head, wondering at the lapse of logic from the pursuing ship's captain.

Without warning, the airship plunged into a deep cloud. All visibility was lost. Nothing but the moist particles with light reflecting on vapour could he see, not even the rails of his own airship. Bonny held out his hand and wondered at the fuzzy image his eyes detected.

This was the moment of danger. No responsible airship pilot flew inside cloud, but it had provided concealment for the airship pirates on many occasions. Captain Bonny trusted no other man but Mister Bale to fly the ship in such conditions. The man's instinct for avoiding obstacles bordered on the supernatural. They were flying too high to concern themselves over church spires and the land below them was too flat to contemplate mountains, but another airship in the clouds could result in a collision that would send both crews falling to their deaths.

The paradox was that no sane pilot would fly into the cloud, certainly not a Company ship pilot. Bonny had never heard of even another airship pirate vessel attempting such a preposterous move. As a result, the clouds had never held any such obstacle... so far. How Bale managed to keep his course through zero visibility was the real mystery. The man had the instincts usually reserved for sea birds.

The clouds began to thin and the patchwork of roads and farmlands became slightly visible below. The bulk of the airship would still be hidden in cloud, but Bale had taken them low enough to see landmarks from the pilot's booth, located at the bottommost point of the airship. The open deck, just above it, had just enough visibility to make out the largest landmarks. The skies were silent. Bale had cut the engines. A favourable wind caught the wing sails to drive them forward, while the silence disguised their position from any who might be listening for them.

Bonny did some listening himself from the vantage point of open sky, or what would be open sky were the airship not buried in the bottom of a cloud. He could see just well enough through the wisps of cloud meeting air that he should be able to detect another airship if it had still been in pursuit, but no matter how hard he concentrated, Bonny saw nothing but cloud formations.

Within that concentration the clouds seemed to form into shapes and Captain Bonny began to wonder if he had inhaled too much of the wake of the dragon from Mister Bale's pipe. At first the fanciful images were vague, resembling mermaids in the sky if he let his imagination add detail. Bonny smiled, enjoying a few private moments of what was essentially a children's game. With only a few crew members on the open deck and those too busy keeping an eye on the wing rigging to take any notice of their captain staring off into the clouds, Captain Bonny allowed himself the indulgence, while remembering that his job was to watch for anything that might be pursuing them.

Perhaps it was this thought that made a particular bank of clouds seem to begin to shape into a dragon. Captain Bonny watched the phantasm closely, picking out the details of an open mouth and sharp teeth. He continued to enjoy the exercise in imagination, watching scales form along an elongated body and bat-like wings forming along the sides, until the head turned a little too quickly and a glint of red glimmered across both eyes at once, then suddenly the dragon regarded the airship with the intensity of a predator stalking its prey.

No clouds could move as fast as the undulating serpent that launched directly towards the airship. Captain Bonny fell backwards, landing on his buttocks with an audible thud, though he did not drop the lifesaving tether that kept him connected to the ship's deck. There was nowhere to run. The gaping maw opened wide as if to swallow the airship whole, then suddenly they were plunging downwards. Mister Bale's evasive move suggested that something real must be behind the hallucination of the cloud dragon. Was the Company ship still in pursuit?

Captain Bonny tried to shake off the effects of whatever opium smoke might be behind his imaginings. His logical mind told him that real dragons didn't form from clouds and what he thought he saw had to be a trick of the mind, yet still the trail of cloud followed, rippling like a snake dropping from the sky. The ship veered to port just as the vaporous jaws would have closed over the dirigible balloon. Then the ground dropped away again as they ascended, plunging haphazardly into another bank of clouds.

Visibility reduced to just a few inches again. Even with his airman's coat, Bonny shivered from the moist chill of unspent precipitation. He hoped his deck crew had remained safe through the sharp manoeuvres and that no one had been lost over the side. He reminded himself that they were sensible lads and knew to grip the safety tethers when Bale was piloting through a pursuit.

Bonny wondered what the others had seen before they had lost visibility. He also wondered what other cloud monsters might be lurking within the dank moisture that surrounded the airship. He shook himself, both to shake off the clinging drops of water and to get a grip on his imaginings. He was not usually given to flights of fancy that would envisage monsters in the skies against all sense. Despite his devotion to a Basque air goddess, Captain Bonny hadn't commanded the most successful pirate airship in history by allowing superstition and hallucination to guide his actions.

The bank of impenetrable fog quickly gave way to wisps above the haze and the airship floated along a sea of white cloud. Captain Bonny looked in every direction as fast as his head would spin. For a moment, he thought they might have escaped. Then the undulations began again along the top of the clouds behind them and the captain could clearly see the scaled loops of the cloud dragon's body. It was gaining on them, fast.

There was nothing he could do except to trust to his pilot's skills. Mister Bale, incessantly under the influence of rum and opium, had proven time and again that intoxication, if anything, enhanced the perceptions of the miscreant pilot and had kept the airship one step ahead of pursuers on every occasion. As much as it went against his nature, Captain Bonny had to admit to himself that Bale had a magic to him that defied all logic. Either that or he lived a charmed life. Either way, Bonny could think of no one he would rather have at the wheel with this impossible cloud formation intent on catching and devouring them.

Again, the cloud dragon closed the distance and opened its jaws wide, intent on swallowing the airship. Captain Bonny gripped his tether for dear life, praying to his goddess Aide that another evasive movement would save them yet again.

As before, the bottom dropped out of the world without warning, but this time a series of twists and turns within the obscuring cloud confused Captain Bonny's sense of direction.

Bonny felt the sensation of the deck rising, fast, then the ship all but popped out of the side of the cloud and rose further into a clear sky, speeding away from all of the clouds towards open sea. Bonny turned and watched, but no dragon-shaped cloud formation tried to follow.

He was just getting enough confidence to release the tether and move about on deck, checking on his crewmen, when Mister Bale strolled onto the deck, looking for all the world as if he had just awakened from a nap.

"Report, Mister Bale," Captain Bonny ordered in his officious voice.

"All pursuers lost, Cap'n. 'Baint no Company airship that'd breech the clouds." Mister Bale took a draw on his pipe and looked out over the clear sky. Captain Bonny smiled to himself, wondering how he had allowed himself to get so caught up in the idea of imaginary cloud monsters.

"'Specially with that cloud dragon on our tail," Bale added.

Captain Bonny's smile dropped. He regarded Mister Bale with a quizzical expression.

"There was no dragon. That was a hallucination!"

Mister Bale turned and looked Bonny in the eye, something he only ever did when making a point.

"You saw it. I saw it. That makes it real." Mister Bale placed the opium pipe back in his mouth and sauntered away, once again, not waiting for dismissal.

For more adventures of Captain Bonny and Mister Bale, read *The Wake of the Dragon* by Jaq D Hawkins.

MODERN DRAGON

BY ASSAPH MEHR

The girl was screaming as the dragon came for her. She had promised herself she wouldn't, that she would bravely fulfil her destiny as a sacrifice to appease the monster, but when the beast appeared she couldn't help herself. Tied to an ancient post in a forest clearing, all her family and friends cowering in their huts a mile away, she felt alone and abandoned. And now this monster, huge and green and scaly, was coming down from the skies with wisps of flame trailing from its nostrils.

The dragon landed, and slithered towards the girl. She sniffed, but managed to get herself in order. The sun shone brightly on her golden curls, highlighting strands of hair in shades from honey to near-silver; her milky white skin almost translucent, and without a single blemish.

"I am ready for you, to fulfil my village's contractual obligations, to appease your anger and preserve our lives and our crops from your wrath!" she spoke the ancient formula drilled into her by the village elders.

"Yeah, yeah, heard all that before," said the dragon, with a slight lisp.

"So will you eat me now?" the girl asked the beast.

"What? Ewww! No," it replied. "I'm a vegetarian."

"Say what?"

"A vegetarian. I don't eat meat."

"So... You terrorise the cabbage farmers, instead of the shepherds?" asked the girl with furrowed brows.

"That is sso lasst ssentury," lisped the dragon. "I get my organically-sscertified quinoa on eBay."

"Eee... what?"

"Oh, never mind, darlin'. Just you come with me quiet-like, and all will be exssplained in due coursse."

"So I have nothing to fear from you?" she said, still hesitant to trust a creature known for its lies and appetite for human flesh, yet reaching gingerly to lay her hand on its magnificent reddish-green scales.

"I ssolemnly sswear I shall do you no harm," said the dragon patiently. "Now, if you'll jusst climb on top, I'll take you on a nissce ride to a magical palace."

The girl climbed hesitantly, and settled on the creature's back. She found the scales slightly warm, yet softer than she had imagined. She made herself comfortable.

"So I'll get to be a princess?" she asked. "Did the fairy tales get it all wrong, and you don't kidnap princesses and lock them up? But take girls and make them into princesses?"

"Well, not quite," said the dragon as it stretched its wings. It flapped a couple of times and then jumped up and kept airborne. "Thiss sscertified organic quinoa is expenssive, you ssee. But on the other sside of the mountainss are a number of rich caliphss of sspesscific tastes. Those haremss you heard about in stories, they don't get populated by exssotic prinsscessesssss cheaply."

The beast's words were growing faint as he flew upwards and started to bear due east, but those who were left hiding in the bushes could still make the last words. "I am what you might call an international import/export entrepreneur…"

THE WYRM IN THE TARN

FROM ESCAPE FROM NEVERLAND BY NILS (NISSE) VISSER

Author's note

The following is an extract from my debut novel *Escape from Neverland*. In that novel unlikely protagonist Wendy Twyner, aka Wenn, seeks to elude her problems in a care home on a dilapidated council estate in a small Sussex town by visiting the nearby mysterious Wyrde Woods. There she spends time with the wood dwellers she has encountered. In this chapter, entitled 'The Dragon Slayers' in the novel, she explores the Wyrde Woods in the company of a boy called Puck, who has made his home deep within the woods and always dresses in green, from top to toe.

The Dragon Slayers

We entered the woods again but these were different kinds of trees. I recognised the serrated leaves at once.

"Oak trees," I said, happy to be able to identify yet another tree.

"Yes," Puck answered. "It's mostly oak forest between here and the Shy Maidens. Some really old parts of the woods."

The oaks had branches along the entire length of their trunks, and these spread out above to form wide, uneven crowns. As we progressed the trees got older and bigger, and some of the lower limbs were easily three or four times as thick as most of the birch trees.

"I'd like to climb one of these," I ventured hopefully.

"Just a few minutes more and we'll be at the Halfhollow Oak, that's a stunner to climb."

"It has a name?"

"Most of the really old ones do," Puck said. "The Halfhollow Oak is about 800 years old."

"Amazing, that's like twelve times a human life?"

I was impressed and even more wowed when we got to the Halfhollow Oak. It seemed big enough to form a forest by itself. The trunk was immensely broad, and, as the name suggested, had a cave like cavity at its base which broadened into a space large enough for some six to eight people to stand in. The lower boughs were trees in their own right. The crown seemed to span a vast area and towered into the sky. Not as spectacularly high as the redwoods at Giant's Grove, but it was elevated above its neighbour's topmost reaches by at least forty feet. I looked at it longingly.

"Better take off your pack, climb high enough and there's a view of Malheur Hall," Puck said, looking pleased with himself and taking off his glasses which he put in his satchel.

"Will you be able to see?"

"Not in the distance, but well *enow* close up, don't want to risk it slipping off," he answered, and then told his border collie, "Stay. Lady, Stay."

Lady whined a protest, and then sank down to the ground by our bags.

The climb was exhilarating, easy going at first as there were multiple options spaced closely together, but, just as had been the case with my chestnut, the higher we climbed the more thought had to be put into where to go next. This included thinking three or four steps ahead, it was useless clambering up a branch to find there was no further way up. As usual the climb required all my focus, though I had time to note that Puck was an accomplished tree climber as well.

I reached the highest branch that seemed sturdy enough to hold me, about ten feet below the topmost part of the tree, and sat down on it, leaning on the trunk with my torso. Puck elected to stay one branch lower; he stood on it and rested his arms on the branch I sat upon. I was aware of his elbow nudging my flank and stayed dead still. I didn't want movement that might alert him to it and make him shift his elbow away.

I liked it; there was both a sense of trust and of intimacy about it. The view was amazing from up here. We looked over a broad valley in which the continuous tree coverage was broken in the centre where a patchwork of open grassy clearings showed. The largest such stretch was bordered by a single long row of trees whose tall crowns were only just overreached by the towers of Malheur Hall.

The tallest tower consisted of a crenelated platform, flanked by two round spired watchtowers from which flew a Union Jack and a red flag with some sort of yellow heraldic symbol on it.

"Malheur Hall," Puck said. "Ever been there?"

"Of course not. I've never had the twenty quid for entry." I shook my head.

"Those chestnuts in front of the castle." Puck pointed at them. "They're magnificent."

"What happened to not seeing the distance?" I hoped I wasn't poking him, but sometimes I just needed to know something and I would blurt out a question.

"I can see a broad green blur," Puck said, then added with a grin. "All around me."

"The Wyrde Woods. Do I get a point for guessing?"

"Sure. I just know what I am pointing at, because I've seen it close up. I've snuck in quite a lot. Can't help the fascination."

I was immediately intrigued. 'Snuck' in sounded like it wasn't allowed.

"Puck, let's sneak into Malheur Hall," I urged.

"Just the castle grounds," he said.

"That would be amazing. Let's go." I lowered myself onto his branch.

"Whoa, hold your horses." Puck laughed. "It closes at five."

"And then what happens?"

"Most of the staff go home, just the three security guards who stay and two of the household staff. But that last lot stay in their quarters in the hall, and the security guys hang around in their own place by the front entrance. Nothing much to steal from the gardens they reckon."

"No CCTV?"

"Only place with alarm systems is the castle proper, the outside doors and windows are wired. Aunt Catt is too stingy for much more, that's why she doesn't like her caretakers to spend too much time in the woods. She wants the gardens in order for when she comes in from London to host a dinner party for business partners. That's all she uses the castle for, about one weekend every month. She doesn't care about the woods at all."

"Is she here now?"

Puck shook his head. "The biggest threat is Fluttergrub; he takes to wandering around the grounds sometimes."

"Who is this Fluttergrub? Is it his real name?"

"No. A local name for someone who likes digging around in the dirt. He's the groundskeeper, in charge of the gardeners and the like, wood maintenance too, though they're too understaffed to do more than the absolute essentials."

"What if we run into this Fluttergrub guy?"

"We run like hell," Puck said happily. I smiled. The prospect of sneaking in was tempting. Running like hell sounded like fun too.

"How do we get in?"

"What time do you have to be back at the Home tonight?"

"Terry is on duty tonight, which means well late for a change. He said nine pm, meaning ten is fine with him too. There's only a minimum of staff in the weekend and Terry is just about the easiest going of them all. And in charge tonight."

"Good," Puck said. "So you're up for it? After five that is?"

"Deffo."

"In the meantime," Puck said, "I'm hungry, let's climb down, grab something to eat, and then see about slaying that dragon. I have some bread and cheese with me."

"I brought warm coffee!" I remembered.

"Splendid," Puck said. I nodded happily and we started climbing down again.

§§§§§§

We shared the bread, cheese, and coffee. Puck had brought a handful of dry dog food for Lady, and poured her some water in a bowl. After lunch Puck put his glasses back on, we packed up and then we walked on through the oak woods.

Some of it was younger, trees crowding each other for space. Other areas were much older and here there was hardly any undergrowth, just broad trunks rising like old Greek temple pillars. We didn't speak much, each of us happy to enjoy the woods in silent contemplation.

After about an hour we heard a rapping, more than a score of rhythmic taps in quick succession. It was almost like somebody was tapping on a drum. This was followed by a similar sound from a different direction.

"Woodpeckers?" I asked Puck. He nodded and left the path in search of the sound. About thirty feet into the woods he put a hand on my shoulder to stop me, and pointed at a large oak with the other. About two thirds of the way up was a bird, strikingly colourful with a beige belly, black and white wings, and a bright red cap and bottom. We saw it rapping the trunk so rapidly that it became a blur, and then it flew off.

"That was the Great Spotted Woodpecker," Puck said with a satisfied smile.

"Why the knocking?"

"Territory, other birds sing, this one drums."

"All we need now is for one to play the fiddle." I grinned. "Then we can teach them Raggle Taggle Gypsy."

The drumming sound resumed as we found our path again.

"How much wood would a woodchuck chuck?" I demanded to know.

"A woodchuck is a groundhog." Puck shrugged.

"Not today it isn't, today it's a spotted pecker," I joshed him. "So how much wood would a woodchuck chuck..." I started tapping out a rhythm on my thighs "...if a woodchuck could chuck wood?"

"As much wood as a woodchuck could," Puck replied, beating his own rhythm. "If a woodchuck could chuck wood."

"Faster now!" I demanded.

"Why not the song of the woodpecker?" Puck asked.

"Never heard of it."

"Kinda old," Puck said, and started whistling a jazzy tune before he began to sing.

Caught this bird in the neighbourhood
Peckin' away on a piece of wood
He pecked and pecked on my front door
He pecked till he made his pecker sore
Peck-a-peck peck-a-peck peck peck
He's the loveliest little bird you ever did see
He'll take a chance on any old tree
The other day he was peckin' in an oak
Making his strokes and his pecker broke

Peck-a-peck peck-a-peck peck peck

"Peck-a-peck peck peck," I said happily.

I liked Puck for not giving a hoot, if he felt like singing he just did. All the green stuff he wore sometimes seemed a bit pretentious, like he was trying to make a statement, but the ease with which he let himself go without abandon was brill. Most Forlorn Hopers from the care home would consider Puck a great deal more cray than they themselves were, and I grinned at that insight.

Our path intersected a dirt road wide enough to accommodate a vehicle. As we crossed this byway I saw the roof and chimneys of a cottage to my left. I stopped and looked at Puck questioningly.

"That's where Willick lives with his Allison, it's called The Cottage," Puck said.

I was about to suggest that we drop by but then I remembered Willick had taken Joy to town.

"That's where I get internet access," Puck added. "Willick's place is modernised, running water, electricity, internet and all."

"What is Allison like?"

"Allison is nice enough."

"Do you think Willick still fancies Joy?"

"He says not, but I don't think a love like that ever really goes away, do you?"

I shook my head, though I didn't really know much of that kind of love from personal experience. Not the ground-shaking, world-upside-down madness I had read about in books anyway.

We continued on the smaller path, heading into a younger area of oak forest again.

Puck stopped. "See this?"

I shook my head, not sure what I was supposed to be looking at. He pointed at a narrow trail which dissected our path.

"One of the routes followed by deer, the woods are crisscrossed by them."

I saw it now, though I would have walked right past it without giving it any notice if Puck hadn't pointed it out.

"What kind of deer?"

"Roe Deer," Puck said. "Look…" He pointed at a branch which hung low to the ground. The tip had been broken and hung on by a strip of bark and there was a little reddish fur attached to it. "Traces of bigger deer like Fallow and Red would have been higher up."

I was impressed by Puck's forestry skills; he was a fount of knowledge on the woods and their history. I thought about the few times I had been in other woods before, and how it had just been a mass of green where it was pleasant to walk. Puck made it all come alive.

"It's your turn now, Puck," I said resolutely. "How did you end up in the woods?"

Puck sighed. For a moment I thought he was going to be evasive again but he wasn't.

"I was a late child. My mother died giving birth to me," Puck said slowly. "My father remarried, but just for the looks. My stepmother had all of two brain cells to rub together. She was half his age and a former model. She married him for the money. It was like living in a cliché."

"But you had a family," I said softly.

Puck looked at me sharply. "A loveless one. My father blamed me for my mother's death, I think. No actually, I know. He told me twice. I think my mother is the only one he ever truly loved. He was cold and distant to me. The step-bimbo couldn't wait to get me out of the house, and like my father I was sent to boarding school when I was seven."

"A boarding school?! You're a toff then?" I was impressed. I had never met a real life toff before. I thought they were all haughty and arrogant. I supposed Puck was like that at times, but in an okay manner, with him it was about all that knowledge he seemed to have soaked up like a sponge. He was dead smart really and wasn't a wazzock in an irritating way. To me anyway, I don't know what the other Forlorn Hopers would have made of him.

"Privileged," Puck conceded.

"What was boarding school like?" I pictured a kind of Hogwarts with young Puck immersed in books like Hermione and honing his intelligence.

"Fucking awful," Puck said. "With the Masters it was all about academic results and I get distracted easily. I can tell you a bird is a spotted woodpecker and I learn the sounds. I like sounds; I guess I collect them in a way. But they have a special name for the feet of a woodpecker, and that kind of information. Pfff."

"Passed you by?" I guessed he probably didn't have Wyrde Woods wildlife classes at school but I understood the comparison.

"The other boys cared mostly about sports; can you imagine me playing rugby?"

The image came to me pretty vividly, and I bit my lip so I wouldn't laugh too loud.

"Well, I had to," Puck pulled a face. "My father combined the academics and sports when I saw him in the holidays. I always looked forward to those visits, hoping that one day we would find some sort of connection. He'd just ask about test results and sporting achievements. That was his indication of well-being. I was forever disappointing him."

At least you had a father, I thought, but didn't say it out loud. What we shared would be the inevitable questions about our mothers. What was she like? What if…? I wondered if Puck blamed himself for her death. That was one hell of a demon to struggle with at night. He must have been pretty miserable growing up. He wouldn't have lasted a minute in Neverland though, far too clever and soft.

"We quarrelled like hell after we visited Joy," Puck continued. "I was fascinated by her and soon after ran away from boarding school. Stayed with her for a year, camped out in the woods mostly, and then went up north where I got involved in local politics. Then I came back here."

"And your father?"

"Disowned me, officially. His lawyer sent me a letter which said that would only be reversed if I went back to school."

I looked at Puck. There was sadness about him now; it wasn't all cheer and fun. I wanted to reach out and touch him, just to comfort him. I admired him as well, and changed my mind about him being soft. He had been fourteen when he made the decision to just drop out. Fuck the system, follow his own rules. Just about everybody I knew at school talked about it, but no one ever dared unless they lost themselves on drugs, topped themselves or got knocked up. It must have taken some courage. Adults talked about it too, but few had the courage to carry it through.

I supposed the Wyrde Woods were a pretty good place to hide, I couldn't see Social Services people running about on the muddy paths in their neat suits or high heels and skirts trying to trace one lost boy.

A thought occurred to me. "Does your aunt have children?"

"Her? No. She never married."

"Soooo, if you went back to school, and your aunty died, and your father relented, you'd become the Lord of the Wyrde Woods?"

"Lord of the Wyrde Woods," Puck said pensively, and I was glad to see him smile again.

"Family tradition after all," I suggested. "Sir Peter, Lord Malheur." I made a curtsey.

"My father and the step-bimbo had a child not long ago, the way things are now I'm not in line for the job. I think I prefer living like an outlaw anyway," he said with powerful conviction. "Puck of the Greenwoods."

"Yes Milord," I made another curtsey and Puck laughed.

§§§§§§

As we approached our destination, the oaks were replaced by alders and willows, and the pervasive bird song lessened significantly. I was stuck by the profusion of anemones which grew some ten inches high, the white star shaped flowers rising above the greenery. It wasn't like the almost continuous haze of the bluebells, here the haze was dark green and broken up by whole constellations of celestial white dots.

"Devil's Tarn." Puck pointed in front of us. The anemone carpet continued right to the edge of a small lake some fifty feet wide, but much longer as it snaked its way around a corner. The banks were lined with anemone beaches and clusters of weeping willows, the pendulated slender branches of which hung serenely over the surface of the lake. The water in the lake was perfectly still and clear. It reflected every detail of its surroundings with the sharp clarity of a mirror, so that clouds seemed to sail in its blue centre surrounded by the inverted domes of the weeping willows which doubled them in visual size.

"It's bloody incredible," I said with admiration.

"Isn't it just?" Puck said, pleased that I liked it. "You should see it in the winter; it's fed by a spring down there so the water never freezes. If there is frost vapours rise from the water like smoke."

"As if something lived in it?"

"Yup," Puck nodded. "There are a lot of lakes like this in Sussex, and they used to believe that they were bottomless, leading all the way to the Underworld from which an occasional serpent-like monster would make its way up. Two of them were killed here."

"Dragons?" I looked around me for traces of epic combat, but everything looked serenely peaceful.

"They call them Knuckers here, Wyrms in the old days." Puck switched to a creepy movie voiceover mode: "A nine footer with a tapered elongated neck and tail. Ebony black scales on its back and a red underbelly with large feet, cold lizard eyes and jaws a foot long filled with a double row of razor sharp ivory teeth. Coming to a woods near you, soon."

"I don't suppose they called them 'Fluffy' then?"

"The first Wyrde Woods Knucker was called Heolstor. It terrorised the countryside, twere middling terrible. It would devour cows, pigs and stray children whole. This was before there were Malheurs here and the villagers of Roreford armed themselves with farming tools and picked a fight with the beast."

"Who won?"

"The villagers lost a few men altogether, the survivors a number of arms and legs."

"So how was it killed?" I thought of a heroic knight in shining armour.

"By a woman."

"REALLY? Awesome, good for her. Tell me!"

"Folk around here were mostly pagan, but a few of the Christians who were here went to the priory and spoke to the prioress, Lewinna."

"Saint Lewinna?"

"Yup, but then she was just a prioress. She said she would rid the Wyrde Woods of Heolstor if folk would convert afterwards, for it would be the power of her God who would drive the Devil's creature from the woods. They agreed and she set out on her own, dressed in chainmail and on horseback. Apparently she was quite handy with a sword. She probably had some kind of martial past before she devoted herself to her God. It wasn't uncommon back then for women to be warriors."

"Girl power." I noted with satisfaction.

"Girl power indeed." Puck nodded. "They say that for a whole day and night the woods echoed with the sound of combat, the clash of sword and claw, the roaring and bellowing of Heolstor, and the strong clear voice of St Lewinna as she recited prayer after prayer. She returned with the creature's head and the pagans duly converted to Christianity. They were baptised at St Lewinna's Pool, I'll show you where that is one day if you want."

I nodded. I wanted to see the whole of the Wyrde Woods. "And the second drag... Knucker?"

"Back in the Middle Ages, that's where I got the description from. They said it was a punishment for people staying pagan on the sly even though their forebears promised St Lewinna otherwise."

"An armoured knight," I said. "Sir Lancelot came to slay the beast."

"Bugger the knights, they were mostly Malheurs around here, not a family with a track record of chivalry I am afraid."

I nodded, and thought about how weird it was that Puck was part Malheur too. His blood was bound to these woods by centuries but also contained traces of a long line of amoral men steeped in evil. I wondered if he ever thought about that, and decided he probably did. His thoughts seemed to reach far and wide like the branches of the Halfhollow Oak.

"Though one of the good ones did try, in armour too, so you're not far off, his name was Richard Malheur, the younger brother of the Lord at the time. Richard carried on the family line though when his brother died without living heirs. The Knucker observed traditions too. You'll be pleased to know he insisted on eating only virgins as dragons ought to."

"Humbug, why always virgins?"

"Maybe they taste better?" Puck laughed. "Possibly because it meant young children. Knuckers weren't the size of Smaug, most of the local Knuckers were even smaller than Heolstor and Drefan. Overgrown lizards really. Kids would have been an easier prey."

"I still think it's because the writers were men and men are obsessed with virgins," I said. "But who killed Drefan?"

"Well Sir Richard tried, but he was grievously wounded and found by the Farisee who nursed him back to health. Folk despaired. If a trained and armoured knight couldn't slay the beast, who could?"

"Please tell me it was another woman!"

"It was." Puck beamed. "Local farm lass, called Ellette Hornsby. Though there was mention that she might be a changeling."

"Changeling?"

"A Faere Folk joke, they'd switch one of their own for a human baby right after birth."

"Maybe I am a changeling," I said dreamingly.

"I wouldn't be surprised," Puck conceded. "Anyway, Ellette means 'little elf' in Saxon and she was about twelve years old at the time and clever. She decided to tackle Drefan on her own and in secret. First she snuck into the grounds around the old castle and visited the Poison Garden."

"Malheur Hall had a Poison Garden?"

"It still does. Ellette snuck in during a full moon so she could see what she was doing and because the plants are at the height of their power then. And there, most carefully and wearing gloves she picked foxgloves, belladonna, poppies, laburnum and hemlock. Ellette took her deadly bounty back home and made a huge pie, filling it with the most savoury meats, but also adding all of the poisons she had prepared from the plants."

"Clever girl!"

"Indeed, and then Ellette loaded the pie on her father's two wheeled cart, harnessed his horse to the cart and drove to the Devil's Tarn singing a particular song to let Drefan know a virgin approached and he duly rose from the Tarn to investigate. Now she was lucky, because first Drefan ate the horse, and then the pie and then the cart and by then he was too full to eat another bite. Ellette waited only a little while before the Knucker began to twist and turn and suffered the most horrible convulsions as the poison began to melt his organs. Drefan bellowed one last time and then fell down dead. Ellette cut off its head and returned home a heroine."

"I can imagine!"

"Sad to say, it did not last long. Ellette had been too careless with the poison, probably when she prepared the pie. Sometimes just touching it with a bare hand is enough and she fell ill and died within a week. She was buried by the side of Tuckersham Church, the grave is still there, covered by a great big sheet of stone they call the 'Slayer's Slab'."

"Poor Ellette," I said. "What was the song, do you know it?"

Puck smiled. "Should I perch on a tree branch for you? Or just sing it here?"

"Sing it here," I decreed.

Puck drew a deep breath and started singing.

A Master of Musick came with an intent,
To give me a lesson on my instrument
I thank'd him for nothing, but bid him be gone
For my little fiddle should not be played on
My thing is my own, and I'll keep it so still
Yet other young lasses may do what they will.

I laughed, Puck grinned but continued singing.

A fine dapper taylor, with a yard in his hand,
Did profor his service to be at my command
He talked of a slit I had above the knee
But I'll have no taylors stitch it for me
My thing is my own, and I'll keep it....

"Hush young maiden!" I laid my hand on Puck's arm and he ceased singing. "I do think the Knucker has heard you. Listen!"

Puck tilted his head and listened intently, Lady looked around in some confusion.

I started speaking softly in a low voice. "Beware the Jabberwock, my son! The jaws that bite, the claws that catch! Beware the Jubjub bird, and shun the frumious Bandersnatch!"

Lady growled. Puck chuckled and was about to say something when I hushed him again.

"LOOK!" I said in alarm and pointed at the water. Lady growled again. "See there, those yellow eyes with black slits, the Knucker has surfaced!"

"Hell's Bells, it's seen us!" Puck said in alarm.

We started backing up to the tree line.

"It's swimming to the shore now, there, it's climbing on land by those willows!" I pointed.

"Quick, arm yourself!" Puck shouted. Lady barked as Puck picked up a long fallen branch and I found a shorter stick.

"There it comes!" I shouted. "Whiffling through the tulgey wood with eyes of flame!"

"And burbling, that's a bad sign, it's about to attack," Puck hissed.

"Attack is the best defence," I replied. Then I shouted "GERONIMO!!" and rushed forwards, beginning to hack at the Knucker with my sword. The beast growled ferociously and lunged at me with its powerful jaws, I smelt a wave of foul decomposition as it snapped its jaws shut, just inches from my face, and fell backwards.

"Help!" I shouted.

"HOKAH HEY!" Puck dashed to my aid, yielding his branch in both hands and thrusting it forwards like a spear. "Take that foul beast!" He shouted and started driving the Knucker back.

I jumped up and rushed to his side, piercing the eye of the monster. It roared and reared upwards, Puck drove his spear through its chest and bellowing it fell, slithering back to the nearby willows.

"He's trying to get away!" I shouted. "Stop him!"

We hacked and slashed our way forwards into the hollow of the willow's dome, the Knucker ineffectively trying to ward off our blows.

"It's done for!" I yelled triumphantly. "Finish him off."

We fell upon the creature, stabbing and piercing its scaly armour until it bled from a hundred wounds and bellowed its death cry.

Puck dropped his branch and let himself fall to the ground, laughing all the way. I dropped my stick and sat down next to him, grinning like mad. Lady came over cautiously and gave us a worried look, causing renewed laughter on our behalf.

"Well that was FUN," I said joyfully when the laughter subsided. Puck looked up at me and smiled his agreement. We looked each other in the eyes and I suddenly felt the urge to lean over, bring my lips to his. This was definitely one of those moments and I thought I sensed an air of expectancy from Puck too. But I didn't dare, what if he was shocked or explained why it was better to friend-zone me? Worse, he might just laugh me in my face and tell Joy it would be better not to invite me again. There was far too much at risk. I couldn't stand to lose the Wyrde Woods like that. A few minutes of awkward silence followed, the air laden with potency.

I broke the spell and stood up, brushing leaves off my legs. "Maybe we ought to go?" I suggested.

Puck nodded silently and stood up too. We were on our way again.

A SOFT SPOT FOR DRAGONS

BY MARC VUN KANNON

-1-

It would have been easier if his opponent had been some giant hulking brute, scaly, stinking and armored, a battle-axe in one hand and a warhammer in the other. This was worse, far worse.

She was six.

"Jasec, plee-ee-ze?" She was sick, too. That's the only time she would ever whine like that. A bad case of thrips, it must have been. She'd been in the sick room for a whole day and it was still almost intact. He'd made a bigger mess, when it had been his turn, and he'd only gotten one thrip, as they say.

"Are you sure you wouldn't rather have an apple?" he asked, holding out a small one. "I stole it just for you."

She stuck out a lip. "Did not."

He took a step–only one, he took very large steps–and placed the appropriated fruit on the small table near her bed. "Did, too."

It was even true. Unfortunately his mother had caught the one he'd tried to steal for himself. This one was much too small, easy enough to palm with hands like his, but what would he do with it afterward?

She sat up and flipped her covers down, suddenly animated. "Cut it," she demanded, her smile wide.

He breathed a loud sigh, as if much put upon, and made a show of getting out his knife. Other men would call it a short sword, but other men weren't over seven feet tall. His little sister loved knives, especially his. It looked so small in his hands, but so large anywhere else. It was like a never-ending magic spell, watching it change sizes like that. With surprising delicacy, he sliced the fruit up, even peeled off the thin skin.

The smell of apple perfumed the air, but he doubted she could smell it. "There you go."

Before he could even stand up, she said, "And tell me a story!"

Right into his ear.

He made a face at her. "You said you wanted the apple."

She hadn't really, but maybe if he said it firmly enough–

It didn't work. Denora heard what she wanted, even with the things she *did* say.

"I want a story," she repeated with great clarity, as if her eldest brother had somehow forgotten, or misunderstood, or something like that.

There was a knock on the door.

I'm saved!, thought the man, clan-Second and Heir.

"Come in," he called out, before his oppressor could do any more than frown fiercely at the interruption.

The door creaked open, his wife and woman on the other side.

"Ah, there you are, Jasec, my beloved. I was just about to seek you out for weapons training."

Her own weapons training, that is. Mirani was the instructor in blunt weapons training for everyone else, but none of her apprentices were able, or willing, to be the subjects of her own practice sessions. "Are you keeping our little invalid company, telling her your tales?"

"Yes, he is," shouted Denora.

Jasec rubbed his arms, felt all the little bruises from the last time he'd 'volunteered' to help his wife, not quite faded. "Of course I am."

Mirani took this news with admirable grace. "Oh. Well, my loss is her gain, it would seem."

She started to bring one of her hands up, holding something. "And I also brought–" She stopped, looking with dismay upon the pile of apple sections, near-identical to the pile on the plate in her hand.

"They're for Denora," mumbled Jasec, as if it weren't obvious.

Mirani swept right past him, scooping the pile of slices onto the platter. "Of course they are. Medicinal, no doubt, in spite of the lack of a plate."

"No doubt," he agreed in low tones. Not a dishonorable ploy to avoid his sister's endless appetite for tales, all the gods of Air forfend.

"Good," said Mirani, settling her burden on the table where the contents had so recently been. "That means my husband is not a thief, and I am not his accomplice." She stepped gracefully around him, as he stood there, blocking the door like a lump. "Enjoy your telling, dear."

Denora waited until the door softly thumped closed before she folded her arms across her chest and pinned him with a fierce scowl.

He grimaced and scratched his head, not quite sure what had just happened. "A story, eh?" She didn't bother to dignify that with a response. "What kind of story?"

"A funny one!" she crowed in her triumph, her scowl gone.

A funny one? Did he know any of those? The tales he told of his great Uncle Tarkas' adventures were many and varied, but not known for their humor.

"Tell her the one about the dirkins," came his wife's voice through the door.

"Mirani!"

Then she opened the door again, just wide enough that only Jasec could see her face. "And do keep it short. I really do need you for that weapons training, with that 'thing' that's coming up."

Not the place to go into what 'thing' it was, but there was no need. She opened the door wider, looked at Denora firmly. "One story, shortbread, then I need him back." She closed the door.

"What's a dirkin?" asked Denora. "And what thing is coming? Is it after the battle?"

Jasec ignored the latter question and brushed a hand through his hair, resigned to his fate.

"A dirkin is…" he paused, gathering himself into storyteller mode, and continued properly, his voice going up, down, and around in dramatic hyperbole with each word, "A dirkin is one of the most deadly, horrifying, fabulous beasts in the entire lifetime of the world."

She looked skeptical. "It's a silly name."

"Oh, that's very true," said Jasec quickly, his voice suddenly mild. He took a slice of apple for himself, and crunched it thoughtfully. A bit too tart for his liking. "But they weren't big, mean, fierce, with great big fangs, broad sweeping wings, and flames on their breath, when they were called dirkins."

He brought up his hand, his fingers just a little apart. "When they were dirkins, they were little tiny things, mean, fierce, with little tiny fangs, small flapping wings…and flames on their breath."

She slapped her arms down on her blankets with excitement. "Really?"

"No, not really," he admitted, "I don't think they were mean, or had fangs, or anything like that."

"So how did they get like that?"

He touched her gently on the nose. "Well, that's the story, is it not?"

She took a quick breath. She loved this part.

"This–" Oops, a little too soon.
"This…is…"
"–Is–" Too late.
"What."
"–What–" Closer.
"Happened," they said together.

-2-

Tarkas bounced down the stony hillside, coming to rest at last on a boulder at the bottom. That's when he noticed that it was raining. From the look of things, it had been raining for a long time, too.

"Crap," he muttered.

"Why did he say that?" whispered Denora.

"I don't know," said Jasec back. "He never told me."

He stepped off of the boulder and immediately sank to his ankles, in cold, icky, slimy mud.

Denora shuddered in sympathetic reaction. "I bet that's why he said 'crap'."

"I think you're right. Now hush."

If he noticed the cold or the damp, he gave no sign of it. Truly, he only reacted to the wind and the rain when it blew or fell into his eyes. So when he set off from his lonely spot, far from the lights and places of men, it was only to find a higher spot, so the mud would not get on his feet.

He walked for a long time. The rain ended, and the darkness fell, as the wind rose. Tarkas had reached some much higher ground, hard and rocky, no mud to be seen or stepped in anywhere. This was good, but it was cold and getting colder, and he could not see his footing very well.

"He should stop," said Denora, who had more than once almost fallen on the stairs while trying to sneak into the kitchen in the dark.

He decided that he really should...well, maybe not stop, but certainly check where he was going. To aid his steps, he summoned a magical light from his mystic sword, a weapon that he, and he alone, could draw safely.

He said: 'Light', and the pommel glowed, about two waxlights' worth. That was how he discovered that he was standing on the very edge of a great cliff, a black and bottomless pit beneath, like a mouth ready to swallow him utterly.

Denora clapped her hands over her mouth.

Yes, he shuddered to think the damage that might have been done had he taken that last step, the breaking, the bruising, the crushing. A fall would be bad, the hole at the bottom worse, and really hard to explain. Why, he might even have gotten injured!

Denora giggled.

What, you think it funny? I assure you, Tarkas did not. Why, I can see him in my mind's eye even now, tumbling down the stone face.

Jasec smacked his fist into his hand. Crunch. 'Sorry.'

He smacked his other fist into his other hand. Splat. 'Sorry.'

Denora started rocking from side to side, clapping her hands. '*Smack, smack.*'

Yes, just like that.

'*Smack, smack.*'

You can stop now.

She stopped instantly, not wanting to give him the slightest excuse to stop, now that he'd started.

So–where was I? That's right, Tarkas was climbing the mountain...

"*He was not! He was over a cliff!*"

But the cliff is boring and the mountain isn't.

"*Why were you talking about the cliff, then? And the mud?*"

Because that's where the story started. I don't make these tales up, you know, I merely tell them. They start where they start. But if it will make you happy, he turned away from the cliff, ran down a hill and up another hill, seven times because seven is a lucky number. Is that better?

"*Did he really?*"

Of course he did. Everything I say is true, I just don't say everything. Do you really want to hear about all the times he ate lunch, or went to the potty?

Denora giggled. "*NO!*"

Okay then...where was I?

"*He was on the mountain!*" *shrieked his sister, laughing.*

Right. Tarkas was on the side of a mountain, climbing the sheer face in the dark, with a howling wind for company and only his sword's light to see by when...

Denora put up her hands and made a scary face. "*A monster!*"

No. Only a great man like Uncle Tarkas would be stupid–I mean, bold enough to climb a sheer cliff face in the dark.

"*A giant bird!*" *shouted Denora. With big, pinchy claws, it seemed.*

In the howling wind? I think not. One more.

She shook her head, out of ideas.

Not even a little guess? Okay then. Suddenly, he was blinded by a great blazing light, bright as the moon, two moons even, fierce as the sun–

Denora frowned. "*You said he was climbing a cliff.*"

He reached the top. And at the top of the cliff he found a great open space, like a field without any grass or plants, and at the far end of the field stood a great big house, made all of..of..crystal, it looked like, backed up against the very wall of the mountain behind. And Tarkas thought to himself, 'Aha, a place, wherein I might seek shelter from the elements and spend the night, shielded from this wind which howls into my ear in a discordant and very minor key.'

"Did he really say that?"

'Think', not 'say', and yes he really did, but don't ask me what it means, because I don't know. Our great Uncle Tarkas has many thoughts that we mere mortals cannot hope to understand.

Her nose scrunched up delightfully in her confusion. "What?"

See? So, Tarkas approached the house–

"He just walked up to it? Wasn't he watching out?"

Yes. No.

"But Septas Tovis says we should always be watching out."

Septas Tovis sounds like a very smart boy, and so do you, but this is our Uncle Tarkas, Champion of the Gods. He doesn't watch out for things, they watch out for him.

Denora's nose crinkled up in confusion again. "I sound like a smart boy?"

Smart girl. Now let me tell my story, or Mirani will never get a chance to pummel me all over.

Tarkas approached the house, not at all worried about a sudden attack even though he wasn't watching out. Creatures of darkness are creatures of darkness, and the house shone so brightly he wasn't worried about them. He worried more about avoiding all the traps that his keen senses revealed to him, mainly pits and such, with who knew what at the bottom.

"What?"

I just said, 'who knew what', didn't I? Our Uncle Tarkas had no great desire to know, since knowing meant he would have to find out, and finding out would have meant he had to fall into one, or set it off, or something, and you can see where he didn't want to do that. He didn't want to know, so he didn't, so I don't either.

What he wanted was to reach the door of the big house, and that he did. The door was set a little back, with a big porch and a roof, just like they have at the temples, so people could wait at the door in the rain without getting wet. It wasn't raining, though, and Tarkas didn't go up on the porch. Instead he picked up a little rock from the ground and threw it at the door, making a big clunking noise that didn't really sound a lot like knocking on it. Well, maybe it did to him, but his hands are much harder than mine.

Anyway, the first knock didn't work, so he made another. And another, until he began to worry about either running out rocks or damaging the door. Just then, however, the door opened, and an attractive young Lady smiled at him as she swung it wide. Ah, I see you narrow your eyes distrustfully, and all I can say is that you are wise for one so young. It will please you to know that Tarkas himself felt much the same, and made no move to go to her.

"Good eve, warrior," the young woman cooed at him.

"Good eve, Lady," said our valorous Uncle. Still he made no move to approach.

She frowned slightly at this keeping of distance. "Would you care to come in?"

"Would you care to turn off whatever traps await on this porch?"

She smiled, as if this request was an amusing joke. "You think my doorway is a trap? Whatever for?"

Our Uncle gestured behind himself. "Those pitfalls back there are far too obvious," he explained, without any contempt. "Their only purpose would be to make a foolish person overconfident, so that they would fall into whatever trap awaited once they appeared to be past. This is the only place such a trap could be, even though I detect no obvious signs of one."

Again she smiled, in appreciation. "You are wise, warrior."

She moved a hand against the wall, and abruptly the entire floor of the porch dropped away, dropping whoever might have been foolish enough to stand on it into a chute leading off to places unknown. Then the floor rose up and appeared normal once again.

Tarkas watched calmly, noting how the rocks fell in the chute but the few apparently randomly-strewn-about objects stayed where and as they were. "Very nice," he said. "But what about the door handle itself? Surely the quick-witted could save themselves with it."

Without a word, she placed her delicate hand on the item in question and pulled it off with hardly any effort. "Inspired," Tarkas said in praise, as she replaced the handle on the front of the door.

She half-turned, displaying her...well, anyway. "And would you care to enter now, warrior?" she asked, a graceful hand beckoning.

"He shouldn't," said Denora.

"Are you going to turn off the trap floor?" asked Tarkas in turn, not distracted by her impressive...distractions.

"Oh," she said, sounding dismayed. "I had forgotten. My thoughts were full of...other things." With that, she moved her hand to much the same spot as she had the first time, but what she did there was hidden from Tarkas' sight. "It is safe now."

"I don't think so," whispered Denora.

Our Uncle Tarkas bent and scooped up a small amount of sand and dirt, and cast it inside the doorway. It scattered all over the floor inside.

"Is that the act of an invited guest?" she demanded, sounding shocked.

"No," admitted Tarkas, not ashamed of what he had done. "It is the act of a man who wishes to ensure that the floor beyond the deathtrap is not itself a deathtrap."

"You could merely have asked me to step aside, warrior." Then the Lady stepped to one side, grit crunching under her feet as she stepped upon the apparently innocent floor.

Tarkas leapt lightly across the dangerous porch to the spot just now vacated by the Lady—

"*No!*" *cried Denora.*

—And whacked his head into something unseen and very hard, even as his feet came to rest safely on the floor. He fell backward, stunned only a little bit, as befits the Champion of the Gods.

"He fell into the pit under the porch."

He fell into the *chute* under the porch, as the Lady triggered her trap even as he was in mid-leap. Even in this event, however, our Uncle might have saved himself, but a projecting stone in the chute struck him yet again, and he missed the rest of the slide to his own doom.

"I told him not to go in there."

"True, and had you actually been there I'm sure he would have been grateful for the warning. But you should also remember that Uncle Tarkas is a Champion, and must sometimes go into a threlk's hole in order to slay the threlk."

When Tarkas came to his senses he was not surprised to find himself chained upright against a wall. There was a man there, watching him, but Tarkas didn't bother trying to talk to him. Most likely he was just there to let the Lady know when her victim had woken up. Sure enough the man walked away as soon as our Uncle's head was raised, but he surprised Tarkas by speaking before he left.

"Don't touch the chains," he said. "They're magic, and will slice your fingers off."

"Did Uncle Tarkas touch the chains?"

"Would you?"

Denora's hands clenched and she tucked her fists under her arms.

"No."

Tarkas heeded the man's warning, but not because he was afraid of his fingers getting cut off. He'd experienced far worse in his time–

Hands came out, thoughts of injury forgotten. "When? What?"

Different story. The point is, that he was waiting for the Lady to appear and make all the threats bad people like to make when they think they're in charge, and so Tarkas had to appear to be in her control.

Denora began to bounce on the bed. "He was setting a trap for her."

So true. Badness is a trap all on its own, one that good people don't even realize they're in until it's too late.

"Don't you mean bad people?"

Badness isn't a trap for bad people. But good people often do things, thinking that they're good, and only find out when it's too late that they're really bad.

"Which kind was she?"

It didn't really matter, you know, as far as Uncle Tarkas was concerned, except that he might feel worse about what he had to do if she was trying to be good.

"Was she?"

Let's find out.

Tarkas passed the time, waiting for the Lady to appear, by examining the old and rotting skeletons hanging on the other walls. Yes, they all had fingers missing, and no, the place didn't smell too bad. It didn't smell too good, either, but a Champion of the Gods isn't as annoyed by such things as you or I would be.

About when he expected, just long enough for him to begin the slide into the deep dark well of despair, but not long enough for him to have fallen asleep, the door opened with a groan that spoke of ancient rust and long hours of practice, opening doors so they sound just like that. Mostly practice.

Tarkas had just heard them shut the door a little while before and there was no rusty creaking *then*, I can tell you.

The Lady stalked in, dressed much less like Lintas Mista and much more like my own dear Lady wife, if you know what I mean.

Denora shook her head.

"Okay, you don't. Don't worry about it. You know my wife, but you certainly won't get to meet Lintas Mista, not if I have anything to say about it."

"What does Lintas Mista do?"

Back to my story. "Ah, still alive, I see, and with all your fingers," said the Lady. "I'll have to have a little talk with Sigur."

Tarkas guessed that Sigur was the man who'd warned him not to touch the chains. He also guessed that her 'talk' with him would not use words.

"Don't bother," he said, "I'm not going to talk, and there's nothing to say anyway."

She smiled back. "Don't be silly. I'm not here to torture you, 'make you talk.' I'm here to apologize before you die."

This was something new. "Apologize?"

She got a funny look on her face. "I knew you were evil, but a barbarian as well?"

Denora frowned mightily. "Uncle Tarkas is not evil, and he's not a 'barian!"

"Just so, and bravely spoken. You make me proud. Now then, where was I?"

"No matter," said the Lady. "The obvious virtue of my act is not soiled by wasting it on scum such as yourself."

"I hope he smites her soon," muttered Denora.

"Denora. What have we told you about smiting?"

Denora pouted. "Fine."

"The virtue of what act?" asked our great Uncle.

"My apology to you, peasant," snapped the Lady. "Now be silent, so that I may continue and have done."

"How is that virtuous?"

"I said be silent!"

"Just trying to help you be virtuous, dear Lady," said Tarkas. "Face of adversity, and all that."

The Lady stepped forward and gripped Tarkas' jaw firmly. "Soon it will be the face of jerked beef, vermin." Then she stepped back, and made an obvious effort to look more like the great Lady she thought she was. "You are going to die here, by my will, so—"

"Are you going to kill me?" interrupted Tarkas yet again.

"No," said the Lady. "Our lore makes it very clear that killing is a bad thing and should not be done."

"Really?" said Tarkas, who'd killed quite a few things in his time. "What does it say?"

"'Killing is bad.'"

"That's all?"

"Word for word. So I cannot in good conscience kill you."

"But you can leave me to die."

"Indeed."

"This is an improvement?"

"No." The Lady looked away, and sighed. "I shall have to detail guards, who will then have to listen to your cries and pleas for mercy." She looked back up at him. "It won't be for long, but still... it's not a popular chore. My guards are quite soft-hearted and prone to be merciful, and the duty will be very painful for them."

"Whereas you are merciless."

"Not at all. The means of my mercy are quite near at hand."

Then Tarkas understood. "The chains." Lop off the fingers and watch the blood spray.

"Sigur did you no favors. It would have been much quicker."

"I must remember to thank him."

"You will never see him again, or anyone." The Lady dragged the interview back to her own purpose. "I apologize for making you die. Our lore also says that to impose our will on another is a double insult, to the other and to the gods. So you have my apology. I will make my apology to the gods in due course."

"Ritual suicide would be good."

"Don't be silly. I'm doing their work. Someone like you wouldn't know it, but there are things in this world that must be done, regardless of the cost to oneself."

Tarkas couldn't stop himself. He burst out laughing. Had the chains not been holding him up he would have fallen to the floor. The Lady, of course, was shocked, but since her apology had been made she felt no need to stay. The door slammed behind her with a most impressive boom. Again, practice.

As you can imagine, Tarkas lost no time escaping from her trap. Then, he–

"*Hey!*"

"*Yes?*"

"*How did he 'scape? You can't just say he did!*"

"*I can't?*"

"*No.*"

So I have to tell you, how he gripped the chain with his left hand, and exerted his mighty, heroic strength to pull the links of the chain apart until–

"*Hey!*"

"*Yes?*"

"*How did he grab the chain? You said the chain was magic!*"

"*That's true, I did.*"

"*So how come it didn't cut his fingers off, like the man said?*"

Because his hand was more magical than the chain.

"*Really?*" *Denora practically shrieked with glee. Something new and special about her Uncle was always good.*

No, not really. It wasn't real magic but something even better, something more powerful than the spell on the chain. It did indeed slice into his fingers, but only enough to give him a very strong grip, not enough to cut off even one finger, much less all of them. And with his grip, and his strength, the chain pulled apart like those little candy strings you like so much. After the first chain broke, it wasn't hard to get out of the rest of them. So he escaped.

"*He was still in the room, though. What about the door, the one that went 'boom'?*" *Denora really loved traps.*

That was even easier. With the first two fingers of his special hand, he opened the lock from the inside and got into the hall before the Lady had even sent her guards down to watch it.

"How?"

He stuck them in the lock and they changed shape to be like the key.

"*I think you're cheating, 'bout his magic hand.*"

Jasec dropped his story-teller's manner abruptly. "No, Denora." He touched her chin gently, raised her sulky face up until her gaze met his. "I am one of the few who know what our Uncle Tarkas suffered, the sacrifice he made, for which his hand was only a small compensation. All the elements, and all the skill the gods possessed, went into the crafting of the hand our Champion bears. But that is not a story I will ever tell."

He'd tried, once, and found that he literally couldn't tell the story, touching as it did upon the affairs of the gods. It sounded better to say 'wouldn't' rather than 'couldn't', though, so that's what he did.

"And I don't cheat, either," he continued, in an offended tone. "His hand does what it does, but it can't turn into a bird and carry him through the air–"

Denora giggled at the thought.

"*Or silly things like that. It doesn't break, it can shape its shape, but only a little bit.*"

"*So how come he didn't just slip his hand out of the chain, instead of pulling it?*"

Trust Denora to think of that.

Once in the hallway, Tarkas made an experimental swing with the length of chain still attached to his wrist. He could have just slipped his hand out of the cuff, of course, instead of pulling it apart, but he had a use for the chain. The magical edge was still good, and it would do for a sword until he could get his own back. It still made that clanking sound that chains make, though, so he'd have to be careful to hold it while he walked.

Like every other prison cell Tarkas had ever escaped from, there was only one way in and out, a narrow straight hall with no convenient outcrops to hide behind. It was also quite long. Tarkas wondered if it was soundproof as well, and touched the wall, but it wasn't.

"*Was it his magic hand again?*" *Denora sounded increasingly skeptical.*

No, it was the fact that the walls of the hallway were solid stone, and Tarkas knew that solid stone echoes very well. If there had been guards at the post at the end of the hall, where it joined with other halls, Tarkas would have been spotted at once. As it was, whatever guards the Lady planned to assign hadn't yet arrived, so he merely walked out of the hall and went elsewhere.

-3-

Denora was overcome with giggles, clapping her hands together with childish glee.

"Yes, it was ridiculously easy, wasn't it?" asked Jasec, quite pleased with her response so far. "And I haven't even gotten to the part with the dirkins yet."

"Oh, yes," cried Denora, her attention brought back to the actual point of the story. "Tell me about the dirkins!"

"As you wish."

-4-

Tarkas was, of course, very worried about whatever 'work of the gods' the Lady was planning to do, mainly because the work of the gods is what *he* did. There were others like him, so it wasn't like he was jealous or anything, but they didn't meet each other much and when they did they agreed on what they were doing. He hadn't ever captured one his fellow Champions and put them in a dungeon.

No matter. The work of the gods is known by the work, not by the worker, and bad men have been known to do good works, although I don't imagine they did them on purpose. And while they may hide themselves on the top of a mountain or in a cave, they don't then light up the night sky with a city's worth of waxlights, or apologize to their victims before leaving them to die.

So our Uncle Tarkas was a bit confused, as he crept carefully up the stairs. It had been a long wait, down in the dungeon, or cellars, or whatever those were. He'd been in a lot of dungeons—different stories, so don't ask—and the one he'd just left didn't really look like the others. Lots of people going back and forth, but they didn't look like guards, talk like family, or act like servants.

None of them had come down here for quite some time, also, and Tarkas suspected that it was late enough at night, or early enough in the morning, that they had all gone to bed. If it was like the other large households he knew, he had a very short time open to him to act, before a morning crew would wake up and start preparing for the coming day. Fortunately the gods' Champion doesn't need much sleep.

"And he got knocked out before."

And he got knocked out before, so he wasn't at all tired. I would have felt sorry for any guards, if he'd happened to meet any.

"He didn't?"

Not yet, he hadn't. That's why he was climbing the steps so carefully, it was just the sort of place for guards to be. Sure enough, there was one there.

"Did Uncle Tarkas smite him?" Denora really liked the word 'smite'.

Uncle Tarkas struck him powerfully, and the man fell down. I do not know if he was dead because Uncle Tarkas did not bother to check. It was enough for him that the man was not able to give warning, and that he hadn't made a lot of noise himself, bringing that about. And he got a sword, so he took his hand out of the cuff and left the chain behind, strung over the door as a trap.

Denora smiled at the ploy. "He should have smited him."

Don't be silly, you don't smite just one man. Smiting is big, much too big to waste on an underling. If he was going to do that to anybody, he was going to do it to the biggest bad person he could find, and all of his warriors, and his evil devices, and his castle too.

Denora looked more and more gleeful at the thought of the carnage he would wreak, until the very end. "But isn't Uncle Tarkas in the castle?"

Exactly. So you can see why he didn't want to do any smiting just yet. No, right now, all he wanted to do was find out what was going on, what the Lady was planning. After all, it may have been something good, and he wouldn't want to destroy that while he was smiting the rest. That's why gods had champions, after all.

So, as he expected, the room at the head of the stairs was the kitchen. Nothing else was as he expected, though. It was dark, for one thing, and quite cold. The fire had gone out.

"Everybody left?"

I don't think so. They had a guard, didn't they? Even if he was the only one in the room. Except for Tarkas, that is.

Now Denora was certain Jasec was fibbing her. "There's gotta be someone there. A cook, or a boy, or someone!"

I'm afraid not. He checked. It was dark, remember, and he didn't want to take a chance on waking someone, so he cast a sleep spell, but it didn't work. He–

"What do you mean, it didn't work?"

As I was about to say, he didn't know how he knew it didn't work, but he could feel it somehow, something different from all the other spells that did work. So he called on his light again, to see what was wrong, until he remembered he didn't have his own sword yet. So he made himself see in the dark instead. That's how he knew there was no one there. His spell had failed because there was no one for it to work on.

I would have been shivered by this, I think, perhaps even you too. An empty house is an unnatural thing. But our Uncle Tarkas isn't the sort of person to get all trembly over a house, no matter how empty it might be. Floorboards creaking. Winds whispering.

Jasec shuddered, not all feigned.

He doesn't care where his enemies are not, he seeks them out wherever they are, and that's exactly what he started to do now. He was halfway across the floor when it happened.

"What happened?"

Are you aware of just how heavy our Uncle Tarkas really is? I don't know if you are.

"Jasec! What happened?"

(Heavy sigh.) If I must. The first thing that happened was that Tarkas felt something small, something soft, under his sandals as he crossed the floor. It couldn't have been large, else he would have, should have, seen it with his new sight, but it was there.

The second thing he felt was the vile, disgusting sensation of the thing, whatever it was or may have been, going *kkkkkhkhkhkhkh–*

Denora winced, making a compassionately pained face.

–under that very same foot, because sometimes I think even our Uncle does not truly know just how heavy he is, and wasn't able to stop pressing down with his foot in time.

The third thing that happened was that Tarkas realized that his foot was on fire. Not merely on fire, but as if he'd stepped on a hot coal. And not just any hot coal, but one that held on to the bottom of his foot, as if to punish him for stepping on it. He knew this because he lifted his foot, which was a mistake.

"*Why?*"

Why do you think? By lifting his foot Tarkas let out all the heat at once, it seemed, and flames came boiling up all about his foot. His sandals didn't burn, of course, made by the gods as they were, but his foot wasn't so sturdy.

Denora reached down and grabbed her own foot through the blanket. "Ow! Ow! Ow!" she shrieked.

Yes, just like that. Only he didn't have a bed under him. He was standing on one foot, waving his other like mad, trying to dislodge the coal that was sticking to it. That would have been the end of it, most like, if something had not happened just then on the bottom of his foot–

"*What?*" *asked Denora with frightful eagerness. She really liked the idea of Tarkas hopping about on one foot, puffing and blowing like an idiot. He would never really do something like that!*

I don't know, it was on the bottom of his foot and he didn't see it. But whatever it was, it pushed against his foot very hard, more than enough to topple him, and he fell very hard against a table and knocked everything on it to the ground, along with himself.

Denora could easily imagine the kind of racket this would make. She'd been responsible for many just like it. Somehow it was funnier when it was someone else's racket.

The good thing was, the fire on the bottom of his foot went out. The bad thing was that he'd just made enough noise to wake the skeletons he'd left behind in the cell, he'd dropped his sword, and he must have hit his head, because he was seeing things. The darkness around him was streaked with little lines and sparks.

It took him a few minutes to realize that he hadn't banged his head, and he really was seeing them. Something was in the air around him, something he couldn't see, and it was making some kind of bright light, blinking and flashing, like those thwimblies you see in summer.

Denora loved those, all the children did. They would race around every summer, trying to catch them. The elders would take note of who succeeded, for further tactical training.

Then the spell he'd used to let him see wore off, or he let it go, or something, because he was once again in the dark, but now he could see that the bright lights were little flames, bigger than a waxlight but smaller than even the smallest campfire. There was something moving up there, lots of somethings, and they were making the flames. They were hard to see, with all the flashes and movement, but he could tell, and with the speed of a threlk seizing its prey he grabbed one out of the air.

"Was it a dirkin?"

Hmm. Well, yes, it was, but Tarkas didn't know that yet. He'd never seen one before, you know. All he knew was that he was holding a squirming, wiggly little thing with lots of points and *Ow!* sharp teeth. So you see, it did have fangs. Then it spit something out, or breathed real fire, and burned him on the arm. He flung it away by reflex.

"*That was stupid.*"

Maybe, but when it comes to fire, our uncle has some pretty strong reflexes, and they were much stronger, back then.

"*Did they attack him?*"

The flying beasts made no move to attack him, merely made their great flashing display, and he did what he was supposed to do. He ran away.

"*He did not! Unca Tarkas never runs away!*"

(Jasec sighed.) He runs away quite a lot. It's not his purpose to harm the innocent or the good or those who don't know better, so when they attack him, he runs away. The dirkins were beasts, and he'd killed one and frightened the rest, so they did what beasts do. Only a fool or a monster kills when he does not need to. Isn't that right?

Denora nodded brightly.

So he ran. Unfortunately, the dirkins followed him.

"*You said they didn't attack.*"

They didn't. Maybe it was because he had burnt-up dirkin left on his sandal, and they were following the smell. But they did have the annoying habit of flying up to each torch, each waxlight, anything that was used to light a room, and set it to burning.

"*They shouldn't do that. Everyone can see him!*"

They were beasts, dear, I don't think they cared about that. I think they were doing what they were supposed to do. Remember how the whole house suddenly lit up, when Uncle Tarkas climbed over the cliff? I think that was the little beasts, lighting all the lights in the house at once.

Besides, it was not as if Tarkas was merely standing in place, stupidly watching as the room got brighter and brighter. No, he was already on his way up a set of steps that he noticed on the other side of the room. He did not know or care what the dirkins were doing behind him.

"*What were they doing?*"

Maybe we'll find out. What Tarkas was more interested in, was the horde of guards coming down the stairs at him. Well, not really a horde, but remember they were on a stair, and it doesn't take a lot of guards to be a horde on a stair.

Denora nodded sagely at this observation.

They didn't stop him, of course.

Denora shook her head. Of course they didn't.

Do you want to know how?

Denora shook her head. She really didn't care about the combat, unless there was something good in it. Jasec knew this, but the only good thing in this bit of mayhem was the way Tarkas used his left hand to disarm his opponents, and he didn't think Denora was all that interested in any more 'magic hand' stories. He had to ask, though.

So we'll just move on to the top of the stairs, then, and what Tarkas saw when he got there.

"*It was the Lady!*"

Well, yes, but that's so obvious it doesn't count. The Lady has to be there, so Tarkas can smite her. What else?

"*His sword!*"

Very good! Very good indeed. Yes, his sword was there as well, and the Lady had it in her hands.

"*What was she doing with it?*"

Oh no, you're not going to trick me that way. We haven't finished with the people yet. Any guesses? No? Very well then, the other person in the room was Sigur, the man who told Tarkas not to touch the chains. Ah, you remember him.

109

Excellent. So you remember that Tarkas said he was going to remember to thank him.

"*Did he?*"

Of course. Tarkas always keeps his promises. I don't suppose poor Sigur felt that being thrown against the wall and flung down the stairs was very grateful, but it had to be better than being run through.

"*Yes it is,*" stated Denora firmly, her head nodding for emphasis.

I'm glad you agree. So at the end it was Tarkas with his ordinary sword against the Lady, who was holding his own magic sword in her hands. That was bad, as Tarkas' sword would cut through anything, including the weapon he held in his hands. So he did what he had to do.

"*He ran away?*"

Of course not. He attacked.

"*But she had his sword.*"

Yes she did. His sword. His magic sword, given to him by the gods themselves. Do you really think that any mere mortal, man or woman, could wield it? I will tell you this, I myself once held that sword, at our Uncle's own urging, and it was all I could do to keep it in my hand.

"*She dropped it?*"

She threw it away, as if it had bitten her. I see you nodding your head. Yes, it was stupid, she should at least have kept it from Tarkas, even if she couldn't use it herself. Well, she was not a warrior, we shouldn't hold it too much against her, especially as it meant she was fleeing the room while Tarkas had to stop to collect what was his. Only then did he go to the doorway she had vanished through, but he was not fool enough to go through it. He was watching out, just like Septas Tovis said. The room beyond, whatever it was, smelled of animals, and he took care not to walk into yet another trap. One a night was quite enough.

Denora nodded firmly in approval.

So when the arrow came out of the room on the other side he was quite ready for it. He raised his hand–yes, his magic hand–and the arrow stuck into it. He was trying to catch it, actually, but this was just as good. Better, if fact. Because the Lady, who had shot the arrow at him with some peculiar looking bow, didn't try to shoot another. I don't think she could, personally, the bow didn't look very fast to load, but she didn't even try.

"Now you die, barbarian," she crowed in triumph. "The poison on that bolt will course through your body, chilling your blood, weakening your limbs, and stilling your very breath."

She gestured about herself, at the many cages in the room, and the horrific beasts they contained. "I will use your body to feed my creations, give them a taste of man-flesh before I release them into the world."

Denora made a face at the thought.

Tarkas stared at the barb in his arm. "Well. Since I am about to die–and a much better death it sounds than to hang against the wall–perhaps you would do me the favor of telling me what you are trying to do here." He pretended to sag weakly against the wall.

"You will be dead before I could even begin to properly tell the tale of my genius," said the Lady.

"Well, then," said Tarkas, standing upright again, "No need to play the dying man." He pulled the barbed shaft from his hand without the slightest flicker of pain or weakness. "I am the Champion of the Gods, madam. It takes more than a mere toxin to keep me from my duty." He stared at the barbed point, as if fascinated by it.

She backed away from him, but he didn't raise his eyes. On the other side of the room was another door, and a handle mounted on the wall next to it. He made no move to stop her.

"*He should.*"

Maybe. He did not, though. When she reached the door and the handle, he was still looking at the arrow's head, standing just inside the doorway.

"Idiot," she cried. She pulled the handle by the door, and the cage doors all came open. "My creatures will rend you!"

"*Will not!*" replied Denora, on her uncle's behalf.

They looked ready to try, though. Teeth and claws in abundance, of course, but there was something…almost human about them. A light in their eyes, the way they moved, all together. And the silence! Not a sound, not even to each other.

"*But why didn't they attack her? Wasn't she meaner to them than uncle Tarkas was?*"

They might have, I think, except for three things. First, Tarkas probably smelled worse than she did, so they were naturally drawn to him. Second, he was standing by an open door, their way out. And third, the place where he was standing had been soaked with the smells of animals in rut.

"*What's that?*"

"Mating season."

"*Oh.*" She *knew what* that *was.*

The Lady was smart. She'd made her creatures smart, too, and she knew they would attack her if they were allowed to be smart and free. Rut has a way of making even the smartest creatures dumb. And mean. I would say that Tarkas was afraid to move, but for the fact that he was moving, waving the arrow's head about like he was the idiot she'd said he was.

Then Tarkas flung his hand back, turning his body towards the door.

"*He was running away again? They'll just chase him.*"

Very true. Certainly the animals thought he was fleeing, and at once they leapt forward, all in a body, to bring him down and tear into him.

Denora brought her hands up to her mouth. "Did they?"

They leapt, yes. But just as they leapt Tarkas fell flat on his face, and they went right over him and through the open door. Well, one landed on his head and bit his ear, but he grabbed it and threw it through the door after the others. Then he stood again, very quickly, blocking the doorway with his own body.

Denora waited a bit, but Jasec said no more. "Well?"

"Well what?" asked her older brother.

"Did the beasts come back?"

"What beasts?"

"The beasts that were attacking him," said Denora, not sure if this was a joke or a trick.

Jasec spread his hands. "Sorry, no beasts here."

Now she knew. "Where did they go?"

That's just what the Lady wanted to know.

Denora settled back, satisfied. It was a trick, all right.

"What have you done with my creatures?" she demanded to know.

Tarkas turned back to her. "There is a place for such animals as those," he said. "This place is not it."

Jasec shuddered.

"What's the matter?" asked Denora.

"There is such a place," he confided, "I have walked in it, one time. It is not an experience I would ever care to repeat."

Denora looked her brother's huge body, still shaking in remembered terror, and shivered a little herself.

Where was I? Oh yes. Tarkas also said, "Such creatures as those, loose in this world, would wreak havoc."

The Lady smiled proudly. "That is why I made them."

Tarkas frowned. "To wreak havoc?"

"An unfortunate necessity," she said, not sounding very unhappy about it. "In order to achieve my holy aims."

"Holy?"

"Yes, holy," she repeated. "You may be the champion of your barbarian gods, but *I* am the living embodiment of the Will of *our* gods, and their Holy Purpose. Does not our lore say, 'bring forth new life'? I have done so. Does not our lore say, 'nurture and strengthen those about you'?"

Tarkas waited for her to say more, but she didn't. "Does it?"

"It does. I was going to nurture and strengthen the whole race of man, as is only right for one of my abilities."

Jasec paused. "Did I mention she was an arrogant bigmouth?"

Denora leaned in close and whispered, "What did she say?"

Oops. Jasec had forgotten to change the words for her. "She said that she had made her creatures to kill men and cause trouble for men, so that men would have to fight and become stronger just to survive against them. And that this was what the gods wanted."

"I don't think so," said Denora.

Tarkas said, "I do not think that this was what they had in mind."

She snorted her contempt. "You would have me give myself to a man, bear his children, raise his family, as ordinary women do? I think not. No man in this world deserves me."

"That's very true," said Tarkas agreeably.

Denora giggled.

"It is not your place to judge me," said the Lady. "I am the gods' chosen handmaiden, through me will the race of men be made strong again. Only the gods themselves are my judges."

Tarkas paused, remembering the fates of those who had invoked the judgment of the gods upon themselves. Almost he warned her against her folly, but he knew she would not listen, and finally he shrugged. "As you wish."

He drew his wondrous sword and held it up, as if in oath. "I am Demlas Tarkas, Hero and Champion of the Gods that are. At this time and in this place, judgment is needed."

Behind Tarkas the room exploded in flames and smoke. He turned to look, just as a swarm of little winged shapes came swirling up the stairway, riding the clouds of smoke and spitting fire from their mouths, setting things afire that were not burning already.

"The dirkins!" cried Denora, clapping. This is where the Lady would get smited.

Yes, the dirkins, left awake and loose on the lower levels of the house, they had quickly run out of candles, fireplaces, and lamps. Like all the Lady's creations, however, they were clever and adaptable.

I don't know why they decided to go into the little room where Tarkas and the Lady were waiting. Perhaps it was Tarkas, with the remains of the squashed dirkin still on his shoe. Perhaps it was the Lady herself, and whatever training or commands she may have given them. Perhaps it was the room itself, reeking of animal smells, the only one in the house not burning. What I do know is that the little winged creatures suddenly filled the room, frenzied and flapping, and puffing out jets of flame in all directions. Tarkas was not afraid of fire, not anymore, and made no move to avoid it.

The Lady was not so lucky, or so blessed. Her clothing was slow to burn, but her hair was not, her skin was not. When she began to scream, it only became worse for her, as the little creatures were attracted to the sound of her voice. With all of them breathing on her, even her clothing was catching fire.

It was, in all honesty, more than Tarkas wanted to see, and very much more than I want to describe. One of the best things about smiting is that it's usually fast–a bolt of lightning, a flood, an earthquake. This was not fast.

So Tarkas decided to make it so. He summoned a fire spirit–no, I'm not going to tell you how–and set it upon her, ending her pain.

"Good," said Denora.

I think so. The death of the Lady and the destruction of all her works—

"What works?" asked Denora, not quite sure what 'works' were. Hopefully something exciting.

Who cares, they're destroyed. And that meant that Tarkas could finally look to his own safety, trapped as he was in a room full of crazed dirkins, atop a burning house.

"I thought you said he wasn't afraid of fire?"

He isn't, but he is afraid of collapsing houses. As it turned out, the door on the other side of the room was an escape, I suppose in case some of the animals in the room got loose and blocked the first door. The animals were gone, now, but—

"Where did *they* go?"

Someplace else, where they would pose no more danger to other things than other things posed to them. And now the door was blocked by the fire, so Tarkas used the escape himself. And that was that.

Denora wasn't about to let him get away that easily. "Where did he go?"

Well, outside, I would think. As I said before, you don't want to destroy the castle when you're inside it, so I'm just as glad the dirkins did the smiting this time.

"Did they get out too?"

A lot of them did. Tarkas saw them all over, after the building fell.

"Did he send them where he sent the other animals?"

Jasec made a pained face. I'm afraid it was too late for that.

"Did they die?"

No, but…I'm afraid Tarkas made a bit of a mistake with the dirkins. You remember how he called a fire spirit to end the Lady's suffering?

Denora nodded brightly.

Well, that fire spirit also saw the dirkins, and it remembered the dirkins, and it brought lots of other fire spirits back to see the dirkins too. And guess what happened then.

"*What?*"

The dirkins started blowing up, into big puffs of fire, like the one on uncle Tarkas' foot in the kitchen.

"*Why? Didn't the fire spirits like the dirkins?*"

Yes, they did. They liked the dirkins a lot. But the dirkins were small, and some of the fire spirits were very strong, and then the dirkin couldn't control its own fire anymore and, well…That was bad. But some of the spirits were just the right size for the dirkins, and those, well, those did something very strange.

"*What?*"

They went into the dirkin, just like a soul goes into a body.

Denora looked confused.

You know how, when a person dies, all their elements get taken away, leaving only their soul behind to go to the gods?

She nodded. Everybody knew that.

Well this was like that, only backwards. And just like you are more than just your elements, the dirkins stopped being dirkins when the fire spirit went into them, and became something else.

"*They turned into little girls?*"

No, they still looked like dirkins, for a while. And they could still do some of the things fire spirits could do, for a while. But they could do some new things, too. Suddenly the new creatures weren't spitting out little bits of fire here and there, they were blowing out great long ribbons of fire, much longer than their own bodies, and setting things on fire or even burning them up as fast as you could blink your eyes.

Denora blinked.

Right, just that fast. Tarkas saw this and thought, 'This is not good.' But as I said before, it was too late. One of the things the spirits could do was go out, just like a waxlight, and then be over there, where some other fire was. The new creatures did the same thing, and started puffing out, but Tarkas had no idea where they were going so he couldn't stop them. I think he managed to catch one of them. One of the fire spirits helped, or maybe the spirit knew him and didn't run away. But then after a while it forgot how.

Tarkas took the new beast back with him to the land of all the Gods that are, so they could see what it was and try to figure out what it could do.

"*What could they do?*"

No cheating. You get one story, like my Lady wife said. Besides, no one really knows, certainly not Tarkas. He felt very bad about what he'd done, and he was needed in other places, so he couldn't stay had he wanted to. In after times, when the new creatures appeared in those other places, much larger, smarter, and meaner (and with a new name), he was one of the few who would not hunt them. Although he was able to talk a few of them into leaving. The other Champions thought it was odd, given his impressive record against all the other monstrosities they faced.

But uncle has always had a soft spot for dragons.

COLD AND WITH DRAGONS
A DRABBLE BY JONATHAN ROYAN

Everyone knew, save a dragon's life, you get four free kills. None knew that better than Brant, the farm hand, as he scrabbled on his back through the ploughed field. Harold chose death for the boy who poured hot wax down his back while at church, when they were both children. Brant whimpered as Harold watched the dragon bare down on him.

"Kill him already," Harold ordered.

Flames spewed forth, igniting screams of terror. The dragon lifted the burning Brant in savage jaws and... a sickening crunch as his back cracked in two.

Revenge was best served cold, and with dragons.

AT THE RED BOAR

FROM HEROES NEVER FADE BY RICK HAYNES

Stealing the horses had been child's play for Grona's band. They immediately rode to Wildside and entered the Red Boar Tavern. To their surprise it was much larger than expected and, even at this late hour, almost full. Some way from the bar they found an empty table and were quickly served by a skinny girl. The locals continued to stare until Grona removed his sword and laid it on the wooden table, but Grona soon eased concerns and loosened tongues when he offered to buy all those around him jugs of ale.

Securing rooms was easy. Grona's men wanted to retire but he held them back. Death came to many in the darkest hours and he hadn't lived this long to succumb to a dagger between his ribs now. He also needed information, mostly about Tarn.

Terryn and Ammett were soon engaged in a game of knucklebones and Grona approved of them losing. He needed information and Ammett could make anyone a winner with his *bones*. The game was simple: bet on the way the bones fell, and the winner takes the pot. The more the two locals won, the more the questions rolled smoothly from Ammett's tongue. As easy as picking ripe apples off a laden tree, as Ammett put it. The two warriors soon learnt much about Wildside and the Tormented King. But there was no news of Tarn.

With over half of the locals departing Grona was undecided about his next move. When the door of the inn opened to reveal a lithe man dressed all in black, he reconsidered his options. Another man followed close behind, smaller than the first and dressed more brightly, his face partially obscured by a cloth. Grona knew he had seen the eyes before, and the golden sword gave Dravino away. Now was the time for action.

Feigning drunkenness he stood up, bowed and shouted. "Now we have a peacock with us! Just look at his bright clothes and the way he struts. Come let me buy you a drink, cock-bird."

No matter his hero status, Grona's exploits had never impressed Dravino. He could not trust a mercenary, no matter what Tarn nor anyone else said. But Ake reached the table first. Sticking his dagger into the table-top, yet maintaining eye contact, he stared directly at Grona even as the old man's right hand gripped the hilt of his sword.

The serving girls ran to the kitchen; the innkeeper followed. The remaining locals slammed the door behind them as they left.

No one moved.

Dravino broke the silence as he walked behind the bar and poured two jugs of ale.

"What took you so long?" Grona roared.

All but Dravino burst out laughing.

"I still don't trust you, Grona," Dravino said.

"As if I give a shit. But I tell you this, I'm glad you're here, their words are bloody difficult to understand and I do need a translator. Still, perhaps you have forgotten the language, you being away for so long."

After the laughter had died away, Grona walked forwards. Dravino hesitated but eventually clasped the proffered hand.

"I have given my word to Tarn and that is enough for you or anyone else," Grona said, his words softer than Dravino expected.

"So be it."

For the benefit of the owner and his girls in the kitchen, Lowis and Terryn continued to raise their voices, arguing constantly. Meanwhile, Grona and Dravino compared notes, lowering their talk to a whisper on discussing anything important. Ammett and Ake said little as they shared out the ale.

As the drinks slipped effortlessly down welcome throats the innkeeper stuck his head around the kitchen door. "Do you... err... any more ale... err... want?"

"No!" the men shouted as one.

"Be careful, men, he must have a spy hole in the kitchen," Grona murmured.

"I have a feeling this innkeeper may be withholding some important information. I'll have a word with him before we leave," Dravino said, with a knowing look in his eye. "If the king's army is as big as you say, then we must find help."

"It is, and I agree we do. But where do we start?"

"I need to find Weylin. He was the only lord brave enough to stand up to King Jarl. Although his influence has diminished, I know he would never follow the Tormented King."

"Great idea, but where do we find him in this vast land?" Grona asked.

"That task is easier than you think, Grona. We only need to find one swordsman, trained at Cpin, and he would know where Weylin is."

"Surely these trained killers – no offence but you were one – would side with their monarch?"

"No offence taken." Dravino looked away, his mind returning to the men he trained with, the intense pressure, and the code of conduct embedded deeply inside his mind. "A few warriors would ignore the code, adhere to the wishes of King Jarl and take the gold. Most would not, but there are no prizes for guessing that they are being hunted to extinction. Remember, Grona, young trainees will also be killed for they would be deemed a threat."

Grona stroked his beard. "How many of these fighters are there?"

"Many thousands have been trained over the years. Whilst few reach old age, I would guess that hundreds are alive and ready to take back the country that they took an oath to defend."

"How many?" Grona pushed for an answer. "You must have some idea."

"The Tormented King believes he is loved by all. In reality, the people hate him, and this hatred is growing daily for too many innocents die on the whim of a madman. There are many here who await the call to overthrow King Jarl. Tarn said he needed an army. I told him there was one ready and waiting and all we have to do is find them."

RED FIRE DRAGON

FROM DEATH OF MAGICK BY BENJAMIN TOWE

Prologue

Envision a naïve young man beguiled, robbed, and ridiculed by a beautiful sorceress. Imagine the young man became the greatest assassin that ever lived. See in your mind's eye an assassin consumed by hatred of all things Magick and committed to their destruction. Visualize the creation through the power of a Wish of an artifact of great power to assist his quest. Picture the assassin's second Wish, a Wish for more time and a labyrinth to keep his treasure forever secure from any that might seek the artifact. Realize the consequences of the imperfect Wish... albeit difficult, a path to the assassin's treasure, the Death of Magick.

Envision the struggle across space and time between a just and powerful sorceress with rainbow tresses and a demon of timeless evil. The sorceress must seek the weapon created to bring about her destruction. The strongest and wisest of two very different worlds attempt to unravel the mysteries of ancient parchments and devise a plan to defeat the demon threatening both worlds. A new generation of Donothor and Parallan empowered by Light, Dark, and Illusory Magick accepts the challenge and assists their king and mentors.

What roles do a beautiful mysterious red-haired elf, the bloodline of an enemy, and artifact of evil play? Will the sacrifices of generations be for naught? If they find the Death of Magick, will the weapon destroy them before they face the demon? But first... can they defeat the Red Fire Dragon Faranzer?

Red Fire Dragon

The room was a square with sides two hundred feet long. They stood on a rectangular eighty by fifty foot area in the lower left corner of the room. Roscoe briefly checked his device and said it was the northeast corner. The dimensions were the same as the room where Cyttia, Erinnia, and Eyerthrein had fought the big bad Man-wolf and the red hooded swordstress. The floor was briefly blue and then changed to black. The black stone sizzled and crackled.

A massive Red Fire Dragon sat in the southwest corner. It appeared to be asleep.

Roscoe peered through the prism. He told what they already suspected. "Auras of Magick fill this room. The brilliant light speaks to this. The greatest auras come from the area where the dragon sits. I can't define..." Roscoe was interrupted when the dragon spoke.

"Well, well, well...what have we here? I've enjoyed a long nap! From the growth of my talons and fangs and the energy I feel, I would guess about eight hundred years. I'm hungry. Would you join me to be my dinner? Your...your essence is familiar. Ah...I have, or had, empathy with my sister Baylexa. You are the scum that ended her beautiful reign of evil. At least, some of you are. You look well for your age! Wait, you have elves! I love the taste of elves! Thanks, Tigarn! This is far more than you promised. You have nowhere to run! Nowhere to hide! Nowhere to run to! If you don't fight, you won't suffer so much!" Faranzer said.

The dragon spoke in old elfish dialect.

"Neither do you!" Dael shouted.

The young sorcerer impatiently cast a Lightning Bolt toward the old Red Fire Dragon.

"If I'm going to take a terrible beating, I'm going to get in the first lick!" Cyttia shouted.

She began to conjure.

The jagged Bolt of Lightning left Dael's hand and coursed toward Faranzer. About ten feet from the gloating beast the bolt stopped! Shimmering luminosity extended around the massive Red Fire Dragon. There was a sound of recoil and the bolt instantly returned to Dael striking the neophyte sorcerer squarely. Dael screamed, fell forcefully backward, slammed into the wall behind them, and dropped to the floor. Gray smoke rose from his fallen body.

Dael was unconscious and near death!

"Stop your spell, Cyttia!" Cara shouted.

"He's covered by a Reflecting Dome," Knarra added. "Your spell will reflect!"

Knarra was on the far end of the rectangular area. She looked at Dael.

She shouted, "He's unconscious! He can't drink a potion! I'm too far away from him! He needs aid now! Eyerthrein, can you do anything?"

Eyerthrein shook his head negatively. The battles with the red hooded swordstress and the big bad Man-wolf had exhausted his components.

Brute placed a hand on Dael and uttered a lyrical incantation in a feminine voice. The Cure Critical Wounds Spell improved the young half-Drelve's shallow breathing. His heart beat became more regular. Some of the burns on his skin healed.

Most kept their eyes fixed on the Red Fire Dragon. Their ears heard Brute's incantation.

"You saved my son's life!" Nigel marveled.

Erinnia had taken two steps toward Dael but Brute had been nearer the fallen half- Drelve. None of the others detected the elf's movements or her quiet sigh of relief when she did not have to cast to save Dael. Cyttia and Eyerthrein were intent on watching the great dragon. Erinnia turned to face the Red Fire Dragon and drew her bow.

Cyttia directed the Magick Missile toward the far eastern end of the room where it burst into the wall. The wall radiated a green glow and yellow ichors flowed from the wall at the site of impact.

Cade drew his bow.

Cara breathed deeply and asked, "Does that mean the entire room is alive? Does this Magick 'live' and 'breathe'?"

Nigel noted his son's respirations were less labored. Dael remained unconscious. Knarra reached Dael, wiped his brow, and nodded positively in Nigel's direction when she caught his glances.

Nigel muttered coldly as he drew a shuriken, "Let it turn to something else."

Cyttia said as she also took a shuriken, "Good idea."

Eomore and Vanni drew bows. Deron was not a proficient archer. He did carry a small throwing axe that he was accurate with up to twenty paces.

Deron said, "Arrows aren't going to hurt that thing very much."

Cyttia asked, "How do we know that projectiles won't return against us?"

Cara answered, "The Reflecting Dome reflects only Magick. Hopefully the dragon does not know Shield and Return to Sender Spells. The Return to Sender Spell is difficult to learn and unpredictable. It would require constant concentration to maintain its effectiveness. I think the Red Fire Dragon will make better use of its Magick.

Cara cast Resist Fire.

Kyrsstina cast Resist Cold.

Roscoe used his staff to cast Protection from Magick.

Cyttia cast Resist Fire.

Faranzer yelled, "Toast!"

The massive Red Fire Dragon emitted a deeper red glow and illuminated the entire chamber with red light. He first inhaled deeply and then exhaled scorching flames that enveloped the entire area where the group was standing.

(Dael was lying.)

Dwarves, elves, and other dragons had innate resistance to dragon fire. Roscoe's Protection Spell halved the damage of Magick and breath weapons. Cyttia's Resist Fire halved the damage from Magick and normal fires. Cara's Resist Fire was additive. Luck played a part as well!

Brute, Deron, Cade, Cyttia, and Dael received one **sixteenth** of the full effect of the breath weapon.

Nigel, Eyerthrein, Kyrsstina, Roscoe, Knarra, Vanni, and Eomore received **one eighth** of the damage.

Cara and Erinnia received **one sixty-fourth**!

Nonetheless, everyone received severe burns and coughed.

Erinnia fired an arrow. The arrow slipped through the translucent Magick shell surrounding Faranzer and hit the dragon in the left eye.

"Nice shot!" Nigel marveled.

The dragon roared and inhaled again.

Cara cast Resist Fire.

Cyttia cast Red Curtain.

Roscoe cast Blue Curtain which was a protection from lightning and Jolt Magick.

Thin wavy red and blue barriers appeared between the group and the dragon.

Cade, Eomore, and Vanni fired arrows. The arrows struck the dragon in the neck, left shoulder, and right thigh. They barely penetrated the thick scales.

Faranzer exhaled and again bathed them with incendiary fires. The intense heat forced them to hold their breath and close their eyes. The roaring of the flames seemed to last forever.

The damage was quartered further by the two fire resistance spells. Cara and Erinnia received **one two hundred and fifty-sixth**; Brute, Deron, Cade, Cyttia, and Dael received **one sixty-fourth**; the others received **one thirty-second** of the full effect of the damage.

The burns still hurt; the injuries were additive.

The full effect of a single burst of ancient Red Fire Dragon breath would kill a hundred unprotected men ten times over!

Searing pain coursed through all their bodies.

"I'm glad these bows and arrows are elfish," Eomore said. "Otherwise, we would be fighting with burned wood and our hands!"

Cyttia hurled the shuriken. The accuracy was reduced due to the distance. The razor-sharp edges dug into the sensitive right nasal passage of the beast. The ichors of the dragon flowed from the wound. Nigel's shuriken hit the beast's tongue as it protruded during the breath attack.

Erinnia fired another arrow and hit the right eye of the beast. She shook off her pain and yelled, "You should have ducked, you big blowhard!"

Cade, Vanni, and Eomore fired again. The arrows scored hits but affected the beast minimally.

Faranzer squinted. The arrows in his eyes did hurt!

"Pesky elf!" he muttered.

The dragon conjured.

Cara fired her crossbow. The bolt followed a true course and hit the dragon in the left eye.

Faranzer uttered lyrical old elfish phrases. A narrow beam of gray light connected the dragon's maw and the elf Erinnia.

Erinnia was not affected by the Death Spell. None of the others saw the tiny green leaves and white berries tucked behind her left ear.

Faranzer roared in frustration.

Cara fired another bolt and hit the dragon in the left jaw but only caused a minor wound. The archers had similar results.

Nigel said, "I have another shuriken, but I accomplished little with the first."

"What would happen if we walked through that dome?" Deron asked.

"Why doesn't he breathe again?" Cade asked.

"Breathing is exhausting for dragons," Brute answered. "The dome may kill you if you enter."

In the excitement Brute's spell that had saved Dael's life was forgotten. Brute passed behind each person and placed a hand on a shoulder of each. Brute uttered an elfish phrase and healed some of the effects of the burns they had received.

Eyerthrein asked, "How can you cast so many healing spells?"

"You are not a normal dwarf!" Deron asserted.

"Healing Magick does not tire me. It is time for me to earn my keep. I cannot watch you suffer, my friends," Brute answered.

Brute transformed.

The scales of the Prismatic Dragon projected all the colors of the rainbow. Taekora's charisma was overwhelming. She could coerce fealty without requesting it! Evil creatures of low intelligence would have fled in Fear simply by looking upon the magnificent creature. Her right wing was withered from age and the effect of an injury received hundreds of years ago from a ballista bolt from the guards of Red Mountain in the Iron Mountains War.

"My life was saved by an assassin, Nigel. Imagine that! An assassin! All these years the lawless have suffered the humiliation of being 'Sniffed by the beast'. His name was Knuth Gainriches. In later life, he was known as Knuth the Benefactor. I'm going to repay the debt I owe him," Taekora said resolutely.

"What can you do that we cannot?" Cara asked.

"Reflecting domes will keep out dragon fire. They will not keep out talons and teeth. The defensive Magick won't hurt me," Taekora insisted.

Knarra pleadingly said, "You don't know that you won't be killed going through the Magick barrier! We don't know the extent of its power!"

"You cannot defeat this beast! Someone or something has protected the Red Fire Dragon beyond your capabilities. Eventually the blasts of dragon fire will wear you down. You have given me some advantage by weakening his vision. I'll press this advantage. Now you must halt your attacks and close your eyes. You won't be able to withstand the brilliance," Taekora said determinedly.

Knarra reluctantly complied and urged the others to do so as well.

Faranzer labored and removed the shuriken from his tender nose and the arrows from his left eye. The arrow remained deeply imbedded in the right eye of the monster.

The Red Fire Dragon roared, "That hurts! I'm going to rip you elves apart!"

Faranzer saw Taekora.

"I...I didn't know you were a Prismatic Dragon when I said I was going to have you for dinner. You can have this lousy potion! It's not even Magick as far as I can tell! I've wasted eight hundred years guarding it when I could have been eating wizards, dwarves, and elves and hoarding treasure. Tigarn didn't tell me I would be placed in temporal stasis; Tigarn didn't tell me I would have to fight a Prismatic Dragon. Tigarn didn't tell me a lot of things. Why can't we be friends? There are plenty of them to go around! You eat half and I'll eat half! Would you mind taking the dwarf? They're chewy! You don't really want to fight, do you?" Faranzer said.

"I'm a vegetarian- and I want to fight! I'm a thirsty vegetarian. I've not tasted good vintage for awhile…no…it's too late to barter. Do whatever you can to defend yourself because I'm going to kick your butt!" Taekora said.

Even with their eyes closed the thirteen sensed the multitude of colors of brilliant flashes of light. Faranzer roared in pain. What Cara and Erinnia had started with their arrows, Taekora finished with the Thousand Points of Light. The Thousand Points of Light was an innate ability of Prismatic Dragons. It was like a breath weapon sent through the skin. Faranzer was blinded by the burst of light. Even a Cure Blindness Spell could not remove the blindness caused by the full force of the Thousand Points of Light.

Faranzer cried, "I'll be a good boy! What harm can a blind dragon do?"

Taekora answered, "You can still smell, taste, hear, feel, and use telepathy."

Faranzer sent a massive fireball at Taekora. It exploded just beyond the location of the thirteen.

Taekora was not hurt. Prismatic Dragons were resistant to fire spells.

Taekora watched Faranzer intently.

Faranzer sent a wave of Cold Magick crashing against Taekora.

Taekora was not hurt. Prismatic Dragons were resistant to cold spells.

Taekora took three steps toward Faranzer.

The Red Fire Dragon bellowed, "I know where you are!"

The Red Fire Dragon sent a lightning bolt crashing against Taekora.

Taekora was not hurt. Prismatic Dragons were resistant to shock spells.

Taekora moved closer and Faranzer belched a Death Cloud toward her. Taekora didn't even cough when the gray smoke surrounded her.

Prismatic Dragons were resistant to Death Magick.

Faranzer fired a Magick Missile toward Taekora.

Twang! The Magick Missile reflected from Taekora. Prismatic Dragons reflected Magick Missiles.

Twang! The Magick Missile reflected from the Reflecting Dome.

Twang! The Magick Missile reflected from Taekora.

Twang! The Magick Missile reflected from the Dome.

The cycle repeated three more times before Taekora tired of the ping-ponging Magick Missile and uttered an elfish phrase. The Dispel Magick did not affect the Reflecting Dome but it did dispel the nuisance Magick Missile.

"I wish I could see this!" Deron uttered.

Nigel retorted, "Dummy, Taekora stopped the Thousand Points of Light ten minutes ago. You can open your eyes!"

"Oh," Deron said.

"Be careful how you use that word!" Cara scolded the dwarf.

Deron saw Taekora and Faranzer standing almost snout to snout. Faranzer was a little bigger. The visual loss reduced the Red Fire Dragon's ability to attack the thirteen, but the beast's other senses empowered Faranzer with the ability to know exactly where Taekora stood.

Faranzer took a deep breath.

Taekora took a deep breath.

Both exhaled. The flames met ten feet from their mouths. The great beasts were scarcely twenty feet apart. The stalemate lasted three minutes before Faranzer weakened. The earlier breaths had taken some steam out of the old boy. Taekora's breath penetrated the Dome and struck the Red Fire Dragon. Faranzer was resistant to breath weapons and was injured minimally. Taekora leapt forward and raked her right forepaw through the translucent dome. The room filled with snaps, crackles, and pops. Although her forepaw was injured by the arcane Magick of the dome, Taekora ripped Faranzer's neck with the injured extremity.

Faranzer howled and backed up defensively. Taekora stuck her head through the dome. Beautiful scales snapped from her body as the anti-Magick shell, the Reflecting Dome, attacked her. Undaunted, she breathed deeply and exhaled icy breath which slammed into Faranzer. The icy breath did hurt the Red Fire Dragon. Taekora next uttered a lyrical elfish incantation and delivered an Ice Storm. Great shards of ice rose from the stone floor and fell from the two-hundred-foot-high ceiling of the room. Faranzer was fully vulnerable to spells cast from within the dome.

The Magick of the dome had been created by the individual who hated Magick and sorcerers more than anyone who had lived before or after him. His greatest wish was to harm, injure, and kill those using Magick. His hatred enhanced the Magick of the dome. Every moment stole irreparably more of the Prismatic Dragon's life force.

Knarra screamed, "Get out of there!"

Taekora instead raked Faranzer with both her injured forepaws. The Red Fire Dragon staggered. Taekora opened her maw widely and delivered a great bite to Faranzer's neck. The bones snapped! The sound exceeded the noise created by the sizzling sounds made by the Dome's Magick attack upon Taekora.

Faranzer died.

The translucent dome disappeared.

Taekora spat over and over again.

Knarra ran ahead of the others toward her and shouted, "Heal your wounds!"

"I used my healing Magick, my friends," Taekora said. She could no longer stand and slumped to the floor.

"I have nothing to help you," Knarra cried.

Eyerthrein concentrated and started to conjure but Taekora interrupted him.

Taekora's breathing was labored as she said, "Your healing spells won't help me, my nephew. The anti-Magick shell draws the essence of life not the life's blood of its victim. Any spell caster who breached the dome was doomed by the Spirit Reaping effect of the shell. We can heal wounds, but we cannot restore essence."

Erinnia's lyrical voice remained silent as Taekora spoke. Tears streamed from the elf's eyes, struck the stone floor, and burst into color.

ARTHUR AND THE EGG

BY LESLIE CONZATTI

I.

They called it The Egg because of its shape: Round, oblong, and slightly pointed at the top. It was the most perfectly formed piece of natural geology anyone had ever seen, casually discarded at the back of Echo Cave like a giant's lost plaything, "Fresh from the stone chicken's butt!" Sam would always say.

"Yeah right," Arthur said this time, as they clambered around the uneven surface of The Egg. "There is no such thing as a stone chicken!"

"Oh yeah?" Sam retorted, pushing the sweaty fringe of his deep-blond mop. "What else could have left this here?"

Arthur sighed, leaning back to let the nylon climbing rope take his weight to ease the soreness in his back. "Nothing left it, you dork," he scoffed. "It's just a rock, shaped like an egg." He stomped on it with his hiking boot. The two friends rappelled down to the ground and started packing up their gear.

"Hey," Sam suggested, "wanna meet for drinks later?"

Arthur shook his head. "Nah; Mom will probably have plenty to keep me busy when I get home."

Sam snorted. "So? You are a grown man, Artie! Just because people tell you what to do doesn't mean you can't have your own ideas!"

Arthur shrugged. He didn't say it, but more often than not he felt it was just easier to be told what to do, rather than make his own choices.

"See you around, Sam."

"Later, loser!"

Arthur climbed into his dad's old beat-up Chevy, turned the key, pumped the gas, and the truck choked and roared to life. His mom kept on saying the truck should have died when his dad passed away, but Artie was bound and determined to keep driving it till it did. He nursed the wheezing, coughing old rust-bucket all the way back home.

His mother—a stern, wrinkled, formidable woman by the name of Esther—was waiting on the porch when he pulled up.

"Bout time you got back!" She barked, hands on her broad hips as she glared at him over the bib of her soiled apron. "What you been doing all day? I've been working my tail off since sun-up, washing clothes, cleaning the house, weeding the garden," she snorted, "pitiful as it is. Well, boy?" She folded her arms. "Have you made yourself useful today?"

Arthur sighed; he'd wandered into town, helped a schoolteacher herd a bunch of rowdy kids, and assisted a perfect stranger with enough groceries for both of them to carry.

"Found a job yet?"

He'd wandered into a few establishments, but they'd immediately asked for some kind of credentials, and Arthur hadn't quite managed to fully navigate the educational field yet.

Esther shook her head and waddled back into the tumbledown shack they called home.

"What am I going to do with you?" She mourned.

Arthur felt his heart turn to lead as he saw the mound of bills and debts they owed, piling up as Esther fought and scrimped for every plug nickel. Mother and son sat at the table, staring at a dinner consisting of two old frankfurters and a single potato.

Esther noticed his miserable silence and wagged her head. "I'm getting paid tomorrow; I'll go shopping right off and get us enough food to last till the next payday."

Arthur chewed the tasteless meat gloomily. "Isn't there some way else we can make money, so we don't have to keep running out of food the day before payday?"

Esther glared at him. "You could go out and get a job," she grumbled.

"I'm trying," said Arthur. "But my people skills are better than my practical ones, and the people in charge of hiring don't often get to see that before they turn me down." He sighed.

"Besides, even if I did get a job, would that be enough?" He gestured to the rickety table piled with red-stamped envelopes.

Esther picked at her potato and sighed. "No," she said softly. "I guess the only other option—"

Arthur knew what was coming and he tensed. "No, ma," he begged, "Don't say it."

"—Is to sell the truck."

"No!" Arthur protested hotly. "That truck is the last thing of Dad's that I still have! It's my only link to ever even finding a good job!"

"Well then," Esther fired back, "why ain't you got one yet? No, Artie; you're selling that rust-bucket first thing in the morning, and you make a profit out of it—and don't even think about showing up back here until you do!" She slammed a calloused palm on the table, and that was final.

That night, Arthur lay on his cot to sleep, but he remained wide awake. He knew the truck wouldn't be worth much to anyone else in the world, but compared to the thought of never having that truck again, no price was good enough.

But what choice did they have?

>>>>>

"Ye tha'un sellin' that-thar truck, m'lad?"

Arthur glanced up and appraised the speaker: he was a vagrant, as evidenced by his motley assortment of clothes, and the dirty, leathery look to his skin. His eyes, though; those eyes drew Arthur in, compelled him to see past the grungy exterior, to the wise man beneath.

"Yes," he answered the man's inquiry.

The strange man tilted his head to one side. "Ye don't sound too pleased with there merchandise."

Arthur shook his head. "Oh no, I'm pleased, all right. It's just..." He sighed, as his despondence detected a willing ear and an open demeanor in the stranger. "I would rather not, but I don't have a choice. I—we need the money."

"Aye," the man nodded. "I den't ha' much o' the moanies mesel', but I kin halps the folk who need it. Ye say ye den't ha' the choosin', but I kin make ye'n offer what gives another way."

Arthur squinted at the strange, glinting eyes. "How do you mean?"

"How would ye like a job, instead o' sellin' tha truck?"

Arthur bounded to his feet. "You would give me a job? What kind of job?"

The man chuckled and leaned against the cab of the truck. "Ever seen a dragon, lad?"

Arthur snorted. "No; dragons don't exist."

The man waggled his eyebrows. "But they might; I be searchin' fer one mesel'. Been searchin' everywhere I can, tryin' ta find one. Legend says they once roamed the world; now all that's left is pieces of their hoard." The man reached under some flap of cloth and pulled out a jingling leather bag. "And that's how I mean to find it."

The tale began to take root in Arthur's mind. The more the man talked, the more the idea of a dragon wasn't so far-fetched, even if it was just a theory. "How do you use the hoard to find a dragon?" He asked.

The man dug into the bag with grimy fingers and pulled out a solid-gold coin. "A dragon's hoard isn't just money that it stole; when a dragon takes, it purifies the gold, melting it with its breath and fashioning it into its own coins." He flipped the coin into the air between them, and Arthur caught it. The coin certainly felt otherworldly, and the miniature dragon etched into its surface more ornate than anything Arthur had ever seen.

"The hoard is always trying to get back to the dragon, y'see," the man continued. "And so a dragon-hunter can search for the dragon by spreading these coins around, holding onto them. In the presence of a dragon, the coins will melt, seeping back into the dragon's scales, where they came from." He poured a handful of the things into Arthur's dumbfounded palm. "Weel ya hilp me?"

Unfortunately, this last petition was one step too far for the man. Arthur felt the weight of the coins, but he also saw the fool's errand he would trade the truck for, and he pushed the man away.

"No!" Staggering blindly, he made for the cab of the truck. "You can't have it!"

The man poked his head through the passenger side window. He waved something rectangular and yellow at Arthur. "But wait, lad—"

Arthur turned the key and cranked the gas pedal, sending the truck bounding forward, forcing the man to pull out or be dragged under the jouncing wheels.

Arthur steeled his mind against protests as he pulled onto the main thoroughfare, the one that would take him to Echo Cave.

Tears stung his eyes, as remorse clogged his throat with a heart stony lump. Of all the interested parties for his beloved truck, the one offer he got had to be the kook with the melting coins! Arthur saw the looming form of the cave before him, and the truck sputtered to a stop without him having to apply the brake. He sat in the cab, gasping and grunting as the tears refused to come when his body so badly wanted to cry. Clenching a fist, he pounded against the door with his arm—

And heard something clank on the floor. Arthur glanced at his hand.

He still clutched two of the dragon-coins. Another had dropped to the floor of his truck, and further inspection revealed one more fallen on the seat beside him and one somehow tucked into his pocket. Five coins in all; whether it was good gold or not, Arthur couldn't tell. His mother was superstitious, and suspicious to boot; if he came back with even one coin she would refuse to touch it, let alone spend it. A yellowed cover caught his eye; Arthur picked up the thing the man had dropped: a small book, more like a pamphlet, really. He read the title: "On the Care and Feeding of Dragons and Their Eggs." On a whim, he opened it and read a few pages:

"No. 1: For best results, store the dragon egg in a cool, dry place, with plenty of room to grow. The larger it can grow before hatching, the better-

behaved your dragon will be. Also, the more remote the location, the less chance of disturbance, which will only serve to exacerbate the incubation period.

No. 2: Proper hatching processes involve the use of gold and fire; gold to protect the hatchling, and fire to cure the shell for an easy emergence.

No. 3: An abandoned dragon will imprint on the first scent it detects upon hatching. Make sure to place a prized possession nearby, as the dragon will likely be as devoted to you as you were to the thing they imprint upon..."

With an angry bellow, Arthur tossed the book out the window. The charlatan had nearly had him; he had almost fallen for that whole dragon shtick. He would just have to find some other means of getting the money they needed.

Arthur sat in his truck, but the idea of that insane book still ate at him. He climbed out of the truck, and stomped on the book, grinding paper and ink into the dust and dirt. But it wasn't enough. Arthur felt the urge seize him: he needed to destroy the book, rid himself of every last shred of evidence that he had ever met the man. Digging into the glove compartment of his truck, he pulled out his dad's old lighter. He picked up the battered book and made sure all five coins were in his pocket as he made his way into Echo Cave, all the way back to the foot of The Egg. Tossing the book down, he dropped the coins on top of it, and torched the whole mess. The book burned quickly, becoming nothing but layers of blackened ash, as the coins seemed to lose substance as well, melting and pooling as if there happened to be a dragon nearby. Arthur watched the blaze.

"Artie?" He looked up as Sam's voice echoed through the cave. "You in there?"

Arthur trudged out of the cave, leaving his act of vandalism behind. "Sam," he said, shaking his head and returning to reality, "what are you doing here?"

Sam clapped him on the back. "Heard you were selling your truck, and I just knew there would be trouble! Why didn't you tell me you were strapped?"

Arthur shrugged awkwardly as they headed back to Sam's car, parked alongside the truck. Arthur smirked; guess nobody was getting his truck now. Tow trucks weren't allowed this far outside the city limits; his dad's memory would be stranded out here till the last bolt rusted away.

Sam nodded toward it. "You wanna—"

"It's dead anyhow," Artie informed him. "What's the point?"

Sam nodded. "Well then let me give you a ride home."

Arthur winced. "Actually," he said. "I think I'd rather spend the day with you, if that's okay."

Sam wasn't rich, at least, not in the traditional sense of the word, but he had a decent pad, consistent work, enough food for two people. He shrugged.

"Okay."

Arthur forgot all about crackpots and dragons as he hung out with Sam, doing odd jobs to assist his friend, and trying to be as useful as he could. He sank onto the "guest mattress" on Sam's floor that night, and merely dropped off to sleep without much preamble.

Whatever his intentions, his psyche had other ideas; that night, Arthur dreamed of his little bonfire in Echo Cave, but in his dream the flames built and grew till they engulfed the entire surface of The Egg, roaring and licking over the rocky surface. Rather than burn out, the flames seemed to leave behind an oily sheen, and when they finally died, Arthur dreamed that they left behind an egg that really did look like a massive shell of glossy black stone swirled and flecked with gold. The "shell" split with a loud CRACK, and Arthur bolted awake.

Sam stood in the small corner that served as his kitchen, looking up sheepishly as he bent over the remains of an eggshell shattered on the floor.

"Sorry about the noise," he said. "I was trying to let you sleep while I got ready for work, but the shell slipped out of my hands."

Arthur placed a hand on his chest to quell his galloping heart. "It's all right," he finally managed. "I just had a really weird dream—"

Sam stood completely still, staring over Arthur's head with a strange expression on his face.

"Dude...." He spluttered.

Arthur stood and followed Sam's gaze to the window. "What are you—oh."

Sam's window afforded a decent view of the skyline—and towering over that was an enormous, scaly form, stretching its neck and flexing its wings and moving its massive head. In the early morning light, the newly-hatched dragon raised its head and roared at the sun.

"Oh, we are so screwed," muttered Sam.

>>>>>>>

II.

In record time, Sam and Arthur had scrambled into Sam's small car and sped toward the edge of town.

"How in the world could this happen?" Sam shrieked.

"I don't know!" Arthur wailed, watching the *real live dragon* wag its head and roar.

"Oh man, oh man," Sam veered off the exit that would take them to Echo Cave. "Half the city's probably freaked out by now. The cops'll be here before you know it." He caught Arthur's frantic gaze and glared at him.

"*How is this my fault?*" Arthur shrieked at his friend. "Believe me, I wish that thing was invisible just as much as you do!"

"Well, just goes to show you how effective wishes are, because it's—" Sam pointed to the massive beast just ahead as they pulled into Echo Cave Park. "*Gone!*" He slammed hard on the brakes, sending Arthur rocketing forward in his seat.

"Ow!" Arthur rubbed his head. "What was that for?"

Sam was still watching the huge dragon in horror. "Arthur, it's gone! The dragon just disappeared!"

Arthur squinted at the massive claws digging up the ground less than a mile away. "What are you talking about, Sam, it's *right there.*"

Sam shook his head. "No it's not! It was there a minute ago—you and I both saw it—but now it's completely gone, like one of those optical illusions or something."

Arthur frowned at his friend. "How are you this dense?" He muttered. "It literally hasn't moved. Keep driving!"

"You know what? No!" Sam took the keys out of the ignition and folded his arms. "I'm not moving. If you want to keep imagining that there's a dragon there, go ahead and walk over there, and I'll believe you!"

Arthur scowled and huffed out his nose. "Fine! I will!" He flung open the door and stepped out, slamming it hard behind him.

The dragon picked up its head and turned toward the sound. Arthur looked back toward his friend, but Sam shook his head.

Arthur felt his heart creep up into his throat as he stepped slowly and calmly through the trees, closer and closer to the dragon with dark-brown scales. It sat on its haunches, with its long tail curled against its legs. The long neck with the blunt head bent down over something in front of it. Just beyond the dragon's bulk, Arthur could see what remained of Echo Cave: a charred husk, like a very deep crater, with shards of The Egg laying in huge pieces around it.

Guess it really was an egg, after all! Arthur thought. He reached the very edge of the clearing when he saw what absorbed the dragon's attention: his dad's truck, still parked just where he left it the day before.

The dragon made a breathy sound, sharp and hissing—and with a low growl, it turned its head and looked right at Arthur! He froze where he stood, not daring to move a muscle as the dragon's head leaned closer. Arthur could feel the movement of its breath as it stopped and peered at him, its snout nearly touching him. It gave one small sniff, and then lunged so fast, Arthur was in the air by the time he screamed. The dragon caught his shirt between its teeth, and swung him through the air till he slammed down on the hood of his truck. Arthur tried to scoot backward, up the windshield and onto the roof, while the dragon waited with claws splayed, bracing itself for—Arthur didn't quite know.

"*Hungry!*" a voice grunted.

Arthur looked behind him, only for the dragon to grunt again, prompting him to turn back to the creature almost salivating over him.

"*Hungry!*" said the voice again, but Arthur had no way of knowing who was speaking.

"Who's there?" Arthur attempted to call over his shoulder.

"Arthur!" That voice was definitely Sam. The dragon didn't turn away from Arthur sprawling on his truck, but it didn't back off either.

"Be careful, Sam!" Arthur called. He could see his friend in his periphery, standing just inside the clearing, only a few steps away from the backside of the dragon.

"What's wrong with you, man?" Sam paused uncertainly. "I saw you walking and then all of a sudden you went flying. Did you break something?" Sam scanned the ground at his feet as if he expected some kind of land mine or spring-loaded launch pad.

The dragon loomed closer, a steady growl building in its throat.

"*Hungry!*" said the voice again, so quiet it seemed to come from behind him. "*Feed.*"

Arthur hardly dared to breathe. "It... It's the dragon," he stammered to Sam. "It's *right here*. Can't you see it?"

Sam glanced around the sky, as if the dragon hovered over the treetops. "I'm telling you, man, that thing is one hundred percent—"

Just then, the dragon slammed its claws down on either side of the truck, causing a small earthquake.

"*HUNGRY. MUST. FEED!*" Snarled the voice.

The dragon looked about ready to eat him; Arthur threw up his hands protectively. "Okay, okay!" He squeaked. "Don't hurt me!"

The dragon actually backed up a few feet. It tilted its head to regard Arthur.

"*Protect Master. Keep Master safe. Master feed.*"

The voice was gentler, not as insistent now.

"All right, whoever you are!" Arthur called to the hungry person behind his truck. "I'm going over there."

Sam began walking toward him. "Dude, what are you talking about?"

Arthur's voice caught in his throat as he watched the dragon swing around to confront Sam, who kept right on walking. The dragon opened its mouth and roared.

"*KEEP MASTER SAFE!*" the voice declared.

"WHOA!" Arthur tumbled off the truck and scrambled around to put himself between the dragon and his friend. "Sam, stop! SAM, STOP! WAIT! NO!"

Sam squinted at him. "What the heck, man?"

"Wait!" Arthur addressed the dragon now. It sat and watched him, amber-colored eyes blinking slowly. "You... you *talk*?"

The dragon huffed and shuffled its foreclaws. *"Master speaks. Master hears the voice of his hatchling."*

Arthur felt his knees wobble and buckle. "Master..." he gasped. "You... you mean *me*? I am your master?"

Sam snorted behind him. "What's going on, Arthur? What are you master over?"

"Shut up, Sam!" Arthur snapped. "I just saved your life, so just hang on a sec while I figure this out!"

The dragon lolled its head over to the truck, cradling it protectively between its claws.

"Thing has scent of Master. Master loves thing, imprinted on thing. Hatchling has imprinted on Master's scent, will serve and obey Master."

"Saved my life?" Sam was muttering behind him. "From what? That would be the first time I've seen you take initiative. What's out there that could have killed me, huh?"

Arthur ignored Sam as he watched the dragon. "Say, are you invisible right now? Why can I see you?"

"Master wished Hatchling to be invisible, but not even Dragon cannot hide from Master. Master will always know where Dragon is."

A slow smile unfolded on Arthur's face as Sam still complained and rambled on behind him. "Do me a favor," he said to the dragon. "Make yourself visible, but only to my friend here."

The dragon turned his head to regard the taunting fellow behind Arthur. "*Is friend? Is kind to Master?*"

Arthur nodded. "Yes; he's a butthead sometimes, but he's nice to me. Please, could you do it?"

"*I obey Master.*" The dragon sat up, planting its claws in front of him.

Arthur knew exactly the moment Sam could see him because the jabbering ceased. "I take you in, give you a bed, and it turns out all you give me is trouble because now we're way out here and Echo Cave looks like it had a bomb go off and— HOLY WHAT?"

Arthur turned around to face Sam. His friend stood, staring over his head as if his eyes would roll right out of his skull.

"Wha… tha—ho-ly…Wh-what??" Sam spluttered.

"Now do you believe me?" Arthur needled, even though he had to admit, it was a little bit strange to go from having *nothing at all* to having *a dragon who would obey and protect him.*

Sam—after he had sufficiently recovered from the shock of actually seeing the dragon materialize right in front of him—wasted no time in pointing out, "What are you going to do with a dragon?"

Arthur shrugged. "I don't know; anything I want, I guess?"

Sam climbed into the bed of the truck, while the dragon regarded him in a manner not unlike suspicion. "I mean, no offense—but it's not like the dragon can find you food or a steady job or anything that you *really* need."

A churning, wet rumble erupted from the spot just underneath the dragon's seat. It bent its head to rest its snout gently against the windshield, so that Arthur could stroke its smooth head-plates from his perch on the roof of the vehicle.

"*Is hungry,*" it murmured to him. "*Master will feed now?*"

Arthur suddenly became very aware of how hungry he was. "I'm sorry," he said. "I don't think there are many animals left in these woods anymore. You probably don't eat trees or leaves or things like that."

"Is new hatchling. Does Master give Hatchling trees to eat?"

Arthur shrugged. "If you're hungry enough, go ahead—"

Before he had finished speaking, the dragon leaned over and wrapped its large jaws around the trunk of a nearby tree. With a small jerk of its head, it snapped the trunk in two pieces, leaving the jagged stump behind and chomping chunks off the end of the felled tree, exactly in the manner of someone biting off the end of a carrot. Very soon, it had consumed the trunk and munched happily on the foliage till all that was left was a scattering of debris.

"Tree is good," the dragon murmured.

Arthur chuckled. "Well, *that* was easy enough! Don't eat all the trees, though," he warned the beast, "because if you do, you'll have nowhere to hide."

"What else does Master give Hatchling to eat?"

Arthur glanced around. Besides the trees, there wasn't much in the area—and with the destruction of Echo Cave, it wouldn't be long till people started to wonder how it came to be that way—and as soon as the wondering began, discovery of his secret wouldn't be far behind. What he needed was a way to dispose of the evidence, to remove any kind of motivation for people to come to this area.

He turned back to the dragon. "Umm, what else can you eat?"

The dragon swung its head around, prompting Arthur and Sam to dodge out of its way as it surveyed the area with wide, blinking eyes.

"All things looks tasty," it murmured. Opening its mouth wide, it bit off a chunk of Echo Cave. The sound it made as it chewed was like sitting too close to an industrial-grade jackhammer. Arthur covered his ears until the beast swallowed.

"Master gives Hatchling stone to eat?" it asked, glancing sidelong at the shards of polished rock piled off to the side.

Arthur was only half-listening to the voice in his head. Sam's cell phone jingled, and he went back to answer it. "Huh?" he said to the dragon. "Oh… sure, I guess."

The dragon hatchling attacked the pile of rubble with vigor. Arthur saw Sam waving to him, so he slipped out of the truck bed and joined his friend.

Sam wagged his head as he watched the dragon. "Man, that is *beyond* cool, right there!"

"Yeah," Arthur responded lamely, scratching the back of his head. "I just hope nothing happens to it while I'm not here."

"Which might be longer than either of us like," Sam waved his cell phone. "That was your mom. She's worried about you being gone all day, especially when you didn't come home last night."

Arthur winced. For as angry Esther tended to get at her son, she also fretted over him with equal ferocity. "Yeah, I'll just... Lemme say goodbye to the dragon."

He trudged back to the clearing. His new pet had polished off the shards of Egg in the time it had taken him to talk to Sam.

"Hey," he said, not quite sure how to address the animal.

The dragon swung its head around to look at him. *"What Master wish for Hatchling to serve him?"*

"Huh?" Arthur had a difficult time following the roundabout sentence. "Oh, er, no, it's nothing I want—well, except... have you got another name besides Hatchling?"

The dragon swung its tail, splitting a crevice into the side of Echo Cave.

"Hatchlings have no names. Master must give Hatchling his name."

Arthur raised his eyebrows. "Really? So... You wouldn't want to be called Spike or Flame or anything like that..." He scratched the top of his head.

Over by the car, he heard Sam holler, "Arthur! We need to go now!"

Arthur looked up at the hatchling. "What do you want to be called?" he asked abruptly.

The young dragon fidgeted with its claws, raking furrows in the dirt. It bent its head down to nudge the truck gently.

"Hatchling only wants Master to love as much as Master loves this thing. Hatchling will take the name of this thing."

Arthur squinted. "Wait, well—that's a truck…"

The dragon perked up right away, laying its head down in front of Arthur. *"Master will give the name Truck?"*

The young man scuffed his sneaker in the dirt and wagged his head. "You're kidding me; you want to be called Truck?"

"Yes; if Master wills it."

"All right, then," Arthur responded with a shrug. "I'll call you Truck."

Truck picked up its head and nudged against Arthur.

"Truck loves Master."

Arthur reached up to stroke the smooth scales of the dragon's snout.

"Good night, Truck."

"Truck will await Master's return."

Sam glanced at the gargantuan reptile as they pulled away from Echo Park.

"So that thing is gonna be okay just sitting there?"

Arthur watched Truck's lumpy form till the trees hid it from view. "He says he'll wait till I come back tomorrow."

Sam smirked. "So it's a *he* now, is it?"

Arthur practically glared at his friend. "Yeah, and *he* has a name. It's Truck."

The car gave a lurch as Sam nearly braked in surprise. "Truck?" he spluttered with a snort. "What kind of a name is that?"

Arthur folded his arms tightly. "It's the name he wanted, okay?"

"Okay, then!" Sam said, wagging the unruly locks of hair out of his eyes. "A dragon named Truck."

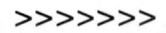

>>>>>>>

III.

The sun was half-set by the time Sam pulled up to Arthur's house. He saw the red flag waving over the front gate and his gut sank. Sam pulled the car to a stop and just stared at the steering wheel.

"Thanks for the ride," Arthur muttered, and sprang from the car as fast as he could.

Esther waited for him on the front porch, her hands on her hips and her face red and blotchy from crying.

"And just *where* do you think you've been all day?" She shrilled, shaking her meaty fist at him. "Here I am, worried sick, trying to work hard to earn the money in my paycheck—where *were* you when I needed you most, boy?"

Arthur would have hugged his mom, but to do so would have been too overwhelming for her anger, and she might have slugged him for it.

"Ma, what happened?" he asked. "Why is there a vacancy flag on our lot?"

"Why, he asks?" Esther barked in his face. "You know good and well what that flag means! It means we don't own our house anymore." She pointed to the door. "It means I can't keep up with that debt your father left behind, so the bank has stepped in, and now we have to move or we won't have a place to sleep anymore!"

Arthur nearly shrugged it off like everything else his mother ever said—after all, Truck wouldn't mind sheltering him for as long as he needed—but he knew that, what with losing the house and his failure to land a secure job, adding a dragon on top of all their struggles would not go over well with her.

"What are we going to do, then?" he wondered aloud.

Esther trudged back into the house. "I've put a call in to Frances. She says they have room for us over at her place."

The words escaped his mouth before he could stop them. "Aw, ma! Not Aunt Frances!"

Esther whirled on her son in a moment. "Now you listen *good*, young man! If you'd have sold that truck for a good price like I told you, if you'd have found yourself a decent wage-paying job like I told you, if the world had been any kind of a fair place for a body to live in without bothering nobody—we wouldn't be in this kind of pickle! But it happened, so I don't give two pins for your opinion of my sister, she's the *last* family we have, so, by jingus, we're going and that's *final!*" Esther emphasized her point with a snap of her apron. "Get washed up, Arthur; I bought us a nice supper."

As it happened, "nice" according to Esther was only a relative term, as compared to the meager pickings they had been eating over the last few days. By that measure, "nice" turned out to be a sumptuous feast of roast chicken, bread, canned peas, and an apple each.

Arthur ate in miserable silence, dreading with each passing hour the impending move to halfway across the country—much too far into unknown territory to even think of working out a way to bring Truck along. And what would the poor dragon do without him? Aunt Frances ran a very strict household, and she loved to be intimately involved with absolutely every detail of the lives of those under her roof. His mother complained a whole lot and she found a lot of things to be mad about all the time, but she was also industrious and gave Arthur space when he needed it. Once they moved in with Aunt Frances all that would disappear.

He lay on the cot that night, pulling the new blanket close around him. He almost imagined, in that dark, star-spangled sky, he could just see the ridges of Truck's back jutting over the trees. Arthur wasn't sure if saying goodbye to his new friend would be any easier to face than trying to sell his father's truck to begin with.

In the morning, Arthur made sure to slip out while Esther was busy with the last bit of laundry. Much of what they planned to bring with them was already piled on the porch. Arthur had taken care to place his backpack on the top of the pile, packed with things like a blanket, a couple packs of food, and bottles of water. Maybe if his mother didn't send Sam out looking for him, he could stay with Truck while she left to go live with Aunt Frances by herself.

Arthur walked right through town to get to the road that led to Echo Cave. Many of the businesses still operated, but nobody wanted to look Arthur in the eye. They all knew who he was—and each one of them had turned him down when he had come to them, desperate for a job: the barber, the mechanic, the grocery, the post office... Arthur blinked and glanced twice at the shady figure leaning up against the back wall of the tiny schoolhouse. The hat, the nose—Arthur felt his chest tighten as he recognized the man who had given him the coins.

The man's head turned. Arthur could feel the gaze like a giant searchlight strobing toward him, but his feet came to a halt and refused to move.

"Eyy, lad!" The creaking voice threaded through his consciousness as the eyes strode closer. "I been wonderin' wot 'appened to ye ever since I gave ye those coins. 'Ave ye gi'en second thoughts to 'elpin' me?"

Thoughts of Truck crowded into his brain; Arthur couldn't make his voice work, try as he might to answer. Didn't the man *deserve* to know what had become of his information? Couldn't they possibly *share* the dragon between them? After all, the man's coins and his knowledge had revealed the dragon in their very midst—he, of all the other people in the city, would be most qualified to see that Truck had a good life since Arthur couldn't take care of him once he moved in with Aunt Frances.

"I—" The word sprang suddenly out of his mouth, like fizzy water from a bottle that had been shaken too much. Arthur wasn't prepared with any other word to say. His thoughts swirled with *Truck—help Truck... Truck, help... Help, Truck help Truck...*

"I don't want to," Arthur finally squeaked, staggering forward as the man reached out to support him.

"Well, then," the man rasped, hobbling alongside the distracted boy. "Ye wouldn't 'appen to 'ave th' coins still on ye? If yer no' gonna take my offer, I'll spend them somewhere else."

"I lost them," Arthur pawed at the air in front of him as darkness seeped around the edge of his vision. What was happening? It felt like plunging into a dream where his legs couldn't function and his eyes wouldn't focus.

"Ye *wha--ooh?*" The man's voice became garbled as Arthur strained to stay upright, to maintain his clarity. The voice in his head took precedence, still repeating the endless *Truck...Truck... Get to... Truck... Must get... Truck help...* Arthur threw every effort into shaking the man off and continuing on his way, but he wasn't at all sure if his body responded. The ground lurched.

"*Truck!*"

The delirious mix faded with the high shriek of a dragon. Arthur caught himself from pitching headfirst into the ground as the fog over his mind lifted. He and the man stood on the trail to Echo Cave. The world stopped leaning, and Arthur felt the wind pick up with the unmistakable leathery flap of dragon wings. The strange old man stared up into the sky, practically ignoring Arthur altogether.

"Blame... simpleton..." he muttered. "Fool boy, wot 'ave ye done?"

Arthur could only watch as Truck smashed through several trees to land before them.

The man cried out, but whether in fear or admiration, Arthur couldn't make out.

He began looking around. "I heard it! It's around here somewhere, as sure as my name's Drake!" He clapped his hand on Arthur's shoulder, and the young man winced at the sudden strength. "D'ye see it, boy?"

Truck reared and let out a terrible scream. *"Truck must save Master from the Monster!"*

"Whoa, whoa!" Arthur twisted away from Drake and held out his hands toward the irate dragon. "Calm down, there's nothing to—"

"Lad?" The old man stared at him with a keen tilt of his head. "Be you four kinds o' daft? Are ye talkin' to the trees now, when there's a dragon about?"

Arthur hesitated to respond; Truck had called this man The Monster—but why? What was so monstrous about the weathered old codger?

"Your name," he said slowly. "Is Drake?"

The man's eyes twinkled and he tapped the side of his thick nose. "Aye, tha' 'tis! Sir Drake the Great, they called me—leastways, till they found I couldn't summon even a single dragon." He rubbed his hands together and gave a chuckle. "But now that I—er, pardon, that *we* have found a dragon, there'll be piles o' gold for the both of us!" Drake took a confident stride forward, nearly into the span of Truck's wings as the hatchling curled behind Arthur. "Now, I 'ave sommat that'll make the dragon so's we c'n see it—"

Arthur gulped. "I already can," he stated.

Drake's twinkling gaze fixed on him. "Ye wot?"

"What does Master think, to make a deal with The Monster?" Truck hissed in his head. Every step forward Drake moved, Truck would cower further and further back into the trees. Arthur was acquiring quite the flattened space behind him. *"The Monster will trick Master, and kill Truck!"*

"I'm trying to save you, Truck!" Arthur thought, hoping that the dragon could hear inside his head, like Arthur could. *"Maybe I can stall—"*

"What is stall?"

Drake coughed, and Arthur realized that the man was standing in arm's reach, peering at him with more suspicion than awe in those beady little eyes. "Can ye *see* the dragon, boy?"

Arthur took an assertive step forward, prompting Drake to step back and regain some space between them. "I can," he answered. "And I can hear him, too."

Drake folded his arms and laughed, a sharp "Ha!" at first, but gradually unfolding into a full cackle. "It speaks, ye say? It *bloody* talks to ye!" Drake wagged his head and eyed the widening clearing behind Arthur. "Wot does it say?"

Arthur heard Truck shuffling anxiously behind him. "He calls you The Monster," he said. "Now why would you have such a name?"

"Monster?" Drake slapped both hands on his belly and guffawed heartily. "Monster, is it? Tell me, lad—do I strike you as a monster?"

Arthur shrugged. "Not to me; what is it you do with dragons, then? Put them on display in some kind of freak show?"

"*Do* with them?" Drake spluttered. "Why, lad, do you know what dragons are capable of? They can turn stone into gold bricks! Metal into precious diamonds! It's not the shows that make the money, it's what the dragons can do!" Drake reached into the pocket of his grimy coat. "Now, if it's just sitting there right behind ye, as I reckon it is, I'll thank ye to get outta the way as I jest slip this little lovely—"

"No!" Arthur didn't want to know what he intended to do with Truck, but judging by the amount of terrified huffing coming from the hatchling, it wasn't anything nice. "Don't come any closer!"

"I'm not going to hurt it, lad!" Drake lied. "Just a small... he won't even feel it—"

Truck's frightened wails in Arthur's thoughts drowned out anything the old man tried to say. Arthur gasped as a huge claw wrapped around his middle and Truck carried him up and away, leaving the dirty dragon-wrangler screaming curses at the sky.

Arthur fought for breath between the rapid change in altitude and the claws pinching his ribs. Truck flew all the way to the site of former Echo Cave, and skidded to a three-legged landing, only jarring Arthur a very little bit. Truck set him down, and Arthur grabbed his sides, though he couldn't help peering into the surrounding forest, even through the pain.

"Do you think he might follow us?" he asked Truck.

The dragon hatchling's eyes narrowed. *"Truck will deal with the Monster. Master will have no fear."* He took off again, leaving Arthur next to the busted truck.

Across the clearing, Arthur noticed something odd. Where Echo Cave and the infamous Egg once stood, there was a pile of neat concrete blocks. He recalled Truck munching on the stone cave—but where did these bricks come from? Was Truck responsible? Shouldn't they have been made of gold then, as Drake insisted?

He was still puzzling over this when Truck returned.

"*The Monster is gone! He will not bother Master any more!*" The hatchling veered in several happy loops before landing.

Arthur squinted at the narrow, scaly face hovering over him. "What did you do to him?" he asked.

Truck settled on his haunches like a puppy that had just performed a trick. "*Truck flew high and silent so that the Monster would not hear his approach. Then Truck blasted The Monster with fire from his jaws!*" To illustrate, Truck let out a great belch of flame that ignited several trees beside the trail.

Arthur edged away from the blaze. "That's all right then; hope he wasn't wearing anything fire-proof—"

"*Then Truck ate the Monster.*"

"You WHAT?"

Truck rumbled deep in his throat and brought his massive head down to rest next to his namesake. "*Truck keeps Master safe.*"

Arthur wagged his head. He could only hope that the strange old man wasn't very well known in the city. He had no idea what he would say if people started asking questions, nor what he would do if someone got it into their head to search for the grimy, wandering vagrant. He shrugged and turned his attention to the other matter.

"Truck," he nodded to the pile of bricks. "Did you make those?"

"*Yes; Truck makes bricks like the Monster says, but they are stone, not golden.*"

Arthur scratched the back of his neck. "So is the other thing true? What Drake said about the metal becoming jewels?"

The young dragon huffed. "*Truck doesn't know. Does Master want jewels?*"

Arthur's mind whirled at the distinct possibilities suddenly opening up before him. "Well, my mom and I, we don't have any money, and we have already lost our home because of all the debt my dad left behind." He sighed, patting the rusted hood behind him. "Its why I came to see you today, to say goodbye."

Truck let out a small moan as he shifted his head closer to Arthur's feet. *"Truck wishes to stay with Master. Truck must keep Master safe."*

"But I can't bring you with me," Arthur protested. "You have to stay out here."

Truck picked up his head and turned to nudge the pile of bricks filling the crater that was once a cave. *"Master can use the bricks to build a new home, with Truck."*

The young man chuckled and approached the pile. Hefting one of the smooth, firm bricks in his hand, he chucked it aside. "I just don't know how my mom would react to having a dragon so nearby," he remarked. "Lots of humans are scared of dragons. I was scared when we first met." How long ago it seemed! Had it really been only a few days?

Arthur flinched out of his musings when the large scaly head bumped gently against his shoulder. *"Truck understands,"* warbled the gentle voice in his head. *"Truck wants to help Master. If Truck must find a new place to live, Truck will do that."*

Lose Truck forever? Arthur's throat clenched at the idea; it would be like watching his father leave all over again—only this time, *he* would be the one leaving someone behind. But what other choice did they have? Arthur glanced from the dilapidated old truck, to the fantastical beast that desired to be named for it. A plan slowly began to materialize in his mind. He looked up at Truck, determination gleaming in his eyes.

"I have an idea!" he said. "Let's go for a ride, Truck."

The young dragon bounded to his feet, knocking over several more trees as he did so. *"Master would like to ride? Where do we go?"*

Arthur beckoned to him. "Put your head down. I want to ride on your neck this time. I'll tell you where to go once we're in the air." Truck lay down, and Arthur clambered up to the hollow at the base of his long, sinuous neck. It was large enough to form a kind of saddle for him. "Oh, and bring the truck, too."

Truck grabbed Arthur's dad's truck, and the pair took off.

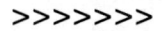

>>>>>>>

IV.

Truck flew at Arthur's direction until the two of them arrived at a wide expanse far outside the city limits. Here, all manner of discarded junk and machinery sat, collecting rust and deteriorating, waiting to disintegrate into the dust they sat upon.

Truck found a wide space on the back end, in the shadow of the towering mountain range, to land, and set the truck gently down in the middle. The dragon laid his head down so Arthur could slide off.

"Well?" The young man asked proudly, spreading his arms. "What do you think? Nobody would *ever* blunder into you here, and even if they did, they would never assume that the invisible thing making noises in the junkyard would be a dragon! Besides," He turned and tilted his head to face Truck, "You can eat the old junk here, right?"

Truck glanced from Arthur to the tall stacks of gears and rubble around him. Experimentally, he bent down and tore the sheeting off an old clothes machine. Munching it like a potato chip, Truck swallowed, then rumbled happily.

"*Is very tasty,*" Arthur heard him murmur.

The young man hesitated, tracing a track in the dirt with the toe of his shoe.

"So..." he prodded slowly as Truck continued to consume the old belts and plates from various discarded items, "Are you ready to try the other thing? The melting magic?"

Truck gulped down a strange bowl-shaped contraption that had an arm for mixing things.

"*Master would like to see if Truck can make jewels for him?*"

Arthur scratched at the back of his neck again. "Well, I just want to see if it's possible. I mean, if not, then oh well—"

Truck's head dipped down closer to Arthur's eye level, and he heard the dragon's voice quietly muse, "*Master wants to use The Truck for his experiment.*"

Arthur turned his back on the vehicle, as if that would make it any easier. "It's... It's time for me to let it go, let it become s-something else," he said shakily, "If it can."

"*Truck will try. For Master's sake.*"

Arthur scurried to a position behind Truck's tail for protection as the dragon opened his mouth and let loose a white-hot jet of flame. Even behind the fire-proof dragon as he was, several yards away, Arthur could still feel the searing heat wafting toward him, stinging his skin. The light dimmed, and the temperature dropped all at once.

"*Master!*" Truck cried happily. "*Has Truck done a good thing?*"

Arthur peeked around the tall, scaly flank. What was once his most prized possession now sat as a pool of burbling, molten metal. Arthur approached it cautiously, well aware of the radiant heat he still felt. As it cooled, he saw the metal contract slightly, revealing small aberrations in the smooth, glossy surface. When it was finally cool enough to touch, Arthur rubbed at one of the geometric knobs. It didn't budge, embedded in the metal as it was. "What is it?" he asked Truck.

The young dragon leaned down, and with the bony tip of his snout, he pounded hard at the knob until the metal cracked and broke.

Arthur staggered back with a gasp. The whole inside of the metal pancake was filled with rough, quartz-like crystals! Truck pounded out the rest of it, and Arthur ended up with a pile of rough gemstones as high as his knee.

"Truck!" He declared happily, filling every pocket on his clothes with as many crystals as he could carry, "You did it!"

"*Does it please Master?*" The dragon still sounded a bit hesitant, if not overly hopeful.

"Does it?" With just these few gems, they could pay off the outstanding debts *and* keep the house—and who knew what else would be possible with the rest? Arthur turned and hugged the nearest part of the dragon he could get his arms around: the huge foreleg. "Thank you, Truck."

Truck bent his head and nudged Arthur's back. "*Master can be safe now?*"

Arthur met Truck's gaze over his shoulder. "Yes; we are definitely safe, thanks to you."

>>>>>

Esther had fumed all morning when Arthur just abandoned her without a word. She had laundry to deliver, packing to finish, and Frances' son would be coming by with a wagon to carry as much as they could away from the house—what had she done to deserve such a punishment, that the men in her life would consistently vanish on her, leaving more destruction in their wake every time?

She grumbled through the deliveries, listening for the creak and rumble of a wagon at any moment. She didn't even hear the crunching, hesitant steps on the front porch, nor the creak of the door—so when she emerged from the back room to find Arthur standing in the kitchen, Esther screamed.

"WHAT DO YOU THINK YOU'RE DOING?" She thundered, as soon as she recovered from her shock. "You've *left* me here, with all the work, and think you can just waltz in when it's nearly done, and you've not had to lift a finger—"

He dropped something on the table while she kept going.

"—and the wagon's going to be here any minute, though there's probably most of these things we won't be able to fit, and... *Land sakes, boy, that's a diamond!*" Her mind, freed of its pent-up worry, finally recognized what Arthur had pulled out of his pocket. Esther didn't utter a sound but her eyes grew bigger and her mouth sagged lower as he just kept pulling out the dingy, translucent crystals, till the pile had taken up nearly half the table.

Esther began shaking all over as she tried to speak. "Wh—where did you get all those, Art?" She squinted at him abruptly. "You didn't steal them, did you? By jingus, if you've added *thievery* to all your father's worthless money-handling—"

"No, ma," Arthur answered softly. "They're ours, fair and square."

Esther rested her hands on the table, both wanting to handle the stones to convince herself that they were real, and not wanting anything to do with illicit goods. "B-but *how?*" she spluttered.

Arthur found his words choked by a sudden lump in his throat, and tears he never realized he had gathered in his eyes. "Th-they were in dad's truck," he said. "He must've found them, and left them there for us."

The gentle pressure on his shoulder reminded him of Truck, but it was his mother, holding him. Arthur fell into his mother's embrace as Esther hugged her son and the two mourned together over their shared loss.

Three months later, Arthur returned to the long road that led to the junkyard. It had been two months since the last trip to the junkyard, to clean up the last of the gems. The stockpile from his dad's truck had netted them more than enough money to pay off the debts, buy back the house from the bank, and even hire workers to renovate the house. Arthur smiled to himself as he recalled everyone's confusion at the random supply of concrete bricks that now formed the walls of their new house. He'd purposely taken multiple trips to cart the jewels out of the junkyard, because it gave him more opportunities to visit Truck while he still could. He had deposited the last of the gems to pay for a college education, relieving his mother of that worrisome burden as well. She still washed clothes, but now it was more of a service, for ready money, since they had plenty to keep and save. Arthur would start classes in the fall, and Sam promised to have job offers for him once he graduated.

Arthur sailed down the long path on his shiny new bicycle. It wasn't quite like driving a car like Sam's, but he knew the wisdom of getting a vehicle that could last, if only so he wouldn't have to walk everywhere. He pulled into the back corner, where Truck lived, noting how wide the open space had become since their first day there.

"Truck?" he called, listening with his mind and his ears. "Truck! I'm here, where are you?"

Silence, and the distant caw of birds answered him. Arthur felt that old heaviness return, the sinking, choking feeling he had hoped to leave behind. He trudged over to the familiar crater that once had been his truck. In the midst of the metal scraps, he spotted something small and green—nearly the same color as Truck's scales had been. Arthur bent down to pick it up.

It was a small bag, one that looked like it had been made of dragon-hide. Arthur weighed it in his palm, hearing something clink inside. He opened it, and the puff of warm air that hit his face nearly reminded him of the way Truck would huff at him. Arthur dipped his hand inside and pulled out a small disc-shaped object that glinted in the sunlight. A dragon coin! The embossed profile of Truck winked at him from the coin's surface. Staring at the coin in his hand, Arthur could hear Truck's voice, as if the dragon himself were there, speaking to him in his mind like he always did.

"*Master is safe, and Truck is happy. Master was gone a very long time, but Truck found other dragons in a place that is not a human-place. Truck has joined the other dragons, but Truck will always remember Master. Truck hopes to someday return to visit Master, but until that time, Truck will leave these coins for Master, so that Master will always remember Truck, and Truck can find Master, as long as Master holds Truck's coins.*"

Arthur gasped as the voice faded, and rubbed the tears from his eyes. He slipped the coin back in the pouch, and tucked it in his pocket. As he climbed back on his bike and rode back toward his house, Arthur reflected on how strange it would seem, that a creature so few would even believe existed would mean so much to him. One thing was certain: if Truck didn't return in his lifetime, he would see those coins passed down through future generations of his family, so that his children, and their children, and their children on and on would know the story of a boy named Arthur, a rock called The Egg, and a dragon named Truck.

THE VIEW FROM THE OTHER SIDE

BY ASSAPH MEHR

A home is more than a shelter, a place to keep your possessions. A home is a place that *matters*. So when someone — or something — threatens your home, you respond. In kind.

The nasty little vermin first started to infest the fields beyond my home over a decade ago. They built their little nests out of wood and straw, felled trees in the forests to make clearings, drove the game away in favour of their filthy pets. I have a delicate constitution, just like father. I can't just eat any old thing, or it gives me terrible gas. So I gave them a warning first, only burned down a few of their houses. I took a few bites of their animals too, and I'll have you know they taste all blubbery and horrible. What can you expect of things that live in mud?

But then the blighters started to invade my home. I have no idea why, but they started to nick my bedspreads. What use could they possibly have for it? I need my bed arranged *just so*, or I can't possibly get a good winter's sleep. And they have no use for it! They just break it down, make it into tasteless decorations. There's no decent use for those metals; too soft, which is why I use them for bedding. Even pilfering ravens are better than that.

And, worst, do you know what it feels like to wake up and find one those critters skittering around in the dark? One minute you're resting quietly, the next you open an eye, and some disgustingly moist thing with undeniably mammalian features is stealing your furniture from right under you! So I roasted the thing, and placed its remains just outside my cave as a sign to others.

You'd think that would turn them away, but you'd be wrong. That only seemed to encourage more of the vermin. I ventured out and burned down whole colonies of them, never mind that I get an awful creak in my wings around autumn. But next spring, just like mushrooms, up popped their nests again.

So I studied them a little, and decided on a different tack. I grabbed what seemed to be their queen bee, something they call a "prin-cess". Well, 'cess' is also the word they use for the pits into which they defecate. That thing smelled no better, if you ask me. Stupid little wet things, they need to wash themselves — no cleansing inner heat, no claws for proper preening of scales.

I was aiming merely to get their attention, open some diplomatic discussions about their immediate surrender and withdrawal from my lands. While I was waiting for their envoys, that moronic prin-cess was making an awful racket. I ended up tying her to a tree outside; I just couldn't bear the noise and the constant flow of moisture from her face.

They sent some representatives by the next day. I wished to speak to them, but they just left a few of their disgusting, pinkish animals outside as an offering. Well, I ate those. Might as well save me the trouble of hunting.

Bad mistake. They came the next day to ask for their princess back. I wanted to explain the terms for them, but I told you that unless I dine on proper stags and deer, I get indigestion. I'm afraid I belched rather indecorously. It was just a misunderstanding, honest. I didn't mean to burn their emissaries to a crisp.

That left me a few more nights in the company of that wailing atrocity, driving sleep away. But then came another envoy. It was clad in an imitation of true scales, some metallic contraption that covered it from head to toe. I started to explain my grievances but it kept charging at me, riding some quadruped beast and brandishing a long pin.

I tried reasoning with it, but its underdeveloped mammalian brain did not allow it true speech. It just kept repeating 'have at thee' and similar drivel. After the third of its passes at me, I admit I got annoyed and lost my temper. On the plus side, turns out that if you cook them in their shells they come out softly broiled. The meat was practically falling off the bones.

Their prin-cess, though, kept fainting. I offered her some of the food to restore her spirits, but that made her turn green and faint again. How this species survives, I have no idea.

When the next such tin-can dolt appeared, I decided I'd had enough. I burned it, the prin-cess, and any of their nest sites I could see in my valley. But the neighbourhood was gone; just not what it used to be. Game has departed, and the smouldering remains of those critters fouled the river.

So I made arrangement with the dwarves under the mountain to move my hoard across the range to a secluded valley much higher up. It cost me a seventh of my hoard, and I'm sure the little buggers pilfered even more — my mattress is decidedly shallower, more gold and gems went missing than the agreed payment.

But at last I shall have some peace, cousin. No more of those pesky humans to disturb my reptilian repose, and the elks here are absolutely delish. So please pass my regards to your mother my aunt, and do come by on the next blood moon for a cave-warming party.

With sincere familial regards et cetera et cetera,

X

ANA'S DREAM OF FLYING

BY MARY R. WOLDERING

The entity formed a crystalline orb and shaped it with what might have been a hand.

Human. As man, it whispered to itself as the dark blue star-filled shape with the emerald bracelet at its wrist became clear, took on the appearance of ruddy skin, and solidified.

He watched Ana grab the broken stub of a much-chewed pencil and scribble a shape on the pale purple scrap of paper.

She bit down on the eraser in a nervous gesture and tucked one of the fat braids that had come loose from her head. A figure emerged. It was a tall and red manlike thing with a long turban-like hat tilted back from his brow. She colored his long robe red, but couldn't decide what to do with the feet so she extended it to the bottom of the page.

The entity smiled and nodded, pleased.

"I will call you Mr. Man," she affirmed. "I know you. You watch over me when I am sleeping." Her teeth flashed in a grin as she pushed the crayon over the surface of her artwork.

She can't see me; not in the light of day, the creature smiled.
The veil is too thick in the cursed sunlight.
At night is when she can see me
I will come to her as a dream,
then carry her away to the lands and places where we walked once when we were gods.
I have watched parts of her shattered soul for centuries.
Tonight, sweet little child, when you dream,
I will take you flying,
I will teach you to fly, and then you will remember even more.

In the thinning distance between worlds, the entity heard a crackly sound of something from another room, suddenly joined by the wispy singing of an older female.

"Some glad morning when this life is o'er,
I'll fly away.

To a home on God's celestial shore,
I'll fly away.
When the shadows of this life have flown,
I'll fly away.
Like a bird thrown, driven by the storm,
I'll fly away."

Then the singing stopped and the crackly sound went abruptly silent with a click, followed by: *"Ana...come to supper, dear."*

Voice from another room, it mused, *the smell of cooking is strong. Fire-treated winged creature – chicken.*

For a moment, the entity wished for a human form; one that would love to eat the older female's fried chicken, mashed potatoes, and green beans.

There will be something she calls pie, afterward.

§ § § § §

"Yas, Muh'dear" the little brown skinned girl muttered, perturbed that she'd have to stop her drawing and put her things away. Her high forehead wrinkled as she frowned. She slapped her crayon on the table, then paused and picked it up. In a quick gesture, as if adding something extra, she scribbled red angel wings sticking out of the sides of the creature's robe. Regarding her work, she changed them so that they looked sharp and pointy.

"That's better. No angel-y wings for you. Now you can fly away. Don't let them see you, Mr. Man. It's our secret. Mwah!" She kissed the paper, then folded it, tucked it in her school notebook, and put away her crayon. She didn't see the red pulse that glimmered inside the spiral bound pages.

Little Ana, not quite eleven, ate her supper, watched the "Outer Limits" with Muh'Dear and Daddy, then took her bath. She put on her pink PJ's, brushed her teeth and went to bed, but couldn't sleep.

Big bad devil is out there, but Cass and Jera'boam will protect me, she thought.

They were her daydream friends. They would always laugh and play with her outside. They took turns jumping off the porch, pretending they could fly. When she was five, they wanted her to jump off the roof of the shed, but Daddy caught her just in time.

They don't believe in you. They say you are 'maginary and to stop fooling around. Be a big girl they say, but I always was *a big girl.* She snickered as she snuggled in her covers. *I just shrinkity shrank like my red sweater in the washing machine.*

Ana loved to draw and dance and play. She didn't like school too much.

The nuns are mean, and always talk about sins and devils and how they come and get bad little boys and girls who cause trouble in class.

Trouble. She thought about school and home a little longer. *Well they made me mad. The kids were talking about me, about my hair and how Muh'dear needed to press it better and pin it down hard before she let me out of the house. I threw the paint bottles at fat old Charise and ruined her dress. That was in first grade. I don't like it when people talk about me.*

Then Daddy got mad when I drew a circle with a star in it. I told him it came from Ma-Maw's book that was supposed to be hidden. I found it way at the bottom of her chest. That night, he took her book and burnt it up with the trash.

Daddy worries I will be "high-minded and proud" like his own Muh'dear, Ma-Maw, was until she found the Lord and started going to the church.

High minded? I can get angry, if that's what it is. In the fourth-grade, Sister Clare was screaming at me about paying attention, but Cass and Jera'boam were goofing around her desk. She put her hand on me. I don't remember what came over me, but I got mad and I growled at her.

Everyone in my class thought it was funny until I growled at her again. Then I got sent to the principal, and then I was sent home for a week to think about my sins. When I came back, Sister Clare was gone. She got put in the crazy house for saying one of her students was turning into a lion or a dragon with big long fangs and claws and was commencing to fly around the room.

None of the other kids said they saw me do that when I asked them about it, but they didn't make fun of me again.

Most nights when Ana lay awake thinking about her life, she watched the shadows from the votive lights in her room dance. Then, right before she slept, her friends would come out to play. The old rocking chair in front of the closed-up fireplace would begin to rock. Her little friends would sit on her bed, and talk in a special language "from outer space" they had invented together. Sometimes they would laugh so loud, Muh'dear would call and tell her to stop talking to herself.

Then everyone would have to be quiet, she thought. When the chair rocked, Ana always felt the rage of the day vanish into peace. Tonight, the movement began as usual.

Ma-Maw is here, she smiled. The chair in her bedroom, the bed, most of the little figurines, and even the model of an altar had belonged to her long dead grandmother. Ana knew very little about her, except she "went to Heaven" long ago.

Muh'dear once told her that the "Fly Away" song she heard her sing had been the old woman's favorite song, and that the elder had rocked her to sleep many nights singing it to her.

The sound of her parents talking in the kitchen suddenly roused Ana. Tonight, their voices were louder.

Daddy's upset about something I did again. What is it this time? I've been good in the fifth grade so far. Sister Patrick is nice. She says my drawings are real talented, and that I will be an artist one day.

"You ain't tell her about my MaMa, did you?"

"No Stan. She's seen the chair, though. You know it still rocks even after we put a block under it so it wouldn't. She takes it out, and she asked about her, but I never have told her much, 'cept she was very old and funny in the head when she passed, and that we should pray for her." Muh'dear quieted the big man.

Ana never liked it when Daddy got quiet after Muh'dear said her piece. It meant he was about to say something angry.

"Unh-huh. Then how'd she come to draw this smiling red devil? And these; look at this one. You know how my Muh'dear looked. Ana was a tiny little baby when she passed. She wouldn't a seen how she looked to draw her like that. And these boys; a little white boy? Where'd she come up with that? Ain't none of them around here unless they's looking for trouble."

Ana tensed, suddenly wide awake. *Daddy found my drawings. But those were in my desk at school. That Sister Patrick double-crossed me.* Her eyes went to the rocking chair and noticed it swaying harder, with attitude.

"Ma-Maw. Shh. Daddy'll hear it if you make it go fast enough to bop the wall." She sat, eyes scanning her bedroom.

The candles' flames on her little altar shot up and began to dance. "This time he might even take your chair out and burn it up like he says he burnt up your book of spells, so I wouldn't get to read them."

Ana heard Daddy continuing to fuss, but his voice had begun to fade.

That Sister Patrick. I thought she was nice, and then she had to go and show my pictures to my Daddy. I bet she told him what I said about them too! I'll get her, I will. Ana remembered Art Class when the rail-thin nun had asked her about the drawings.

"That's my Ma-Maw, and that's Cass and Jera'boam, and on this one is Mr. Man. He looks like a man sometimes, but other times he looks like a dinosaur or a dragon." And then she, feeling quite self- assured, added "Raaah!"

Being mad at someone always woke her up, but tonight, no matter how hard she tried after she had calmed down, she kept thinking about Sister Patrick sneaking cigarettes, and a trash can fire in the convent.

Bad things happen to double-crossers, she thought as she tried to focus on Daddy rambling. She fought the approaching drowsiness.

"We ain't having no VooDoo in this house. We ain't no devil worshippers, and Ma-Maw wasn't either by the time she passed. She got right with God. And that show we looked at on the TeeVee; that 'Outer Limits.' That's too scary for a innocent child to watch."

VooDoo? Who says? She thought about the drawing she made today with the big red bat wings. *Wasn't VooDoo or the devil. Well,* she reconsidered, *he* did *have four horns on his head covered up by his big tall hat, but I haven't seen him really; just in my dreams. I know he can look like a tall man, or also be like a snake with little bitty legs and big old leathery wings.* Then she thought about the show.

No Daddy, I wasn't scared by that show. I know what was on the TeeVee wasn't real.

Little one, get up. Don't worry about what your Daddy's saying. A woman's voice in the dark sounded oddly familiar.

Ana's eyes shot open. She clutched her covers tightly over her chest.

"Ma-Maw?" she whispered so quietly that she thought only her lips were moving and no real sound was coming out.

Yes, child. Just get up very, very quietly and come to the window. Cass can't open it by hisself.

Ana looked at the rocking chair and noticed it had stopped rocking. In the distance, she heard dogs outside begin to howl. Their sound circled around the group of homes again and again. Each time, the noise came closer and the barking got louder.

"Ma-Maw?" she quietly called, more than worried. She sat and stared at a ray of moonlight that meandered over the roof of the house next door to a small spot in front of the window.

Here child. Cass and Jera'boam are with me, but you have to help us open this window.

October in Memphis was just beginning to be crisp enough for windows to be shut by dawn so that the chill wouldn't overtake the house. When Ana went to bed, it was always warm and the windows were left open. Muh'dear would come in later to check on her and to close them.

Muh'dear closed them early tonight because Daddy was fussing about the VooDoo.

"Ma-Maw?" she plaintively whispered into the moonbeam.

Something was standing in the edge of the light. It was a person, and it was dark.

Daddy. She wanted to shout. *Maybe I can get up and go to the bathroom, or get a glass of water. Can't. He'll think the show we saw scared me. He'll just be mad about my 'maginary friends.*

"Damn hounds causing a ruckus out there! What got them started? If we still lived in the country, I'd shoot me one of them, coming for our cans again. Stacie, you put the lids on tight after the chicken bones went in?" She heard Daddy's upset voice again; this time from his bedroom.

A mumbling answer came from Muh'dear, but Ana didn't care anymore. The shadow by the window moved closer. An old woman clad in a long black dress stepped forward. Beside her, as if they were clinging to her generous skirt, was a brown-skinned boy with fat little curls and a white boy with sun-bleached hair. She'd only seen and talked to them in her thoughts and drawn them a few times, but knew at once who they were.

"Ma-Maw! Cass! Jera'boam!" she wanted to cry out at the not quite opaque forms, but slapped both hands over her mouth and buried her head in her own lap. "I'm dreaming or crazy. You ain't real. Daddy says so."

Oh, that Stanley! My goodness, what a doubter he grew up to be. Thought him going to the war would have showed him some things about the spirits in some of the old cities. I've a mind to... she started, but paused, turning to the window and gently scolding. *Child. Come help Cass with this window.*

Ana raised her eyes and blinked. The dark dressed figure of an old woman moved toward the sash, more solid in appearance. She towed the boy Cass and his friend Jera'boam with her. The boys' expressions appeared ever so slightly scared, but excited.

You sure? She sent a thought. *Is Ma-Maw making you do this?*

Child. The old woman's voice grew stern. *I told you to help them with this window.*

Ana paused as she threw back the light coverlet and sat on the edge of her saggy little bed. Her feet grazed the floor and searched for her slippers. *If they are ghosts or spirits, why can't they go through the wall like they do in books and on the TeeVee. Why do I have to open the window?*

So you can get out easier, and without Stanley, er, your Daddy knowing. He wouldn't understand, the elder woman answered in her thoughts.

"Out? Out this window? At night?" Ana whispered in the air as if she was talking to a fully real old woman and not a spirit or a dream. "Oh, I *know* Daddy would kill me!"

Ana...Ana, the boys called out in sing-song, high pitched giggles that echoed in the near midnight updraft of autumn air. Cass touched her arm so suddenly that it felt like a poke.

She jumped at the chill.

Tiptoeing forth ever so quietly, she unlocked the thumb latch on the top of the window sash so that it didn't make a sound.

The dogs had grown nearly silent, but still yapped occasionally in the distance. Down the street someone had put a platter on: "Tossin' and Turnin'."

Ana grinned, because her nights were like that most of the time. *"I didn't sleep at* all *last night..."* she affirmed and wondered how school would be tomorrow now that she knew about Sister Patrick talking to Daddy.

Even farther down on the main road, horns honked, and beyond that, she heard the scream of an ambulance or a fire truck siren and wondered for an instant about the trash can fire.

Crossing herself to make that thought go away, she turned to the three figures behind her who had coaxed her to the sill.

"It's open. Now we can all get out," she whispered, but the images had become like smoke. The young girl's shoulders sagged in disappointment. She thought she had finally woken and had caught herself sleepwalking. For a few moments, she stood taking in the fresher air of night and the city sounds.

1961. Memphis. The colored part of town, with modest porched bungalows and shotgun single-family homes near the river's ridge. Another song entered her thoughts.

"Long distance information, give me Memphis, Tennessee," Chuck Berry sang in her memory from the static-filled old radio on the kitchen table.

"Help me, information, get in touch with Ana Marie
She's the only one who'd phone me here from Memphis, Tennessee
Her home is on the south side, high up on a ridge
Just a half a mile from the Mississippi bridge."

Ana Marie? *Wait a minute.* Ana reviewed the parade of words to the tune that everyone knew. Kids always sang it in the schoolyard. *It's supposed to be 'my' Marie, not 'Ana' Marie.*

> *"Help me, information, more than that I cannot add*
> *Only that I miss her and all the fun we had..."*

But it wasn't Chuck Berry. And her name wasn't Ana Marie. It was just Ana Lena Thomas. The voice moved farther from her window. At that moment, she realized she wasn't listening to a neighbor's record. It was a man's voice, but it was deeper and grindy; almost growling. It sounded as if it spoke from the sky.

Ana stuck her head out of the open window, looking first up, then right and left for the source of the song, but she couldn't see anything.

Come out. Sit on the sill, my little one. Sit and remember how it used to be, the voice that had sung now spoke to her.

Ana frowned, then cast her eyes toward the dancing candle flames on her mantelpiece altar. What she saw, instead, shouldn't have been there.

It was tall, nearly as tall as the room so that its elegant headdress grazed the ceiling. It was red, and now it took a step. Ana backed up to the sill and began to climb out, biting her lip and glancing out at the overturned and broken flowerpots below.

Must be still dreaming. I won't scream. If it's only a dream, Daddy will be so mad. Her thoughts rushed, but whatever it was in her doorway seemed to understand everything she was thinking. Worse than that, it didn't care.

Go away. You ain't real. You're just a drawing. You're just Mr. Man that I put wings on today so you could fly away. She gripped her arms and wondered if she would be able to get out of the window and onto the ground in her side yard without scratching herself up or making a commotion that *would* get Daddy to run out, get her, and "tan her hide."

If I get out, where am I gonna go? Ain't nobody will believe me anyway. The Po-lice will just get me and call my Daddy.

The tall figure took another glide forward, his long-nailed, but strong-looking hands extending to her. They almost touched her, but she shrank back just in time.

Don't fall out, he told her, *just sit there until your eyes see into the past. Ana Lena. So many wonderful memories wait for you.*

"You..." Ana started to ask about him knowing her name, but stifled her words.

"You can speak words with your mouth if it's easier for you." His left hand swirled in the direction of her parents' bedroom. "They won't be able to hear you."

She saw him staring at his hand as if he was thinking, and noticed it had only three clawed and birdlike red fingers, not four fingers and a thumb, as men are supposed to have. He shrugged and touched her with that bird hand.

"Aahhh!" Ana screamed because the man's grip was strong and firm and she noticed his hand had scales. The nails weren't just long, they were talons. "Daddy's right! You *are* the devil!" she shrieked and struggled, knowing her parents certainly should have heard her.

"Old trick," he affirmed, still gripping her in two sets of claws.

His face does too *look like the one on the potted meat can.* Ana noticed he grinned like he had in her drawing.

"Making the silence around us. Do you remember when we used to do that, sweet child? And this 'devil'?" He sighed as if dismayed. "I wish they..." He stopped, looked at the little altar, and plucked one of the two plastic crucifixes from its holder. He regarded the little Jesus figure stretched out on it and twirled it absent-mindedly between two of his fingers before replacing it.

Must not be the devil then, Ana thought. *The sisters told us the devil can't touch blessed things, and Father Wall came to the house after I got in trouble, so he could bless it and get rid of Ma-Maw's spirit and anything else bad that was staying here. It didn't work. They just stopped coming around Daddy. Everyone still talks to me, though.*

"Because you are special to us, and very special to me," the red figure continued her earlier thought. He looked more like an ordinary man now, a little redder version of her own brown color. His hands were normal again. His long red robes looked like a fuller version of a priest's frock, with sleeves that looked like flames.

"Come sit with me in your window for a while." He led Ana back to the sill and sat beside her, his hard, strong arm around her back so she wouldn't slip.

"Special?" Ana looked into his face, searching his blackest eyes but noticed there were no whites around the color part. It made her want to look away. She tried, but, "I don't know you, and I shouldn't be talking to you, even if you made a spell so Muh'dear and Daddy can't hear us. I know about spells from Ma-Maw's book before Daddy burnt it up." She stared at her own hands, and at his changeable hand that wrapped around her arm.

"You called me, through your magic wish drawings. It was your *own* spell," he whispered. His voice invaded her soul and made her feel so warm inside as if he too, was her Daddy. "Your heart has been asking for me to come for a long time."

"My drawings?" Her mouth stayed open in surprise. "Well... Sister Patrick and Daddy say I made you up 'cos I'm lonely. Ma-Maw is real, though. She was my grandmother and she was a VooDoo witch, too, Daddy says."

Mr. Man chuckled, but shook his head as if none of that was exactly the truth.

Ana knew he was getting impatient, but didn't know *how* she knew.

"I've made drawings of lots of things before. *They* didn't come alive. Daddy knows I like to draw, and he brings me paper from his bosses' office that they are throwing away." She shook her head. "Cass and Jera'boam were these kids I played with when I was tiny. They say I made them up too."

"There is so much you don't understand, young Ana. Your Cass and Jera'boam are guardians given to you, old friends of yours, making themselves appear as boys. They have been here all your life. But it was *your* waking memory and *your* magic that gave me life to make it more than the image on the paper." He nodded paternally, then went on. "Your wise Ma-Maw knew about your soul when you were born. She knew you had a gift. She didn't want us to lose you the way we lost her boy; your Daddy."

Ana reflected on everything Mr. Man said, and it made her wonder even more about her Daddy. She knew he had worked on a farm in Mississippi, but he never spoke of it. He went off to the Army when it was time to fight the Nazis, then came home and married Muh'dear. He bought the house in the city and took a job that made enough to support her and Ma-Maw, who was sick by then.

"Lost? Called You?" Ana asked, but the words of the song drifted through her thoughts this time, instead of coming from Mr. Man or the neighbor's record player. "How?"

"Help me, information, get in touch with Ana Marie
She's the only one who'd phone me here from Memphis, Tennessee
Her home is on the south side, high up on a ridge
Just a half a mile from the Mississippi bridge"

"I could show you, instead." The red creature had changed into something not quite human.

Ana didn't want to look at him. He was red and scaly.

"But you have to be ready to believe everything you see. Your Daddy, even though your Ma-Maw wanted him to learn, couldn't. And when he went to fight the war, the things he saw made him lose hope for anything beyond the skin he wore. We could not reach him after that."

"Can you fly?" Ana suddenly asked. She hadn't understood everything Mr. Man said, and her thoughts had moved on. "I drew wings on you so you could fly."

She had no idea what had inspired that question until she saw Cass peeking from behind her dresser with a big grin, as if he had put the thought in her head.

Cass. She sent a thought, but knew Mr. Man was waiting impatiently for an answer. *You made me ask that.* Ana shivered, because this had to be a dream. *In real life,* she thought, *I'd never be talking to a strange man in my bedroom in the middle of the night. It'd never be someone whose hands keep changing into red scaly claws and who wears a funny red hat and robe with fire sleeves.*

"Show me you can fly." she ordered, aware that the wings she had drawn on him were nowhere to be seen. *I'll do drawings of* that, and hide them in the trunk. At school from now on, it's going to be hearts and flowers for Sister Patrick.

"Then you'll have to trust me," Mr. Man quipped before he held onto her and fell backward with her out of the window.

"Whoa!" she cried, waiting for the inevitable pain of crunching and bouncing only two feet into a bunch of noisy flower pots from a first-floor window. But the falling didn't stop. Mr. Man had a mighty grip on her as they fell farther and farther down, as if the ground beneath them both had vanished.

Wind rushed past them with such a force that her pajama top had begun to shimmy up her chest and was about to show him the places her Muh'dear said no man except her husband should ever see. All her fear and doubt came back in a flash.

Dragging me to Hell. It is the devil!

"Help! Stop! I'll be good! Daddy, save me!" she squalled as loud as she could.

They fell until she realized they weren't falling at all. Mr. Man wasn't a man anymore. He looked like a picture of a giant red dragon from a fairy tale book, only much bigger. His great and powerful wings were just like the bat wings she had drawn on him that afternoon. His robe had become magnificent, flame-colored golden and red scales, and his hat a spiked and bony head with four horns. His voice made the triumphant call like that of a great hawk on a TeeVee nature show.

"Help! Put me down! Where are you taking me? I wanna go home!" Ana cried, her tears blasted away by the speed of the wind in her face.

The deep and comforting voice spoke in her thoughts again as the mighty creature gripped her against its chest so she could see the city where she lived slipping fast away.

Ana Lena. It is still me. I am your forever friend. Don't be afraid, or close your eyes to what you know is truth. Climb up on my back and fly with me for a little while, and then I will go. In time, I will show you even more things. His mighty head glanced down at her in his grasp.

Chuck Berry's song echoed, this time with static-filled sound as they shot past the twinkle-topped radio tower:

"Help me, information, more than that I cannot add

Only that I miss her and all the fun we had…"

He paused, and circled in what now looked like purple sky and mountains. The city was gone.

"I really *didn't* imagine you then, did I?" Ana felt her voice growing small and afraid.

"No. I was always here, waiting for the day you would wake. Perhaps…" he started to say something, then as if it had been an afterthought, shook her free from his back before she could grab his horns.

Somewhere in the recesses of her mind, she remembered something about falling in a dream and dying if you hit bottom before you woke.

"You dropped me! I'm falling!" she screamed again.

His voice in her heart whispered the same old gospel song she'd heard on the radio one Sunday morning, the one Muh'dear said Ma-Maw liked to sing to her:

I'll Fly away…
I'll fly away, O Glory,
I'll fly away.

Like someone drowning, Ana flailed her arms and began to move up into a distant round light in the sky. She was older, not shrinkity-shrank, and clad in a black, billowing garment. The skirt of it grew and transformed into smoky trails that she knew might serve as her own wings if she could only get control of them.

Try. The great red creature circled above her, waiting. *Your heart remembers when we flew together. When we ruled, and formed the world of men. Try Ana Lena. Please, try…*

"Fly away…I can fly away" she cried out and half sang. Her skirt flapped and took the form of wings, lifting her for only an instant before she thought, *this is crazy,* and began to fall again.

The great and burning red dragon swooped beneath her and let her settle on his back. They flew in brilliant light growing large enough to circle the sun, but they were never burned by the heat or light. Their shadow cast upon the Earth inspired terror in all who lived below. They flew backward—or was it forward?—through time itself. She closed her eyes and buried her face in the hard ridges of the red dragon's neck.

"Will I turn into a dragon, just like you?" she sniveled, feeling a little ill. *This dream is too long. I want to wake up. I want to fly away. I'm gonna burn those drawings.*

She felt as if her heart might break, because drawing had been one of the few solaces in her life. If it made her dreams real; if these things she saw and did *were* real, but forgotten, it just didn't fit in with being a little colored girl who often got in trouble at school in 1961 Memphis, Tennessee.

I'll Fly Away

"No, you won't burn them, Ana Lena, and you *won't* fly away. Nor was I *just* a dragon. We were god and goddess toying with men, teaching some, creating others. Men of Earth saw us as such; great ones, like gods when they walked as men. A thousand, thousand years ago, I found you and loved you, but we were pulled apart. I looked for you everywhere in space and time, and then I heard your call."

"Long distance information…give me Memphis, Tennessee"

And suddenly they were sitting on her window sill. Ma-Maw was sitting in her rocker, contentedly rocking and making a veil of black lace. Cass and Jera'boam were teasing and smacking each other.

Mr. Man hugged her and kissed her brow, then her eyes. She was falling again; floating and resting but not screaming any more. She turned and began to fly, high above the rooftops. She knew the "dream," if she could even call it that, was ending. It made her sad, because of his words drilling through her thoughts.

"Only that I miss her and all the fun we had."

Her bedroom was empty and still. *Knew it was a dream,* she grumbled, relieved but still disappointed.

No, it wasn't, Ana Lena. I am still here as are all the others. She heard his voice sounding gently in the back of her thoughts. *We will still be here waiting for you to draw us from time to time. Meet kindred souls as you grow, and tell them these stories. They will have stories to tell just like you do. One of them may even write about it one day.*

"But, I don't even know your real name..." Ana sniveled.

"Oh, that. I have thousands. For now, Mr. Man will do." The creature appeared briefly in her doorway, elegant headdress poised on his head and hands up in a magical gesture. "Another time, perhaps, when we meet again." but he had faded. In her corner chair, Ma-Maw quietly sang:

"When the shadows of this life have flown,
I'll fly away.
Like a bird thrown, driven by the storm,
I'll fly away."

Epilogue

Ana Lena Thomas (not her real name) never had such a powerful dream again, although she had many and always remembered enough about flying and seeing to teach it to those who were ready to learn.

Sister Patrick was right. When Ana grew up, she became a talented artist with the power to evoke magic in her art and to seek others in her "family." She told her stories just as Mr. Man suggested. From time to time, she sang old church songs like "Amazing Grace." At night, I think she still sings "I'll Fly Away."

"To a land where joy shall never end,
I'll fly away."

THE OFFERING

BY JONATHAN ROYAN

Sir Helix sat atop his shuffling mare, in front of the gaping maw of the dragon's cave. The horse whinnied, pulling at its reins. Sir Helix however was made of sterner stuff. He barely shook under his gleaming armour. He could feel the sweat beading on his brow and trickled down his back. This was merely from the heat of this winter's morn; not from any nervous disposition. His churning stomach however, did give him some cause for concern.

"Come on now, Helix," he chided, "fear is just something to overcome. Just another hurdle before greatness."

His words sounded weak, even to himself. Not unlike the first time he'd spoken to his lady love, Rebecca, all those years ago. She had laughed into her handkerchief at the time, causing Helix to turn scarlet, under the dappled shade of the arboretum. It was a pleasant sound he remembered; a tinkling laughter that warmed the soul, as well as his face. The sun shone pale green light through the leaves, accentuating her faultless complexion. He had fallen for her right there and then. It was because of her that Sir Helix found himself in his current position. Rebecca had the terrible misfortune of being chosen for the offering for this Winter Tide. A hideous tradition of sacrifice to the monster that once terrorised the land. A deal had been struck to bring peace to the kingdom years before. The offering.

Sir Helix had learnt of Rebecca's fate from Sir Gerald of Cline, also a Knight of the Realm. Unlike Helix he was a noble, and a weasel of a man in Sir Helix's opinion. Gerald had had a brief desire for Helix's true love, Lady Rebecca. Helix had seen off this love rival without too much trouble. He had stood over Sir Gerald on the jousting field, after unhorsing him at the first attempt. Helix could have killed the man easily enough, but had chosen to aim for the chest rather than the head. Ever the compassionate man. Helix had been knighted by the king during the War of the Thistle. His skill on the battlefield had awarded him praise from his commander, however it was his compassion for the wounded and his attempts to help the injured that earned him his knighthood.

After the joust, Sir Gerald had reluctantly ceased his advances on Rebecca. Although he claimed to have no further interest in Rebecca, Sir Gerald would turn bashful in her presence and excuse himself at the first opportunity whenever their paths crossed. It had amused Helix, much to Rebecca's displeasure.

"It is not becoming of a Knight to gloat," she had said. And of course she was right.

Sir Helix had learnt of Rebecca's fate in the great hall, while at yet another tiresome castle function. Sir Gerald's man servant had bustled past Helix in search of his master, who at the time sipped from a goblet while having his ear chewed off by an irate Lord. Helix had become bored listening in on the conversation long ago, but his attention was drawn back by the look of concern on the man servant's face as he sidestepped, shuffled and dodged his way past the other guests towards his master. Helix watched as Sir Gerald's face visibly slackened after hearing his servant's words. Gerald's eyes flicked towards Helix as his servant spoke. The look alone would have been enough to concern Helix but he had also heard what the servant had conveyed to Gerald. Ice coursed through Helix's veins at the words.

Rebecca had been chosen as this year's offering by random selection. Helix was horrified by her bad luck. No noble's daughter had ever been selected before. It had, fortuitously, always fallen to the peasants of the realm to fulfil the obligations of the agreement. It took all of three great hammering heartbeats for Sir Helix to decide what was to be done; the dragon needed to be slain, and he would have to be the one to do it. He wasn't going to allow such a fate to befall his Rebecca, not while he had breath in his body. He left the hall immediately, speaking to no one in his great haste

Now at the dragons cave, Sir Helix dismounted. He slapped the horse's hind quarters. His mount needed little encouragement to leave, breaking into a gallop, back in the direction of the castle. He instantly regretted releasing his horse. He would need it when he came back out, victorious. The doubts started building in his mind in earnest now. He swallowed the large lump in his throat and walked towards the cave.

Darkness seeped out of the cave's opening like spilt ink on parchment. The vile stench of carrion filled his nose. His feet crunched on gravel, as he made unsteady progress into the darkness. Once inside, the echoes of his foot falls joined the sound of dripping moisture from the unseen roof of the cave. The light behind him faded away with every step forward into the mountain. He lifted his visor; it did nothing to improve his vision. Reaching into a pouch, Helix produced an alchemical vial. He shook the vile vigorously. Green light slowly radiated from his hand, revealing a huge cavern, littered with bones and skulls of a multitude of beasts. Skin and fur still clung from the piled bones, accounting for the almighty reek of rotting flesh.

Helix shone his light along the cavern walls, looking for any sign of a way further into the mountain. After some searching, the emerald glow of the vial revealed an opening in one wall. It was large.

Large enough for a huge lizard to fit through, Sir Helix mused.

This had to be the way to the dragon's den. Sir Helix pushed himself on, before his better judgment kicked in. But who then would save his lady love? Helix pressed on.

The vial's glow illuminated the walls of the passage, warn smooth by the passing of time and scales. As he crept along the passage, the air became noticeably fresher. He could still smell the rotten remains of the cavern behind, but the air was getting cleaner. Up ahead he saw flickering red and yellow flames, dancing against the passage wall. This must be it, he thought. He drew his sword. It whispered from its sheath, glinting green from the vial's glow.

Sir Helix came to what appeared to be the end of the passage. He peered in from the opening. This cavern was as far away in appearance from the last one as he could have imagined. It was bright, almost dazzling. Flaming pools dotted randomly in the smooth stone floor. Stalactites hung low from a high ceiling, many joining the floor creating thick pillars of rock. These were impressive in size, however it wasn't the rock formations that drew Sir Helix's gaze right now, rather the huge, scaled tail that snaked its way around the base of a number of the pillars. His eyes traced the tail to its source. Sir Helix's eyes widened.

He had seen the dragon only once before, when he was just a boy. While walking with his father one evening he had seen the flying lizard pass across the night's sky and through the pale circle of the moon. The young Helix had thought the dragon to be a manageable size. His father laughed after Helix said he thought he could catch the beast in the palm of one hand.

He later learned more about dragons, and though he came to understand their vastness, nothing could have prepared him for his first sight of a dragon up close. He stared, jaw dropping at the sight before him. The dragon's scaled mass lay a hundred yards away, filling an entire corner of the cavern. Reds, yellows and greens made up the mottled colour of the huge lizard. The fire danced and shimmered along the dragon's flanks. Wings of leathery skin were folded up tight on its back. A slender neck lead to the multi horned head that laid on the ground, A forked tongue escaped the collection of razor sharp teeth to lay curled over the snout of the great beast, the nostrils of which flapped open and shut with the dragon's slow breathing.

The constricting grip of fear halted his breathing. Helix realised he'd made a huge mistake. He needed to leave, now! Helix took one slow, one very careful step back into the passage way. Another plan formed in his mind.

I'll take Rebecca away, yes, that's it. I'll take her far away. Why didn't I think of this before? Helix thought, instantly feeling idiotic. He shook his head at his foolishness.

"Going so soon?" came a voice from the cavern. "Can we not at least speak before you crawl back down the latrine?" The voice sounded ancient, commanding, and terrifying all at the same time. "I know you are there. I can hear better than you would imagine, being that you made such a racket on your way here. You woke me actually."

Sir Helix froze. Surprise had been his first plan. It had been a terrible plan he now realised. Helix felt a word bubbling up inside him.

"Sorry," Helix found himself saying.

Something in the dragon's voice had compelled him to speak. The word came out unbidden. Helix's emotions roiled inside him. Helix felt, panic, fear, but also compassion, embarrassment and love all at the same time. His emotions were all vying for control of him. None fully succeeding. What was happening to him? Was this some sort of magic? He'd heard of dragon magic, but didn't know its nature.

"Sorry," the voiced mocked in return, "Sorry indeed."

The dragon's voice had a smooth quality to it now.

"You can talk?" Helix said dumbly, taking in the massive pile of scales that was the dragon.

The beast laughed, his huge mass shaking with the sound, causing scales to click with the movement.

"I'm over a thousand years old. You pick up a few things after a while," the dragon said, eyes now open, dark red and catlike. They fixed on Helix, holding him in place as surely as iron manacles. "Now tell me, human, what brings you out of the depth of my lavatory to stand here, before me?"

All Sir Helix wanted was to bolt down the passage, but something stronger than his, now dominant fear, held him in place. His waring emotions fought for supremacy within him. The fear subsided, allowing his thoughts to coalesce, he remembered Rebecca.

"Love," he said.

The dragon laughed again, this time a great booming laugh that reverberated around the walls, loosening dust and stones from above.

"I'm flattered, I really am, but I need not any love from the cattle," the dragon declared.

"NO!" Sir Helix barked, more forcefully than he'd intended. "No," he repeated in a more respectful tone. "I'm here to protect my lady love, my Rebecca." Helix couldn't believe what he was saying. Why could he not master his own words? *Am I really going to tell this dragon I am here to kill it?* "I'm here to slay you." *Dear god. I am!*

"Slay me? I'm offended," the dragon replied, sounding neither surprised nor offended.

"Sorry," Sir Helix found himself replying again.

What was happening to him? Words were coming out unbidden. This dragon was playing with him, governing his emotions, forcing words from his lips. Like a puppet on a string, he had full control over Helix now. *Definitely magic! it has to b*e.

"Tell me of this *love* of which you speak. And how has it brought you to your demise," the dragon said.

The knight was choosing the words on how to explain his love for Rebecca. The dragon watched as Sir Helix mulled the words in his mind. His passion for Rebecca flooded his mind. He opened his mouth to speak.

"Sh..."

"Don't tell me," the dragon interjected, "She's the most beautiful human you have ever seen, and so on," it added with bored sarcasm.

Sir Helix snapped his mouth shut and just nodded in reply.

"I see. Why do *I* need to die, for this *love* of yours," the dragon demanded.

"The offering, it's her," he said, plainly.

"I see," said the dragon. "So killing me is the solution, is it?"

The knight nodded, unable to stop himself. He felt hot tears running down his face now, the last vestal of control he had maintained.

"Well you are in luck then," the dragon said cheerily. "You can take your lady love's place as the offering, how does that sound?" The dragon did not wait for a reply. "I can smell you are not of noble birth, am I right?"

Sir Helix nodded again.

"Good, good. I can't digest anything noble, far too rich for my stomach you see. I demand offerings from the peasant quarter only. They have such a lovely, gamey taste, and they don't cause me any trouble on their way out, if you pardon my crudeness."

Sir Helix tried to speak but was unable, his throat closed up. A cold chill ran down his spine, and was now spreading to numb his limbs.

The dragon spoke again, but this time the voice was more commanding, more compelling, and more coercive than before.

"If you wouldn't mind dropping your sword, and remove the armour," asked the dragon. "Metal plays havoc with my teeth you see."

Sir Helix let the sword slip from his fingers, it clattered to the ground. Next his helmet dropped with a clank. He proceeded to saunter towards the dragon, tears streaming down his cheeks, dropping to the floor, along with plate after plate of his armour. His heart was a riot in his chest, as he looked into the open mouth of the dragon, with its razor sharp, glistening wet teeth. Sir Helix was powerless to stop his march into the jaws of death. Sir Helix of Rammenshire, the only common blooded knight of the realm, stepped into the dragon's mouth.

***

Up in the noble quarter the streets were packed with human traffic, all attempting to make their way to the castle gates, for the announcement of this year's offering. Sir Gerald struggled against the flow, not interested in the ghoulish intrigue of the masses. He had someone important to see.

Sir Gerald knocked on the door. After a wait, it opened. Lady Rebecca stood, framed in the doorway, a vision of beauty. Well she would have been if not for the puffy eyes and red nose. It was safe to say she'd received the bad news.

"Sir Gerald," Rebecca sniffed. "What are you doing here?"

"My dear lady Rebecca, I heard the news. I'm here to offer my deepest sympathies," Sir Gerald said, bending at the waist in a half bow.

This brought on a fresh bout of weeping. He allowed them to subside before speaking again.

"When Sir Helix came to me and told me of his plans to slay the dragon, I tried in vain to stop him. But you are aware of what he is like... was like. Honour before anything else. He said to me that he could no longer stand by while innocents were being offered as sacrifice to the evil resident of the Craggy Mountains. When his horse returned rider-less I assumed the worst."

Lady Rebecca used a sodden handkerchief to wipe the tears away. More quickly took their place.

"Before he left he had the presence of mind to see to your care while he was away. Now Sir Helix and I have not seen eye to eye on some things in the past, but he knew when he asked me to look out for you, that I would take the best of care of you in his absence. I know he expected to return, but..." he frowned, and bowed his head.

Lady Rebecca nodded, "I understand. That was just like Helix," she added with a wry smile.

"Then it is settled, I will return tomorrow. We can arrange everything then," Gerald said. "But for now I must return to the castle for the offering ceremony, I believe it's a farmer's daughter again this year."

Sir Gerald turned on his heels and made his way towards the castle. His smile started at the corner of the street, but by the time he had rounded it, his smile stretched from ear to ear.

The End

GOLD IS EVERYTHING
BY RICK HAYNES

I know I'm big, big headed as well as big boned, but I never walk away from a fight as walking forwards is more honourable than the other way around. I'm proud to carry the name of my forebears and no one will find any scars on the back of Olav, son of Olav Avang.

Like any man I have desires, but one can consume me, eating away inside my head. If I see a flash of yellow, I want it. Grabbing a young girl and forcing her to the ground satisfies my lust for sex, but I'll go sword to sword with anyone if gold is offered. I'm sure others want the precious metal, but I doubt they have my cravings. Simply seeing a golden sun turns my head, my heart races away with desire. What if I could reach out and pull it from the sky? Would I be sated, or would my longing finally destroy me?

With age comes experience and if you don't learn, you perish. I could walk away from many things but when gold is mentioned, my longing overrides all logic, and my mind is consumed with greed.

Sitting here with my back against the wall, I stare at the large golden rings on the wrist of my left hand and ponder.

If only I had listened to my father, but the arrogance of youth took hold of me, refusing to compromise. And now, Olav Avang, was dead, my mother and family slain. I remember the vacuous stare of my beautiful sister, Rigmar, her naked body lying in the dirt covered in blood, the flies swarming.

If I had ordered my men to stay with my kin, then King Erik would be the one in Valhalla and my clan would be dividing the gold. But I didn't want to share the King's gold with anyone, especially my father.

So how could I later refuse the offer of fifty gold pieces for the first man to cast down the standard of King Erik Bloodaxe? His army numbered less than two hundred men, whilst those following Harald held over a hundred more swords. The slaughter should be swift, victory assured, yet I knew that numbers mattered little when the blades clashed. Mercenaries were fickle fighters and easily turned when their own blood began to flow.

Apart from my small band of chosen men, I wouldn't have faith in a one legged man tending my horse, let alone a rag tag bunch of paid soldiers with my life. Trusting them in battle would be akin to believing that a viper wouldn't bite your arse as you sat on it. Yet, Harald owed me a debt and was sworn to me. And I had called on him to honour his word.

Fate is a fickle mistress and soon she will decide my future, but for now I wandered back in time and remembered my sword shield, Sigismund.

He had fought well, too well, for my missing finger had pained me for weeks. After the fight I had spots of blood, both his and mine, all over my face, and smears of crimson on my leather jerkin and trews. I knew we were both drunk that night, but a bet over a single piece of gold had to be collected, even from a good friend. The tree of the eagle, as he was known, would never see the sun rise again. I missed him then, even more so now.

I stretched out, easing my position on the ground, and thought of a different life, a life away from constant battles and death.

At my age, I should be taking a young maiden as wife and retire to a farm in the valleys. I had given it much thought. I was richer than anyone I knew, so why should I be so stubborn? No one lives by the sword forever. I want to sire many sons, even a daughter or two, and with my wealth all would defer to me as I pass.

Alas my eyes saw only the colour of yellow for the lure of gold was stronger than any other desire, and even now I craved for more and more of the drug.

My thoughts brought me back to the present. I would never be satisfied until I could hold the severed head of King Erik in my hands. My revenge would be complete and perhaps then, I could journey north, to find that special place to live until the gods welcome me to Valhalla.

I once more thought over the actions of this morning. The strong wind had fallen to a stiff breeze, the clouds racing across the sky. Grey with menace and with the sun unable to show its face, the air was cold. Hands would need to grip swords tightly. Yet all in all, it was a good day to kill.

I had to give Harald his due, he led the charge and I followed. As we struck soon after their midday meal, many of Erik's men were asleep. They died where they lay.

The ring of iron on iron echoed off the rock walls as individual battles broke out, but I ignored them all.

Snarling like a wild dog I ran forward towards the banner of King Erik, my seven trusty warriors alongside me. With our long dirty hair flowing behind us and our stinking clothes covered in dirt and shit, we looked more like savages than trained swordsmen. We cared little for only the gold mattered, and the split was always the same. I took half, and they shared the rest.

I couldn't see Erik, but his sword shields surrounded his huge standard. With a golden eagle woven into a dark blue background it stood out like a beacon and we couldn't miss it.

I swung my broadsword against a helm and missed. Stumbling forward I ducked under a thrust and hammered the boss of my shield into the man's groin. To move was to live, so I stamped on his face and rushed on quickly.

My ears had learnt to ignore the grunts of those fighting, and those already down. Instead they concentrated on the sounds of those closest, the ones trying to kill me.

No matter what, that banner was mine. I could already feel my fingers running smoothly over the gold pieces. I surged onwards knowing it was the only incentive I would ever need.

A soldier swung, I blocked and managed a vicious riposte which made him fall. I slashed my sword across the throat of another. The banner was ahead, calling me to take it down and kill the king. I had less than twenty paces to go and none stood before me now. Looking around I saw my men fighting but they were being edged farther away from me. Reassuringly, I could see Harald behind, rushing to join me. He wanted to share in the glory but it would all be mine.

With only ten paces to go it was now or never.

A shadow fell across my path and King Erik stepped from behind a rock, a mighty sword in his hand. I knew this was my defining moment, win the battle - take the prize.

Grinning, I rubbed my tongue over the gaps where my teeth should be. I really hated people that looked so clean. I wanted this peacock to realise who he faced and to know the name of the man who killed him.

I remember saying, "I am Olav, son of Olav Avang, and you will die."

But then the sky went black.

When I awoke, I found myself unclothed, resting against this wall. It took a little time for the haze in my mind to clear away and longer before my eyes could make out the glint of swords inches away from my chest. Surprisingly, I was unbound, and without thinking tried to stand. The sharp stab in my thigh prevented any further movement, but I did manage to wipe a little sticky blood from my eyes.

To my right I could just make out the bodies of my men tied to wooden stakes. Their hands had been cut off leaving them to bleed to death. King Erik had condemned them to eternal misery, for without swords in their hands, my men would never drink ale with their friends in the great halls of Valhalla.

I could hear laughter behind me and the taunts of the victorious warriors. I blinked rapidly, and for the first time in my life my body trembled as I shrank back against the wall. I screamed for my sword.

A shadow moved slowly towards me. I espied the form of King Erik, but another, lay hidden.

The tears fell as I cried out in anguish. I begged for my sword to be placed in my hand but only laughter greeted my plea.

A familiar face loomed over me.

As the sword fell I knew that I should never have trusted anyone ... especially Harald.

FREE WILL

FROM <u>THE BLACK KNIGHTS OF CROM CRUACH</u> *BY NAV LOGAN*

Chapter One: Free Will

Maerlin stood with her toes curled around the very edge of the cliff, her hair flowing freely around her. She looked down at the jagged rocks far below. This was a fitting place to defy the gods. It was here that her mother had died. Maerlin had tried to warn her, but to no avail. Like everything Maerlin tried, it went awry. People got hurt. People died.

On her way here, Maerlin had flown over Manquay and seen the remains of the funeral pyres after the recent battle. She wondered if Uiscallan was amongst the burning bodies, and tears rolled down her cheek. Her great-grandmother deserved better than a mass pyre. Dragania owed her that much, at least. After all, Uiscallan had lost everything in her service to the goddess Deanna and in the service of the Dragon Clan, and yet still they had demanded more. Eventually, they had demanded her very life-blood.

Then, there was the other matter: Duncan Gambit. He was missing and Maerlin had promised to find him. He could be anywhere. He could be lying dead under a bush somewhere on the mountain, or he could have been eaten by wolves. No one had seen him. She had promised Auntie Millie that she would find him, but like so many promises she made, she had failed.

Maerlin wiped away the tears that refused to stop flowing and roared her frustration into the sky. The dark clouds echoed her anger with a rumble of thunder and a howl of wind. With a bitter twist of a smile, Maerlin realised that she was not in fact alone. She would never be alone. Wherever she went, her Elementals were always at hand. She hadn't even noticed the storm brewing overhead; she had been too engrossed in her own dark thoughts, but the Elementals, as always, reacted to her inner turmoil.

Shaking away those thoughts, Maerlin braced herself for action. She had come here for a reason. Maerlin was fed up with being a puppet to the gods, and she would no longer play their games. She would not become another Uiscallan, hiding away in a cottage in the middle of nowhere, afraid of her own destiny. Maerlin would make her own destiny. Having seen the slaves on the Dragonship, she refused to become one of them: to man or god.

She had for some time suspected the manipulation of the Seven Greater Gods in the world around her. They had been subtle, but the more she thought about it, the more she realised that things were not as they seemed. It was all a little bit too convenient. Slowly, one by one, the gods had become embroiled in her life. Some were more obvious about it than others.

Deanna and Macha for example. Macha's trick to steal Nessa to her side was a stroke of genius, and Maerlin still didn't fully comprehend the motive behind that. She had always believed Macha to be on the side of darkness. After all, hadn't Macha been worshipped by Dubhgall the Black? Macha was guilty of helping Dubhgall to survive for all those years, and she had actively taken a part in his continued existence after his defeat at the burial mound. Therefore, she was in no small part responsible for the many lives sacrificed on Dubhgall's altars. However, Maerlin had seen a different aspect of Macha's personality during her visitation at the Broll's deathbed. She had sensed an empathy and kindness within the goddess. It seemed that good and evil meant different things to different people, and the gods made up their own rules as they went along.

Then, there was Deanna: the goddess of life. Normally associated with benevolence, Deanna had kept Broll alive despite the pain that it had caused him. Could she also have had a hand in Dubhgall's longevity? Surely, Dubhgall could not have been granted his powers of rejuvenation without Deanna's consent? Was she as implicit in Dubhgall's continued existence, and therefore, his continued evil acts, as her dark sister: Macha? Were her hands also tainted with the blood of innocent children?

The deeper Maerlin looked, the more she saw the hand of the gods in past events; events that spanned centuries. Were the lives of men all one big game to the gods? Did they really care about the people whose lives they toyed with?

She considered the other gods and goddesses of the Seven. Arianrhod, the goddess of the moons and the tides, for example. Immediately, Cora's beautiful face came to mind. Could Cora have been Arianrhod's pawn all this time?
Cernunnos, god of the hunter and the warrior. It wasn't hard to see Vort as his knight. She thought of Lugh, the sun god, and immediately Conal's bright face came to mind; how his smile could light up a room.

She suspected that even Cliodhna, the goddess of love had recently got in on the act.

Maerlin remembered her Dream-catching of the ceremony of the bees on the first night that she had made love to Cora. Maerlin had woken from that dream still wracked in her first orgasm, and she found herself kissing Cora with a hunger that she had never known before. Later, during the festivities after the Gathering of the Clans, she had seen the woman who had sung to the bees in Conal's camp, sitting by the fire. She had directed Maerlin to where Conal and Cora were making love. That left only the All-father: Dagda.

Maerlin remembered Nessa explaining the powers that each of the gods was attributed with.

Dagda was called the god of all things magical and of time.

Maerlin wasn't sure which of her companions the All-father had been using, but she felt sure that he was somehow involved.

Could she be paranoid?

She doubted it. She had sensed the hands of the gods in her life too often, and she would have no more of it. The gods could all go to the Nine Hells.

This was why Maerlin was standing on the edge of that particular cliff.

As she was returning to Manquay, she had slipped into another Dream-catching, and she was confident that this one was not a flight of fancy. It wasn't a portent of the future either. This Dream-catching was of the past; not the distant past, but Maerlin's own recent past. It was when Maerlin's mother had left to head up the mountain. It was when Maerlin had first dreamed of a coming storm. Her mother had died that day. Up until now, Maerlin had always believed that she was responsible for that particular storm. She had certainly taken the blame for it, but after recent revelations, she wasn't so sure. Her Dream-catching had given her a new perspective.

In her dream, she had watched her mother walk the mountains, checking on the cattle and enjoying the pleasant sunny day. That in itself was no surprise. However, what came next was a shock. Riding out of the cloudbank that covered the peak of Sliamh Na Dia, Maerlin saw seven horses. They rode down to where her mother stood waiting. As they came closer, Maerlin recognised at least two of the seven riders. One, riding a grey unicorn, was definitely Deanna. Her sister, Macha, rode alongside her on a feisty jet-black nightmare with bloodshot eyes. She had seen both goddesses before, and she was certain of their identities.

The other five riders she had not seen before, but they were surely the other greater gods. As she looked closer, she noticed that the lady in the aquamarine gown was not riding a normal horse at all. Her mount had no legs and seemed to float above the ground as if in water. It had a horse's head and neck, with an extra-long nose that ended in a snout. Its body ended in a long, curly, almost snake-like tail and it used this to bounce along the ground.

Looking more closely, she could identify the riders by the descriptions she had been taught. The tall handsome man with the flowing mane of golden curls and the beaming smile must surely be Lugh. The older man with the grey hair and beard must be Dagda. The rider on the stocky Pectish chestnut stallion, dressed in furs and armed with a bow and spear, could only be Cernunnos. The beautiful lady on the palomino must be Cliodhna, and the lady on the strange legless horse must therefore be Arianrhod.

They stopped before her mother and started talking. At first, the conversation seemed to be pleasant enough, but soon, it became evident that her mother was not happy. She was gesticulating and shaking her head, and her face was becoming flushed as their conversation became more heated.

The Seven seemed equally unhappy by the way the conversation was going, and finally with a gesture from Deanna, they turned and rode back into the mist. It was then that the clouds darkened and the first rumble of thunder sounded.

Maerlin had been unable to get close enough to hear what had been said, but she was near enough to understand that her mother had clearly refused them.

She watched, unable to help, as the storm grew quickly in intensity. Her mother must have sensed the danger as she had fled down the mountain. Maerlin had been unable to follow and could only stand by and watch helplessly as her mother disappeared into the heavy rain that shrouded the landscape.

Now, Maerlin stood, above the very spot where they had later found her mother's body. Taking a deep breath, Maerlin leaned forward. Forcing herself to relax, she leaned farther and farther out over the ledge until the weight of her body was no longer being held by her legs. Quickly, gravity snatched her away and dragged her over the edge ...

Maerlin had never considered leaping to her death before, but she imagined that for most people the difficult part would be the initial jump, willing the muscles of their body to the point of harm knowing that once passed a certain point, death would be inevitable. Once someone had fully committed to the act and was in mid-air, the rest would be only a matter of gravity. The fact that many suicides died before they actually hit the ground due to heart failure was neither here nor there. There would be no turning back once they step off that ledge. Gravity will simply ignore them, no matter how loud they yelled, "Stop ... I've changed my mind!"

Although one small step is enough to complete the task, mentally, it is a marathon.

Nevertheless, Maerlin had been gifted with Wild-magic, and with the merest thought her ever-present Elementals could sweep down from the skies to cocoon her in their love and adoration. She would float gently down to earth under their magical embrace. For her, stepping off the ledge was not the end of it.

Maerlin had to use all of her will to deny her Sylphs and defy the very gods themselves. She stubbornly refused to draw her magical powers to save herself from death. Her heart beat like a hummingbird as time slowed and she fell down the mountainside. Rocks flew past, only inches away from her face, and the wind howled in her ears as the Sylphs screamed out in horror at her decision to end her life. Yet, they were powerless to resist her will as she refused their offers of assistance. They screamed their love of her, but she hardened her heart and closed her eyes.

Quickly, Maerlin retreated into the white room she had created within her head. She refused to witness her own demise. It was too hard to watch; too tempting to interfere and deny gravity's embrace. The only way she could stop herself from halting her fall was to shut her mind away from the reality of what she was doing.

Any moment now, the floral curtains would disappear, the hearth fire would go out, and Maerlin would cease to exist. Sitting as calmly as possible in one of the battered old chairs she had created, she waited for the end.

She knew that time could be deceiving, but after a while she started to wonder. Surely, it couldn't take this long. It was a big drop, true, but she had been travelling at quite a speed. She waited, getting antsier the longer it took. Finally, she got up and started to pace her mental room.

Something was wrong. Had the gods interfered? Had they denied her the one thing that mankind still had: free will? Could they do that? Could the gods break that unwritten law? She didn't know, but she dreaded finding out so she paced the room for a while longer. When it finally became unbearable, Maerlin braced herself and opened her eyes.

She was still in the air, but the cliff was no longer before her. Instead, there were acres and acres of open grassland. Off to her right, Maerlin could see a half-built fort on a rocky hillock and beyond that, she saw the familiar shape of the burial mound with the Twelve Warriors and the Maiden Stone on its top. She was flying over the Plains of the Dragon ... but how could that be?

She looked up and saw shimmering silver scales above her head. Then she heard the distinctive sound of sails rippling in the wind, and the boom as they tightened to capture the wind: Dragon wings!

"Sygvaldr! Is that you?" Maerlin demanded, barely containing her temper.

"Ah good! You're awake. I thought you'd passed out for a while there. That's a dangerous thing to do, you know, standing on the edge of a cliff like that. It's not a good place to pass out. It could have turned nasty if I hadn't come along!"

"I didn't pass out, you idiot ... I jumped! How dare you interfere!"

"Jumped? Good gracious! What on earth would you want to do that for?"

"Never you mind why. That's none of your business. Anyway, how did you know that I was standing on the edge of a cliff in the first place? Have you been spying on me?"

The dragon cleared his throat, ignoring her question, hoping it would go away.

"Well ...? I'm waiting ... no thanks to you."

Sygvaldr cleared his throat again, a sound similar to a small avalanche.

"Erm," he said finally. "I just happened to be passing by ... that's all ..."

"Passing by! Passing by on your way to where exactly? What business does King Sygvaldr Frost-Breath have on the Mountain of the Gods?"

"Well, I say! There's really no need to take that tone of voice with me!"

"Yes, actually there is. I think you were spying on me. Go on ... admit it!"

"I wouldn't call it spying ... well not exactly. I was merely worried about your well-being. Your mind has been very troubled lately ..."

"You mean you can read my mind, too! Stay out of my head, Sygvaldr. Do you hear me? That's an order."

"It wasn't intentional. It's only when I'm thinking about you, which is rather a lot recently, now I come to think about it ... anyway, that's beside the point. I didn't intentionally mind-read. That'd be impolite. It's just that you have a poor shield wall up when you get upset, and your thoughts are zipping around like comets. I can hardly help it. It's not my fault!"

"Put me down this instant!"

"I will, once you calm down. Then we can discuss this rationally."

"I don't want to discuss anything rationally ... or any other way for that matter. Now put me down or I'll be forced to make you."

"I really don't think that's a good idea, Maerlin."

"I'm counting to three ..."

"That's all well and good ..."

"One ..."

"Maerlin, please ..."

"Two ..."

"If you'll just compose ..."

"Three ... right that's it. You asked for it!" Maerlin pulled from her inner pool of magic and summoned a Salamander.

"Spirit of fire, come to my aid," she murmured and a ball of flame quickly settled above her outstretched palm. "Last chance, Sygvaldr, let me go right now or you'll regret it!"

"Don't be silly, Maerlin. Please calm yourself."

Maerlin focused on the scaly claw and directed the Salamander to burn the dragon.

Much to her annoyance, Sygvaldr started to laugh. "That tickles, Maerlin. You can't harm me with Wild-magic. Dragons are creatures of the Elements. Your magic won't work on us.

Only Dragon magic can harm dragons, and we've sworn not to use that against each other since the Dragon Wars."

Maerlin glared at the scaly claw that was wrapped around her waist, and released the Salamander. Instead, she tried more traditional methods. She thumped it. This only resulted in a bruised knuckle, but still, it made her feel better to vent her frustrations.

They fell silent for a few moments while Maerlin pouted sullenly. "So, you're immune to the Elements."

"We are creatures of the Elements so there is very little that can harm us," Sygvaldr admitted apologetically. "Have you calmed down now?"

"I guess so, but I'm still not happy about you spying on me."

"I wasn't spying on you. I was only trying to help. I can teach you how to block your mind if you'd like, and then you can keep your thoughts to yourself. No immortal will be able to pry on your innermost secrets then."

"You mean to say that the Seven can hear my thoughts too?"

"Probably, why?"

"And you can teach me how to stop that from happening?"

"Certainly, but you'll need to calm down first. I'd like to talk to you about some of your recent dark thoughts. I'm sure that I'd be able to help you if you give me a chance."

"I doubt you can, Sygvaldr, but finding a way to keep the gods out of my head would be a good start." Maerlin looked around and found an isolated hillock just ahead. "Land on that hill over there, and we can talk."

Sygvaldr tilted his wings and banked into a smooth dive before settling on the crest of the hill. Gently, he released Maerlin from his grasp and sat back on his haunches.

FEAR AND HEAT
FROM DEMONIAC DANCE BY JAQ D HAWKINS

Chapter Four

Fear. Heat. There were no words, only emotions as Haghuf watched his own image torn limb from limb in the searing reflection of volcanic fires. The claws, rending and tearing. The other, his twin, shredded into nothing but meat for the dragon's feast. Blood everywhere. Fear. No words, just emotion. Fear. Run, run, run…

Haghuf awoke with a start. His eyes opened. His body flinched as if he would run, but he lay safely among the sleeping furs in the coolness of his familiar cavern. There were no dragons here. No fires. The world of the Foringen had been left behind long ago. Haghuf had never gone back to his mother's people again.

The dream had been more than a dream… it was a memory. For a moment, Haghuf lay still, shivering. For the first time in a very, very long time, he allowed himself to remember what life had been like in the Foringen caverns. It was accepted among them that some would be lost to the dragon's feast, just as many of the dragon's eggs would feed the goblins, but this had not prepared Haghuf to actually watch his twin being eaten.

Twin birth was very rare among goblins. Haghuf wondered if his grotto had allowed themselves to mourn that loss. Unlike other deaths, feeding the dragons was accepted as part of the cycle of life and death. For this, they were more fertile than many of the other species, yet Haghuf was still seldom chosen in the Dance. Talla had once told him that it was because the females found him too distant and unapproachable. Haghuf accepted that having been a part of the grotto at Krapneerg for many generations, his bloodlines already filled the veins of many of the younger goblins.

Haghuf had never been one for conversation beyond necessity. Among the Foringen, there were no names, no verbal language. Haghuf didn't remember how long it had taken him to learn to speak when he first came among the Deep Dwellers. The first noises he had been able to form were no more than guttural grunts, which is how he had gained the name that was the only sound he had been able to utter for long after his acceptance within what had become his grotto amidst the Deep Dwellers.

He had been accepted easily among them. Haghuf had the look of the ancient earthen goblins, enough to suggest that his mother had likely been seeded by one of them. Sometimes the Foringen were known to travel to other levels, to bring weapons among the fighting goblins and collect gifts of food to take back with them. Dragon eggs would be a stale diet on their own. All forms of goblins did as they needed to for survival. That had no doubt been how the symbiotic relationship between dragon and goblin had started. Goblins needed underground fire to forge weapons to protect them from humans. Both dragons and goblins needed food.

Now Haghuf was not sure if he would be able to tolerate the heat. So much time had gone by. To go among a people who had no names, no language to speak aloud, was his task alone. He knew their unspoken language still, as he had remembered when the Foringen had brought the sword to Count Anton. Some terms he had to struggle to remember, but the knowledge was still there, as was the fear.

Much time had passed since the sword had been bestowed on the human... an unprecedented event. Those who had been younglings then were nearly grown now. Haghuf had never understood the reason for the gift. He wanted answers. His resolve to seek them among the Foringen had remained since that day, but still his feet did not travel the deepest passages.

It came down to this: He was afraid of the dragons.

The nightmare had not been his first, but there was only one way to make it his last. It was time to conquer the fear and to go among the people of the dragons, the Foringen. Weapon forgers, fire goblins... his mother's people.

Haghuf roused himself from the sleeping furs and took the first step. That one was hardest. The rest would follow more easily, but not too easily. As he passed the opening to his sleeping space, his instincts cried out to turn left, not right. So it was with every choice where passages converged. Haghuf knew these caverns as well as anyone – better than many. Every junction gave him visions of possible destinations and imaginary business that he must attend to that would distract him from his path. He had, in fact, tried this route twice before and had allowed himself to be distracted by other diversions.

Not this time. For this journey he allowed himself only one detour, to collect a bag of apples to take with him as a gift to the Foringen. The golden apples that the goblins grew specially on an island that only one human had ever seen and lived to remember. These would be a welcomed gift indeed.

By force of will, Haghuf kept himself on the path that would take him to the deepest places. Nothing was going to distract him this time. No excuse would be allowed to stop the journey that must come. He had delayed it far too long already.

He needed to know. And that drove him forward. Forward and down, down narrow passages that grew warmer and noisier as he drew closer and closer. The walls themselves seemed to change as he travelled, growing redder in hue. The sound of sizzling and bubbling things permeated his consciousness increasingly, as did the smell of sulphur. It was no wonder that the humans thought of the deepest places in the Earth as a place of punishment in their mythologies. If only they knew the truth.

Sweating, feeling the heat too strongly as his destination drew near, Haghuf began to wonder if he was on a fool's errand. What matter was it if the Foringen should choose to bestow gifts on a human? The sword could never be used on a goblin anyway. Let the creatures kill each other more efficiently. What was it to goblin kind?

But that was exactly the point. Haghuf knew well that 'goblin kind' did nothing without reason. It had been too long a journey to the surface just to bestow a gift on a creature that was of no importance to the forgers of metal. A human would not have thought to offer food in return. Only the goblins kept the metal forgers supplied with food besides their staple diet of giant eggs. Haghuf was grimly aware that the dragons must not be allowed to die out, or the forgers would starve.

The rhythm of the earth had changed steadily during his journey. Now suddenly the intermixing of the rhythms of hammers echoing off of volcanic rock became noticeable. He was near the world of the forgers. The heat was almost unbearable. How had he lived here as a youngling? The larger cavern openings reminded him all too well of his fears. He felt exposed, more here even than on the surface world. There was much more room in the spacious passages here than in the comforting enclosed caverns of his adopted grotto. Room for a dragon to move about.

Even as the thought occurred, Haghuf turned a corner and found himself face to face with a pair of huge, fiery golden eyes. He froze in place. Thoughts of retreat mixed with realisation of futility... there was no escape. But the dragon turned and ambled away nonchalantly. It had obviously eaten recently.

It was then that Haghuf identified the blood stench mixed with the sulphur on its breath. He clutched the wall for support.

His knees wobbled shamefully. Such abject terror was unfitting to a goblin, especially one of his mother's people, but it was in the nature of all living things to fear death at the claws of such a beast. He wondered for a moment how many of his people knew such fear when the dragon actually took them. It was too easy to be philosophical about something that happened to someone else.

A few more turns and suddenly he was amongst them − the forgers. Dozens of the dark, fire toughened goblins were to be seen working among the cacophony of noisy hammering that had been the only sound Haghuf had known in his youth. One of them broke away from an assembly line to greet him. They bowed to each other casually, then Haghuf handed the bag of apples to the Foringen. The dark goblin bowed again in thanks.

Then the dance began. Haghuf remembered the movements he needed. He had indeed run them through his mind many times over as he had descended the paths to this realm. The Foringen answered in his own dance of communication. The explanation was straight-forward. No riddles this time, only answers. At last, Haghuf understood.

BITERS

FROM SONGS OF AUTUMN BY GUY DONOVAN

Author's note

The following sequence is excerpted from *Songs of Autumn: Book Three of The Dragon's Treasure*. Talorc is the titular dragon of the series. In book one, *The Forgotten Princess of Môna*, he befriends a young Welsh princess, Cerys, and later saves her from certain death. Through most of book two, *A Cold, White Home*, the two live together in the wild, occupying a series of caves on both sides of Hadrian's Wall in fifth-century Britannia. After the revelation of a dark secret on Talorc's part ends their friendship, he roams the world, seeking out other dragons, while Cerys remains in Britannia. During the events that follow, he has failed to find any others of his kind and has been adopted by a pod of Humpback whales. As a sort of family, they swim south to the whales' breeding grounds in the waters surrounding what we know today as the Hawaiian Islands.

Early Winter, 447 A.D.

Though Talorc was no stranger to swimming, he had never ventured so far from land before. Since recovering from his long flight across the seemingly endless sea, he and his new friends had been swimming south for a full week. In all that time, he had eaten nothing but fish and seals, and he had begun to miss the variety of sheep, goats, and swine from his life on land. Still, he had no desire to disappoint or, worse, offend the bulbous-yet-sleek, winged creatures he now lived with and thought of as his "family."

That word brought back memories of *her*, and those brought back all the old anger. At the same time, their continued separation, both mental and physical, brought back the hurt as well. They had once counted on each other, and even loved each other in their own ways, but now he felt at odds with himself, conflicted over the way they had become something bordering on enemies. Then his friends' continuous song cut through his thoughts, their tone growing more urgent.

What is wrong? He asked, aware that his own mental tone had begun to resemble their slow, warbling cadence. *Your song is different now...less sad, more...frightened.*

They have come. They are near and growing closer, his friends chorused in his mind.

Who? Who has come?

Biters, they answered in unison.

He did not understand completely, but he felt their urgent need to flee. They all stroked harder at the water with their broad, flat tails, and he did his best to match them. His own tail being more adequate for flight than for propelling him through water, he gradually fell behind.

Talorc wondered how his friends even knew of anything pursuing them. Through his transparent inner eyelids, he could see nothing behind them but the endless expanse of blue water and the occasional silver cloud of fish. His sense of smell, so acute above the water, was useless to him below it. His ears, too, did little good; only the sound of the water rushing by and the lower register of his friends' increasingly agitated song was audible to him. For many long minutes, they continued their attempt to outpace the unseen "biters." Even the youngest of them pulled farther and farther ahead of him.

I am not as fast as you are, he thought as the last of them disappeared from his sight. *Will you all leave me?*

It is you who must leave us, a lone voice answered in his head. *We will continue, even if some do not. You will not continue unless you return to the air.*

I do not think I can, Talorc responded, his strength flagging.

A feeling of warmth grew in him as a bulky, winged shadow appeared from the blue gloom ahead, slowing so he could catch up. The song directed him to lie atop the back of the creature. Propelling himself forward, he unfurled his wings and gripped as gently as he could onto the smooth, dark hide.

Then the larger animal nosed upward. Arching its back, it gave a powerful sweep of its tail that sent Talorc above the waves in a spray of seawater that sparkled brilliantly in the clear sunshine.

Talorc leaped upward. With a mighty stroke of his wings, he shot back into the air for the first time since falling out of it more than a week before. Looking down, he saw the dark shape of his friend disappear beneath the foam upon the sea's heaving surface.

Your true home is the air, that friend said, even as its tail slapped against the waves with a loud clap, *though you are always welcome among us.*

Far ahead, Talorc saw the telltale mist of the rest of his friends' breath as they tried to outrun whatever pursued them. Barely a dragon's length above the waves, he looked back and saw other such spouts, and a number of tall, glistening black triangular shapes slicing through the water toward his friends. He did not know what they were, but he understood that they belonged to the "biters."

Back in his natural element, he felt reinvigorated. In the distance, he saw an island within easy reach. It was green, heavily wooded, and large enough that it might have animals on which he could subsist until he decided what to do and where to go next.

He also made out with greater clarity the things that had frightened his friends into their mad dash for survival. Their shapes were similar, including their tails, but they were shorter and even darker, with oblong white markings to either side of their sleek black heads. Where his friends had long, knobby wings, the biters possessed fins that were smaller and nearly round. Like his friends, they too sang. Their song was faster though, and composed of high-pitched notes and clicks. More than anything else, he sensed from them an overriding hunger.

Flipping up onto one wingtip, he turned to face his friends' enemies, who had now become his enemies. He dropped downward, fixing the speeding black shapes in his sight while also adjusting his angle so the wind was at his back. As he raced up on them, he opened his mouth wide and then exhaled a long gout of his white-hot breath. It washed over the top of the water, but also licked at a number of the tall, thin fins that sliced toward him. His claws broke the surface just as he and the biters came together, slashing deeply into one dark monster's back and sending bloody water spraying into the air.

Flapping his wings, he rose back into the sky and arced about in a wide circle to judge the effectiveness of his attack. He saw a clear trail of blood and even some bits of thick, fatty flesh in the water where he had clawed the one creature. Those whose fins he had flamed had scattered, but three others continued unscathed to pursue his friends, now growing very near to them. It was toward those three that he aimed himself next.

Talorc was upon them in seconds, sending another hellish blast across all three fins before snapping at the one in the middle, shearing away most of what showed above the water. As he glided past, he slashed again with one clawed foot, resulting in another geyser of blood and more rent flesh. With a roar, he dropped the fin from his mouth and flapped away.

Another broad circle revealed that two of the first creatures he had flamed were again on the attack. The others, he saw, seemed in disarray, neither retreating nor attacking. The skin of the fins that still showed above the water appeared bubbled and cracked. That satisfied Talorc, and he prepared to attack again.

Lining up the two fins as best he could in the whipping wind, he dropped low to the water. When he was close, he let out another gout of his flame and saw both fins shrivel up on themselves. They steamed and spit as the biters dove deeper. Turning quickly, Talorc dragged one wingtip through the water as he sought another target.

Only one blistered, smoking fin still showed, and he angled toward it, intent on ripping it from the beast's back. In order to make the turn, he had to slow down enough not to overshoot. That left him closer to the surface than before, and his wingtips slapped the water with each flap. Just as he reached out with a grasping claw, the water to his left seemed to explode as a massive, dark shape leaped upward and drove into him.

As the biter's forceful impact drove him to the right, Talorc felt the black and white creature's razor sharp teeth rake across his leathery skin. It had failed to rip out his throat, but succeeded in knocking him from the sky. Dragged down by the creature's bulk, Talorc let out a surprised bellow and a blast of flame that scorched his attacker badly before the seawater extinguished it in a steaming flash. They both disappeared beneath the waves, Talorc's wings wrapped about the enraged and horribly burnt animal. Mindless of his own survival then, concerned only with the safety of his friends, he bit savagely at the powerful creature within his embrace.

The water turned red as Talorc sank his fangs into the fatty skin behind the biter's left eye, but the beast refused to submit, twisting and thrashing about in an effort to free itself. Talorc's breath began to fail. If he did not kill his opponent soon, he knew it might yet be he who died.

Just as his vision began to dim, he felt another impact from the struggling creature's other side. The shock if it shook him loose and he sank deeper into the water. He saw that it was not another of the biters coming to the aid of its companion, as he had supposed. It was instead his knobby winged friends come to his rescue once more.

Then he felt others buoying him up toward where the sun shone through the bloody water in spear-like shafts. When his head broke the surface, he drew in a deep breath of the sweet, cool air, and saw a great commotion upon the wave tops as his friends pummeled their one-time pursuers with their massive tails. The water all about churned with a pinkish froth, only a pair of the ruined, black fins speeding away.

Talorc's head lolled to one side to look into the eye of one of his rescuers as he thought, *Now all of us will continue.*

THE DRAGON RAID

A DRABBLE BY NAV LOGAN

The dragons glided silently through the early morning mist, slipping upriver. They were seeking adventure, seeking gold. Ahead, in a sleepy hollow, lay the abbey and its nearby hamlet. Dawn was lighting the sky as the first of the dragons beached on the shingle and spewed forth its wrath. Death had arrived with the coming day. With a blood curdling roar, they fell upon the poorly-armed farmers and monks, slaughtering in a blood frenzy any who dared resist. Some were raped or dragged into slavery. Gathering up their treasures, the dragon riders headed back to their ships. Another successful raid.

FREÓSAN DRAKA TREÓW

A WYRDE WOODS TALE WRITTEN FOR GERRIT, ANNA & ROZEMARIJN BY NILS NISSE VISSER

The Wyrde Woods, Sussex, 878 AD

The Draka have arrived at the edge of Wyrdwuda to wreak havoc. Lewinna Wulfgardohter yearns for her father's comforting presence, but Wulfgar Roransun is far away. So are the men who carry the swords and spears needed to protect her home. Without them, it seems impossible to halt the tide of naked steel and voracious appetites that have spilled out of the Draka longships.

At dawn, the girl climbs to Herne's Horns, two sandstone pinnacles protruding from the edge of a near vertical cliff that marks the end of a river gorge. The cliff is mirrored by its twin across the Rorian River. The river rushes out of the gorge between the two cliff faces before settling down into a broader and calmer stretch of water. This curves around the settlement of Rorianford, a collection of thatched wattle dwellings huddled around Wulfgar's hall. At the village's east edge, an old stone bridge stretches across the river. The Rorian becomes turbulent again at the waterfall beyond Rorianford, before settling down to meander out of the dark green Wyrdwuda, through the light green Downs, to the white cliffs, and then into the grey sea many miles to the south.

The breeze stirs Lewinna's long blond hair. She reaches into her blue woollen summer tunic to take out the small silver amulet suspended from her neck on a sturdy string. The amulet represents Meolo, the hammer of the Thunder-God Thunor, and Lewinna clenches it in her hand.

The sky over Wyrdwuda should have promised a bright sunny day, but is marred by ugliness. Columns of dirty smoke billow upwards from the southern edge of the woods, harbingers of death and destruction. Lewinna's face displays grim tension as she watches the smoke rise. A steady breeze blows land-inwards, north towards the woods. It is still fresh, untainted by acridity so the fires are newly lit.

A messenger had come from the settlement of Odesburh the day before. He had reported a coastal sighting of the feared Draka ships. The smoke rising up confirms that the Draka weren't passing by on one of their patrols, as they had been wont to do this summer. Instead, they have landed on the coast to raid northwards. They have come far inland in a short time, cutting deep into the nearly defenceless *scir* – the shire of Suth-Seaxe in the Kingdom of West-Seaxe.

Lewinna grips the folds of her simple wool tunic as her mind's eye provides glimpses of that which she can't see from this distance. Beneath the rising smoke, the settlements of Nihtlícburh and Odesburh will be in the grip of sheer terror. Their morning disrupted by brutal violence when the Draka descended upon them with cold fury, drawn swords, and sharpened spears. Those who tried to defend their families…cut down. The old killed, the young rounded up for transport to the slave markets of Frankia, the livestock slaughtered. The girls and young women…

…Lewinna shudders as she thinks of the screams and wails which would be competing with the rush of crackling flames devouring the thatched roofs. Women and girls she knows by name. Their bodies might heal, but minds and souls will be ever after scarred. They are now also condemned to the drudgery and short life of a slave. Lewinna doesn't doubt that it could be her own fate.

If the Draka extend their raid northwards, they will enter Wyrdwuda. There are three settlements under her father's protection: Rorianford, Thurgisham, and Wulftun. If the Draka come and find the Wyrdwuda folk in their villages, Wulfgar's people will suffer the same cruel fate which destiny has dealt to Nihtlícburh and Odesburh…blood spilled…screams renting the air…souls torn asunder.

"*Myne Frowe* – Milady?"

Lewinna takes a deep breath.

"*Myne Frowe*? Lewinna, lass?" It's the old hunter, Aldred Dræfendsun, who addresses her. He and his sons have accompanied her to Herne's Horns, but are waiting at some distance behind the sandstone pinnacles, having provided her some space.

Why me? Lewinna shuts her eyes. She murmurs brief prayers to Frig and Ēostre in the hope that both goddesses will deem Lewinna worthy. Composing herself, the girl turns around to face Aldred, Ryce, and Beorn.

Ryce is fifteen, two years younger than Lewinna, and Beorn a scrawny eleven-year-old who stares at her with wide eyes. Like Lewinna, they all wear simple but robust knee-length wool tunics, although theirs are dark green. All have knives dangling from their belts. Lewinna, Aldred, and Ryce are also armed with a saex, the short Saxon stabbing sword which signify they are free-born. Aldred's belt sports a quiver from which goose fletched arrow shafts protrude, and in his hand is a long, thick, yew bow stave.

Aldred gives Lewinna a nod and a brief smile. The silver-haired and grey-bearded hunter is well past his physical prime, but his eyes retain sharp wariness and he exudes calm confidence. Lewinna adapts her posture to mimic his.

She is struck by brief wonder. Aldred is a close friend and confidant of her father. As young men, they had stood shoulder to shoulder in many a *scild-burh* – shield wall, and that had created a sense of kinship between the two men which Lewinna envied. Aldred has also been her teacher for many years, teaching her the secrets of his woodlore. There is nary a corner of Wyrdwuda which she hasn't visited in his company. He has always been the undisputed leader of their expeditions around Wulfgar's domains, but now refrains from taking the initiative, signalling that he is ready to defer to Lewinna's authority. She is startled by his unspoken recognition but also struck by the sense of responsibility. She has yearned for this as long as she can remember, but now it weighs heavily upon her shoulders. The Draka are coming.

She breaks the silence. "Beorn, you will have the most important job."

Beorn digests this and then shoots his older brother a triumphant look. Ryce tries to look disgruntled, but gives Lewinna a cheerful wink. Aldred nods when his youngest son looks up at him for confirmation.

"Get down the hill as fast as you can," Lewinna instructs Beorn. "Tell the others it is time. Womenfolk to Ēostre's Cleofa. All the boys and menfolk to drive the livestock to Stonley. You will lead them."

"*Jā Myne Frowe* – Yes, Milady," Beorn confirms. Stonley is secluded deep in Wyrdwuda, but the boy can find the clearing with its spectacular circle of dancing stones blindfolded if need be.

"What do you do if the Draka come?" Lewinna asks Beorn.

"Abandon the livestock and leap away faster than hares, so that we can live to return strong as bears," Beorn answers.

"It is not cowardly," Aldred says in his deep, gnarled voice, "to yield Stonley to the Draka in this manner, as long as you return to fight the Draka when you have grown into a warrior."

"*Jā, Fæder* – Yes, Father." Beorn nods his understanding with the impatience of a youth who can recite by heart lessons which have been incessantly hammered home. Rorianford has long prepared for a possible Draka raid, the plans revised after the Draka warlord Guthrun had driven the King of West-Seaxe into exile in the Sumorsaete marshes, far to the west.

"Then what are you waiting for?" Ryce asks. "Fool."

Beorn snorts at Ryce, "I'll not obey an *aersling*..."

Beorn ducks to avoid a swipe from Ryce, then turns to Lewinna, puffing up his puny chest and drawing his shoulders back: "I'll only obey the chieftain."

"Go," Lewinna tells him. "Fly faster than a hawk and stay safe."

"*Jā, Myne Frowe.*" Beorn runs off.

Lewinna inhales deeply through her nose. The air is still fresh. The Draka likely still in Nihtlícburh and Odesburh, poking about for hidden silver or gratifying their lusts.

She turns to Ryce, who is in charge of half-a-dozen older lads. They are on the threshold of manhood, too old to be boys, too young to be men. In Suth-Seaxe they are called *frumbyrdlings* – first-time-beard-growers, in mockery of the fluff they invariably sport on their chins, Ryce included.

Lewinna fights a smile and then says: "Thurgisham."

"Menfolk to Stonley, womenfolk to Ēostre's Cleofa," Ryce confirms the message he will deliver to the hamlet of Thurgisham. It's farther south than Rorianford and Wulftun, but hidden away in the woods and hard to find. Ryce and his fellow *frumbyrdlings* will reach Thurgisham long before the Draka might accidentally stumble upon the small huddle of huts. Still, the Thurgisham folk will be far safer in the assigned hiding places.

"And after....?" Aldred asks.

Ryce grimaces.

"You're to join Beorn at Stonley," Lewinna says. "Immediately after warning Thurgisham."

"I can fight," Ryce protests.

By rights, he should have followed Wulfgar after King Ælfred and his warlord Uhtred had summoned the Suth-Seaxe militia, the *fyrd*, to face the Draka horde that had invaded the west. When Wulfgar had led the Wyrdwuda *fyrd* away to rally around the Kingdom's dragon banner, Ryce had been incapacitated by a fever and unable to travel. Lewinna knows it torments the boy, for he will not be counted a man until he stands in a *scild-burh*.

"Nā – no. Not against the Draka," Aldred says. "Each man and woman aboard the Draka ships is a trained and experienced warrior. You cannot stand against such without the *fyrd* around you, not yet."

Ryce turns to Lewinna, desperate appeal in his eyes. "You don't know what it's like."

Lewinna glares at him. "I don't know what it's like?"

Ryce wants to become a warrior, and if he lives long enough that wish will be granted sooner or later. Lewinna wants to become chieftain, like her father, but she's a girl and destined to be lorded over by a husband. She should have been wed years ago, but so far Wulfgar has indulged Lewinna in her nuptial procrastination. She is keenly aware that the indulgence cannot last forever. She has confided these frustrations to Ryce on a few occasions, and he should have known better.

"But you are going to fight," Ryce objects. "You and *myne fæder.*"

"Enough," Aldred growls.

"We will not be using sword, spear, and axe to fight the Draka," Lewinna says as calmly as she can, because uncertainty and fear are gnawing at her belly. "Now go. Be off to Thurgisham before it's too late."

"*Já, Myne Frowe,*" Ryce says sullenly. He opens his mouth again, as if to say something, then changes his mind and runs down the same track Beorn has just taken, back to Rorianford.

Lewinna gives Aldred a questioning glance, which he answers with a nod and reassuring words. "You did well, *Myne Frowe*. The people will be safe in Eostre's Cleofa and Stonley."

"*Thancas, myne lareowa* – thank you, my teacher."

Aldred smiles at the acknowledgement of what has, since this morning, become their past. "*Georne, myne leornere* – you're welcome, my pupil."

"Still, I'll not have my father return to find his hall in ashes. You and I will ride to Wulftun."

"Raedan is unlikely to listen to reason, *Myne Frowe*, and Crawa awaits you at the Úlehús..."

Lewinna turns to view Wyrdwuda from her perch at Herne's Horns one last time. The dark smoke billowing up from the southern edges of the woods has risen higher, dispersing wider in the sky. When the screams of the survivors are hoarsened by terrified exhaustion, when the meagre hoards of hidden silver are found and divided, when the monstrous Draka appetites are temporarily sated...where will the steel-helmeted Draka go next?

"Raedan is unlikely to listen to reason," she agrees. "But I have to try one last time and we will go to the Úlehús straight after."

"*Já, Myne Frowe.*"

The two hasten down the slope towards the trees where they have tethered their horses.

§ § § § § § §

There is no time to stop in Rorianford but the evacuation seems to be running smoothly. The greybeards and lads are herding nervous livestock over the bridge, and then northeast towards the secret byways which lead to Stonley. Some of the menfolk turn their heads to watch the smoke rising to the south, or cast a last look at their home which they might never see again because the Draka are coming.

Almost all the women and girls are headed towards the gorge where they will follow the Rorian upstream until they reach the dark cave opening of Eostre's Cleofa. The youngest children fret, sensing the fear around them but not understanding why. Some of the older children are wide-eyed with guilt, having been told often enough that if they were bad, the Draka would come and get them. This notion has been lent a terrifying credence now that they have to flee their homes, the only world they know, because the Draka are coming.

A handful of women and girls are hastening north-west, taking a path through the evergreens of the Singrénewold towards the Úlehús, Crawa's home near the spiritual heart of Wyrdwuda. Although Crawa is likely to already know, they carry the dire news that the Draka are coming.

Lewinna and Aldred urge their horses into a trot on the Woldweg, a dirt road which leads west towards Wulftun. To their left is the Bécanwold, broad swathes of beech trees, their ample foliage shading spacious carpets of last year's fallen leaves. These woodlands are dotted with ash and chestnut, and intertwined with denser copses of hazel and hawthorn. Beneath the protection of the foliage, the Bécanwold is mostly open and airy, a pleasant place to be, this in sharp contrast to the woodlands on the other side of the Woldweg.

The Seolforwold is so called because of the predominance of silver birch trees. These shimmer eerily on moonlit nights, the preponderance of pale trunks resembling the silent ranks of a ghostly army. There are a few darker copses of quaking aspen, the aspens' leaves trembling at the slightest hint of a breeze as if frightened by the doleful presence of scattered alder trees. The whole is completed by the occasional whych elm, and impenetrable colonies of spiny blackthorn.

Lewinna's arms become covered with goose bumps as she begins to feel the menacing presence of the Seolforwold. It is more commonly known as the Ghaestdenn, the lair of lost spirits and broken souls which can find no rest. Most folk hasten their journey when they pass, and few ever venture into the Ghaestdenn voluntarily.

She recalls the occasion when her father had condemned a murderer to be abandoned in the Ghaestdenn at sunset. The man was a local, well aware of the woodland's dire reputation, and had screamed his terror when he had been dragged off to be tied to a solitary and ancient oak in the Ghaestdenn.

Lewinna had seen thirteen winters at the time. Wulfgar had no living sons, and had chosen to train Lewinna as his heir. Sometimes, he had told her, dealing with matters of extreme justice to right a wrong was the unfortunate duty of a chieftain. Wulfgar had encouraged Lewinna to go with him into the Ghaestdenn the next morning. "Always face the consequences when you have made the decision about another person's life…or death. Whatever you will see today, remember that a good chieftain bears the burden of responsibility for that."

They had only found shreds of the condemned man, near unrecognizable bloody strips of this and that spread out over half-a-mile, leading away from the sacrificial oak. The red droplets sprayed on birch trunks had formed a bright, but grim contrast on the silky white bark.

"*Púcan?*" Lewinna had asked, referring to the Pooks whose antics often caused minor mishaps around Rorianford, especially if the villagers forgot to leave out treats for the mischievous spirits.

Wulfgar had shaken his head. "*Nā, myne deórling* – my darling, these were the *Nihtgengan*."

Lewinna had shivered all over at the mention of the *Nihtgengan*, the night stalkers and the shadow walkers, the twisted creatures that roamed parts of Wyrdwuda at night. It is a relief when she and Aldred emerge in a clearing that marks the far corners of the Ghaestdenn and the Bécanwold. Another dirt road intersects the Woldweg here, the Æcerweg running north to venture deeper into the great expanse of the Suth-Seaxe Wold, and south to Nihtlícburh, and after that the Downs and the white cliffs of the coast.

Lewinna and Aldred pause briefly on the crossing, called Innanley, to gaze southwards. If the Draka decide to raid further inland, this is the most likely way they will come. Like the rest of the Suth-Seaxe Wold, Wyrdwuda doesn't offer easy access. Many roads lead nowhere at all, their purpose to function as droves for the annual autumn trek of herders and pigs to acorn rich clearings called dennes. The droves are deceptive. Countless pigs have deepened and widened them for centuries so that they look like established highways, whereas some of the main thoroughfares through Wyrdwuda, like the Woldweg, resemble inconsequent byways. If the Draka strike out blindly, they might lose many hours wandering about in the pig-made maze. If the Draka interrogate survivors, those will likely point at the Æcerweg, which would lead them straight to Innanley.

Nothing Lewinna sees gives her immediate cause for worry; the only creatures using the Æcerweg are a pair of rabbits nibbling at the grass on the road's verge. Nonetheless, there is discomfort in continuing east towards Wulftun. If the Draka do appear, they will cut her off from the Wyrdwuda woodlands.

The landscape across the Æcerweg changes into a patchwork of small fields and copses which makes Wulftun the most vulnerable settlement in Wulfgar's domains. Thurgisham, it is joked, can only ever be found by its own inhabitants as long as they are sober, nobody else stands much of a chance, sober or drunk. The only usual tell-tale sign of Rorianford is the smoke from the cooking fires, and those are doused, but the small steeple tower of Wulftun's church is visible from stretches of the Æcerweg.

Lewinna reflects grimly that the same building is divisive in other ways as well.

They ride past the chequered fields and copses until they reach the edge of Wulftun. Three men stand astride the road at the edge of the village, their manner and countenance one of fierce determination, ingrained Suth-Seaxe stubbornness at its worst.

They slow, and then bring their horses to a halt. Aldred sighs and shakes his head, muttering a muted "*Aerslingas*" into his beard.

"*Wass-hael* Raedan. *Wass-hael* Yrre," Lewinna greets Wulftun's elderly blacksmith and his son. There is no warmth in her greetings. She ignores the third man called Wynnstan, dressed in the ankle-length black gown of a Christian priest.

"Oh Lord!" The priest wails. "Oh Saviour! Save us from temptation, shield your faithful servants from the wicked wiles of the heathens."

"Wicked wiles?" Lewinna asks, bemused.

"You dress unseemly," Raedan grumbles into his beard.

"Like a boy," Yrre adds.

Aldred rolls his eyes in exasperation. Lewinna glances down. Her knee-length tunic, trousers, and leggings, rather than a woman's ankle-length gown, are far more practical in the woods.

"Your priest," Lewinna says, "dresses in a gown like a woman. Is that not offensive then Yrre Raedansun?"

Yrre looks thoroughly confused, as she knew he would.

"The shape of your legs show," Wynnstan complains, "and you're not wearing your headrail, letting every man who cares to look see your hair."

"This offends you?" Lewinna asks. "Just because Christian women tolerate your church's demands that they dress like your nuns, Priest, doesn't mean you get to tell the rest of us how to live our lives."

"It's wanton and lewd," Wynnstan insists.

Aldred growls, Lewinna gestures at him to ignore the insult to her honour. She feels perfectly capable of returning the insult.

"If I had time, Priest," she says dismissively, "I'd dismount, bare my naked arse at you and fart in your face."

Aldred grins. Lewinna knows he is always amused when she demonstrates that she grew up in the company of Wulfgar's *huscarl*s, his small band of household warriors. "It's not seemly for a girl, all that battle-talk," Aldred had once confided to her, "but I reckon you can't help taking after your father. All the more so since he has refused to remarry after your mother's death, so Wulfgar is to blame."

Raedan scowls. His son Yrre smiles with anticipation, as if to encourage Lewinna to carry out her threat. The insult drives Wynnstan into renewed wails. "Lord save us! The temptress seeks to turn our thoughts to sin!"

Lewinna looks at the priest with disdain. Wynnstan is in his thirties, and most in Wulftun consider him to be touched by the Christian god, but everybody else in Wyrdwuda reckons he is merely insane. Although he is not ugly Lewinna finds his calculating eyes and snivelling demeanour repulsive.

Yrre, on the other hand, is spectacular to look at. Broad-shouldered and muscular, he is in the prime of his early twenties, with a blond beard trimmed meticulously short to show off his square jaw line. He exudes masculine confidence that, as far as Lewinna is concerned, is misplaced because he is as stupid as the rear-end of a cow and possesses less personality than a goat turd.

Yrre had been conspicuously absent when her father Wulfgar had mustered the Wyrdwuda *fyrd*, and he had seemed relieved, rather than disappointed or angry.

She glances at Raedan. When she had been a child the blacksmith had always seemed a tower of strength, hulking over her like a friendly giant. In the last few years however, he has started to shrivel, his muscular bulk in decline. His mind too seems to be diminishing, becoming ever more suspicious and shrewish, increasingly encouraged by Wynnstan's poisonous words.

Lewinna has an axe to grind with all three men. Two days after Wulfgar's departure, Wynnstan had convinced Raedan and Yrre that the ancient standing stone which marked the Innanley crossing was an icon of the Christian Devil. The men of Wulftun had cast the stone down and dragged it to their village, where a stonemason had started chiselling Christian crosses on the stone's face. Lewinna had ridden into Wulftun, full of fury, but her demand that the stone was restored had been ignored even though Wulfgar had publicly decreed that Lewinna would take on his responsibilities during his absence. She's still furious about this, uncertain enough about her role as it is without Wulftun's open defiance to contend with.

Lewinna reminds herself that Wulfgar is absent, and the Draka menace upon them. This is not the time to bear a grudge. Regardless of their casual betrayal of the old gods, the inhabitants of Wulftun deserve the protection of the Chieftain of Wyrdwuda.

Wynnstan can't keep his eyes off Lewinna's legs. "Oh Lord, save me from wicked temptation!"

"You flatter yourself, Priest," Lewinna says, "if you think I would ever lower myself to lead you into temptation."

Aldred chuckles. Lewinna turns to Raedan. "The Draka have landed. They are less than half-a-day away, maybe even closer."

"*Já*, we know, we've seen the smoke from Nihtlícburh and Odesburh," Yrre exclaims with a disturbing amount of enthusiasm.

Raedan answers, "We are taking precautions. All the womenfolk are in the church, praying that the Good Lord delivers us from evil."

"Hallelujah!" Wynnstan exclaims.

Aldred spits on the ground. "They are fools, *Myne Frowe*."

"And we will fight the Draka," Yrre boasts, thumping his chest. "They will beg for mercy."

Lewinna ignores the young man. She tells Raedan: "Bring your folk into Wyrdwuda, they will be safe there."

"Witchcraft!" Wynnstan exclaims. "The very thing that has brought the Draka demons upon us, drawn by sinful, naked cavorting around the Devil's stones…"

"Aldred," Lewinna says. "One more word from that priest, and I'll have his tongue so I can nail it to a nithing pole."

"*Já, Myne Frowe*," Aldred answers. "With great pleasure." He draws his saex and gives Wynnstan a withering look that makes the priest go pale.

"And who are you," Raedan addresses Lewinna, pride in his voice. "That I should bow my head so low?"

"Lewinna Wulfgardohter speaks on behalf of Wulfgar Roransun," Aldred hisses. "Your chieftain."

"*Ná* Aldred, a fool who has taken all the fighting men away," Raedan says, "leaving his land in the hands of a mere girl. And look what's happened! The folk are unprotected, at the mercy of the Draka savages."

"Not unprotected," Lewinna counters. "There is protection in Wyrdwuda."

Raedan ignores her. "How low the mighty have fallen, Aldred Dræfendsun, when in their old age they meekly bow their head to a girl. Is that the manhood you teach your sons?"

"*Jā*, that is right. I am oath-sworn and bow my head to my chieftain, pleased and proud that my sons see me do so," Aldred answers, adding the worst insult imaginable: "I will not be a *waerloga* – an oath-breaker. You, Raedan Edricsun, will wear the shame of that in this life, and the next."

"How dare you insult my..." Yrre fumes.

"Shut your mouth," Raedan snaps at his son before turning back to Lewinna and Aldred. "The folk are desperate for leadership. Marry my son, Lewinna Wulfgardohter, and Wyrdwuda will have a chieftain to follow and fight for. Accept the one God in your life, and Wynnstan can wed you here and now. Unite all our folk, Christian and Pagan alike."

"*Jā!*" Yrre agrees, his eyes roving over Lewinna's body with the greed of a magpie and the subtlety of a drunken ox.

"*Nā!*" Lewinna retorts. "I'd rather rut with a dozen pot-bellied, sweaty, and hairy *Wealsh*-men."

"Wyrdwuda has a chieftain," Aldred declares. "And Lewinna Wulfgardohter orders the folk of Wulftun to the woods. Pay heed to the voice of your chieftain, Raedan."

Raedan shakes his head. "We will stay in Wulftun and pray."

"And fight if need be!" Yrre adds.

"We are wasting our time then," Lewinna concludes. "*Bēo gesund* – goodbye."

Without a further word, she turns her horse and begins riding back to Innanley, followed by Aldred.

When they are some distance away, Wynnstan finds his courage and hollers a stream of curses at them, mostly unintelligible but the gist of the words is clear.

"You tried," Aldred tells Lewinna. "It was all you could do, *Myne Frowe.*"

"They bring death upon themselves," Lewinna responds. "I failed."

"*Wyrd bið ful aræd,*" Aldred says. "Fate is wholly inexorable."

"*Já,*" Lewinna agrees. "*Wyrd bið wended hearde* – fate is hard to change."

She bites her lip. Aldred hasn't denied her failure in his response. No matter how obnoxious the Wulftun men had been, a chieftain was ultimately responsible. Aldred and her father's other old *scild*-brothers would be loyal unto death, that much she can rely on, but there are more folk in Wyrdwuda. Folk who talk and gossip. There are women in all three of Wyrdwuda's settlements who resent Lewinna's temporary elevation, and their tongues are sharper than a well-honed sword edge. Even the smallest failure will be magnified and multiplied to be counted against her.

At least, Lewinna consoles herself, Aldred gives good council, not afraid to present her with things she might not like, just as he had during their woodlore lessons. Such council, Wulfgar had impressed upon her, was rare and invaluable.

They pause at Innanley to look south. Though the woods restrict their view, they can see two columns of smoke still rising into the sky added to which are two smaller plumes, north of Nihtlícburh.

"The first farmsteads on the Æcerweg," Lewinna says. She feels faint for a moment, drained by a sinking sensation that threatens to drag down her spirit. She clutches Meolo and sends a short prayer to Wodan, the All-father.

"They are headed this way." Aldred's voice sounds grim. "We must make haste."

They turn their horses and follow the Æcerweg north. As they urge their horses into a canter, Lewinna's thoughts turn to her own fate. Although she yearns to live, she's less afraid of death than the prospect of being captured alive by the Draka. Nonetheless, she knows that her own capture is precisely the bait she will have to offer the Draka. Lewinna isn't sure yet if she will have the courage to do so. All she knows for certain is that nothing will ever be the same again, because the Draka are coming.

§ § § § § § §

The Úlehús is a long thatched hut built on a small clearing called Uley, between the evergreen Singrénewold and the yew woodland called Wiccanhyrst. The modest dwelling is home to Crawa, her daughter Æmma, and half-a-dozen tawny and screech owls. Crawa is a *Wicce*, a wise woman and sorceress. Æmma is a year younger than Lewinna, and the two are close friends.

Neither Crawa nor Æmma are in sight when Lewinna and Aldred ride into the clearing, but there are others. A dozen greybeards from Rorianford and Thurgisham, as well as a score of *frumbyrdlings* from both settlements and outlying farmsteads.

"*Hwaet* – Look!" Lewinna shakes her head with disbelief as she points at Ryce. The boy sees them and stands straight, shoulders drawn back, all trembling defiance as he watches his father and chieftain approach.

Aldred curses. "That disobedient little cur. I'll have to knock some sense into his head."

"*Nā* Aldred," Lewinna says. "You don't fool me; you pretend anger, but I hear pride in your voice, *myne frēond* – my friend."

Aldred shrugs.

Lewinna makes a decision. "Let him join us then, Aldred, seeing Ryce is so intent on it that he's willing to risk your displeasure. We will need that kind of courage."

"*Ellen sceal on eorle* – Courage belongs in a warrior."

"*Jā*, it does. And the apple never falls far from the tree."

Aldred beams at that when they dismount, but when he turns to face his defiant and disobedient son his face is all scowl again.

Ryce bites on his lower lip but neither looks away nor withers under his father's stern gaze. Aldred hands him the reins of the horses. "See to it that they are watered, rubbed down, and tethered safely where they can graze."

A smile of relief flashes across the *frumbyrdling's* face. "*Jā, Fæder.*"

Lewinna is relieved too, but for a different reason because she has spotted Æmma emerging from the Úlehús. Her friend is barefoot and not wearing a tunic, just a plain white, knee-length, linen shift, offset by the cascade of her wild tangle of red hair.

Æmma greets Lewinna with a brief hug. "There you are, at last. Crawa awaits, we must hurry."

Lewinna looks at Aldred, "Prepare your men."

"*Jā, Myne Frowe.*"

Lewinna follows Æmma, who leads them through the extensive vegetable plots at the back of the Úlehús, past squawking chickens and a hissing goose. A thick wild hedgerow marks the border of the Uley clearing. To Lewinna's surprise, Æmma marches straight at the hedgerow as if charging an enemy *scild-burh*. Only when it is practically under her nose does Lewinna realise that there's a narrow gap in the hedgerow, a dark breach half concealed by a single layer of young leafed twigs which are supple and bend easily enough. She follows Æmma through the narrow gap that allows them to squeeze through the thick hedgerow and emerge into the Wiccanhyrst – The Witch Woods.

Wiccanhyrst consists almost entirely of yew trees. The top of their crowns lock out all sunlight. It is strangely dark beneath the yews; the air is cooler, almost cold, and there is a notable absence of the usual forest sounds. Lewinna is far less sensitive to the Unseen than Æmma, but she readily perceives the tangible sense of sanctity. Even though the red-barked yew trees at the edge of Wiccanhyrst are still young and single stemmed, they already exude their presence with a demand for reverence. The *eow treów*, the yew tree, is the tree of life and death, its components medicinal or poisonous and its lifespan seemingly eternal because of yew's power of regeneration.

Although Lewinna has never been in the Wiccanhyrst, she knows that Æmma can only be taking her to one place, the *Heorttreów*, the Heart Tree, mother of all the trees in the Wyrdwuda. No man, it is said, has ever been allowed to lay his eyes on the *Heorttreów*. Only a small number of women have, those selected as *Heorttreów's* guardians. They are called the *Waerwyrd* – those wary with their words, keepers of secrets, the Wyrdwuda Guardians.

"I may be Lord of the Wyrdwuda," Wulfgar had once told Lewinna. "And the *Wicce* Crawa may seem no more than a trusted councillor. But I am only Lord of the tangible Wyrdwuda, that which the eyes can see, the ears can hear, the nose can smell; that which you can touch and behold in daylight. The *Wiccan* – the wise seers, perceive a different world which most of us never witness or only catch glimpses of...but the Unseen is as real to them as the world you and I know, *myne deórling*, and far more dangerous."

"The *Nihtgengan*," Lewinna had said, her skin crawling as she had recalled the fate of the murderer in Ghaestdenn.

"Já, the *Nihtgengan*, the Pooks, and more. Crawa and the *Waerwyrd* protect us from the Unseen, and in that sense, Crawa is more than an advisor. She is the moon to my sun, ruler of the night where I oversee the day. Do you understand *myne deórling?*"

"I think so, *Fæder*. Guardianship of the Wyrdwuda happens on different levels, and the folk's safety is a shared responsibility. You are equals in that."

"Well spoken. Almost equal, for the *Wicce* is far wiser than I am. If you are ever in doubt, go to the Úlehús and listen to Crawa. If what you desire is best for Wyrdwuda and its folk, you cannot find a better ally. If your interests diverge, you will not find a worse foe."

Lewinna feels a moment of peace as she recalls her father's words. Æmma is taking her to Crawa to seal an alliance, and Lewinna is sure her father would have approved had he known.

The path they are on begins to descend into a low vale. The yew trees are older here, the trunks squat and stout, pulled down by the weight of their heavy boughs.

"Æmma, are you taking me to *Heorttreów?*" Lewinna breaks the silence.

"*Já, myne sweostor* – my sister," Æmma answers. "They are all waiting for you, impatiently I should imagine."

"I went to Wulftun."

"And they spurned you, no doubt?" Æmma stops and turns, fixing Lewinna with her fierce green eyes. "They were doomed from the moment they cast down the Innanley Stone. There is a price to be paid for provoking the gods. The ravens will roost at Wulftun and they will be well fed, mark my words."

Lewinna shivers at the intensity of Æmma's conviction. "Their priest made me out to be a whore, predictably, but I had to try."

Æmma's demeanour changes and she smiles at Lewinna. "Their priest is a turd. You did your duty. They made their own choice, the rest is fate."

"Do you think…," Lewinna blurts out. "Do you think all this is going to work?"

"It will only do so if you believe it will, *myne sweostor*," Æmma answers before turning again to continue down the path.

Lewinna sighs as she follows. Like her mother Crawa, Æmma tends to speak enigmatically; winding circles around the point she is making and speaking in riddles, answering questions with questions of her own.

"Did you see Yrre?" Æmma asks cheerfully. "Is he still a Christian?"

"*Já*, and still as dull as a swine's rear-end, though slightly less intelligent."

"Shame, he would be welcomed at the Beltane fires."

"Æmma!!"

"What?" Æmma laughs. "He wouldn't be needed for his conversational skills, dullards can be useful in other ways."

Lewinna laughs as well, if only to break the tension that has been building up in her all day.

Tendrils of mist start rising from the moist earth when the path evens out into the vale. It's barely noticeable at first, but before long they are wading through a ground fog and there is no more time for jesting, as the girls have to focus in order not to trip on the uneven pathways.

Occasional glances tell Lewinna that the yew trees here are far older. Massive in their circumference, many of the old trunks have started rotting but have been ringed by younger trunks rising high like the stately columns of the old Roman temple in Odesburh. Humongous boughs have been dragged down by their own weight, curving down to the ground only to branch out and rise again, the most recent siblings of the original yew seeming to dance in a circle around their parent.

Æmma leads them into the ponderous embrace of one of the yew trees. The path underneath the curved boughs winds into another such yew-limbed dome, and then another. They appear to be circling inwards, shielded now by a veritable tunnel of yew.

"We're in *Heorttreów's* embrace," Æmma says, "not long now."

There is bright light ahead. After walking through the odd twilight of Wiccanhyrst, Lewinna is dazzled when they step into a large round clearing devoid of mist and awash in sunlight. She blinks, trying to take in the spectacle that greets her. Her eyes are first drawn to what can only be the *Heorttreów*, the largest tree Lewinna has ever seen, rising tall in the middle of the clearing. The massive circumference of the yew is hard to comprehend. The main trunk has been hollowed out by time and rot. The size of the hollow is emphasized by the tall standing stone which rises within. The stone reminds Lewinna of the stone circle at Stonley. New trunks have formed around the old tree, but they too are gnarled by age, as are the giant boughs curving down around *Heorttreów*.

Taking a deep breath, Lewinna tears her eyes away from the magnificent yew to cast a curious look at the many people gathered around the giant tree. They are all women and girls. Seven of them are dressed in black woollen robes and black cloaks, including Crawa. Lewinna knows the other six women too, there's Cille from Thurgisham and others from both Thurgisham and Rorianford. Lewinna recognises some of those who have not donned the black robes, like Cille's daughter Elswide, and Lufe and Tova, thirteen-year-old twins from Rorianford. Yet most are people Lewinna has never seen before, dressed in strange clothes, some resembling the familiar *Seaxe* tunics, but others outlandish to her eyes. Some wear long trousers even, tight ones or loose and baggy. Lewinna is close enough to the nearest of them to overhear their conversations, spoken in a strange but somehow familiar language.

The talk dies down when the newcomers are spotted, replaced by a few reverent whispers and curious admiration which make Lewinna feel awkward. All these people clearly know who she is, even if she is left puzzled by their origins.

"*Wass-hael* Lewinna Wulfgardohter! *Frowe* of Wyrdwuda," Crawa calls out by the base of *Heorttreów*, partially concealed by the shade of the yew's multiple trunks and curved lower boughs.

Lewinna and Æmma walk towards her. Like Æmma, Crawa's face is framed by long red hair. The hair colour isn't common in Suth-Seaxe. The women's gossip in Wyrdwuda is that the *Wicce* is descended from the *Wealsh* tribe which had inhabited the woodlands before the *Seaxe* crossed the Narrow Sea. Lewinna isn't sure how old Crawa is, but she has fine lines around her eyes and mouth and grey hair at her temples. Lewinna knows from experience that Crawa's face can crease with merry laughter, or emphasise stern authority.

"*Wass-hael* Crawa, *Wicce* of Wyrdwuda," Lewinna greets Crawa when they halt in front of her.

"You are welcome at *Heorttreów*, Lewinna Wulfgardohter," Crawa declares formally.

Lewinna glances at the yew tree, even more formidable now that she is so close. "I am honoured to be here. *Ic thee thanci* – I thank you, *Frowe* Crawa."

Crawa drops the formality. "And you're later than I hoped for." The *Wicce* gestures outwards. "There will be no time for formal introductions."

Lewinna turns to see that the other black-robed women are distributing white shifts to the others. "Who are they Crawa? Where are they from?"

"I called, they answered," Crawa says, before casting her eyes on her daughter. "Æmma, *myne maeden* – my girl, can you fetch Lewinna's things?"

"*Jā Mōdor* – Mother."

"How? Who?" Lewinna asks. "I am beholden to them."

"*Jā*, that you are. And in time, some may call on you for help. Will you be prepared to answer their call when that time comes?"

"Of course, if I live that long. But…?"

"Always impatient to know things, ever since you were a little girl." Crawa paradoxically tut-tuts with proud approval. "There …are…were…will-be… many devoted to the guardianship of Wyrdwuda, *myne maeden*. They all have their own battles to fight, sometimes with help from the others. All have been chosen by Niada, *Frowe* Seolforswan. She who performed the rites of renewal with the great Myrrdin himself."

"Myrrdin?" Lewinna spits on the ground to avert evil, and for good measure grasps her Meolo amulet. The *Wealsh* wizard's name is used still, along with that of the Draka and the dark monster Ulemanna, in that time-honoured tradition of composing songs and stories designed to impress and terrify young children. Her father's retainers have taught Lewinna a few coarse and colourful phrases as well, to describe the old and feared enemy Myrrdin, most of them related to sexual perversions, and Lewinna utters one of them now.

Æmma, returning with various bundles, laughs heartily, as does Crawa.

"It is partially true," Crawa says. "Myrrdin was overly fond of the fertility festivals, but I assure you he didn't attend them because of a special interest in goats. His name is honoured in some places…there where other rules apply…," Crawa's arm sweeps the clearing.

Lewinna nods, thinking about the Unseen her father had spoken of, the realms beyond the visions of most folk, places where the likes of the *Wealsh* Myrrdin and *Saexe Wiccan* can walk as allies, stalking a different kind of foe, a common foe to all folk. She looks around the circle of girls and women around the *Heorttreów*; they are all changing into white shifts like the one Æmma is wearing.

"Time to get dressed," Crawa says.

Lewinna's eyes grow wide as Æmma retrieves a folded rectangle of shining mail from one of the bundles and shakes it out into an open-ended mail coat.

Crawa bundles Lewinna's hair and secures it into a tail with a length of string. Lewinna stares at the rarity in Æmma's hands. In Wyrdwuda, Lewinna's father is the only person to own a mail coat, but its iron rings seem dull in comparison to this one. Cruder as well, for the coat in Æmma's hands is an exquisite piece of work although it looks far too delicate for the brunt of battle.

"*Seolfor* – Silver," Æmma clarifies. "Useless in a *scild-burh*, but it might dazzle a few Draka into submission."

"It will not protect you from the Draka," Crawa says. "But it will keep you safe from other foes in the Ghaestdenn. Hold out your arms."

Lewinna shivers as she thinks of the *Nihtgengan*.

Æmma and Crawa help Lewinna push her arms through the mail coat's sleeves. Crawa ties together the leather laces at the back of the coat whilst Æmma holds up her friend's ponytail to keep Lewinna's hair from entangling with the small silver ringlets. The mail coat seems to fit perfectly, though it causes the Meolo amulet to poke sharply against her chest, so Lewinna lifts it out to wear it over the mail. She is amazed at the relative lack of weight. She had secretly tried on her father's mail coat once, only to be nearly dragged down to the ground because of its great weight, much to her father's merriment.

"So all of these strangers, they were...are *Waerwyrd?*" She asks, referring to the Guardians of Wyrdwuda.

"Or similar, *jā*," Crawa confirms. "And all those I summoned came."

The *Wicce* starts to recite a list of names, some familiar to the *Seaxe* ear, others strange: "Ellette, Līzzie, Bettie, Særah, Prīs, Æsc..."

Æmma produces a stout plain leather belt and secures it around Lewinna's waist. "*Nafath aenig mann freonda to fela* – no one can have too many friends."

Crawa rummages in the pile of bundles. "...Wēnn, Djēy, Djōy, Anna, Mēsie, Rōse...and more. All came."

A *grimhelm* appears from one of the bundles, bright even in the shade. The helm, cheek-pieces, fixed half-visor, and neck-guard are all covered with intricately decorated silver foils. The crown of the helmet is protected by a ridge which ends with a stunningly fashioned silver swan's neck and head, rising above the eye-holes of the visor.

"Oh!" Is all Lewinna can say.

"A *grimhelm* fit for a Queen, a *heregrima* – war-mask, to drive fear into your enemy's heart." Crawa places a leather cap on Lewinna's head. "A gift to you from *Frowe* Seolforswan, as is the mail."

Æmma places the helm on Lewinna's head and fastens the chin-straps. "The Draka will go mad with greed and desire."

Those words bring Lewinna out of the daze of wonder she has experienced ever since she has arrived at *Heorttreōw*. Paling at the thought of the approaching Draka, Lewinna peers out at the clearing. It is odd at first, to behold the world through the eyeholes of the *grimhelm's* half-visor. She can see most of what is happening in the clearing right in front of her, but has to turn her head to perceive what has hitherto always been provided by the corner of her eyes or a side glance.

Barring the black-robed women, everyone else is now dressed in white shifts, with white bands tied about their waists. The black-robed women move around, inserting leafy twigs into the bands.

Looking at Æmma, Lewinna sees that she is fastening a similar band around her waist, Crawa standing by with a handful of twigs.

"Hazel," Crawa explains, "for protection. You won't need it, as you are wearing *Frowe* Seolforswan's armour. Tell me, Lewinna, who do you pray to?"

"Mostly Frig and Ēostre."

"Good," Crawa says as she starts poking hazel twigs into Æmma's waist band. "But on this day it may help to say a few words to Thunor, Tiw, and Hel."

"The Gods of Thunder and War," Æmma adds rather needlessly, "and the Goddess of Death."

"I will do so," Lewinna says.

Æmma presents a round shield, made of wicker with a leather covering and a thin iron rim. It depicts a white dragon on a red field, the Dragon of all *Seaxe* folk, East, *Suth*, and West.

"You are not only fighting for Wyrdwuda today," Crawa says, "but for Suth-Seaxe and the Kingdom of West-Seaxe. You owe your fealty to King Ælfred."

Lewinna nods as Æmma helps her slip her left arm into the leather loops at the back of the shield.

"And finally...," Crawa lifts up a scabbarded sword. The scabbard is decorated with deep red velvet and silver thread. The sword's guard and pommel are finely decorated too, and the grip wound with leather strips.

"Not the scabbard," Lewinna says. Wulfgar's retainers had frequently mentioned that they discarded their scabbards in a fight, to avoid tripping over it in the heat of battle.

Crawa nods her approval, holding out the grip to Lewinna. The girl draws the sword out reverently, because swords have a magic of their own and demand due respect. Released of the sheath's embrace the weight of the sword feels perfect in her hand. It is longer than a saex, but not as long as Wulfgar's sword. Lewinna swings it experimentally, pleased to find it has a good balance.

"Does it have a name?" She asks.

"No, it is new, Wulfgar had it made for you," Æmma says.

"Did he?"

"Just in case you would need it one day," Crawa confirms. "It is for you to name it."

Lewinna raises the blade, her father's most generous gift, and points it at the sky, marvelling at its perfection. "I shall call her... *Wælcyrie* – Valkyrie."

"*Wælcyrie*. Maiden of Battles and Chooser of the Slain," Æmma says thoughtfully. "It is an apt choice, Lewinna."

"It is an excellent choice," Crawa says. "Just remember, Lewinna, that *Frowe* Seolforswan's armour protects you against the Unseen, not so much against either Draka blade or axe."

"I know that you've had some sword training," Æmma says. "But don't go charging the Draka."

"I know," Lewinna says. "I know my role."

Crawa steps back and admires Lewinna. "You look every inch the warlord. If the folk of Wyrdwuda see you today, they will know they have a chieftain ready to defend them."

"If..." Lewinna answers.

"*Wyrd bið ful aræd*," Crawa says, and the girls answer as one: "*Wyrd bið wended hearde.*"

"It's time, it's time," Crawa says with a sudden burst of renewed urgency. "The Draka are coming. A last embrace *myne maedens* – my girls."

Æmma and Lewinna take turns in giving Crawa a hug.

"Wulfgar would be bursting with pride if he could see you now," Crawa murmurs into Lewinna's ear as she clasps the girl to her bosom. "*Bēo gesund*, Lewinna."

"*Thancas*," Lewinna answers softly. "*Bēo gesund*, Crawa."

When she lets go of Crawa, Lewinna finds Æmma in front of her, spreading her arms out and the girls clasp each other in a tight embrace.

"Let's get started," Crawa says. "May Ēostre watch over you."

§ § § § § § §

Crawa steps out of the partial privacy granted them by *Heorttreōw's* shadow-play and takes a few strides into the sunlight. She raises her arms to the sky, and the folk in the clearing grow silent.

"I call upon all the Gods to bear witness...," Crawa speaks, letting her voice ring loud, "...to this day in Wyrdwuda. For on this day, we question the right of an invader to be here, on our soil, in our woods. A new champion of the Wyrdwuda arises: Lewinna Wulfgardohter!"

Æmma gives Lewinna a gentle shove. "Go, *myne sweostor*, strut like a peacock. Pretend you're Yrre."

Lewinna Wulfgardohter starts to walk towards Crawa's beckoning hand. The weight of her armour is unfamiliar, but feels manageable. Its magic must be working because Lewinna walks with a confident stride, suddenly a lot more sure about the outcome of her task. She feels like she can take on the whole world.

"Lewinna Fréodohtor – freeborn daughter." Crawa continues.

Lewinna Fréodohtor reaches Crawa and comes to a halt.

"Lewinna Seolforhelm!" Crawa bows her head, takes a step to the side, her hands outstretched to Lewinna. The women and girls cheer briefly before waiting in expectant silence.

Lewinna Seolforhelm raises *Wælcyrie* in the air. A ray of sunlight seems to dance upon her, dazzling her as the armour, helm, and sword explode into brilliance. There is absolute silence, and Lewinna realises she should say something inspirational to bolster courage, but she cannot find any words, none whatsoever. How do you encourage people to walk into danger and possible death?

A rising panic threatens to overcome Lewinna, fed by the prospect of ruining this important moment. Thinking fast, Lewinna resorts to the war-talk she has come to know so well from eavesdropping in her father's hall. She shouts: "The Draka have come like cowards. The Draka think we are helpless. When the Draka find out we are not helpless, they will fart with fright and then soil their *aerse-endan* with their own turds!"

Æmma bursts out in laughter behind Lewinna. "They will *skitte* themselves. You tell them, *sweostor*!"

Lewinna punches *Wælcyrie* into the air. "Then we will rip out their stinking guts and feed the Ravens. We will be Raven-feeders. Raven-feeders for Wyrdwuda!"

There are cheers and the call is taken up: "For Wyrdwuda!"

Lewinna looks at Crawa questioningly. The *Wicce* shakes her head in mock disapproval, but her eyes are laughing. Then she raises her arms again, turning slowly to face *Heorttreów*. The other six women clad in black drift around the expansive tree, forming a wide circle with their backs to everybody.

Lewinna feels her friend's hand on her shoulder.

"Come," Æmma says, "it's time; we must go."

They move towards the clearing's entrance as Crawa begins to sing.

> *Mod sceal thee mare,*
> *thee ure mægen lytlath.*

The other six around the tree answer in unison.

> *Beam sceal on eorthan,*
> *Leafum lidan,*
> *Leomu gnornian.*
> *Fus sceal feran,*
> *Fæge sweltan.*

Crawa picks up her lines again, and the song is repeated as Lewinna and Æmma walk into the rising mist that greets them on the winding path which takes them away from *Heorttreów*, followed by the other white-clad women and girls, Lewinna's *maedens*.

§ § § § § § §

Æmma doesn't lead them back to the Úlehús, but takes a different path which winds its way south through the Wiccanhyrst, straight towards the dreaded Ghaestdenn. To her surprise Lewinna, continues to hear Crawa and her black-robed companions sing as loud as if she had still been at *Heorttreów*.

"Æmma?"

"In a moment, come stand here with me," Æmma answers and draws Lewinna aside. As the others pass, quick introductions are made, allowing Lewinna to put faces to the names of Crawa's earlier roll-call. Most just state their names, smile at Lewinna's *"thancas,"* and murmur what sounds like a short encouragement for the task at hand. A few say more words, leaving Lewinna with nothing but a responsive smile to communicate with. She is unable to understand them, but perceives the positive tones.

One girl, whose lack of height seems to belie her real age, launches into a stream of cheerful chatter until she is pulled away by her apologetic, red-headed companion who reminds Lewinna of Æmma. Another, one of the women Lewinna had earlier seen wearing long trousers, steps forward to give Lewinna a brief hug. She murmurs gratitude whilst her young companion, the youngest girl in the company, beams cheekily at Lewinna with a mixture of pleasure and awe.

Lewinna and Æmma form the rearguard when the last have passed. The singing is still loud in Lewinna's ears.

"I couldn't understand most of them," Lewinna confesses.

"I will teach you the basic of their tongue," Æmma promises. "The one who hugged you…"

"Wēnn? Is that right?"

"Jā, that is right. She was thanking you for saving her daughter Djēy. Before that, the short girl…"

"Mēsie?"

"Jā. Mēsie was recounting one of the times you two fought shoulder to shoulder, like *scild-burh* brothers."

"Æmma, I haven't done any of these things!"

"You will."

"But Æmma, how…if…when?"

"Time is a funny thing," Æmma says as if that explains it all, then indicates the air above them with a finger. "Ah, the drums. About time."

Lewinna cocks her head and then she too can hear drumming, a deep bass rhythm accompanied by lighter and faster patterns setting a beat for the songs she can still hear.

"You can hear the singing as well?" Lewinna asks.

"Of course," Æmma answers. "Listen!"

Lewinna can hear a chant fusing into the musical whole; it sounds like a great many women and children singing.

Sitte ge, sigewif,
Sigath to eorthan,
Næfre ge wilde
To Wyrdwuda fleogan.

"Æmma..?"

"We're all together now, Lewinna, all the folk in Wyrdwuda. *Hédan* – heed! The *Waerwyrd* Guardians circle Heorttreów and sing for *Frowe* Seolforswan. *Hédan!* The menfolk and boys light a fire in the centre of the Stonley circle. They drum to summon the sky. *Hédan!* The womenfolk and children are deep within Eostre's Cleofa, where they gather around and dip their hands in the cold water of Ēostre's Spryng and chant to summon the earth."

"But I can hear it all so loud, just as if they were here...?"

"They are here." Æmma supplies one of her mysterious smiles. "I told you, Lewinna, we're all together now, and will be until this day comes to an end."

"Or else I've gone *wéding* – mad," Lewinna suggests.

The sound of a solitary flute mingles with singing, chanting, and drumming. Its tune is melancholic and martial at once, with deep, unearthly, pure notes. Æmma looks surprised at first, but then her face becomes one of pure delight. Out of sheer joy, she clasps an arm around Lewinna's shoulders and plants a kiss on her cheek. "*Hédan!* The *Aelf-folc* – Elf folk! The *Wylde-elfen* of Wyrdwuda hear us and join us!"

"That's it, I have definitely gone *wéding*."

"There'll be far worse things to get your head around in the Ghaestdenn," Æmma says. "Just remember, anything that isn't a Draka will not harm you. Do not fear them; do not try to harm them. Any other day, run like Grendel himself is chasing you, but not today."

"The *Nihtgengan*." Lewinna shivers.

"Today they'll be as sweet as a handsome young farmer with a belly full of mead at a Beltane fire," Æmma promised.

"I'll take your word for it."

Æmma stops and grasps Lewinna's hands, pulling Lewinna around to face her. "*Myne sweostor*, are you sure you are ready for this? The folk are safe, the Draka will not find them. Wulftun is lost at any rate, and beyond that they might torch Rorianford. But your folk are concealed; the Draka will never find them. We can still withdraw into safety."

Lewinna looks her friend in the eyes. Is she ready? Is anybody ever ready for a moment like this? Her father thinks she is, otherwise he would not have nominated her to rule in his stead during his absence. Aldred, the wisest man she knows, thinks she is ready and follows her lead. The *Waerwyrd* Guardians, women who have known Lewinna since her birth, have deemed her ready. Crawa has so much confidence that she has summoned help from far away and told Lewinna that Niada Seolforswan herself held Wulfgar's daughter in high esteem.

Thinking on this, Lewinna feels strength spread within her like a tide. Raedan and Yrre can doubt her qualities all they want – but who are they in comparison to all these fine folk who so clearly believe in her? The Wulftun men are just self-righteous and small-minded fools. Lewinna takes a deep breath. *Thunor, Tiw, and Hel, hear me now, heed me as I go to meet my destiny. Wyrd bið ful arǣd.*

"Come, Æmma," Lewinna says. "We must catch up with the others, *myne sweostor*. The Draka are coming, and there are ravens to feed."

§ § § § § § §

A number of long, broad vales mark the boundary between Wiccanhyrst and Ghaestdenn. The vales are called Fernsæ. Few trees grow there. Fernsæ is home to dense colonies of tall common cotton and bracken growing waist high, if not higher, though now much of it is concealed in the mist that has thickened and risen. The day's sunlight is broken as clouds are drifting in from the south, the horizon is dark with them, and there are ominous rumblings in the sky as the wind picks up.

Lewinna's *maedens* emerge from the Wiccanhyrst and assemble along the yew woodland edge. Lewinna and Æmma are the last to appear. In front of them, they find the greybeards and *frumbyrdlings*. The menfolk are not recognizable, for they have transformed into Herne's Wild Hunt, their faces are blackened and they are swathed in black and brown capes and hoods. They carry yew bows, filled quivers, axes, saexes, and each has a horn. All are liberally adorned with hazel twigs. Lewinna identifies Aldred by his great bow, and walks towards him in *Frowe* Seolforswan's war-finery.

"*Wælcyrie*," one of the men whispers hoarsely, and it is taken up by the others. "*Wælcyrie. Wælcyrie!*"

They sink onto one knee and bow their heads, Aldred included. Lewinna is delighted that they perceive a Valkyrie, but feels awkward with the obeisance.

She bends forwards to lay her hands on Aldred's shoulders. "Please rise, *myne frēond*." She turns to the others, "Rise, *frēondan*, there is work to do for Wyrdwuda."

"For Wyrdwuda!" Æmma punches a fist into the air. The battle cry is taken up: "For Wyrdwuda!"

Lewinna strides purposefully towards the bracken. She is prepared for a struggle. There are no paths other than animal tracks and the ground will be soft and boggy between the harder knolls from which bracken and grass sprout. Moreover, the mist is so dense that she can barely see the ground at all. To her concern, she discerns vague movement by her feet.

Reminding herself of Crawa and Æmma's council not to fear anything other than the Draka on this day, Lewinna continues to stride forward. She is surprised she doesn't encounter any resistance whatsoever, no knolls for her feet to contend with, the bracken fronds parting to allow her passage. All around her, the others too are moving through Fernsæ without trouble.

They enter the Ghaestdenn, ranks of pale birch trees looming out of the mist. The singing, drumming, flute play, and chanting continues unabated, added to by the caws from rooks and crows, as well as the chatter of jackdaws, all of which roost in the Ghaestdenn in large numbers.

Lewinna can hear the Waerwyrd Guardians sing.

Beam sceal on eorthan, leafum lipan, leomu gnornian –
A tree on the earth must lose its leaves, the branches mourn.

Lewinna strides forwards through the feared Ghaestdenn without hesitation. Here too, her feet find a path wherever she walks even though the fog blocks out her view of the forest floor. Æmma and Aldred are close at hand, but the others begin to spread out.

Fus sceal feran, fæge sweltan –
Those who are ready must go, the doomed die.

The drumbeats increase in intensity. The singers and chanters speed up too. Crawa sings.

Mod sceal thee mare, thee ure mægen lytlath –
Mind must be the greater, as our strength diminishes.

Lewinna grins as she repeats those words. It is indeed a matter of mind now. If they tried to form a *scild-burh*, the Draka would batter through it without even making an effort, and the Wyrdwuda defenders would be slaughtered en masse. So they must use other weapons to achieve the impossible, a different way to ensure the Draka would end the day as raven-food.

The women deep in the earth's womb at Ēostre's Cleofa chant.

> *Sitte ge, sigewif, sigath to eortha –*
> *Settle down war-wives, go aground.*

Crawa had explained her plan in detail when Lewinna and Aldred had visited her the previous day, after the Odesburh messenger had sped on to spread the alarming news that the Draka might be coming.

Lewinna hadn't understood everything Crawa had described, inevitably enigmatic as some of Crawa's words had been, but the girl knows the *Nihtgengan* are likely to be trailing their progress through Ghaestdenn.

> *Næfre ge wilde to Wyrdwuda fleogan –*
> *Never be wild and fly to Wyrdwuda.*

The sky starts to darken as clouds drift over Wyrdwuda, blocking it from the sun's view. The mist intensifies, growing denser and higher. The crows and rooks caw their encouragement at Lewinna and her companions, rather than flocking up in startled alarm as a warning that untoward things are moving through Ghaestdenn.

Some of Lewinna's companions come to a halt, both *maedens* and wild hunters. They will wait amidst birch, aspen and alder, whych elm, and blackthorn, until it is time to resume their part.

Before long, they are only seven strong, Lewinna in the centre, flanked by Æmma and Aldred who in turn are flanked by Mēsie and Djōy on one side, and on the other side two *maedens* who had introduced themselves as Anna and Rōse.

The singing, drumming and chanting, hypnotic in repetition, begin to fade and even the mist seems to be dispersing. Lewinna falls into a careful crouch as she moves forward, seeking out the cover of Ghaestdenn as she senses they must be nearing Innanley. For a short while, they will be on their own.

They hear Innanley before they see it. Loud shouts and then the unmistakable clash of metal against metal, roars, screams of pain.

The four *maedens* melt away in the undergrowth. Lewinna, Æmma and Aldred rush forward, hastening to the last concealment offered by the undergrowth of Ghaestdenn. When Innanley comes into her view, Lewinna sees a grim spectacle that leaves her breathless, her heart pounding in her chest.

There are a great many men and a few women on the crossing: Draka. The raiders' faces are partially concealed, shaded by the long nose guards of their steel helmets, or else half-visors covering their upper face. The men have frumptious beards, woven into braids and decorated with iron beard rings. They wear mail or leather armour, and are further clad in furs. Many carry round, iron-rimmed shields. Some have bare upper arms almost wholly covered in tattoos depicting either sinuous dragons and serpents or stylised wolves and bears.

There are about two score Draka on the crossing, with another similarly sized party coming up the Æcerweg. There has been a brief fight, which is reaching its conclusion. Broken and bleeding bodies lay scattered on the hard dirt, some of them mere boys and none of them Draka. Lewinna can see Raedan, one of the last Wulftun men standing, desperately attempting to fend off three Draka at once, and failing. A sword thrust bypasses his defences, the blade sinking into the old man's chest. Then a swung axe cleaves into his skull, and Raedan crumples to the ground.

"*Nā! Fæder! Fæder!*" Yrre comes charging to his father's side, resplendent in his war-gear but giving no thought to his approach. His is the furious blind charge of an enraged bull, and he plunges straight into four waiting spear blades.

Lewinna clenches her teeth as she sees the almost comically surprised look on Yrre's face. He coughs, and then blood rushes out of his mouth in a great stream. The Draka wrench their spears loose out of his chest and belly, and Yrre sinks to the ground as the life in his eyes fades.

Of Wulftun's men, greybeards, and *frumbyrdlings*, only Wynnstan is still alive. The priest screams and begs for mercy as the Draka drag him to an oak tree on the other side of the Æcerweg. The Draka laugh, some imitate Wynnstan's feeble resistance and pathetic wails, mocking his cowardice. Others retrieve saexes from the fallen Wulftun men and hammer these through the priest's arms to pin him to the tree. Wynnstan howls in agony and reflexively kicks out each time the flat face of a Draka axe blade thuds against the saex hilts. One of the hammering Draka curses loudly when he is kicked hard against the shin by Wynnstan, and other Draka rush in to hammer saex blades through Wynnstan's legs for good measure.

Two ravens sail through the air to settle on a bough just above Wynnstan. They croak and peer down at the screaming priest with beady-eyed interest. Lewinna shudders. She tears herself from the shock which overcame her at seeing Raedan and Yrre slain before her eyes, the brightness of the blood seeping into the dirt around the lifeless bodies, the screams still echoing in her ears. Lewinna recalls Æmma's prediction that ravens would feed on Wulftun's men. She tells herself that it isn't Wulftun which has become a *Ræfen Róst* – A Raven's Roost. Instead, Innanley now bears that burden.

Wynnstan begins to scream anew as the Draka start to carve into him with blades. They seem intent on prolonging the priest's death. Some of the Draka lose interest in Wynnstan's torture and shrill shrieking. Lewinna sees them point at

Wulftun's church tower, calling out to each other in their strange tongue. As the second group on the Æcerweg reaches Innanley, members of the first group start to drift west on the Woldweg, heading for Wulftun.

Lewinna recalls the vivid images her mind's eye had provided earlier this day, the cruel fates of Nihtlícburh and Odesburh. She thinks of the Wulftun women and children praying for salvation in their church, easy and defenceless prey for the Draka. They are Wulfgar's folk, and no matter how much hostility and disobedience they had displayed, they were Lewinna's own folk too. The last shreds of her doubts disappear. Lewinna has arrived too late to do anything for Wulftun's menfolk, but she can save the womenfolk and children from rape and enslavement. All she has to do is draw the Draka away from Wulftun.

"Aldred," Lewinna calls in a low tone, casting an eye on the dark clouds overhead.

"*Myne Frowe?*" Aldred creeps to her side, his face grim.

"Please end the priest's misery."

"*Ja, Myne Frowe.*" Aldred wastes no time. He has already strung his bow, and now notches an arrow to the string before drawing it back to the corner of his mouth. He waits two, three seconds, and then looses the arrow. It flies so fast Lewinna can't see it, but she hears the pluck of the bow string, the swoosh of the wind rustling the fletching, and then the fleshy thud as the arrow strikes home, straight into Wynnstan's heart.

The priest stops screaming and his body slumps against the restraints of the saexes driven through his limbs. Draka voices call out their startled surprise before they turn around to look at the corner of the Ghaestdenn from which the arrow flew.

Countless eyes, shining fiercely on either side of nose guards or through visors, and furious animalistic snarls convey ravenous bloodlust Lewinna has only ever been able to conceive of in nightmares. The day's fretting and worrying loses all meaning. Now that the moment has come, Lewinna decides, it boils down to the very simple act of standing up straight, and then stepping out of the undergrowth into full view of some eighty battle-maddened Draka.

§ § § § § § §

Æmma steps forward to stand beside Lewinna, and together they look at the Draka, who look astonished at the sight of Crawa's *maedens*, one armoured in splendour, the other in a simple white shift.

The Draka ranks part as a tall, broad man strides forward, holding a huge battle axe in his hands. He isn't wearing a helmet, and his shiny, bald skull is covered with serpentined tattoo patterns. Half concealed by a plaited moustache, his mouth is formed into a bare toothed snarl and his icy eyes spit cold fire. His beard reaches down his chest and has been forked with beard rings. A matted bear fur hangs from his shoulders, and his bare, muscled upper arms are tattooed with stylised bear claws. A sword and smaller axe dangle from his belt. The battle axe has a five foot long shaft as thick as Lewinna's forearm. The axe head is double bladed rather than the usual single bearded blade the Draka carry to war. Its face is marked by engravings of intricate decorative patterns encircling Draka runes. Its edges look sharper than an eagle's claws.

The clearing seems bereft of any sound for a moment. Even the ravens have stopped croaking. When Lewinna swings *Wælcyrie* up above her head, she can hear the sword whistle as it cuts through the air.

"I bid you gone," she shouts. "In the name of King Ælfred of West-Seaxe."

The Draka seem to recognise that name, for they growl and take a few steps closer to Ghaestdenn's edge. Their formidable chief spits on the ground and laughs derisively.

"*Ut* – Out! *Ut* of Wyrdwuda." Lewinna roars with anger. "Get your *skitte* faces *ut*! In the name of Thunor…"

The dark clouds above rumble, then everything lights up briefly in blinding light as a bolt of lightning zips down, striking a Ghaestdenn tree mere hundreds of yards behind Lewinna. There is an almighty crash, the ground shakes briefly, and the noise seems to reverberate across the Wyrdwuda for an eternity.

The Draka edge backwards, fumbling for amulets, the names of their Thunder-God Thor and Valkyrie on their lips.

"A bit too effective," Æmma murmurs. "You're meant to draw them into Ghaestdenn, not scare them back to their ships all by yourself."

Lewinna laughs. She has never felt so alive and is delirious that Thunor has chosen to honour her. Nonetheless, her friend is right. "Aldred, three arrows."

Concealed in the undergrowth behind them, Aldred looses the first of the three arrows, followed seconds later by a second, then a third.

The two Draka on either side of the chieftain sink to the ground, fletched arrows protruding from their chests. Aldred's last shot wasn't a clean loose. The arrow deflects from one of the metal plates sewn into the leather of the chieftain's body armour, and then buries itself in a fold of the fur cloak.

The chieftain rips the arrow out of his bear cloak, gnashing his teeth with fury. He holds the arrow up, perhaps to demonstrate to his followers that they are facing mere human foes, whilst he spits out a torrent of words. It ends with a barked command as the chieftain points his axe at the two girls. The Draka charge almost as one, roaring.

"*Ryne* – Run!" Aldred hollers. Lewinna and Æmma turn and flee into the Ghaestdenn as fast as their legs can carry them, followed closely by Aldred. Behind them are eighty enraged Draka in pursuit, hell-bent on killing the archer and capturing the girls and precious armour.

"Well that...worked well," Æmma gasps after a quick backward glance to make sure that the Draka horde are tailing them. Lewinna doesn't dare such a glance, with sword and shield in hand, and less visibility because of the *grimhelm's* visor, running requires her full concentration.

They pass the places where the four *maedens* are concealed.

"Mēsie and Djōy," Aldred hollers as he passes. "*Ryne! Nú –* Now! *Ryne!*"

Æmma shouts, "*ryne* Anna and Rōse! *Ryne!*"

Behind them they can hear the chieftain bellow at his raiders. They are too close for comfort although the seven gain some headway, as all but Lewinna are unencumbered by armour, helmets and shields and her war gear is far lighter in weight than that of the Draka.

The storm rumbles and thunders. Bright flashes light up the dark sky. The seven run back into the mist, low and barely noticeable at first. Then it envelops them as does the harmony between song, chant, flute-play, and drums.

They start to pass the others. Already warned by Draka yells and the drumming of Draka feet, these *maedens* and wild hunters are up on their feet and fall in pace with Lewinna for a while before dispersing left and right.

Æmma cautions Lewinna to slow down. The Draka are losing speed, encumbered by the lack of visibility and unseen roots and rocks tripping them up. It becomes a deadly game of catch, with Lewinna's companions moving through the Ghaestdenn effortlessly, pausing to taunt their pursuers just long enough to enrage them into further headlong pursuit, deeper and deeper into the Ghaestdenn.

The drumming speeds up to a frenetic pace, followed by the rest, the flute oddly playful now, and all song becoming a fast chant as the women at *Heorttreów* and Eostre's Cleofa rap their words. Crawa is the exception. She whispers her lines. She screams them out. She moans them in fevered frenzy. She howls them as if she is a wolf. She whimpers them as final words spoken on a death-bed. She barks them like a rutting stag. She loads them with seductive promise. She hisses, croons, screeches, cajoles, and ululates.

"*Nú*, it is time," Aldred says, and they halt by a whych elm.

Lewinna looks around. Æmma is still with them, as are Anna and Rōse, but apart from a few flitting shadows in the mist there is no sign of the others. A score of Draka are on still on their trail, but to judge by Draka shouting and cursing, the rest have spread out over a considerable distance. The raiders are following glimpses they catch of a girl in a white shift, always skipping away into the mist when the Draka get too close. Or disappearing to almost immediately re-appear somewhere different.

"It's working," Lewinna exclaims.

"*Já!*" Æmma's eyes shine. "And there's more to come."

She points at Aldred, who has lifted his horn to his lips and blows three deep blasts into the Ghaestdenn. Other horns answer, one after another and then all together. The nearest Draka stagger to a halt, looking left and right, unsure what surrounds them other than dense fog.

The sky rumbles. Lightning flashes. Thunderclaps echo across Wyrdwuda. The first drops of rain fall down. The horns call out. The Wylde Hunt is let loose. The first arrows fly out of the mist. Shouts of Draka anger are now intermingled with screams of pain.

Ryce comes running through the mist. The *frumbyrdling's* saex blade is red with blood, and he has acquired a round, Draka shield. He is followed at a distance by a dozen Draka driven on by the unmistakable bellow of the bearded chieftain.

"Geirtyr Odderson," Aldred says, nocking an arrow to his bow.

"What?" Lewinna asks.

"The chieftain's name. He was with Guthrum at Werham two years ago, but he first made a name for himself at Readingum fighting for Halfdan Ragnarsson." Aldred draws and looses the arrow in the general direction of the vague shapes pursuing Ryce.

There is a yelp of pain, followed by a stream of curses.

"I know because I was at Readingum, fighting side by side with your father, fighting for the King," Aldred says. "Come, we must be on the move. That larger group is getting closer."

Lewinna's group run again, inspirited by the now frenetic chants and drumming, as well as the knowledge that the fearsome Geirtyr Odderson is not far behind them. They run, turn and taunt, and then run again. The horns sound repeatedly, rain is falling steadily, arrows come spitting out of the mist, Draka keep on tripping over rock and root.

One of the younger and more daring Draka spurts ahead of the others, sprinting towards Lewinna. Anna and Rōse crouch in the mist, each holding the end of a long, sturdy branch. Bent low they rush forwards when the raider comes near and the Draka goes tumbling down in the mist, pounced upon by Ryce wielding his saex. A short scream, and it is over, time to run again.

There are more such screams when arrows pierce Draka, or they stumble and fall to find a wild hunter's saex at their throats. Gradually though, the nature of the screams changes. Something other than *maedens* and wild hunters awaits some of the Draka who trip over unseen obstacles...or are wrenched down. Something far worse, to judge by the sound of the anguished shrieks of terror and screeches of prolonged pain.

Lewinna catches a few glimpses of dark, low shapes hurtling through the mist. Fur, scales, feathers, claws, fangs, reptilian eyes, beaks and snouts lined by rows of deadly teeth. The *Nihtgengan* are amongst the pursuers, clawing down Draka right, left, and centre.

Several times, a *Nihtgengan* passes close enough for Lewinna to smell their pungent odour and hear their paws or hooves pounding the ground. Now and then, there is brief eye contact. *Nihtgengan* eyes are unlike any living creature's Lewinna has ever seen. A reddish, glowing film covers their pupils, regardless of the type of creature, and Lewinna is beheld and then rejected as possible prey with a cold and singular calculation that chills the blood in her veins.

When Lewinna's group reaches the Fernsæ, the rain becomes a deluge and all are thoroughly soaked in mere seconds. Aldred curses. Bowstrings are vulnerable to intense rain, and this downpour renders his bow virtually useless.

The mist is fragmented by the heavy rainfall, slowly beaten back to the ground. All along the Fernsæ, Lewinna can see small groups of *maedens* and wild hunters wading through the bracken. Here and there the Draka pursuers are perilously close, but when the first raiders plunge into the Fernsæ the vegetation becomes obstinate, resisting their every move. A few low, dark shapes dart out of Ghaestdenn to disappear beneath the bracken, unerringly making their way to lone Draka who are yanked down, out of sight, leaving only their horrific screams to indicate the location of their dance of death with the *Nihtgengan*.

The pace of the music slows, and the volume diminishes. The singers and chanters and drummers have been at it for a considerable time, and Lewinna doesn't doubt that they are beginning to flag.

"We make our stand here," Æmma shouts as they scramble up the slope leading to Wiccanhyrst. "We make our stand here!"

The cry is repeated up and down the thin line of Wyrdwuda defenders.

Lewinna's group emerges from the Fernsǽ and halts by the edge of the yew woodlands. They turn to view the Fernsǽ. Draka are emerging out of Ghaestdenn, dispersed along a considerable distance just as Lewinna's defenders are. The Draka pause to catch their breath, keeping a wary eye out across the vale. Their numbers appear diminished, about half of what they started out with at Innanley. The largest group, a dozen Draka, are opposite Lewinna. The girl can make out the hulking form of Geirtyr Odderson. He paces up and down, glowering across the Fernsǽ, never ceasing to issue booming orders. The long line of Draka on Ghaestdenn's edge starts to contract, those on the wings coming nearer to close the wider gaps with the centre. The Wyrdwuda defenders mimic the manoeuvre on their side of the vale.

One Draka attempts to rush into the sea of bracken, but when Geirtyr Odderson barks a command at him, the running Draka stops dead in his tracks and slinks back towards his fellows.

"Odderson knows; he's figured it out," Aldred says.

Lewinna takes stock of the Fernsǽ. There are no more people wading through the bracken, and the mist is being beaten down further by the hammering rain. The clouds rumble; there is a flash and thunderclap. In the brief illumination of cold blue light, Lewinna can see *Nihtgengan* scuttling away. The grotesque creatures are using the gaps between the Draka to make their way back into Ghaestdenn before the mist disappears entirely.

One of the wild hunters looses an arrow across the vale, but the arrow spins crazily and then tumbles into the bracken.

"*Skitte!*" Aldred voices Lewinna's thought.

Crawa's voice sings out: "Mind must be the greater, as our strength diminishes."

The drums have slowed to a heart-beat, the Guardians follow Crawa, "Those who are ready must go, the doomed die." The flute player blows a funereal dirge and those around Eostre's Spryng add their chant: "Never be wild and fly to Wyrdwuda."

Lewinna guesses that it's all supposed to mean something, but there seem to be a hundred different ways of interpreting the words. She casts a look over her shoulder into Wiccanhyrst, wondering if more safety lies within. She feels exposed here, in full view of those intent on the capture or death of the Wyrdwuda defenders, half of whom are unarmed womenfolk. The Draka jolt into action across the vale and start forming a number of wedges.

"They'll come across," Aldred promises. "We have humiliated them. If the Draka don't extract revenge, there is no point in them returning to whatever rotting swamp they have sprouted from – they would never live down that they were defeated by women, children and a handful of old men."

Æmma lays a reassuring hand on Lewinna's shoulder. "It's not over yet, *myne sweostor.*"

"Crawa said to make our stand here…," Lewinna says, looking at Geirtyr Odderson striding to the front of the nearest wedge, thundering encouragement at his Draka as if in competition with the rumbles and crashes from the storm clouds. It's an odd thought to have, but Lewinna wonders if Thunor and Thor are one and the same or opposing Gods, now fighting for dominion in the dark sky above their heads.

"*Já*," Æmma says. "Stand fast. She...the Guardians need to know where we are."

Lewinna nods her understanding and shouts as loud as she can. "WE HOLD HERE! WE HOLD HERE! FOR WYRDWUDA! HOLD FAST."

Lewinna tightens her hold on *Wælcyrie* and hefts her shield. She feels wet and cold, but it must be worse for the *maedens* who don't have helmets or hoods to keep their heads dry, nor wear extra coverings to provide at least a bit of warmth. She looks at Æmma, whose usually exuberant, long hair is listless and bedraggled, then at Anna and Rōse who have clutched each other for warmth but are still shivering.

Geirtyr Odderson howls and the Draka wedges start to edge down the slope, slow at first but then gathering speed. The drums beat a faster rhythm, and the flute's melody picks up urgency. Crawa, the Guardians, and the women in Eostre's Cleofa start singing a new verse as one.

Three lifetimes of the yew
For the whole wide world
From its humble beginning
To its violent end.

The Draka plunge into Fernsæ, the flute shrieks, the drums speed up to reach a mad frenzy.

Three lifetimes of the yew...

"The Draka are coming," Ryce says, a tremble in his voice.

They are, but not as they had intended to because their formations break up in the bracken. They slow down, lose cohesion, and a few stumble. The already boggy ground has turned into a quagmire under the rain's onslaught. Mud sucks at Draka boots and the bracken resists their passage, some of the Draka begin to hack at the fronds.

...for the whole wide world...

Odderson seems the least affected; he ploughs through the bracken, still howling his bloodthirst. The chieftain struggles at times but continues to breach the Fernsæ, leaving the other Draka straggling behind him.

...from its humble beginning...

Aldred unstrings his bow and lays it on the ground. He undoes his quiver to throw it next to the bow, and then draws his saex from its scabbard and pulls his axe from his belt.

...to its violent end.

"Odderson is mine," Aldred says. The soot with which he had blackened his face earlier has been partially washed away, leaving the old hunter with black stripes on his grim face.

Æmma joins in the singing.

Three lifetimes of the yew...

Anna and Rōse fall in.

For the whole wide world...

Lewinna and Ryce pick up the song as well.

From its humble beginning to its violent end.

The other defenders join in, one huddle of wet, shivering defiance after another. Soon, the edge of Wiccanhyrst resounds with their voices, becoming one with the voices at Heorttreów and Eostre's Cleofa.

Three lifetimes of the yew for the whole wide world,
From its humble beginning to its violent end.

The clouds still rumble, but the lightning has stopped and the rain, at last, begins to diminish in intensity. Geirtyr Odderson has reached the slope leading up to Wiccanhyrst, and without looking back, rushes towards Lewinna's group with great leaps and bounds.

"*Mōdor*," Æmma says hoarsely. "Be quick."

Lewinna glances at her friend, it's the first time she's heard fear in Æmma voice today.

"*Nú*, Crawa," Lewinna whispers. "*Nú*."

Without warning, Aldred rushes forwards to meet Odderson's attack.

"ODIN!" Odderson hollers as he swings his giant battle axe with both hands.

Aldred seems to slip, but it is a feint allowing him to dodge the arc of the menacing axe, and then leap closer to Odderson, too close for the Draka chieftain to use the axe. Aldred and Odderson collide with a crash, and Aldred sinks his saex into one of Odderson's thighs. The Draka roars with fury and then shakes Aldred off like a cornered bear swipes away a hunting hound. Aldred falls backwards, the saex still buried deep in Odderson's thigh. The chieftain steps forwards, seemingly oblivious to his wound, and lifts his battle axe high above his head.

"*Nā!*" Ryce yells. "*Fæder!*"

Odderson brings the great axe down, aiming straight for Aldred's chest. Aldred lifts his own axe, one hand on the shaft's end and the other on the axe head, thrusting the shaft up to meet Odderson's swing. The shaft breaks on impact, but it slows down the Draka axe head and deflects it so that it buries itself into Aldred's braced forearm, cleaving through leather, skin, and flesh until it strikes bone.

Aldred cries out in pain. Odderson grunts and pulls the axe head's edge out of Aldred's wound, revealing a horrid gash. The Draka's wounded leg buckles, and he stumbles backwards.

Æmma grabs Aldred and pulls him back. Lewinna and Ryce rush forward to place themselves between the hunter and the Draka chieftain. They raise their shields.

Odderson has regained his balance and stares Lewinna straight in the eyes as he slowly draws the Saex out of his thigh without a blink or a whimper.

Behind him, the first of the other Draka raiders begin to emerge from the bracken, making their way up the slope. It is getting lighter as the worst of the storm passes over, reducing the rain to drizzle.

"Ryce! *Scild-burh!*" Lewinna shouts, and Ryce immediately closes in on her to place his shield edge so that it overlaps Lewinna's.

She can hear Aldred groan behind her, but doesn't turn to look, much as she wants to. Instead, she keeps her eyes fixed on Odderson. The Draka chieftain snarls, laughs at their *scild-burh*, and then raises his axe high above his head again. Lewinna stares at the great axe head and tenses her shield arm. Odderson steps forwards, the axe beginning its downward swing.

Quick as thieves, Anna and Rōse slip past Lewinna and Ryce in a crouch. Anna is holding Aldred's great yew bow and passes one end over to Rōse. Holding it low, the *maedens* scurry forwards and trip Odderson, who stumbles and the girls dart away.

The downwards stroke of the axe can't be stopped, but is robbed of much of its power and instead of the sharp edge, the flat face of the axe head impacts the shields. There is a loud crash, and Lewinna feels pain shoot through her shield-arm. She bites on her lip hard enough to draw blood. The axe, bereft of its edge and Odderson's full strength behind it, has still shattered most of Lewinna's shield and splintered part of Ryce's shield.

"Hold the *scild-burh!*" Lewinna shouts, and she and Ryce move closer together to compensate for their battered shields, what is left of the rims still overlapping.

Odderson curses at the two *maedens* who have circled back behind Lewinna and Ryce, throws a murderous look at Lewinna, and then briefly glances backwards to see the first of his Draka followers appearing just behind them, with more starting their journey up the slope. Lewinna can see Draka straggling up towards Wiccanhyrst all along the vale's slopes.

Odderson grins at Lewinna as four Draka raiders flank their leader, forming a shield wall of their own. The grin is full of grim promise, and Lewinna feels her heart sink.

The singing and drumming continues unabated, the unearthly flute wild and manic now. The defenders on the edge of Wiccanhyrst continue singing along, their voices loud and pure.

Three lifetimes of the yew for the whole wide world,
from its humble beginning to its violent end.

Odderson unleashes a stream of words at Lewinna, none of them sounding friendly.

To her surprise, Lewinna feels no fear, not anymore. They tried, did their best, and now it was time for the doomed to die. She feels a strange calm within, dulling even the throbbing pain in her shield arm. The clouds above break open and sunshine streams upon the Fernsæ. Never has the warming caress of the sun felt more welcome.

Lewinna smiles at Odderson and says: "*Wyrd bið ful aræd.*"

"*Wyrd bið wended hearde,*" Aldred voice sounds weakly behind her.

"It has begun," Æmma says inexplicably.

The Draka start beating their swords against their shields. Lewinna grins, because she can see that even Odderson has lost the confidence of having an easy prey and regards her warily.

Lewinna grips *Wælcyrie's* hilt and crouches behind her tattered shield, holding the sword close by her side, ready to parry or strike. Ryce's side presses into hers, and she can feel how tense he is.

"Your *fæder* is watching you," she says to Ryce. "Make him proud."

Ryce nods, and Lewinna can feel some of the pressure melt away.

Odderson shouts a command, and the Draka make to step forwards, halted almost immediately. They look down at their feet. Lewinna follows their gaze.

"The Dryads are here," Æmma explains. "I told you it's started."

The earth around the Draka's feet has sprouted tendrils, thin as hairs and pale as ghosts. The strands rise up, tentatively exploring the air before surging towards Draka boots, where they coil upwards fast as snakes. More and more new sprouts rise from the wet earth to start spiralling towards the Draka. Their boots look like they are covered in fine spider's silk. No matter how hard the Draka try to wrench themselves loose they seem incapable of breaking free. They start to hack at the strands around their feet with their swords, Odderson with his axe, but for every strand they cut, three more start their winding course around Draka boots, and then Draka legs.

Lewinna heaves a deep sigh and her tension eases up a little, although she remains alert. The drumming works towards a climax. The singing voices are filled with triumph.

All the Draka stretched out along the Fernsæ's slopes have lost interest in their quarry, hacking, cursing, and shouting at the strands instead. These start thickening along their base, growing string-sized, and the Draka become ever more entwined. Lewinna watches with wide eyes as the threadlike tips start creeping up and around thighs. The first Draka begin to panic.

The drums and singing stops; only the flute continues to play a melancholy tune.

Deeming it to be safe, Lewinna turns to look at Aldred. He is propped up between Anna and Rōse, who are supporting him. His pale face looks tired beyond his already considerable years, and beads of sweat stand out on his forehead. Æmma is crouched next to Aldred. She has taken off her waist band and is using it to staunch the wound. Hazel twigs are spread about her feet.

"*Fæder?*" Ryce too has turned.

"Eyes to the front," Aldred says.

Both Lewinna and Ryce turn around again, to see the Draka raiders' unnatural dances as they wrestle with the strands and strings whilst steadily losing control of their lower bodies.

"If I die, Ryce," Aldred tells his son. "I will vouch in Waelhalla that I saw you stand in a *scild-burh* and hold your ground. You are a man now."

Ryce swells up with pride. Lewinna snorts. She can't help but turn again. "What does that make me then, because I can vouch that I haven't suddenly sprouted a pair of hairy balls."

Aldred smiles at her through his pain. "*Frowe* of Wyrdwuda, mistress of eloquence."

"Enough of the dramatics," Æmma says. "You will live a while longer old man, if you stop talking long enough for me to treat you."

Aldred nods weakly. Æmma casts a concerned look at Anna and Rōse. The two *maedens* are staring wide-eyed at the root-bound, twisting and shouting Draka raiders.

"Anna, Rōse," Æmma says, and then instructs the *maedens* in their own tongue. They pull up Aldred's cloak and bunch it behind him, then carefully lower him so that his head rests against the makeshift pillow. After that, they run into Wiccanhyrst.

"I told them to collect a dozen long branches. We need to build a stretcher and take Aldred to the Úlehús," Æmma tells Lewinna before taking Aldred's knife and cutting a broad strip from the end of her shift, which she uses to bandage Aldred's torn arm.

One of the Draka begins to scream, a high-pitched squeal.

Lewinna and Æmma share a glance.

"You don't have to look," Æmma says.

Lewinna shakes her head. Wulfgar has taught her to always face the consequences of her actions. She turns around.

The roots have continued to advance upwards, getting ever thicker at ground level. The tips are winding about hips and stomachs now and tightening their hold, squeezing as they expand. One of the Draka has dropped his sword and ineffectually claws at the roots with his hands until they too are encircled and then drawn tightly to his body. Blood is seeping out between the few narrow gaps in the lower mass of roots.

Odderson however, is still swinging his fierce axe in broad swathes, managing to cut a great many strands. Lewinna can see veins pulsating on his forehead and bare skull as the Draka struggles hard, jerking his legs with furious bursts to slow the roots' progress. Lewinna recalls how he had ploughed through the bracken and fears he might work himself free. She crouches, waits for the axe to be mid-swing when even Odderson can't stop the momentum, and then springs, thrusting *Wælcyrie* at the Draka's arm. The sword pierces through the tattoo of a snarling bear and then sinks into Odderson's flesh. He roars and drops the axe. Lewinna ducks and then scuttles backwards to avoid the Draka's other arm, his hand formed into a formidable fist.

Odderson bares his teeth and then hurls curses at Lewinna. She stares at him, weathering his expletives. Without his axe, the Draka is unable to stop the tide, and roots are curling up his legs in ever-greater numbers.

Æmma screams.

Lewinna turns to see that scores of threads have wound around Æmma's ankles. They tug, then jerk and pull Æmma off balance, onto the ground where she is immediately grasped by dozens more.

Odderson barks laughter.

"Nā!" Lewinna shouts.

The root tips curl around her friend's arms and legs, slither across her belly, get entangled in her hair, and start to explore Æmma's shoulders and neck.

Æmma struggles, but the more she tries to move, the tighter the roots wind around her. She stares at Lewinna with wide eyes and open mouth, incomprehension on her face.

"What's happening?" Aldred calls, trying to prop himself up on his healthy arm.

Odderson laughs again, then roars at his men. The screamer has stopped, but the other ones shout and yell in panic.

"Lewinna!" Ryce rushes to Lewinna's side. "The hazel! The hazel!"

Lewinna understands at once, shakes off the remnants of her shield, and falls to her knees next to Æmma. She scrambles for the hazel twigs which littered the ground after Æmma had untied her waist band to begin treating Aldred. For a terrifying moment, emerging root tips reach out for her before recoiling when they come too close to the silver ringlets of the mail coat.

Æmma screams again, but this time the scream is cut off and she starts wheezing, gasping for breath. The roots which have wound themselves around Æmma's chest and belly have begun to expand in size, constricting her breathing. Thin thread-like tips have circled the girl's throat like skeletal fingers clawing out of a grave.

Odderson roars with laughter, then shouts some Draka words, his tone rich with sarcasm.

"Ryce, here!" Lewinna thrusts two handfuls of hazel twigs and dirt into Reece's hands. "Apply them to her neck, quick."

While Ryce does so, Lewinna moves both arms so that the lower part of the mail sleeves sweep over the writhing mass of roots enveloping Æmma's rump. There is a hiss, and the roots start pulling back, disentangling and then sliding back into the ground altogether. The hazel in Ryce's hands wins the same result. Lewinna clears an arm and hand next. As soon as Æmma's hand is clear, Lewinna thrusts a few hazel twigs into it. Her friend clasps them, and more of the roots start to recede even before either Ryce and his hazel or *Frowe* Seolforswan's silver ringlets come near them.

When Æmma has been released from the roots' grasp altogether, Lewinna and Ryce help her sit up, holding their arms around Æmma's shoulders as the girl gulps in deep breaths.

There is a loud crack, followed by others, and the Draka shriek in renewed pain. The roots have enveloped most of their upper bodies now, their arms either pinned against their bodies or frozen in odd positions, held there by the tenacious grip of the unstoppable roots. There are more cracks. One of the Draka starts coughing out blood. Lewinna realises that the cracks she can hear are ribs being broken. Even as the roots wound about the Draka's legs become as thick as fence posts, more fresh shoots emerge from the earth and wriggle their way to the captives.

Geirtyr Odderson is the only Draka not reduced to terrified panic. Nor does he scream. He is no longer struggling. Instead, he stares at Lewinna balefully with rancour in his eyes as the roots wind about his chest. She holds his gaze, withstanding the sheer hatred directed at her as she holds on to Æmma. Her friend has regained her breath, but is quietly sobbing, her face turned away from the Draka agony, her forehead pressed against Ryce's shoulder.

Odderson directs a few more curses at Lewinna before he starts to struggle for breath. One of the other Draka has emitted a stream of blood from his mouth before his eyes roll in their sockets and then become lifeless. Another is blue in the face, choking as he is strangled by roots tightening around his neck. The others are all screaming their unbearable pain, but they too, one by one, are silenced by death.

Lewinna stares at them. It seems a horrific way to die, but she recalls the agony of Nihtlícburh and Odesburh, Raedan falling lifeless to the ground under the gaze of the roosting ravens, Yrre's expression of surprise as Draka spears drained his life blood, her own fate had she fallen into Draka hands, that of Æmma, Elswide, sweet Lufe and Tova, as well as the others from a long time away…and feels no pity or compassion.

Odderson starts to turn blue in the face as the root tips, weaving up through his beard, caress his cheeks almost tenderly, like a lover's fingers tracing the contours of a beloved face. His eyes finally lose their enmity, and Lewinna can read a silent plea in them. Untangling herself from Æmma's embrace, she scrambles to her feet and picks up the Draka's battle axe. Its weight is astonishing, but Lewinna lifts it off the ground. One of Odderson's arms has disappeared beneath the twitching mass of roots. The other is held up and outstretched, immobile in the crushing grip of the roots but his hand is free of all but the first exploring root tips. The Draka grasps the axe shaft when Lewinna places it within reach. The root tips respond immediately, weaving their way around the shaft and thus binding it to Odderson's hand. The Draka chieftain's eyes convey gratitude at Lewinna and then shut, never to open again.

Lewinna turns back to the others. It was neither compassion nor pity which had moved her to give Odderson his battle axe, but a code of honour, a duty one warrior owed another on the battlefield.

Aldred, wincing with pain, nods. "He will feast in Waelhalla."

The roots, thick and sturdy now, spiral up, interweaving as they do so, swallowing the Draka whole. By the time Anna and Rōse return with branches for a makeshift stretcher, the whorled roots have fused, growing red, scaly bark and sprouting branches and evergreen needles. The only sign of the Draka are gnarled whirls of yew trunk, which suggest wide-open, screaming mouths and gaping eyes.

Lewinna can see similar frozen Draka trees to her left and right. The solitary flute player lets a last low note die down, and blessed silence follows.

Maedens and wild hunters make their way to the centre, some stunned into shock, others jubilant. Now that it is over, Lewinna feels exhausted, fatigue seeping into her very bones and a great weariness reducing clarity of thought to a muddle.

One of the wild hunters, Tilian, a greybeard from Thurgisham, is escorting a Draka who has escaped the gruesome fate of the others. His hands are tied behind his back. He is young and frightened.

"This turd here," Tilian says, "told me that there's just a dozen of them left, at Nihtlícburh, guarding the captives, those from Odesburh as well."

Lewinna digests this and sheds her fatigue.

"Ryce, take the *frumbyrdlings* to the Úlehús, fetch all the horses, and bring them to Innanley. We'll meet you there. Be as quick as you can."

"*Já, Myne Frowe.*" Ryce and Æmma rise to their feet and the boy summons his companions. After bidding a farewell to his father, Ryce leads his pack of *frumbyrdlings* into Wiccanhyrst at a run.

"Æmma," Lewinna turns to her friend, who seems to have regained her composure. "Get the *maedens* to build that stretcher, and take Aldred to the Úlehús."

"*Já, Myne…Frowe.*"

"Tilian," Lewinna says. "Gather the greybeards; we walk to Innanley through the Ghaestdenn. Make sure everybody still has hazel. When we meet up with the *frumbyrdlings* and the horses, we will ride south to Nihtlícburh."

"*Já, Myne Frowe,*" Tilian answers. "And the prisoner?"

Lewinna looks at the prisoner, helpless and scared, and then looks at Æmma. Her friend says, "There's a price to be paid for magic, Lewinna. Always a price."

Lewinna nods. "We take him with us, Tilian, and bind him to the Blood Oak."

"*Já, Myne Frowe.*"

The *maedens* are nearly finished constructing Aldred's stretcher when Lewinna turns her back on the frozen Draka trees and leads the greybeards and the solitary captive into the Fernsæ and then the Ghaestdenn. They make good speed, pausing only briefly at the Blood Oak, where the captive is tied to the old sacrificial oak and then left behind. At Innanley, they disrupt a raven's banquet and bury the dead by the roadside in hastily dug graves. Soon, the lads will come thundering down the Woldweg with the horses, and all will mount and head south, following Lewinna Seolforhelm as she rides into legend.

THE END

Author's Note

The story of the frozen dragon tree has already been briefly touched upon in *Secrets of the Wyrde Woods: Forgotten Road*, when Joy relates the confrontation to Maisy and Chunmani. I had intended to work out the actual story more elaborately one day, and when I saw Nav Logan's drabble 'The Dragon Raid', I was reminded of this intention. Participation in the *DREAMTIME DRAGONS* anthology allowed me to work it out in far more detail, and I hope you've enjoyed my efforts.

The story is based on a Sussex legend and folklore about Kingley Vale, in the west of Sussex. Kingley Vale is a deep and narrow valley, much of it covered by yew woodland, with at a series of yew groves at its centre containing some 40-60 ancient yew trees, all well over 1,000 years old. Local legend has it that the four barrows on top of the hill overlooking the vale are the graves of Danish chieftains, whose men died here after their Viking raid went awry and they were defeated by local Saxon militia men.

The Anglo-Saxon Chronicle actually records a battle in this area between the local *fyrd* and a Danish raiding party in 894 AD, with the Suth-Seaxe men victorious at the end of it. The Chronicle doesn't mention the specific location of the battle, but it is a probable source for the legend.

Some say that the yew groves were planted to commemorate the victory, others that they were planted over Danish graves. One version suggests that the marauding Danes were transformed into the yew trees by an Anglo-Saxon sorcerer, and there are whispers that the trees come to life at night. There are occasional Pook sightings too.

Walking through the groves, I could not help but notice that the gnarled trunks of the yew trees depict faces, scores of faces, many with their mouths opened in horrified howls, eyes wide with inhuman fear. Evidence enough for me that the legend of the Anglo-Saxon sorcerer is the most realistic explanation of the lot, and how could I not transfer this Sussex tradition to the Wyrde Woods?

Liberties were taken, as they must when you uproot local folklore and shift it to fictional Sussex woodlands a fair stride to the east of Kingley Vale.

One such liberty was that I placed the story 16 years earlier, to coincide with events before the Battle of Edington, namely King Ælfred's exile in the Somerset marshes. This gave me a chance to pay homage to Bernard Cornwell's excellent Warrior Chronicles, and also to draw away most of the Wyrde Woods' fighting men, for a great part of the Suth-Seaxe *fyrd* fought at the Battle of Edington. I've also taken liberties with the Saxon language, liberally mixing various words ranging from Old High German, to Old-Saxon, to Saxon, to Old English, and also tweaking them to try and make their digestion a bit easier. The words are in the story to enhance the time period, not to teach a language lesson. I offer my sincere apologies for any distress caused to linguistic scholars.

Cair, Anna, Rozemarijn and Gerrit: Wrestling through a stubborn Fernsæ in Ashdown Forest and rushing for the breach of a Bronze Age fortress at Devil's Dyke in torrential rain on one of Thunor's bad hair days does have its uses. ;-)

ABOUT US

BRIEF BIOS & LINKS

LIA REES (cover design)

Lia Rees had the pleasure of designing the typography for the cover of Dreamtime Dragons. She is a book designer and cover artist based in London, and enjoys using her imagination to convey the spirit behind a book. Lia also writes memoir and poetry, with future plans for fantasy, sci-fi and a journalistic project. She makes art and jewellery and has strong feelings about people who put others in boxes.

Business page (for authors): http://freeyourwords.com/
Everything else: https://liarees.com/

CORIN SPINKS (cover design)

Corin Spinks is a talented photographer with a wide range of interests, including nature, street portraits, abandoned buildings, churches, street art, steampunk and anything quirky and odd. He has previously designed a few Wyrde Woods book covers and is experimenting with photoshop to get compositions which are prime book cover material.

Visit him at:
https://www.facebook.com/corin.spinks/photos_albums

https://www.flickr.com/photos/corinography/

https://nl.pinterest.com/nilsvisser/corin-spinks-photography-book-covers/

GUY DONOVAN (author & editor)

In the 1990s and 2000s, I worked on both television and feature films as an animator and storyboard artist/designer for Marvel Films, Hanna-Barbera, Sony Pictures, DreamWorks SKG, and Warner Bros Feature Animation, among others. With the demise of hand-drawn animation in the early 2000s, I started working a job that offered financial security, but little creativity. On the advice of my wife, a fellow Hollywood expatriate who writes both screenplays and novels, I turned to writing as a creative release. That led to my current obsession with fifth-century Wales, which is the setting of my Dragon's Treasure Series. The first three novels, *The Forgotten Princess of Môna*, *A Cold, White Home*, and *Songs of Autumn*, are currently available as e-books through Amazon. The fourth and final instalment, *Memories so Distant and Brief*, is nearing completion, with an estimated release in the winter of 2018.

You can find the books on my Amazon author page.
Author.to/GuyDonovanAuthor

I'm also on Facebook.
https://www.facebook.com/search/top/?q=the%20dragon%27s%20treasure%20series

ASSAPH MEHR (author)

Assaph grew up in Israel, where wherever you dig you'll find historical relics from the dawn of civilisation. His favourite spot was the port of Jaffa, where layers of cultures could be dug down to the ancient Egyptians, and the many citadels remaining from the crusades and Ottomans. That probably explains why he lives in the past and far distant worlds, and only pays attention to the present when he has to cross the street. He now lives in Sydney, Australia with his wife Julia, four kids and two cats. By day he is a software product manager, bridging the gap between developers and users, and by night he's writing – he seems to do his best writing after midnight. You can find more of him and his works on egretia.com, and all over the net.

JAQ D HAWKINS (author & editor)

Jaq D Hawkins is a published writer with 10 books in publication in the Mind, Body, Spirit genre published by Capall Bann Publishing, as well as four Fantasy novels in print and E-book; *The Wake of the Dragon, Dance of the Goblins, Demoniac Dance,* and, *Power of the Dance,* published by Golbin Publishing. A combined edition of the Goblin Trilogy is also available. Her next release, The Chase For Choronzon, is due in 2017.

Information on all titles can be found through her website at http://www.jaqdhawkins.com

Samples from various projects occasionally appear on her blog at https://goblinsandsteampunk.wordpress.com/

Amazon page http://www.amazon.com/Jaq-D.-Hawkins/e/B0034P4BFI

NILS NISSE VISSER (author & editor)

I was born in Rotterdam in 1970 and grew up in the Netherlands, Thailand, Nepal, Oklahoma, Tanzania, England, Egypt and France. I've taught English at various Dutch secondary schools for 18 years but my firm belief that education is most effective when it is fun raised a few eyebrows. Having been told too often that I live in my imagination I took the hint and moved there on a full-time basis. I now live in Brighton, England. Rather confusingly I sometimes write as Nils Visser, Nisse Visser or Nils Nisse Visser. It made sense at the time. My sincere apologies.

Do visit me online:
Pinterest:
https://nl.pinterest.com/nilsvisser/the-wyrde-woods/
Facebook:
https://www.facebook.com/NilsNisseVisser/
HubPages:
http://nilsvisser.hubpages.com/
Twitter:
https://twitter.com/NilsVisser

BENJAMIN TOWE (author)

Benjamin Towe is a vintage (epic) fantasy writer, Whovian, Dungeon Master, and lover of all things Magick and make believe. Ben was born in Carroll County, Virginia, and graduated from Mt. Airy, NC, High School in 1968, Davidson College in 1972, and the University of Virginia School of Medicine in 1976. Ben has been married to Libby Dawson since 1973. Dr. Towe served in the United States Army Medical Corps from 1976-1981 and now practices Family Medicine in Augusta, Georgia. The eleven books of the Donothor and Parallan series are Dr. Towe's prescriptions for sci-fi/fantasy: *Thirttene Friends*, *Dawn of Magick*, *Lost Spellweaver*, *First Wandmaker*, *Wandmaker's Burden*, *Emerald Islands*, *Mender's Tomb*, *Deathquest to Parallan*, *Orb of Chalar*, *Chalice of Mystery*, and *Death of Magick*. Magick should be more than pointing a wand and saying shazam! Escape to an Elfdream!

Facebook:
https://www.facebook.com/elfdreams/?hc_location=ufi
Amazon:https://www.amazon.com/Benjamin-Towe/e/B002PN9FAG/

Or visit my blog at https://benjamintowe.com/

JONATHAN ROYAN (author)

Jonathan lives in a leafy part of Oxfordshire with his wife and three children. He is a writer of Drabbles, short stories, and full length novels. Fantasy is his genres, of which he is a ferocious reader. In between working his day job in the printing industry, he has developed his writing skills, building an impressive body of work. You can view some of it for free here: https://drablr.com/jroyan He is currently working on a number of novels, all set in his fantasy world, Kareen. He hopes to finish all three before releasing them to the world.

MARC VUN KANNON (author)

Marc Vun Kannon, after surviving his teen age years, entered Hoftstra University. Five years later, he exited with a BA in philosophy and a wife. He still has both, but the wife is more useful. Since then he almost accumulated a PhD in philosophy and has acquired a second BA in Computer Science. After dabbling in fulfilling pursuits such as stock boy and gas station attendant, he found his spiritual home as a software support engineer, for CAMP Systems International.

Mark puts his degrees in Philosophy and Computer Science to good use writing stories about strange things that happen to ordinary people. His wife and three children think it's harmless enough, and it keeps him out of trouble. As a philosopher (his first novel demanded he write it while was in Graduate School), his main interest is in the characters, and as a Computer geek his technique is to follow the characters and story's logic to 'grow' a story organically. His main rule when writing is to not do again what he's already seen done before, resulting in books that hard to describe.

LESLIE CONZATTI (author & editor)

Leslie Conzatti, the writer behind "Arthur and The Egg", has (to date) one published work, a novella titled "Princess of Undersea" that is a re-telling of the classic fairy tale, The Little Mermaid. She is an avid writer and a voracious reader residing in the Pacific Northwest. Equipped with a vibrant, active imagination, Leslie has been crafting stories and creating fantasies out of the world around her and the one within her mind since before she learned to read. From the start of the very first story, Leslie has been committed to the production of lasting literature intended to invest in the lives of her readers, motivating them to become more involved in the world around them.

For more stories by Leslie, excerpts from longer works, updates on current projects, and book reviews, check out her blog, "The Upstream Writer"

www.upstreamwriter.blogspot.com

MARY R. WOLDERING (author & editor)

Mary R. Woldering (nee Reynolds) wrote stories and illustrated them as a child. Later she studied Art in college but soon moved into Art History. For many years she enjoyed being and Arts Official in the Society for Creative Anachronism. Her notes and sketches from meditation and studies of reincarnation which she developed with friends became the source of even more stories.

She married Dr. Jackie Woldering and raised children Ruth and Thom and now has three grandchildren with a fourth on the way. After retirement from various part time teaching jobs, she began to write full time.

At present, she has published three books of a five part series entitled <u>Children of Stone</u> which is an alternative story inserted in ancient Egyptian history and mythology. She is also working on shorter works in related universes. She has a blog for writers at:

Https://www.maryrwoldering.com

and you can find her at a number of Facebook sites. Her Amazon page is:
https://www.amazon.com/Mary-R.-Woldering/e/B00OND7QMU/ref=dp_byline_cont_ebooks_1

AJ. NOON (author & editor)

AJ Noon is a writer from Portsmouth, England, who can usually be found skulking around the historic ships there. He writes fantasy and sci-fi and occasionally dabbles in bad rhyming poetry, which he has been known to perform around the city.

You can find him on
https://www.facebook.com/AuthorAJNoon/

NAV LOGAN (author & editor)

Many years ago, when I was just a small boy gazing in wonder at his first chest hair, I decided that I was going to become a tramp. I was going to drop out and go to Strathclyde. Why Strathclyde? God only knows, but every man must have a goal in life. Being an engineer or a pilot didn't cut it for me. My soul was filled with wanderlust and the need for adventure.

So, after leaving home, I dropped out. I even went to Strathclyde, passing through it in a sleepy haze while being rocked gently to slumber in the passenger seat of an unknown truck.

Since then, I have done many things and seen many places, always following my instincts and trusting in my destiny. I am self-taught in many things; a jack of all trades and a master at none, but I've always got by. A strong self-belief has brought me through many adversities. I try to be the best I can be and often fail, but I continue, nevertheless.

I've been writing since I was that small boy, mainly poems and an occasional short story. *Maerlin's Storm* was first written over a decade ago. It wasn't something I planned to do. I didn't wake up and say, I'm going to be an author. Far from it. Like many things in my life, it all started with a dream. The next morning, I wrote a poem. Later, it became a story, and this small seed became my beanstalk. People read it and enjoyed it, but then life became busy again. For many years the story sat, collecting dust. It would have stayed on the shelf, forgotten, but fate had other plans.

I now have 5 published novels. Three are part of the Storm-Bringer Saga, an Epic Fantasy series. I also published a collection of drabbles and poems: Little Words ... Full of Big Worlds, a collection of short stories and drabbles: Bananas In My Shorts, and a collaboration short story: Happy Halloween.

Website and blog page: http://navlogan.com/
Facebook Page:
https://www.facebook.com/StormbringerSaga?ref=hl

RICK HAYNES (author)

Hi, my name is Rick Haynes. Let me welcome you to the world of my imagination. If you like Game of Thrones, you'll love, Heroes Never Fade, my latest fantasy novel, for as one reviewer posted:

'Prepare for a nerve-tingling ride through a fantasy world of medieval warfare, a world that springs to life under the skilled pen of an author who has thoroughly researched his subject. The characters are full-blooded, their relationships to each other clearly drawn. The warriors leap off the page, wielding their weapons with skill and courage as their battle of right against might is mirrored by a power struggle between their gods.'

https://www.amazon.co.uk/Heroes-Never-Fade-Maxilla-Book-ebook/dp/B06XYS1RBX

https://www.amazon.co.uk/EVIL-NEVER-DIES-MAXILLA-TALES-ebook/dp/B011GP1LQO/

MICHAEL CRITTENDEN (cover art)

From a very early age, Michael has enjoyed 'creating art' from building and painting models to oil paintings of the beautiful Berkshire countryside. His first commissioned piece was to paint a cigarette lighter for a friend, while studying at Reading College of Art and Design; payment of which was reported to be 20 Marlboro Lights. He has since created many more works of art, some of which can be viewed on his Facebook page.

https://www.facebook.com/andsometimespencils/.

Most recently he has created cover art in the fantasy genre and is strongly considering a move into the medium, as he really enjoys it.

DREAMTIME DRAGONS

AUTHORS OF
DREAMTIME TALE FANTASY